An

Amish Harvest

OTHER NOVELS BY THE AUTHORS

BETH WISEMAN

AMISH SECRETS NOVELS
Her Brother's Keeper
Love Bears All Things
(Available October 2016)

THE DAUGHTERS OF THE PROMISE NOVELS
Plain Perfect
Plain Pursuit
Plain Promise
Plain Paradise
Plain Proposal
Plain Peace

THE LAND OF CANAAN NOVELS
Seek Me with All Your Heart
The Wonder of Your Love
His Love Endures Forever

OTHER NOVELS
Need You Now
The House that Love Built
The Promise

OTHER NOVELLAS
A Choice to Forgive included
in *An Amish Christmas*
A Change of Heart included
in *An Amish Gathering*
Healing Hearts included
in *An Amish Love*
A Perfect Plan included
in *An Amish Wedding*
A Recipe for Hope included
in *An Amish Kitchen*
Always Beautiful included
in *An Amish Miracle*

Rooted in Love included
in *An Amish Garden*
*When Christmas Comes
Again* included in *An
Amish Second Christmas*
In His Father's Arms included
in *An Amish Cradle*
A Love for Irma Rose included
in *An Amish Year*
Patchwork Perfect included
in *An Amish Year*
A Cup Half Full included in
An Amish Home (Available
February 2017)

AMY CLIPSTON

THE AMISH HEIRLOOM SERIES
The Forgotten Recipe
The Courtship Basket
(Available July 2016)

THE HEARTS OF THE LANCASTER GRAND HOTEL SERIES
A Hopeful Heart
A Mother's Secret
A Dream of Home
A Simple Prayer

THE KAUFFMAN AMISH BAKERY SERIES
A Gift of Grace
A Promise of Hope
A Place of Peace
A Life of Joy
A Season of Love

A Plain and Simple Christmas
Naomi's Gift

OTHER NOVELLAS
A Spoonful of Love included
in *An Amish Kitchen*
A Son for Always included
in *An Amish Cradle*
Naomi's Gift included in
An Amish Christmas Gift
Love Birds included in
An Amish Market

KATHLEEN FULLER

THE AMISH OF BIRCH CREEK
A Reluctant Bride
An Unbroken Heart
A Love Made New (Available
September 2016)

THE MIDDLEFIELD AMISH NOVELS
A Faith of Her Own

THE MIDDLEFIELD FAMILY NOVELS
Treasuring Emma
Faithful to Laura
Letters to Katie

THE HEARTS OF
MIDDLEFIELD NOVELS
A Man of His Word
An Honest Love
A Hand to Hold

OTHER NOVELLAS
A Miracle for Miriam included
in *An Amish Christmas*
A Place of His Own included
in *An Amish Gathering*
What the Heart Sees included
in *An Amish Love*
A Perfect Match included
in *An Amish Wedding*

Flowers for Rachael included
in *An Amish Garden*
A Gift for Anne Marie included
in *An Amish Second Christmas*
A Heart Full of Love included
in *An Amish Cradle*

VANNETTA CHAPMAN

THE AMISH VILLAGE MYSTERY SERIES
Murder Simply Brewed
Murder Tightly Knit
Murder Freshly Baked

THE SHIPSHEWANA AMISH
MYSTERY SERIES
Falling to Pieces
A Perfect Square
Material Witness

OTHER NOVELLAS
Where Healing Blooms included
in *An Amish Garden*
An Unexpected Blessing
included in *An Amish Cradle*
Love in Store included
in *An Amish Market*

OTHER AMISH NOVELLA COLLECTIONS
An Amish Christmas
An Amish Gathering
An Amish Love
An Amish Wedding
An Amish Kitchen
An Amish Miracle
An Amish Garden
An Amish Second Christmas
An Amish Year
An Amish Market

An Amish Harvest

Four Novellas

Beth Wiseman
Amy Clipston
Kathleen Fuller
Vannetta Chapman

Thomas Nelson
Since 1798

Published in Nashville, Tennessee, by Thomas Nelson. Thomas Nelson is a registered trademark of HarperCollins Christian Publishing, Inc.

Thomas Nelson titles may be purchased in bulk for educational, business, fund-raising, or sales promotional use. For information, please e-mail SpecialMarkets@ThomasNelson.com.

Scripture quotations are taken from the Holy Bible, New International Version®, NIV®. Copyright © 1973, 1978, 1984, 2011 by Biblica, Inc.™ Used by permission of Zondervan. All rights reserved worldwide. www.zondervan.com. The "NIV" and "New International Version" are trademarks registered in the United States Patent and Trademark Office by Biblica, Inc.™

Poems "The Autumn" and "How Do I Love Thee" (Sonnet 43) by Elizabeth Barrett Browning are in the public domain.

Poem "Sonnet LIV" (Sonnet 54) by William Shakespeare is in the public domain.

Publisher's Note: This novel is a work of fiction. Names, characters, places, and incidents are either products of the author's imagination or used fictitiously. All characters are fictional, and any similarity to people living or dead is purely coincidental.

Library of Congress Cataloging-in-Publication Data

Names: Wiseman, Beth, 1962-author. Under the harvest moon. | Clipston, Amy,
author. Love and buggy rides. | Chapman, Vannetta, author. Mischief in the autumn air. | Fuller, Kathleen, author. Quiet love.
Title: An Amish harvest: four novellas / Beth Wiseman, Amy Clipston, Vannetta Chapman, Kathleen Fuller.
Description: Nashville: Thomas Nelson, 2016.
Identifiers: LCCN 2016008308 | ISBN 9780529118530 (paperback)
Subjects: LCSH: Christian fiction, American. | Amish—Fiction. | Romance fiction, American. | Pennsylvania—Fiction.
Classification: LCC PS648.C43 A46 2016 | DDC 813/.01083823—dc23 LC record available at https://lccn.loc.gov/2016008308

Printed in the United States of America

16 17 18 19 20 21 RRD 6 5 4 3 2 1

CONTENTS

Under the Harvest Moon

Beth Wiseman

To Sharon Hanners

GLOSSARY

ab im kopp—off in the head; crazy
ach—oh
bruder—brother
daadi—grandfather
daed—dad
dochder—daughter
Englisch—non-Amish person
frau—wife
gut—good
kapp—prayer covering
kinner—children
lieb—love
maedel / maed—girl(s)
mamm—mom
mammi—grandmother
mei—my
mudder—mother
nee—no
Pennsylvania Deitsch—the language most commonly used by the Amish. Although commonly known as Pennsylvania Dutch, the language is actually a form of German (Deutsch).
Wie bischt—How are you? / Howdy
ya—yes

Prologue

Naomi squeezed concealer into the palm of her hand, then gingerly dabbed it beneath her eye, smoothing it into her skin until the black circle was almost invisible. If anyone said anything, she'd feign lack of sleep and ask the Lord to forgive her lie. Again.

Growing up, Naomi's father had rarely laid a hand on her and never in anger. Maybe twice she'd received spankings for acting out, but he'd never hit her in the face. In the beginning, it was confusing why Stephen seemed to take out his frustrations on her, but her husband was a good man. Stephen was a hard worker, a pillar in their community, and a handsome man whom others took notice of when they were out and about. He was a good father too. He wasn't like other Amish husbands who left all the child-rearing to their wives. Stephen played with the children, and when they were infants, he'd even changed a few diapers.

They'd married when Naomi was seventeen, and over the past nine years, she had come to think that the problem must be her. She'd done her best to be a proper wife, even though she wasn't a very good cook and her housekeeping skills could only be described as mediocre. But having two young children kept her busy, along with the list of daily chores that Stephen encouraged her to keep up with.

Naomi leaned closer to the mirror in the bathroom, proud that she'd learned how to apply the *Englisch* makeup she'd found at the market. It had taken several purchases before she'd found the color that matched her pale skin almost perfectly. She jumped when there was a knock at the door and quickly stashed the tube in the pocket of her apron, in case she needed a touch-up between worship service and the meal.

"You ready?"

She opened the door, faced her husband, and smiled. "*Ya.* All ready."

Stephen looked at her, and for a few seconds, she thought maybe she hadn't done a good enough job covering the black remnant of their argument a few days ago. But Stephen kissed her on the cheek, stepped back, and smiled.

"You are the most beautiful woman ever born. I'm a blessed man to have you as *mei frau.*" He pushed back a wayward piece of hair that had fallen from beneath her prayer covering, a gesture that used to make her jump. But she'd learned long ago that being timid only angered Stephen, so she'd trained herself not to flinch or cringe, no matter what might be coming.

"*Danki,*" she said. "I'm a blessed woman to have you also."

He grabbed her hand and together they went downstairs. Abby and Esther Rose were sitting on the couch, dressed and ready for church. It would be a grand day of fellowship and worship, and like always, Naomi would ask God to help her be a better wife, someone who didn't anger her husband so often.

Naomi followed Stephen and the girls down the porch steps, knowing her pace would be slow today, and probably for the next couple of weeks. A broken rib tended to slow a person down.

Chapter One

Four months later

Naomi stood beside Stephen's headstone; wooden and plain like the rest of the unmarked graves in the Amish cemetery. Her husband was laid to rest next to Adam, the baby Naomi had lost in her second trimester the year before. She and her children would make their final resting place here also, their souls journeying on to heaven where they'd all reunite someday. Stephen would be a different man by the time they got there. God would see to that. For now, Naomi would continue to bring her girls to the cemetery as often as she could.

"Do you think *Daed* can see us?" seven-year-old Abigail said. "Do you think he is with baby Adam? Do kids have toys in heaven?" Naomi's father had once remarked jokingly, "*That* one's going to keep you on your toes. She's wise beyond her years and would question a grape if it could talk back to her."

"I don't know. What do you think?" Naomi pulled her black sweater snug atop her black dress and apron. She'd be glad to shed her mourning clothes for brighter colors, although she wasn't sure when it would be appropriate to do so. Her mother had said the choice was hers, but if that had truly been the case, Naomi would have chosen to wear a maroon dress, symbolic of the fall harvest that would soon be upon them. Even though she had no idea how she would bring in the crops Stephen had planted months ago.

"I think *Daed* and baby Adam can see us and hear us from heaven, and that they are together. And I just know there will be toys in heaven!" Abby smiled brightly, unbothered by the fact that there was a black hole where her two front teeth had been until recently. Her oldest daughter had dimples that made her always look happy, even if she wasn't smiling. Abby was the only person in the family with curly, blond hair and blue eyes. Everyone else had dark hair, on both sides of their families, except for one of Naomi's cousins whose hair was red and her eyes green.

Naomi wasn't sure if Stephen and Adam could hear and see them, she only hoped her husband couldn't read her thoughts. She folded her arms across her stomach. It saddened her that Abby, Esther Rose, and the child she now carried would grow up without a father—but it was hard not to feel a sense of relief.

Esther Rose sat down in the overgrown grass by Stephen's headstone. As she'd done a dozen times before, Esther Rose put her hand on the earth where her father was buried and said, "I miss you, *Daed*." Then she did the same thing where Adam was laid to rest.

Naomi's five-year-old hung her head, and she suspected that tears were forming in the corners of her daughter's eyes.

"But remember, *Daed* and Adam are with Jesus now." Naomi wondered how much Esther Rose would remember about the brother she'd lost and the father they'd buried four months ago. Naomi's earliest memories ran back to when she was five, and she hoped her younger daughter would remember her father for the good man the child believed him to be.

"We must go now. *Mammi* is coming by later this morning." Naomi looked forward to her mother's visits, which had become more frequent since Stephen's passing. No one said it aloud, but it was obvious that people were waiting for Naomi to either get remarried or have a nervous breakdown following the loss of her husband at such a young age. *If they only knew.* Some days, Naomi could picture God looking down on her and shaking His head at the wicked thoughts that trolled through her mind. But for the past four months, Naomi had felt more at peace than she had in years. It was awful to think that way, but she was getting reacquainted with a life she barely remembered. She no longer had to worry if the meat was undercooked, the pasta oversalted, or a host of other things that might set off her husband. She could stretch to the ceiling if she felt like it and hang clothes on the line without a pinching pain in her side. She could skip certain chores and opt to play with her children instead.

She placed a hand on her stomach again, knowing that with each pregnancy, Stephen had kept away from her for fear of hurting each unborn child. He could control his temper, she'd come to learn. He just didn't want to or need to unless she was with child. When she'd been pregnant with Esther Rose, her husband had put a hole through the wall with his fist and also thrown a trinket box that had belonged to Naomi's grandmother across the room, smashing it into tiny slivers of wood.

But Stephen had nothing to do with Adam being called home before his life had a chance to begin. Not even the doctor had a good explanation, saying only that a small percentage of miscarriages happen in the second trimester. But amid the whirlwind of emotions she'd felt about Stephen's passing, fear had reared its ugly head in a different way. She didn't think she could bear losing another baby.

Naomi and her girls returned home from the cemetery later that morning, but it wasn't her mother waiting on the front porch, it was her father. A rare visit for a Tuesday morning. As Naomi walked across the yard toward him, Esther Rose and Abby almost knocked her over, blowing past her and into their grandfather's arms. Her parents would be excited to hear she was having another child, but she hadn't shared the news with anyone yet. Even at five months, her pregnancy was easy enough to hide beneath her baggy dresses. At first, she'd wanted to wait until she felt more certain she would carry her baby to term, or at least longer than she'd carried Adam. Then Stephen died, and it just didn't seem like the right time to celebrate this new life. Sadness still fell over her when she recalled miscarrying her son. It was the only time she'd seen Stephen cry. She would tell her parents about this baby soon.

"What are you doing here on this brisk September morning?" she asked her father, waiting for him to quit smothering the girls with hugs and kisses. Most Amish men weren't affectionate, but she loved that her father wasn't afraid to show his love.

"We need to talk about the harvest," he said, giving each girl a final hug before he sent them inside. "Girls, I need to talk to your *mamm*. You both go find something sweet for *Daadi* to eat when I'm done here."

Naomi smiled. There wasn't a person on God's beautiful earth who liked sweets more than her father. She suspected that was the reason he'd had to get false teeth a few years ago. But it hadn't curbed his love of sugar.

She sat on the porch step beside her father. "Where's *Mamm*? She said she was coming by this morning."

Daed ran his hand the length of his dark beard, now salted with white specks that seemed to have appeared overnight. Or maybe Naomi just hadn't noticed her father getting up in age until Stephen's life was cut short so suddenly. Despite the horrible thoughts she'd been having, she was reminded that the Lord giveth and the Lord taketh away. In addition to praying that she'd carry this baby to full term, she found herself praying for good health for both of her parents, sometimes begging God not to take either of them for at least a couple more decades, until her children were raised and on their own.

"Your *mudder* had to take Barbara Byler to town." Her father rolled his eyes. "Your *mamm* is a *gut* woman because I couldn't do it. That old widow never closes her mouth." He tapped his fingers together against his thumb. "Yap, yap, yap. That's all she does." Her father scowled as Naomi stifled a smile. "And Barbara doesn't even talk about nothing important. She just rambles on about the weather, a sale she found at the market, or whatever floats her boat that day."

"Floats her boat?" Naomi couldn't hold back her grin any longer. She'd never heard her father use the *Englisch* expression.

"Don't you turn into her, you hear me? You might have lost your husband . . ." He paused, glancing at her with sad eyes before he went on. "But if you get so lonely that you have to ramble on like Barbara, I won't be coming around much." He pointed a finger at her. "Another reason we need to find you a husband."

It was their way to remarry quickly, but it was the last thing

Naomi wanted. *Never again.* Although, lots of folks in town were already trying to match her up with someone, and she hadn't even shed her mourning clothes yet. But no one knew what had gone on in Naomi's house. She'd been much too proud, even if pride was frowned upon, to let anyone know that she'd failed miserably as a wife. "It's too soon for another husband," she finally said.

"*Ach,* well . . . that's a conversation for another day. Right now, we need to figure out how we're going to pull in this harvest. We're at a bit of a disadvantage since your *bruder* has a broken ankle, and he'll be struggling to get his own crops harvested. And I must have been *ab im kopp* when I decided to plant double the alfalfa that I usually do, so I'm going to be struggling as well."

Naomi hung her head. This wasn't the first time she'd felt like a burden since Stephen died. "I'm sorry, *Daed.* I don't want to cause extra work for anyone."

Her father chuckled. "Well, ya gotta eat, don't cha?" He waved a hand in the air. "Don't worry, *mei maedel.*" He put an arm around her and pulled her close, kissing her on the forehead. "By this time next year, I'm sure you will be married. And we will all get by until then. I've decided to hire someone to harvest your alfalfa for you. And he'll help dry and bale it too. He's an *Englisch* fellow whom I trust to be around my daughter and granddaughters. The man is a good worker, comes from a farming background, and I know he'll do right by us."

"*Daed,* I have a little money left if—"

Her father shook his head. "*Nee, nee.* I will bear the expense, but I do ask that you prepare his meals—breakfast, dinner, and supper. He'll be working alone, so he'll start at sunup and work until he's out of daylight."

"What about his own family? Those are long hours, especially for an *Englisch* man."

"He doesn't have a family. Well, not nearby anyway. I think he has a *bruder* in Oklahoma, but otherwise he's alone. His wife died a couple of years ago, and he quit farming after that. He sold their place and lives in Paradise now, in a smaller home. He told me once that he missed farming, so that's why I thought about him. He's a strong man of faith, and when I say *strong*, I don't mean just in his faith." Her father laughed. "He is a *big*, strong man. He's not as old as I am, maybe seven or eight years younger than me, but he's as fit as someone your age. Brock is a *gut* man that will pull in the harvest at a fair price."

"Brock? That's an odd name."

Her father moaned as he lifted himself to his feet. He'd had trouble with his knees for as long as Naomi could remember. "*Ya*, that's his name, Brock Mulligan. So, when you see a big fellow show up early next Monday morning, don't be alarmed."

Naomi nodded and stood up too.

"Now, let's go see what those *maed* have found to feed my sweet tooth." He pointed a playful finger at Naomi. "*Ya, ya*, I know. I don't have any real teeth."

Naomi giggled. She recalled the guilt that she'd felt the days following Stephen's burial. When a few church members had gathered at her house, her father had whispered something in Naomi's ear that had tickled her. She couldn't recall what it was, but she'd burst out laughing. She'd felt some glares from some of the women in the room and realized how inappropriate she'd acted.

She couldn't imagine life without her parents, and yet . . . she'd settled into a life without Stephen quite easily.

Chapter Two

B rock parked his truck in Naomi Dienner's driveway just as the sun started to spread orange hues across the fields of alfalfa surrounding him. The dew on the grass dampened his boots as he walked, and he was glad to see that the equipment he'd rented had been delivered and parked by the barn. He was anxious to get to work, but Gideon had insisted he take all his meals with Naomi and her children. Brock wasn't much of a breakfast eater, not since Patty died, but an early-morning feast would give him the energy to put in a hard day's work. He'd always respected Gideon, so he didn't want to disappoint his Amish friend.

There were two doors leading into the house from the front porch. He chose the door that was open since he could see through the screen and into the kitchen. Two young girls were seated at the table, and a woman—presumably Naomi—was stirring something on the stove. One of the girls scurried to the door and pulled the screen wide.

"Are you the farmer man who will harvest our crop?" She was a cute kid, missing her two front teeth and with a smudge of something purple on her chin, maybe jelly.

"Yes, I am. I'm Brock Mulligan." He stepped over the threshold just as Naomi turned to face him. He'd known Gideon for years, but he'd never met the man's family. Breathing in the welcoming aroma of bacon cooking, he extended his hand to the woman. She was a tiny thing, and she didn't look like she could be even thirty. Brock remembered how he'd felt after Patty died, and some days he still reached for her in the bed beside him, even two years later. Naomi must still be wracked with grief since she'd lost her husband only a few months ago. And she was mighty young to have gone through something like that. It seemed there were more and more buggy accidents in Lancaster County each year.

Naomi motioned to a place already set at the head of the table. Brock figured her husband had probably sat there for meals, and the thought caused him to shift his weight uncomfortably in the chair.

"We're having bacon, scrambled eggs, and biscuits, Mr. Mulligan." Naomi set a plate of bacon in the middle of the table. "What can I get you to drink? Milk, orange juice, or I have fresh coffee ready?"

"Coffee, please. And it's just Brock. No need to call me Mr. Mulligan. That makes me sound older than I feel." He smiled and reached for a biscuit when one of the girls pushed a basket toward him. The bread was still steaming, and he was happy to see a bowl of gravy nearby.

Naomi placed a cup of coffee in front of him, wiped her hands on her apron, and sat down in a chair at the other end of the table. Brock bowed his head with them. He knew the Amish folks prayed silently. He thanked God for the food, especially since people were starving all over the world, and he was truly grateful for a good meal. He didn't do much cooking these days. But he hadn't prayed with heartfelt vigor since Patty died. He raised his head at the same time as Naomi.

"We're glad you were able to accept my father's job offer." She passed him a bowl of scrambled eggs, then she nodded toward the little girl with the missing front teeth. "This is Abby, my older daughter." She tipped her chin to the left. "And this is Esther Rose."

After introductions, they ate in silence, but Brock could feel the younger of the girls, Esther Rose, staring at him. He glanced in her direction. She was nibbling on half a biscuit, but her eyes weren't roaming, they were locked on him.

"So, how old are you girls?" he asked when the silence grew a bit awkward. Brock was wondering if he had something on his chin since Esther Rose couldn't seem to take her eyes off him. He picked up his napkin and ran it once across his chin just to be safe. But the little girl kept staring at him. The Amish folks did their best to keep their children away from outsiders as much as they could. Maybe the child was just curious about him.

"I'm seven," Abby said as she sat taller in her chair. She pointed across the table at her sister. "And Esther Rose is five."

"So, you'll both be leaving for school soon, right?"

Both girls nodded, Esther Rose's eyes still on Brock even as she took a sip of her orange juice.

Brock cleared his throat, scratched his chin, and shifted his weight in the chair again. "This is a fine breakfast, Naomi." He would be enjoying it more if the little one could focus on her food and not him, but he continued to try to ignore her. He wasn't particularly comfortable around children, maybe since he'd never had any of his own.

"You are a big *Englisch* person." Esther Rose's eyes widened as if Brock were a superhero, but he knew how to field this comment. He'd hit six foot five by the time he was seventeen, a tall and lanky lad for a while. But after his weight caught up with his height, he filled out. He was used to being the biggest guy in a room. "You have big arms like *mei daed* had," the girl added.

Brock glanced at his arms, then back at the child. "So, he was a big man too?"

Esther Rose shook her head. "*Nee.* He was a little man with big arms."

Brock nodded, hoping Esther Rose would focus on her food. But when she laid her fork across her plate, her eyes drifted back to him.

"How many *kinner* do you have?" Abby asked.

The younger girl, Esther Rose, grunted. "*Mamm* already told us he doesn't have *kinner*."

"Why don't you have *kinner*?" Abby frowned and folded her arms across her chest.

Naomi cleared her throat. "That's enough questions, Abby. Let Mr. Brock eat his breakfast in peace."

"It's okay," Brock said, even though he was glad Naomi had spoken up. But when it got quiet again, the awkwardness returned, so Brock decided to answer the girl's question. "There was a time when my wife and I wanted children, but it just wasn't in God's plan." He wasn't sure if Abby would understand his answer, but he was going to stop there, and hopefully she would too.

"Sometimes when babies don't come the normal way, the *Englisch* buy their own." Abby gave a taut nod of her head. "Right, *Mamm*?"

Brock looked across the table at Naomi, and she smiled.

"That's not exactly how it works," she said. "You're talking about adoption. But I told you to let Mr. Brock eat his breakfast. Let's hush." She put a finger to her lips.

When they were all done eating, Naomi told her daughters to go brush their teeth and grab their school bags, and Naomi began to clear the table. Brock carried his plate to the sink, then went back for the girls' plates.

"*Nee*, Mr. Brock. I'll do that. Please. You have a long day ahead." She took the plates from him.

Brock considered arguing with her. He'd always helped Patty clear the table after a meal, although they'd been known to eat on the couch in front of the television plenty of times. He also thought about asking her to call him just Brock, not Mr. Brock. But maybe it made her more comfortable since he was considerably older than her.

"Thank you for a wonderful breakfast." He turned to leave, but slowed his steps when he heard someone following him. Turning around, he waited for her to meet up with him on the porch.

"Was the breakfast to your liking? I can make pancakes tomorrow morning or anything else you might fancy for breakfast." She folded her hands in front of her and narrowed her eyebrows as if this was the most important question she'd ever asked.

"Don't go to any trouble for me, ma'am. I eat anything. And the breakfast was really good."

She blew out a big breath of air she'd seemed to be holding, but the serious expression remained. "What about dinners and suppers? There must be something you don't like."

Brock thought for a moment. He was thrilled to be getting three home-cooked meals per day, and after a breakfast as grand as the one he'd just had, he didn't want to cause a fuss and mention the one thing he didn't like. He was pretty sure people didn't cook liver and onions much anyway. Brock could barely stand the smell of liver cooking, much less the thought of eating it. "Anything will be fine."

Naomi watched Brock from the porch as he made his way to the equipment he'd rented for the harvest. In the past, Stephen used mules to pull his rigs, and he'd hired several teenage boys who lived nearby to help harvest the alfalfa. It seemed like a big task for one man, but Naomi supposed his fancy equipment would get the job done.

Abby and Esther Rose joined her on the porch, and after she'd adjusted Esther Rose's *kapp*, she kissed each of them and sent them off to school. She was tempted to remind the girls to wait at the corner for the older children before walking the mile to the schoolhouse, but Abby had told Naomi that she didn't need to tell them that every morning. *My girls are growing up.* Naomi made her way to the barn to milk the cows and goats.

When Brock showed up for dinner several hours later, Naomi could smell him the moment he entered the living room. It was similar to the way Stephen used to smell when he was out working in the fields, the aroma of freshly cut grass combined with perspiration, but minus the manure that Stephen always managed to step in. But Brock wasn't using mules for the harvest. He was atop a big tractor.

"I probably need to clean up," he said as he held out his dirty hands.

Naomi pointed him toward the bathroom down the hallway,

then finished cooking the grilled cheese sandwiches. When he returned, she placed a sandwich in front of him, along with a bowl of steaming tomato soup.

"Aren't you going to eat?" He took a seat at the head of the table, the spot she'd assigned him at breakfast.

"*Ya.* I wanted to make sure you had everything you needed first. I poured you a glass of meadow tea, but I also have juice or water if you'd prefer that."

"Tea is fine." He smiled before he took several large gulps from the glass. Naomi sat down at the other end of the table and bowed her head. She opened one eye after she'd finished her prayers. Brock still had his head down, and she wondered what he was praying about. Naomi had thanked God for His many blessings, and prayed that He'd continue to help her become a better person. She didn't want another husband, but she suspected one would be forced upon her at some point. Her parents wouldn't understand her desire to be alone with her children. If and when that time came, Naomi wanted to have improved herself, not be someone who angered a man the way she had Stephen.

Naomi cleared her throat and laid her napkin across her lap. Brock lifted his head and opened his eyes. *Esther Rose was right. He really is a big man.*

"I love tomato soup and grilled cheese sandwiches. I'm not sure I've had this combo since my wife died." He spooned the soup, then blew on it. Naomi wondered if Brock had been happily married.

"Mr. Brock, do you mind me asking how your wife died?"

He finished chewing a bite of sandwich and swallowed. He took a deep breath. "It was a freak accident, something that happened in a split second." His gaze drifted to somewhere past

Naomi, and she already regretted asking him the question. "Patty fell off of our porch and bumped her head while she was hanging a potted plant. She hit her head in just the right spot to cause her to hemorrhage." He hung his head for a few moments before he looked back up at Naomi. "You just don't think something so random can happen."

Did you push her off the porch? An illogical thought, but one that entered her mind just the same. "I'm very sorry for your loss."

"By the time I got home from work, she'd already passed." Brock refocused on his sandwich, but he paused, then cleared his throat. "I'm sorry about your husband also. It's terrible the way people drive around here. I spoke to the city council a few years ago, imploring them to widen the buggy lane on Lincoln Highway in an effort to give the buggies more room, but my requests fell on deaf ears."

Naomi didn't want to talk about Stephen's death. It only fueled her guilt for not missing the father of her children. "How do you know my father?"

Brock smiled. He was a handsome man with kind gray eyes and dark wavy hair. When he smiled, one side of his mouth crooked up higher than the other, and at first glance, he seemed like a man Naomi would trust. But Stephen had been handsome too.

"I met your father at that same city council meeting I just referred to. He was the only Amish man in the room, and after I'd addressed the council and the meeting was over, he followed me to my car and thanked me for my efforts." Brock shrugged. "We went for coffee and pie at the diner next door, and following an hour-long conversation about things we'd like to change around here, I knew we'd end up being friends. The coffee and pie at the diner ended up being a weekly thing. Your father threw a lot of construction work my way, and when Patty died, he was at the funeral. He's a good man."

"The best," Naomi said, recalling her father's mention of coffee and pie at the diner with an *Englisch* friend.

Brock chuckled. "And he makes me laugh. Most folks don't realize what a good sense of humor the Amish have. But your father has a joke for me almost every time we meet."

Naomi took a sip of her iced tea, then nodded. "I love that about my father. He makes me laugh too. There's not enough joy in the world, but it warms my heart when I hear laughter, especially coming from *mei daed* or my girls."

Brock stared at her until Naomi felt self-conscious and looked away.

"Naomi, you'll find happiness again in your life. It probably doesn't seem like it right now, but you will. After Patty died, I was sure that my life had ended. But, as cliché as it sounds, time really does have a way of healing."

Naomi nodded. There were times she missed Stephen, brief recollections of the good times they'd had. But what saddened her most was that his passing was so painful for her daughters. But Naomi was determined to give her girls a good life, to instill in them traditional values, and to school them about choosing a husband wisely. One who wouldn't hit. But as she thought back, her love for Stephen had overshadowed everything else about him, and she'd overlooked some early warning signs. *Do you ever really know someone until you are sharing a life with them?*

Brock was looking over her shoulder again. Naomi turned to see what he was looking at. An old woman was standing in the backyard, looking at them through the kitchen window.

Chapter Three

Naomi poured Pearl King a glass of tea, then sat down across the kitchen table from the elderly *Englisch* woman. Pearl's gray hair was twisted in a loose bun on the back of her head, strands dangling on either side of her face, the lines of time suggesting she was at least eighty years old.

"I love the taste of the meadow tea that you Amish folks make." She smiled before taking another sip. "The sweet, minty flavor is unlike tea you get anywhere else."

Naomi took a sip from her own glass. "This is the last batch until the spring, the last of my mint."

"Well, I thank you kindly for sharing it with me. And I apologize again for being a peeper." Pearl dabbed at her mouth with the napkin Naomi had placed underneath her glass, then she set the tea down and sighed. "I thought it would be a lovely day for a walk." She eased her chair out and stretched out one leg, which was covered by a thick gray stocking and boasted a bright red running shoe. "I even bought these at the store for this very purpose, so I could enjoy the fall weather before it gets too cold for walking." She pulled her leg back under the table. "But sometimes I get confused, and I'm not quite sure how I ended up here." She leaned forward, frowning. "This is what happens when you get old."

"I'm grateful you wandered our way and didn't get lost in one of the fields surrounding us." Naomi studied the woman as Pearl used both hands to lift her glass to her mouth. She was wearing a faded blue dress and black sweater. The only jewelry she wore was a watch on her left wrist.

"Is the man you just introduced me to of a relation to you?" Pearl nodded toward the kitchen window where they could see Brock in the distance on the tractor.

"*Nee.* My father hired him to harvest our crop of alfalfa." Naomi swallowed hard. "My husband died recently, so I needed some help this year."

"Oh, sweet child of God. I'm so sorry to hear that." Pearl shook her head as a couple more strands of hair spilled from her bun. "He won't get to meet his unborn child."

Naomi stiffened and cocked her head to one side. "How did you know that I'm"—she put a hand on her belly—"in the family way?"

Pearl was missing a few teeth, but unlike Abby, the dark empty spaces were farther back in her mouth, only visible when she stretched her mouth into a wide smile, like she was doing now. "You're glowing, my dear." She shrugged. "I just know these things."

Naomi scratched her cheek, grinning. "Hmm . . . that's strange you would know. I haven't even told my parents yet. I was waiting until the right time." She glanced down at her stomach again and pressed a hand against her baby beneath the baggy black dress.

"You're a small woman, but you won't be able to hide the

bump for much longer. Baby will gain lots of weight these next four months."

Naomi's spine prickled. "How did you know how far along I am?"

Pearl chuckled. "Oh, dear girl. It would take decades for me to learn you about such things." She winked at Naomi.

"I suppose I need to tell my parents and my daughters. I was trying to wait until we were done mourning my husband's death, so that this new life would be an occasion to celebrate."

"Might we bow our heads and pray for your unborn son?" Pearl reached her weathered hands across the table, but Naomi stiffened.

"You couldn't possibly know I'm having a son. Even at the doctor, I asked them not to tell me the gender when they did a scan of the baby."

"Oh. Did I say son? I meant baby. Of course I couldn't know the sex of your child." She wiggled her fingers until Naomi's hands found hers, then Pearl closed her eyes and bowed her head. "Dear Heavenly Father, we ask for Your divine blessings on this unborn child Naomi carries. May he—or she—be born healthy and well, destined to live a long life serving You." She raised her head, smiling. "Amen."

"Thank you, Pearl." Naomi's doctor had told her to be careful with this pregnancy. She'd already lost one child, and that automatically put her at a slightly higher risk for another miscarriage. And he was worried stress would play a factor following Stephen's death. Naomi noticed the woman's empty glass. "More tea?"

Pearl shook her head and stood up. "No, dear. I should be getting home. But thank you for the drink and the company."

The woman was about the same height as Naomi, and when Naomi wasn't pregnant, they probably weighed about the same. Naomi felt like she was looking at herself in fifty or sixty years.

Naomi followed Pearl to the door. "Let me drive you home in my buggy. It won't take me long to hitch the horse."

Pearl kept going, pushed the screen door open, and waited for Naomi to join her on the porch. "No need. It's a beautiful day, and I have these wonderful running shoes." She chuckled. "They might be running shoes, but for me, I will only be walking in them." She rocked from heel to toe a few times, just like Esther Rose did the first time she put on new shoes.

Naomi wasn't comfortable letting Pearl take off on foot again, but the older woman told her where she lived, and it was less than a mile away.

"Which house do you live in on Black Horse Road?"

"It's the small blue one that sits between a red brick house and a white house with green shutters, just before you get to the T in the road."

Pearl held the handrail as she made her way down the porch steps. Naomi followed close behind, wondering if she should walk with her at least part of the way. But Pearl seemed steady on her feet, and Naomi had a full day planned.

"Be safe." Naomi waved to Pearl from the bottom step, raising a hand to her forehead to block the sun. She could see Brock on the tractor at the far end of the field.

Pearl waved over her shoulder. "Stay dry when the rain comes."

Naomi scanned the cloudless skies, while her new friend moved at a slow pace down Naomi's driveway, then onto the gravel road that led to Black Horse Road.

Naomi put a hand across her belly again, deciding that she was going to shed her mourning clothes and tell her parents that she was pregnant next weekend. As she walked back into the house, she couldn't help but wonder if Pearl was right in her prediction that the baby was a boy.

Brock raised and lowered the handle on the water pump in Naomi's front yard until a steady stream ran long enough for him to wash his hands. He looked over his shoulder when he heard giggling in the distance.

"*Wie bischt*, Mr. Brock." Abby stopped by the water pump while her sister crossed the yard to the house. She ogled the tractor and baler parked by the barn. "*Mei daed* used mules for the harvest."

Brock dried his hands on his jeans as best he could. "Did your father harvest the hay by himself?"

"*Nee*. My uncle helped him, and then he helped my uncle. My uncle has a hurt foot this year." She hung her head for a moment before she looked back at him with her bright blue eyes. "And my *daed* went to be with Jesus."

Brock swallowed. "Um . . . yeah. I know. I'm sorry about that." He wasn't sure how much a child Abby's age understood about death.

"He used to play Life on the Farm with us. It's a board game." Abby smiled. "It's fun. You buy cows and run a farm." She sneezed before she went on. "Esther Rose isn't very *gut* at it. She almost always loses."

"Bless you." Brock ran his hands along his pants again. "I

better get back to work. I was just taking a break, but I'll see you for supper."

"Have you ever played Life on the Farm?" Abby squinted against the sun's glare.

"No. I haven't. It sounds fun though." Brock smiled before he turned to head back to his equipment. Abby got in step with him.

"Maybe we can play after supper. *Mamm* doesn't play it with us anymore. I think she used to let *Daed* win anyway."

"Maybe." Brock opened the gate that separated the front yard from the field and stepped on the other side, closing the gate between him and the child.

Abby peered through the wooden slats. "Do we have any weevils this year, Mr. Brock?"

He slowed his step and turned around, surprised Abby would know about such things. "Nope. It seems to be a healthy batch of alfalfa."

She nodded. "That's *gut*. You're going to wrap it in plastic to keep it dry, right? *Daed* used to put some in the big barn too." She pointed to a red barn on the far side of the property.

"I'll put some in there for your horse, and I'll make sure it stays dry." He waved and started walking to his tractor. He glanced up at the sky. *All clear.*

It was two hours later when Abby came back to the fence, waving him down for supper. He'd just draped a tarp over the last bale of hay, just to play it safe, even though it didn't look like rain.

"Something smells good in here," he said as he walked into the kitchen.

Naomi looked over her shoulder and smiled. "A simple meal. Just roast and potatoes. And steamed broccoli."

Naomi was a pretty woman with dark hair and big brown eyes. Brock was sure she'd have plenty of Amish suitors soon. It was their way to remarry quickly following the death of a spouse. Brock didn't foresee another wife in his future. It was a lot of work getting to know someone, and he didn't have the energy for romance these days. He'd settled into semi-retirement with ease, even though he took on enough extra jobs that it wasn't really like retirement.

Naomi's girls were already sitting at the table. Brock took a seat in the same place again, where a big glass of iced tea awaited him. He thought about all the meals he'd shared with Patty, just the two of them at a dining room table that could seat six. Sometimes, he'd known Patty wanted to eat on TV trays as opposed to looking at the empty chairs they'd hoped to fill with children someday.

Abby rattled off something in *Pennsylvania Deitsch*. Young Amish children seemed to speak their native dialect in front of outsiders since it is the first language they learn, so he didn't think it was rude. But the context of what Abby was saying was a bit shocking. Brock brought a hand to his mouth, hiding the smile on his face, wondering how they would feel if they knew he understood what they were saying.

Naomi spun around with a spoon in her hand, slinging droplets of brown gravy across the wood floor. She answered her daughter in the same dialect, her eyes wide. They went back and forth several times.

They all turned their attention to the window when pellets of rain dotted the glass. Brock was glad he'd been proactive enough to cover the hay bales.

He finished his last bite of roast, wiped his mouth, and

recalled the conversation between Naomi and her daughter. He couldn't help but smile.

"Was supper okay?" Naomi had the hint of a smile on her face, surely wondering why Brock was grinning. He cleared his throat and forced a solemn expression.

"Yes. It was wonderful. Thank you."

Brock's grandparents were Amish, so he'd understood the dialect since he was a child. The poor woman would be horrified if she knew Brock had understood them.

"*I think that maybe you should marry him,*" Abby had said, nodding at Brock. "*Then you can kiss him to make a baby. I bet he wants some* kinner."

"*Abigail! I don't even know this man, and we don't speak of such things.*"

"*He's old, like* Daadi."

"*He's not that old, and we are not talking about this anymore. Do you hear me?*"

"*I'm going to pray for a new* daed *and a new* boppli."

Naomi had glanced at Brock several times throughout the exchange, but Abby wasn't done.

"*We can't handle a farm by ourselves. We need a man in our lives.*"

It was at that point that Brock had the hardest time holding in his laughter.

"*Abby, I will not have you shopping for a husband for me. Do you understand? So, hush now. I'm just thankful this man doesn't know what you're saying!*"

If she only knew.

Chapter Four

Friday morning, Naomi had just gotten the girls off to school when Brock came up the porch steps and knocked on the kitchen door. Like most of their guests, everyone seemed to migrate to the kitchen door as opposed to the other door, which led into the living room. Maybe because it was the closest entrance when you came up the porch steps. Usually, Naomi only saw Brock at meals, so she was surprised to see him now.

"I need a part for my tractor." He ran his sleeve across his forehead. It was unseasonably hot for September and Naomi had opened all the windows, filling the house with a cool cross breeze.

"I'm so sorry I haven't been bringing you something cold to drink. I forget how hot it can be out in the fields, even this time of year. Can I get you something now?"

"No, no. I bring a small cooler every day with water or lemonade. So I'm fine. I just wanted to let you know I'll be gone for a while. I have to go to Lancaster for the part."

Naomi didn't get to Lancaster very often. It was too far to go by buggy. She thought about the list she'd been adding to, things she couldn't find at the nearby businesses. Abby needed a new tire for her kick scooter, the reason the girls had been walking to the schoolhouse. Esther Rose was allergic to something outside and occasionally got welts on her legs. The homeopathic doctor has suggested a salve to make, and Naomi made it just like he'd said. But when it didn't stop the itching, the doctor suggested an over-the-counter medication that Naomi hadn't been able to find.

"I am so sorry to ask this, and I don't want to trouble you . . ." She bit her bottom lip, flinching a little. "Is there any way I can go with you? Could we go to Walmart?" It was the best kept secret in her community. Amish women loved Walmart.

"Of course. It's no problem at all."

Naomi was surprised that Brock didn't question her about it. Most *Englisch* thought that the Amish only shopped at markets nearby, and there was a tiny store similar to Walmart in Paradise, but they had a limited selection.

"I can hire a driver, I've just been . . ." She was trying to be frugal with money, but decided not to share that with Brock. ". . . busy and haven't gotten around to it." And that was the truth too.

"Naomi, I don't mind taking you anywhere you want to go. Really. I retired early because I was more or less forced to when the company I'd worked for my entire life went belly-up. So, I farmed full-time for a while, but after Patty died, I thought I'd be better off with a smaller place." He scratched his forehead as he shook his head. "But I got bored pretty quick. Besides, idle hands makes for idle minds, and I'm only forty-one. I take on construction jobs, or sometimes even harvest hay for someone who needs help." He smiled. "But I still have more free time than I'd like. So, even after I'm done with the harvest, you can call on me for rides if you need them."

"We all pay drivers. Maybe that's something you could do

to occupy some time. I could spread the word around to friends and family."

Brock shook his head. "I don't want to do it all the time for everyone. I prefer jobs where I work outside." He winked at her, which was a bit unsettling. "But I'll take you wherever you want to go."

Naomi wondered if he was flirting with her. It had been so long since Stephen courted her, she barely remembered what it felt like. Surely not, she decided. He was fourteen years older than her and a friend of her father's. That made him safe. And safe was high on her priority list.

⁓⁓⁓

Brock silently reprimanded himself for winking at Naomi. She'd blushed right away, and he didn't want to do anything to make her feel uncomfortable. He enjoyed bringing in their hay. Something about being on a tractor made a man feel like a man, and when the weather cooperated, there was nothing better than a hard day's work. He was thankful the rain hadn't lasted.

"I'll just get my purse." Naomi scooted around the corner, but peeked back around a few seconds later. "Will we be back before school is out?"

"I'll make sure we are."

She smiled and was gone again, returning with a small black purse. "Ready."

Brock noticed she didn't lock the door when they left, just pulled it closed behind her.

"I appreciate this," she said after they'd turned onto Lincoln Highway. "Stephen built the girls' scooters from extra bicycle parts he'd found here and there, so the tires are a special size, not typical of the scooters people buy around here."

"No problem at all." He glanced in her direction for a moment and noticed she'd shed her mourning clothes. "So, no more black clothes?"

She pressed her lips together, frowning a little. "Do you think it's too soon? *Mamm* said it was up to me when I chose to move on, but maybe I should have waited longer."

"I think that's a personal decision, totally your choice." Again, Brock wanted to tell her that time would heal, but he recalled how he hated hearing that after Patty died.

"I loved my husband." She raised her chin and stared forward. "I did."

Brock sensed there was more to the comment, but he just nodded.

"He was *gut* in many ways. He was a *gut* father to the girls." She turned to Brock. "And he had a strong work ethic."

Brock wondered why she felt the need to convince him about her husband's character, a man Brock hadn't known.

"But I'm done mourning him," she said in a whisper as she faced forward again. And there was no mistaking the finality in which she made the statement. Brock stayed quiet, unsure what to say.

"Do you think that makes me a bad person?" she asked after a while.

Brock cleared his throat. "No. Like I said, a personal decision."

"*Mei* parents liked Stephen. I think my father respected his work habits. He got along well with my *bruder* and his family also." She sighed. "*Ya*. Everyone liked Stephen."

Her words held an undertone, a demeanor Brock couldn't quite grasp. "Well . . . that's good."

"I guess." She stared out the window and didn't say much for the next few minutes. Then she twisted in her seat to face him. "I'm pregnant. And no one knows."

Then why in the world are you telling me? "Uh, are you happy about that?" It sounded like a dumb thing to say, but he wasn't sure where their conversation was going, so he wanted to tread lightly. Her face brightened.

"*Ach, ya.* Very happy. A child is a gift from God."

Brock supposed that was true. It was God's choice who He blessed with children, not a given. For a while, Brock had felt cheated since he and Patty couldn't have children. But he'd grown to accept it. More so than his wife. Looking back, Brock was sure that's when his communion with God began to slip. He couldn't understand how the Lord would deny Patty the chance to be a mother. Brock hoped she had lots of children to care for in heaven.

"A baby needs a father." Naomi sighed. "So do my girls. But there's not one man in our district that I could even think about dating." She turned to face him again. "I don't want to date or get remarried. But it's the right thing to do, *ya?*"

Brock shrugged. "That's another one of those personal decisions." He stifled a grin as he recalled Naomi's conversation with Abby about not shopping for a husband.

"I want to do what's right."

Brock nodded. He decided he was going to pray for Naomi to find a good man for her and her children. Maybe praying for someone else would help him get right with God again. He didn't ask for much these days. If he didn't ask, he wouldn't be let down. He still had a strong faith, he just felt a little disappointed with how God had directed his life. His attitude was like a bad habit he needed to kick. But he still went to church most Sundays, hoping that God would just let him live in peace.

"Why haven't you told anyone you're pregnant?" Brock wondered how far along she was, but a pregnancy was easy enough to hide beneath the loose dresses the Amish women wore.

She leaned her head back against the headrest and closed her eyes. "I don't know." Sighing, she raised her head. "Having a baby is such a joyous occasion. I wanted everyone to be happy about the news and I didn't want that to supersede their mourning of Stephen." She folded her hands in her lap atop her purse and turned to him again, her eyes soft and inquiring. "Do you want to remarry? Do you date? I mean I know you're older and all, and maybe it—" She paused and bit her lip. "I don't mean *older*, like really old, like you can't remarry, or—"

Brock held up a hand and chuckled. "It's okay. It's been two years since Patty died, and I dated a few women in the past year, but none of them were right for me. Believe it or not, I have a fairly young heart, and I like to stay active and busy . . . for an old guy." He laughed again.

Naomi grinned. "You're not old. Just *older*."

Brock reached in front of her to point to her side of the highway. She instantly threw her hands in front of her face. "Sorry, I didn't mean to make you flinch. I was just pointing to that carnival going on over there. How many old guys do you know who would ride every single ride there?"

She lowered her hands. "I just saw your arm . . . and . . . sorry." She smiled. "My girls have always wanted to go to a festival like that."

"Is it allowed?" Brock knew a lot about the Amish because of his grandparents, but they had been gone a long time, and the Amish modified their rules, which also may differ by district. Cell phones were evidence of that, and most families had at least one of those. Brock could remember the shanty his grandparents shared with two other families. A phone booth of sorts that housed a rotary phone strictly for emergencies. Those days were long gone.

"The festivals are allowed, of course. Our bishop doesn't really encourage the rides that are powered with electricity, but I overheard him say one time that he was willing to overlook it." She paused. "Stephen didn't like heights, though, so I guess he didn't think the rest of us would either." Frowning, her voice had slipped back into a place Brock was having trouble translating. *Bitterness* was the word that came to mind. He understood that. Brock had gone through the gamut of emotions after Patty died. Mad at God, and even mad at Patty for a while for leaving him, which made no sense.

Brock turned in the Walmart parking lot, deciding to drop Naomi off while he went to the tractor supply store for his part. "I'll come back and get you in about a half hour. Is that enough time?"

Naomi nodded. It was easy to see how her father was such good friends with Brock. Gideon Huyard was a man who didn't befriend *Englisch* folks easily, and he was generally distrusting of outsiders. If he trusted Brock enough to bring in Naomi's harvest, that told her a lot. Maybe that's why she'd told Brock she was pregnant. He wasn't mourning Stephen, and she'd felt the need to tell someone. She was surprised word hadn't gotten out since Dr. Noah was her doctor, and he was local. But it was time to share the news. This baby was coming in less than four months.

Standing on the sidewalk thirty minutes later, she parked

her cart, filled with two small bags and a bicycle tire across the top. Brock pulled up to the curb, and before Naomi could even open the back door of his big truck, he was opening it for her and loading her things.

"I'm starving," he said as he shut the door. "We should have time to grab some lunch and still get back way before your daughters get home from school. You hungry?"

Naomi's stomach growled. What a treat it would be to eat out, but she'd spent almost all of the money she'd brought with her in Walmart. "Um . . . I am. Uh . . ."

"My treat," he said as he opened the front door for her, shutting it once she was inside. "Where do you want to go?" He put the white truck in drive and started out of the parking lot.

"I-I don't know. Stephen usually chose a restaurant on the few occasions we went out to eat." She pondered the possibilities, thought about all the places she'd always wanted to try, but maybe Brock just meant that they would get a hamburger at a fast-food type place.

"Have you ever been there?" Brock pointed to his left. "They have steaks, chicken, burgers, seafood . . . a little bit of everything."

Naomi twirled the string on her *kapp*. "That's a fancy place."

Brock grinned. "It's really not all that fancy, but if you think you'd be uncomfortable, we can go somewhere—"

"*Nee.* That place is fine." Naomi decided to grab on to this opportunity.

During the meal, she and Brock settled into a casual conversation. He was easy to talk to. And a good listener. She decided then and there—while eating the best steak she'd ever had—that she was going to pray for Brock to find the peace he seemed to be searching for. She liked his thinking. He only had one goal, not a long list of expectations or desires. Just a desire for the peace of Christ.

On the way home, he slowed down as they went by the festival again. "Well, if you weren't pregnant, I'd beg you to go ride the rides with me tomorrow at that carnival." He chuckled.

Naomi thought again about how much her girls would enjoy something like that, even if they were too small to go on some of the larger rides. But she was sure Brock wouldn't want to take a pregnant woman and her two children for the day.

Brock let out a deep breath, then turned to her. "I don't even know if I should ask this. I'll be the first to admit that I don't know a whole lot about kids. I've only been around my brother's children a few times since he lives so far away. But you said your girls would have fun at a carnival like this. Are they big enough to ride any of the rides?" He laughed. "Look at me, trying to round up little kids to go on rides with me."

Naomi smiled, but festivals—or carnivals, as he called them—cost money too. "Do you know, um . . . does it cost a lot?"

He shrugged. "I've got plenty of money, just not anyone to ride the rides with me."

Naomi studied his expression for a moment. He looked like a little boy with his crooked smile and all the excitement in his voice. He sure didn't act like a forty-one-year-old man. Her girls would love an adventure like that. And Brock was her father's friend. He was older and *Englisch*. No one would push her into dating someone like that. He might become as good a friend to her and her children as he was to her father, and that sounded nice.

"I think the girls would love to go," she finally said.

Chapter Five

"Esther Rose, go upstairs right now and get dressed." Naomi gave her daughter a gentle pat on the behind. "Scoot. We're late."

Abby dropped onto the couch like a sack of potatoes, then tossed her head against the back of the sofa. "Why can't we go to the carnival *now*? Why do we have to wait until this afternoon?"

Naomi scurried from place to place in the living room, picking up empty glasses, a pair of dirty socks, some books, and Esther Rose's doll. "Because we need to go see *Mammi* and *Daadi* this morning. I already told you that."

Esther Rose hopped with both feet down each step, something Naomi had told her repeatedly not to do. "I'm ready," she said, holding her socks and shoes in one hand and her blanket in the other. The tattered, pink material that Esther Rose clung to could barely survive the wringer washing machine these days. But each time Naomi tried to separate Esther Rose and her beloved blankie, tears ensued. Naomi wasn't up for the battle today.

"That's *gut*. But now go back upstairs and put on one of your pretty pastel-colored dresses. Remember, I said we're not going to wear our black dresses anymore."

Naomi wished it was acceptable for an adult to wear pastel

colors. But she was happy in a dark green dress, glad to be wearing color again. She handed the books and doll to Abby.

"Please carry these upstairs to your sister's room. I'm having a hard enough time getting her ready to go."

Abby huffed and didn't move from the couch. "Why? Esther Rose left them down here. Why do I always have to clean up after her?"

"Please, just do it," Naomi said, wondering when her children had become so argumentative.

Both girls were upstairs when Naomi caught a glimpse of someone walking up the driveway toward the house. When the woman got closer, Naomi recognized Pearl King.

Naomi hurried onto the porch and down the steps to where she'd already hitched the horse to the buggy. She was hoping Pearl would sense that Naomi was in a hurry to leave and not expect to come in for a visit. But Naomi wouldn't be rude to the old woman either. Pearl was toting a bag in one hand and waved to Naomi with the other.

Naomi returned the gesture and waited in the yard until Pearl reached her. "Hello, Pearl. How are you?"

"I see you must be on your way out, so I will not keep you." Pearl smiled as she handed Naomi a small brown bag with handles. "I wanted to repay your kindness with something I'm told is my specialty, Florentines."

"*Ach*, this is so nice of you, but it wasn't necessary." Naomi pulled out a batch of cookies in plastic wrap with a pink ribbon tied around the opening. "But I know my girls will love these."

"I usually make them during the holidays, but I had a craving for them, so I made a double batch for sharing."

Naomi started to put the cookies back in the brown sack

when she saw something else. She lifted a purple mesh bag held together by a dark blue ribbon. "What's this?"

"Oh dear. I'm sorry about that." Pearl eased the bag away from Naomi. "That was meant for someone else. I get so many orders this time of year, and I must have put this one in your cookie bag by mistake."

Naomi studied the small bag that fit in the palm of Pearl's hand. "What's in there?" It looked like an oversized purple tea bag filled with herbs, and a lump of . . . something Naomi couldn't identify.

Pearl slowly untied the blue ribbon and widened the opening. "You see, there is an amethyst inside."

Naomi leaned closer until she saw the tiny rock. "Are those herbs in there with it?"

Pearl nodded. "But not just any herbs. They're organic. There's a bit of lavender, a pinch of white sage, some St. John's Wart. And in that small vial is a special blend of oils that are a family secret." She carefully tied the ribbon back around the opening. "During the waxing phase of the moon, I'm always overloaded with orders. I'm sorry one of these found its way into your cookie bag." She grinned. "I'm a careless old woman."

"Why do people order them? I wouldn't think you could cook with that since there is a rock inside." She pointed to the bag, still cradled in Pearl's hand.

"Oh, no, dear." Pearl's forehead wrinkled as she drew her mouth into a frown. "This is not for eating, it's for protection. This packet, along with dozens of others that I have at home, have been prayed over and specially prepared, as we grow closer to the rise of the harvest moon in a few weeks."

"Protection? From what?" Naomi glanced at her horse when

it whinnied, a reminder that she needed to excuse herself soon. "We've always looked forward to the harvest moon and thought of it as a blessing. The extra light it provides allows farmers to work longer, and it's symbolic of our hard work. *Mei daed* calls it the Full Corn Moon."

Pearl continued to frown as she shook her head. "I'm afraid it has many names with much superstition attached to each one. Some Europeans call it a Gypsy Moon. Historically, the Norse believed that it was the most powerful moon of the year because it was associated with the trickster god Loki." She paused and looked at her hand, gingerly running a wrinkled finger across the bag. "Moon superstitions abound, my dear, but everything is magnified this time of year with the approach of the harvest moon." She moved a bit closer to Naomi. "There was a time when your people were my biggest customers. The Amish have always been known to have deeply rooted superstitions."

"I've never believed in such things." Naomi looked over her shoulder toward the house and hoped her girls were ready to go.

"I'm surprised no one has mentioned this to you, to take precautions during this time of year. Especially now, since you are with child."

Naomi snapped her attention back to Pearl. "What? Why does that matter?" She couldn't help but think about the baby she'd lost, even if she'd never been superstitious.

"No worries, child. I'm sure all will be well." Pearl stuffed the small bag into her purse. "I can see that you are preparing for travel. Be safe and well, and enjoy the cookies." She waved and turned to leave.

Naomi glanced back and forth between Pearl and her house, knowing she and the girls needed to get on the road. "Pearl, wait."

The old woman slowed her pace and turned around. Naomi walked toward her.

"How much for one of those little packets?"

"These treasures are sixty dollars." Pearl smiled, but Naomi's jaw dropped.

"For herbs and a rock?" She brought a hand to her chest. "How can that be?"

"I told you." Pearl raised her chin. "These aren't just regular old herbs, and the combination of oils is a special potion, and all of it has been prayed over by many different people."

Alarms were going off in Naomi's head, especially at the mention of the word *potion*. "Like a witch's potion?"

Pearl chuckled. "I assure you, dear girl, I'm not a witch. Just someone who believes that extra protection at certain times of the year can give a person peace of mind."

"Can-can I buy that packet in your purse?" Naomi swallowed hard. Sixty dollars would buy grocery staples for two weeks, things they didn't grow on the farm or make by hand.

"I thought you didn't believe in such things."

"*Ach*, well . . . I don't. Not really." Naomi wasn't sure she was willing to take the risk. She couldn't bear it if anything happened to the baby she was carrying. She asked Pearl to wait while she went into the house to get some cash. Both her girls had shed their shoes and socks. Esther Rose didn't have her *kapp* on yet, and it appeared that the blankie would be making the trip with them today.

"Girls, get your shoes and socks on, and Abby help Esther Rose get her prayer covering on."

Abby grunted. "I hope you're not going to let her take that blanket."

Before Naomi could answer, Esther Rose screamed, clutching the worn cloth to her chest. It was probably time for Esther Rose to give up her cherished possession, but Naomi had given her younger daughter some leeway since Stephen's death. "We're not going to worry about it today," Naomi said above Esther Rose's wailing, which stopped right away.

After Abby moaned, both girls started pulling their socks on, and Naomi found three twenty-dollar bills and went back outside.

Naomi handed Pearl the money in exchange for the packet.

"You must keep this on your person the entire time," Pearl said. "And at night, you should sleep with it under your pillow. And it's best not to sleep with the moon shining on your face, so keep that in mind when it is time for bed." She paused, holding up a finger. "That is something you should always avoid, even when a harvest moon isn't approaching."

Naomi nodded, put the packet in her apron pocket, and said good-bye to Pearl. By the time she rounded up the girls and traveled to her parents' house, they were an hour late.

"I was getting worried," Naomi's mother said after she opened the front door. She showered the girls with hugs, then Abby and Esther Rose scurried to the kitchen, where they knew they'd find freshly baked cookies and lemonade already set out for them.

"Where's *Daed*?" Naomi wanted to tell both her parents that she was pregnant, along with her girls. But her mother frowned as she sat down on the couch next to Naomi.

"I didn't want to say anything in front of the *kinner*, but I noticed you've all stopped wearing your mourning clothes." Naomi's mother was still donning a black dress and apron.

"Um, *ya*, we have. You said it was a personal choice when we chose to stop mourning."

The lines on her mother's forehead deepened even more as she folded her hands in her lap. "*Mei maedel*, it is a personal choice, but it's only been four months. What will people think? I expected you would go at least eight or nine months." *Mamm* shook her head. "It's too soon. Men in the district will think you are available for courtship. *Ya*, it's *gut* to remarry, and it's encouraged by the bishop after the loss of a spouse, but I'm sure you are not ready after only four months."

"People are already trying to play matchmaker anyway. But *nee*, I'm not ready." Naomi didn't think she would ever be ready for that. How could she trust another man? And she'd obviously failed at being a wife, driving her husband to levels of anger that resulted in violence. As much as she wanted to tell her mother about the baby, it was not turning out to be the joyous announcement she'd hoped for. She'd wanted to tell her parents so many times, and she was surely anxious for Abby and Esther Rose to know. Naomi had been careful not to change clothes around her daughters, and she watched how she sat, making sure her dress wasn't taut against her tummy.

Mamm patted her on the leg. "A few more months, I think, at least."

In less than four months, I'll have a baby. She reached into the pocket of her apron and touched the packet of herbs she'd gotten from Pearl. Her stomach roiled when she thought about the money she'd spent, but she wasn't willing to take a chance of anything happening to her unborn child. Naomi knew such superstitions were rubbish, but still . . .

Mamm started to talk about a small lap quilt that she was

making for a friend who was ill, but Naomi's thoughts were still on the baby growing inside her. She lost track of time as her mother carried on the conversation.

Abby rushed into the living room with Esther Rose on her heels about thirty minutes later. Esther Rose sported a red mustache and carried her blanket. *Must have been cherry Kool-Aid today instead of lemonade.* Naomi wondered how many cookies they'd eaten.

"When is Mr. Brock going to pick us up to go to the carnival?" Abby bounced up on her toes. "I'm ready for rides!"

Naomi and her mother exchanged glances, then Naomi stood up. "Soon, so we best get back on the road." They were leaving earlier than Naomi had planned, but the visit hadn't gone as she had hoped.

"What's this?" Her mother lifted herself from the couch and put on a false smile. "Mr. Brock? Your father's friend? Why is he taking you to the carnival?"

Naomi heard insinuation in her mother's tone. "Girls, tell *Mammi* bye and go wait for me by the buggy."

When they were gone, Naomi said, "I know what you're thinking. This isn't a date. Stephen never wanted to take the girls to a fall festival or carnival, and when I mentioned that yesterday in his truck on the way back from town, Brock said he loved carnivals and would be happy to take them. We passed by a carnival. That's how the subject came up."

"In his truck? Why wasn't he working? And why were you traveling in his truck?"

Naomi silently reprimanded herself for making things worse. "He needed a part for his tractor and was going to Lancaster. I asked if I could go along. Abby needed a tire for her scooter and I had a few other things on my Walmart list."

"I know all of you younger people love Walmart, but I'm not sure it's a *gut* idea to go there. We should support our local vendors and friends."

Naomi breathed a sigh of relief, glad the conversation had shifted. "I know, *Mamm*. But we can't get everything we need around here."

Her mother shook her head. "Times are changing and that scares me. Almost everyone is toting a portable phone now too."

"You have one." Naomi folded her arms across her chest. "So does *Daed*."

"For emergencies."

Naomi grinned. "Cousin Sarah Mae in Ohio must have a lot of emergencies."

Smiling, Naomi's mother gave her a gentle push toward the girls. "Go, now. Have fun at your carnival. Don't let the girls ride anything dangerous. They're not big enough for many of those rides, I'm sure."

Naomi kissed her mother on the cheek and left, excited for their afternoon, but upset that she'd disappointed her mother by shedding her mourning clothes. And even more unhappy that she hadn't felt comfortable telling her mother about the baby. Naomi laid a hand on her tummy as she walked to her buggy where the girls were waiting, knowing it wouldn't be long before her belly popped out and it'd be impossible to hide.

Chapter Six

Brock had a bounce in his step as he walked the length of Naomi's yard, then up her porch steps. He heard giggling coming from inside. He almost always knocked and went in through the kitchen, but the laughter was coming from the living room so he veered toward that door. Abby opened the door before he knocked.

"We're ready for rides!" She clapped her hands and pushed the screen open. Brock had to jump back so it didn't hit him.

"I'm ready for rides too." It was fun seeing Abby so excited, and Brock felt like a kid again. He couldn't remember the last carnival he'd gone to. It was a beautiful, cloudless day with just enough breeze for a nip in the air, but when the warmth of the sun comingled with the coolness, it was just right.

"The girls are very excited," Naomi said when she and Esther Rose came up behind Abby. Esther Rose was carrying a pink blanket. He'd noticed the child toting it around. He was a little surprised to see her bring it today, but he remembered his brother carting around a stuffed bear until he was much too old to be doing so. He hoped the blanket would stay in the truck while they walked around; he didn't want to be searching the carnival grounds all night if she lost it.

Brock noticed they were all in black clothes again, but he didn't say anything. Apparently, Naomi wasn't ready to move on yet. Maybe Brock could give the three of them a fun day, even if his own boyish motivations had instigated the plans. The alfalfa needed another day to dry out anyway.

~⟶~

Naomi and Brock didn't talk much, mostly because Abby and Esther Rose kept up a steady chatter from the backseat of Brock's truck. Naomi was glad that there didn't seem to be a need to make small talk since two things were sitting heavy on her heart. She reached into the pocket of her apron and touched the bag Pearl had given her, feeling silly for spending the money on such nonsense. But what if there was an ounce of truth in what Pearl said? Naomi was also still upset about her mother thinking she and the children should be in mourning longer. *I thought it was my choice.*

Brock got out of the truck with as much energy as the girls, and it was cute the way each of them grabbed one of his hands, even though it appeared to have caught Brock off guard as she saw him startle. Brock had mentioned that he didn't know anything about children, but one thing about *kinner*—they had an uncanny ability to know adults, seeming to latch on or avoid without anything more than an instinct. Her girls liked Brock. Naomi lingered a couple of steps behind the trio and felt herself blush when her gaze found Brock's backside. He wore dark jeans, and his red T-shirt stretched nicely across his broad shoulders.

From behind, he looked like he could be her age. She'd noticed the first day she met him that he was a handsome man.

Naomi's daughters looked even tinier than they were on either side of such a big man. *He could really hurt someone if he was mad.* Naomi hated that the thought popped into her mind. Brock was a friend of her father's, and he seemed to have a gentle spirit. But after rolling it over in her mind, she sighed. Stephen had been a friend to everyone too. There hadn't been a problem with anyone but her.

Brock should feel ridiculous riding a Ferris wheel with a seven-year-old, but as the breeze blew his hair and the sun warmed his face, visions of his childhood rose to the surface, and he suddenly missed his brother, the only family he had left. He was going to call Andrew and schedule a visit.

Abby's bright eyes shone, and the smile on her face looked permanently affixed. Brock figured she wouldn't be asking for her two front teeth for Christmas since the Amish holiday celebrations didn't usually include Santa Claus. Strands of curly blond hair fell across Abby's face as they neared the top of the ride.

It was more than just the rides that fueled Brock's thoughts. It was the feel of family, the memories he'd made with Andrew when they were young, and the smell of popcorn, cotton candy, and funnel cakes. The weather, the scents, the laughter, the families . . . it all screamed of fall harvest time. He was glad that today he had borrowed a family to share the day with.

When loud screeching grinded the ride to a halt, Abby twisted to face him, her eyes wide as saucers . . . then she screamed. Brock had no idea that much noise could come from a child her size. He stared at her, held his breath, and had no idea what to do. The scream went on forever.

"Abby, it's okay. We're just stuck for a minute. We're okay."

That didn't deter the child's fear, and Brock found Naomi in the crowd below them with Esther Rose by her side, both of them looking up. Naomi had a hand to her forehead, blocking the sun, but the fear in her wide eyes prodded Brock to get control of this situation. He grabbed Abby's hand and squeezed.

"Abby, Abby. Listen. This happens all the time." He forced a smile, having no idea if that was true. He shrugged. "No big deal at all. Just part of the fun." He looked down at the rungs that led from the top of the ride to the bottom, wondering if he'd be able to carry the child to safety if it came to that. *Surely not.* But in all his carnival memories, he couldn't remember ever getting stuck on a ride.

"How long will we be here?" Abby's bottom lip trembled. "Is this ride broken?"

Brock breathed a small sigh of relief that she'd stopped screaming. "No, it's not broken, and we'll be moving again soon. Then we can celebrate our adventure with some cotton candy or something."

"What's that?"

"Cotton candy?" Brock wasn't sure how to explain it to her. "Um, it's sweet. Lots of sugar. You'll like it." He decided distracting her was working. "That's part of the fun of a carnival, eating all the foods they have."

"Like ice cream?"

"Yep. I'm sure they have ice cream."

Abby finally looked at the ground below them, and Naomi

blew her a kiss and smiled. Brock took in another deep breath, wondering if she was going to scream again, but wondering even more when they would be moving again. Even Brock was beginning to feel unsettled, his stomach churning a little.

"*Mei daed* didn't like ice cream."

"At all? Not even plain old vanilla?" Brock had never heard of anyone not liking ice cream.

Abby shook her head. "Are we going to fall off this ride and die?"

Brock squeezed her hand again. "No, no, no. Of course not. Sometimes these things just happen with rides. Maybe they had to put grease on a part or something. Abby, I won't let anything happen to you."

"*Mei daed* died."

Brock swallowed hard. "Yeah. I know." He glanced at the little black dress and apron she was wearing again. "I bet you really miss him."

She was quiet, but then waved to her mother, and thankfully, the ride slowly started to move again. "*Ya*, I miss him."

Brock didn't say anything, deciding to enjoy the view of Amish country as they neared the top of the ride again. Abby eased her hand from his, but her smile didn't resurface.

"He was a *gut daed.*"

"I know. That's what I heard. You probably have great memories of him." *Help, Lord. I really don't want to mess up this conversation.*

Abby turned to him, her lip quivering again. "He wasn't always nice to *Mamm*, though." She jumped when the ride stopped again, leaving them near the top.

"It's okay." He pointed to the ground. "See, they're stopping to let people off. This is normal." He thought for a few moments.

"Well, even couples who love each other have arguments sometimes. But that doesn't mean they don't love each other."

"When *Mamm* was bad, *Daed* would hit her. Not like a spanking." Abby hung her head, sighing as if she had the wisdom of an adult, before she looked back at him. "Esther Rose doesn't know, I don't think. And that's probably *gut*."

Brock thought back to the conversation in *Pennsylvania Deitsch* between Naomi and Abby. *This child is wise beyond her years.* But had she misread her father's actions somehow? "I'm sure he didn't . . . hit her. Maybe you misunderstood what you saw, your dad was probably playing or something?"

"*Nee.*" Abby kept her eyes locked with Brock's, even when the ride moved and stopped to let people off. She moved a strand of hair from across her face again. "He made her cry sometimes. Don't tell Esther Rose. She's too young to understand."

You're too young to understand. Brock glanced at Naomi, who had a hand to her chest, as if she were holding her breath, waiting for their turn to exit the ride. When it finally came, Abby ran straight to Naomi, threw her arms around her, and began telling Naomi about being stuck at the top.

Brock slowly caught up to them, but the conversation with Abby was just starting to catch up with him, and as he looked at Naomi and her children, he had to assume that Abby had misread something in her father's actions. Brock didn't want her to store those memories if they weren't true. His thoughts were interrupted when Abby threw up, much of it landing on her sister's pink blanket. It turns out that Esther Rose could scream louder than her sister.

Brock was mostly quiet on the way home, he couldn't stop think-ing about what Abby had told him. When it started to rain, his thoughts shifted, wondering if he had covered the alfalfa well enough. Either way, rain could set the hay baling back several more days, if it lasted.

Both girls had fallen asleep within minutes after they'd left the carnival, despite a massive overconsumption of sugar; from cotton candy, to ice cream, and everything else they set their sights on. Once Abby had purged, she was ready to match her sister's sugar intake bite for bite. Naomi said Abby probably had too many cookies earlier in the day when they were visiting with their grandma, then the ride triggered the upset stomach. *The resilience of youth.* Naomi had cleaned up both girls, washed the blanket in the bathroom sink, and maintained the patience of a saint. He'd noticed that about Naomi. Even when the girls had bickered occasionally, Naomi was calm but firm. They were sweet kids, fun to be around, so the occasional tiff hadn't both-ered Brock.

"It's hard to believe it's raining so hard when it was so beau-tiful earlier." Naomi glanced in the backseat. "Still sleeping."

"Yeah, the rain kind of puts us behind schedule a little." Brock shrugged. "But what can you do? Can't control the weather, I guess."

He thought about Abby again. The Amish weren't immune to abuse, infidelity, addictions, or anything else that the rest of the world dealt with, but as he glanced at Naomi, he couldn't imagine someone laying a hand on her, especially someone who should love and cherish her. And she was so tiny. And pregnant. Almost as upsetting was that Abby knew about it. Or thought she did. Brock was holding out hope that it wasn't true.

It was pouring when they pulled in, and both girls were still sound asleep in the backseat. "Do you want to carry the smaller one and I'll get the bigger one?" He realized right away he should have used their names. "I mean, I can get Abby if you want to get Esther Rose."

She pointed to her stomach. "I-I can't really carry Esther Rose being this far along. They'll be okay walking."

He knocked himself gently on the forehead with his hand. "Sorry. I forgot. No problem, I'll get them both. There's an umbrella under your seat, so use that for yourself, and I'll try to keep the girls covered best I can with my coat." He reached for a jacket on the back floorboard of the truck.

"Really. They can walk. I don't know how you're going to carry them both." She found the umbrella, but looked over her shoulder. "Abby's awake. We'll make a run for it if you can get Esther Rose, and it won't be the end of the world if we all get wet." She smiled, then pulled the door open.

Once they were all in the house, dripping on the wood floor in the kitchen, Naomi handed him a kitchen towel while she dabbed at the girls' faces, then sent them upstairs to bathe and change clothes. Naomi had done a pretty good job cleaning the girls and the little one's blanket at the carnival, but Brock had caught a whiff of unpleasantness every now and then during the ride home. *Probably Esther Rose's blanket.* If Brock hadn't known better—and he didn't—he might have thought Abby intentionally aimed for her sister's treasured blanket.

"Well, thanks for sharing your kids with me today. It reminded me of when my brother and I used to go to carnivals when we were young. Good memories."

"They had a wonderful time. And who knows when they'll

have the opportunity to go again." Naomi reached down and flattened her palms against her stomach, then she looked up at him and smiled. "He's moving."

Brock stared at her hands, wondering how incredible it must feel to have a life moving inside you. "He? So, it's a boy?"

Still smiling, she shrugged. "In my mind, it's a he. But if it's a girl, that's *gut* with me too."

Brock nodded. "Well, I hope you girls have a good night. I guess I'll be back to work on Monday, weather permitting." He walked onto the porch and sighed. *Pouring.* He turned when he heard the screen door slam behind him.

"Mr. Brock, do you want to stay for supper? It's nothing fancy tonight. I was just going to make some chicken and dumplings, an easy version of my grandmother's recipe."

Brock's mouth watered at the thought. Every meal Naomi had prepared had been nothing short of great. "Are you sure? I didn't work today, so you don't owe me a meal."

She laughed. "After everything you did for my girls today, I owe you a lot more than a meal."

Brock felt himself blush a little, unusual for him. Thankfully, Naomi didn't seem to make the statement in the same way that he took it, which made him want to either laugh or knock himself upside the head. But either way, he was hungry and not looking forward to heading back into the downpour. "Sure. I'd love to stay."

After they were back in the house, he offered to start a fire. The temperature had fallen as night grew near, and he and Naomi were still damp from the rain.

～✺～

Naomi was tired, and the baby had been active the entire time she'd prepared supper. She loved feeling him—or her—moving inside of her. She recalled when that had stopped happening with Adam. She would do whatever it took to carry this baby full term. She'd been careful about not lifting anything heavy. She'd forced herself to calm down, even when Abby and Esther Rose took to bickering. And if a bag filled with herbs and a rock gave her peace of mind, she wasn't going to beat herself up about the purchase.

While she finished supper, Brock read a book to the girls, at their insistence, sitting on either side of him on the couch. It was nice hearing him read to Abby and Esther Rose, something she hadn't done enough of since Stephen died.

As Naomi placed rolls on the table, she called everyone to the kitchen, and once they were settled, they bowed their heads. Naomi silently recited her usual prayers and remembered to include Brock.

Her new friend had said that all he wanted was a quiet, peaceful existence, but Naomi had noticed some things about Brock that he perhaps wasn't aware of himself. He'd said he didn't think he would get married again. But he was so good with children, any family would be blessed to have him. But after thinking about it, Naomi decided it was not her place to make choices about the man's future, so she prayed for his peace and happiness.

It rained all through supper, and as the wind whipped against the house and thunder rattled the windows, it felt gloomy in the dimly lit room. Naomi had never liked storms, even though they didn't seem to bother her daughters. She turned up both the lanterns in the middle of the table to brighten the area. Brock went to put another log on the fire, sending orange sparks shimmying up the chimney, casting a distant glow in the living room.

Naomi sliced the chocolate cake she'd made early that morning, and they all ate it in the living room by the warmth of the fire. Shortly thereafter, despite the rain, Brock thanked her again for the meal, but said he should head home. Abby and Esther Rose each hugged Brock and thanked him for the fun day at the carnival. Neither one of her girls were overly affectionate, except with Naomi's parents, and rarely with someone they didn't know well.

Yawning, she got the girls all tucked in upstairs, then readied herself for bed. It had been such a good day. She put a hand across her stomach as she crawled into bed and felt her baby moving. Then she remembered the packet Pearl said to keep under her pillow when she slept. She got out of bed and dug through her laundry basket until she found her clothes from today. When the packet wasn't in the pocket of her apron, she dumped all of the clothes on the floor and searched through each piece. *It's not here.*

She carried her lantern through the living room and into the kitchen, looking everywhere. Next she tiptoed upstairs, wondering if somehow she'd leaned over when she tucked the girls in. After a quiet inspection, still nothing.

Silly superstition.

But as she climbed into bed, there was a sense of dread that she couldn't shake. She curled onto her side and placed a hand across her stomach.

Chapter Seven

Naomi was anxious all through worship service the next morning, and she was glad when her mother agreed to watch Abby and Esther Rose for a while in the afternoon. Naomi told her parents she wanted a nice quiet nap, which was true. But before she'd be able to rest easy, she had an errand to run.

She knocked on Pearl's door and waited as a dog barked from inside. After a while she heard Pearl shushing the dog, then the older woman opened the door, a small brown dachshund beside her.

"I lost my packet." She brought a hand to her chest, choosing to bypass any type of formal greeting. "I'm sorry to bother you on a Sunday, but can I please purchase another one?" Reaching into the pocket of her apron, she pulled out a hundred-dollar bill she'd stowed away for an emergency. She wasn't sure this qualified as such, but Naomi pushed the money toward Pearl until she took it. The woman's bun was tousled, loose strands dangling on either side of her face, similar to how she'd looked when she showed up at Naomi's that first day. And Pearl was wearing a blue housecoat with matching wooly socks. She stared at the money and frowned.

"I'm sorry, child. I don't have any more of those. I'm sold out." Pearl lifted a crooked finger. "Wait here, and I'll go see what else I might have." She closed the door and returned a few moments later. "I have this."

She handed Naomi a similar bag, but it was almost double the size.

"How much is this one?" Naomi thought about how her emergency fund was shrinking, along with her everyday operating money as well. Even though Stephen had accepted plenty of jobs outside of just farming, they hadn't saved much, and Naomi was going through what was left faster than she'd intended. Several times, she'd made a list of things she might consider selling on consignment at various shops in the area. But that's as far as she got. Running the farm and taking care of the girls, along with the few animals they had, took most of her time.

"This larger packet has two amethysts, you see?" She held the purple mesh bag closer to Naomi. "There are more herbs, special oils, and blessings and prayers attached to it. This one is one hundred and fifty dollars."

Naomi's heart thudded, but maybe this was a sign to walk away. She let out the breath she was holding and reminded herself that she didn't believe in superstitions. "*Ach*, all right. I don't have that much." She forced a smile. "I'm sorry to have bothered you on the Lord's day."

"I'm not going anywhere, dear, if you'd like to go home and come back with the other fifty dollars." Pearl edged her dog back with her socked foot when he tried to slip out the door. "No, Mutt."

Naomi felt her eyes widen.

Pearl chuckled. "I know. Seems like a strange name for a dog. But that's just what he is, a mutt. He showed up on my doorstep one day in a snarly mess and covered with fleas. I told him, 'Go home, Mutt,' but he kept coming back, and eventually"—she raised her shoulders, then lowered them slowly—"we grew to love each other, but the name stuck."

Naomi nodded, thinking about how much Abby and Esther wanted a pet. Naomi was sure she couldn't take on anything else. Three goats, two cows, six chickens, and the horse . . . they were enough to feed and tend to. *And two children, soon to be three.*

"Hon, I'm going to let you have this treasured packet for just a hundred dollars because you are in the family way. That just seems like the right thing to do. We want to protect that precious bundle you're carrying." Pearl stuffed the hundred-dollar bill into the pocket of her housecoat.

Naomi had talked herself out of buying it, but the lower price made it seem bearable. *But it's still forty dollars more than last time.* She hesitated as she accepted the bargain bag of items from Pearl. "*Danki,*" she whispered, knowing Pearl was being thoughtful of Naomi's situation.

Brock went to church on Sunday morning, then took a long nap, and when he woke up, it was raining. And it rained for the next four days. This weather was messing up the harvest for everyone, not just him, but it wasn't just that. He could feel the walls closing in on him by Thursday, and if he didn't get to the grocery store soon, he was going to starve. He missed Naomi's three meals per day.

He leaned his head against the back of his couch as rain pelted the window on the far wall. For the second time, he scanned the hundreds of television channels available to him, then clicked the TV off and closed his eyes. It was too late for a nap and too early to go to bed, so he walked onto the front porch and watched it rain for a little while, then walked back in and paced his living room until he decided he needed to go somewhere, even if it was pouring rain and a flash flood watch was in effect.

Fifteen minutes later, he was parked in front of Naomi's house. He'd sensed that she didn't like storms, so maybe she'd welcome the company. And maybe she'd offer him a meal. That was the best reason he could come up with, but if he faced the truth, he missed spending time with Naomi and her girls, and his fond recollections of their time at the carnival had stayed with him. Most of Brock's friends were married with children, and even on a rainy night, Brock didn't want to intrude on them. *Yet it's okay to intrude on Naomi and her children?* He sat in the truck pondering until he saw Abby's face peering out at him from the living room window, boasting her toothless smile. Moments later, both girls were on the porch waving. Maybe they were as bored and restless as he was.

By the time he ran through Naomi's soaked yard in the downpour, he was drenched. Naomi met him at the door with a towel.

"Am I interrupting anything?" he asked as he ran the towel across his face, then down his arms. "The walls were closing in on me at my house, and I thought you and the girls might want some company."

Esther Rose spoke to her mother in *Pennsylvania Deitsch*. "Please let him stay and play with us! Maybe he will play Life on the Farm."

"I'm sure he didn't come over to play games," Naomi said in

her native dialect before she turned to Brock. "I'm sorry. Esther Rose hasn't been speaking English all that long, so she tends to revert back to the *Deitsch*. She's not meaning to be rude."

"It's perfectly fine." Brock wasn't ready to let them know he understood the dialect. It would only embarrass Naomi when she realized he'd understood Abby's comments awhile back.

"I still think he would make a good daddy," Abby added in *Deitsch*, then folded her arms across her chest as her lip curled under in a pout.

Maybe I should clue Naomi in before this goes any further. Brock stifled a grin.

"I think he would be a good daddy too." Esther Rose carried her blanket with her as she sidled up next to her sister, both facing off with their mother.

"Thank goodness he doesn't understand you girls. Now stop this silly talk. You don't get to pick out a new daddy. It's too soon anyway. And he's not Amish." Naomi turned off the burner on the oven and turned to Brock. "I'm heating up some chicken soup. Are you hungry?"

Music to my ears. "Yeah, sure. That would be great."

Esther Rose tugged on Naomi's apron, again talking to her in a language they didn't think Brock understood. "Can you at least think about making him our daddy? He can turn himself Amish to be with us. We need a dad. We might turn out bad if we don't."

Naomi glanced at Brock, then back at her daughter. "It isn't nice to talk *Deitsch* in front of someone who doesn't understand. And you are not going to turn out bad if you don't have a new father soon." Naomi shook her head. "Where do you hear such things?"

"As young scholars, we need disciples," Abby said from across the room.

Naomi put a spoon in the sink and wiped her hands on her apron. Brock had heard some of the older Amish folks refer to school-aged children as scholars, but it was cute to hear Abby say it in such a way. It was getting harder and harder not to laugh.

"I think you mean *discipline*, not disciples. No more of this talk," Naomi said.

"Will you just think about it?" Esther Rose looked up at her mother with pleading eyes, holding tightly to her blanket.

Brock had to put a hand over his mouth to hide his smile. Naomi stared at Brock for a moment. He needed to tell them now, but as soon as he opened his mouth, Naomi spoke up.

"Fine. I will think about it."

Brock lowered his hand from his mouth although his eyes felt like they were bugging out of his head. He blinked a few times in his effort to gain composure.

Naomi stared across the table at the large, and handsome, man who sat in Stephen's place. How could her girls possibly be ready to have a new man in their lives? Naomi wasn't sure she'd ever be ready. But she couldn't help but think about how different things were since Stephen died. She stayed busy. But on the days she felt it was more important to play with her girls or give them her undivided attention, she was able to do that without fear of Stephen's wrath. There were still days she missed him a little, days when the happy memories fought their way to the surface. But each time that happened, it was never long before the bad recollections bubbled up, drowning out joyous times.

Naomi could see why her daughters would latch onto Brock Mulligan. He was a good man. But it still struck her as odd that

Abby and Esther Rose didn't hold tighter to the memory of their father, especially Abby. Maybe they were just too young to fully grasp the permanence of death. And had her daughters forgotten that the man wasn't Amish?

Naomi glanced at Brock, but looked away when he caught her gaze. If she could ever get past her fears of marrying again, she would want a man like Brock. In her mind, she listed all of the things she liked about him again, and she decided that when someone did come calling, she would pull out that mental list and make sure that any suitor held all the qualities that she'd grown to endear in Brock.

"May I be excused?" Esther Rose pushed her chair from the table.

Naomi nodded, and her younger daughter went to the end of the table and stood by Brock. Naomi held her breath. *Please don't ask him to be your daddy.*

Esther Rose whispered in his ear, and Naomi felt the color slipping from her cheeks.

Brock smiled. "I guess you need to ask your mother about that."

Naomi knew better than to stand up, fearing she might pass out from embarrassment.

Brock wiped his mouth with his napkin, then stood up. "But if it's okay with her, I'd be happy to play Life on the Farm with you girls. I've never played, though."

Naomi slowly released the air in her lungs and slid her chair from the table. "*Ya, ya.* It's fine. But please don't feel like you have to."

"We will teach you." Esther Rose tossed her blanket over her shoulder, found Brock's hand, and along with Abby, they all went into the living room.

Naomi leaned against the kitchen counter and decided that

she might have to date someone, if for no other reason than to keep her children from getting ideas about Brock.

⁓✻⁓

The rain had been over for about an hour when there was a knock at the door. Naomi glanced at the clock on the mantel, knowing eight o'clock was much too late for anyone to be calling on them. The girls were already up past their bedtimes. But Naomi had stretched the rules tonight since they were all having so much fun teaching Brock how to play the game. It warmed Naomi's heart each time he intentionally let one of the girls get ahead of him, often causing them to squeal with delight. Naomi lifted herself from the floor. They'd chosen to sit around the square coffee table in the living room, closest to the fire.

Naomi picked up a nearby lantern and walked to the front door. "*Daed*, what are you doing here?" She stepped aside as her father crossed the threshold.

"Your *mamm* has been calling you on her mobile cell smartphone." He took off his hat. "Whatever that thing is called. And you don't answer, so she sent me here to make sure you weathered the storms okay."

"Um, well . . . for starters, the cell phone is for emergencies." She grinned.

Her father rolled his eyes. "*Ya*, if you say so."

Naomi closed the front door. "Besides, with all this rain, I haven't been anywhere to charge it up. It's been dead for several days."

"That's the difference between young people and old people. Your mother keeps a close eye on the weather and makes sure her phone is charged prior to a weather event." His eyes darted to Brock. "Speaking of old people . . ." He crossed the room and extended his hand to Brock. "What are you doing here?"

"I missed Naomi's cooking," Brock said as he shook Naomi's father's hand. "And then when the girls asked me to play Life on the Farm, well . . . I didn't even realize the rain had stopped."

Abby and Esther Rose went to their *daadi* and wrapped him in double bear hugs. "He is losing," Esther Rose said in a whisper, then giggled.

"Is he now?" Naomi's father raised an eyebrow. "I noticed you've all been spending a lot of time together. *Mammi* says you even went to a carnival. And I think I heard about a trip to Walmart . . ." Her father's eyes met Brock's as he pressed his lips firmly together.

"*Ya*, Brock was nice enough to take me to the store one day, and the girls were thrilled about going to the carnival."

Her father stroked his beard. "Well, I can report back to your *mudder* that all is well then." He kissed Abby and Esther Rose each on the cheek. "And maybe still get home before it's completely dark."

Naomi was glad her parents lived close so her father didn't have far to go. Her heart rate picked up as she recalled the night Stephen was late coming home, but as always, her emotions tugged and pulled at each other. She remembered her father standing on her porch crying as he told her about Stephen. But she could also remember the last words Stephen had said to her that morning before he left for a construction job. *I hope this house is clean when I get home.* She could still feel the tightness in her chest when she'd told him, *It will be.*

After her father left, she sent the girls upstairs to get ready for bed, promising to tuck them in shortly.

"Can Mr. Brock tuck us in?" Esther Rose asked from halfway down the staircase about fifteen minutes later.

Naomi stood up from where she was sitting in the rocking chair, and after Brock tossed another log onto the fire, he looked over his shoulder. "I don't mind tucking them in, if it's okay with you."

"Um, okay." Naomi wasn't sure how she felt about this. "We say prayers aloud together at bedtime."

Brock nodded and was already moving toward the stairs, and Abby and Esther Rose each took one of his hands.

Naomi poured herself and Brock each a cup of coffee and was sitting on the couch when he returned.

"They are sweet girls," he said as he sat down beside Naomi. "And thank you for the coffee. I'll drink it quick since I know I've already kept you all up too late."

Naomi set her coffee cup on the table after taking a sip. "I don't go to bed this early, so you're not keeping me up." She looked at the clock on the mantel and wondered why she had just told a lie. It was nine o'clock, and she was almost always in bed by eight. *Oops. Sorry, God.*

"Okay, well, I'm appreciative of the good meal and the fine company this evening." He blew on the steaming cup, then took a sip. "I guess I'm not ready for it to end, but the girls have school tomorrow, and now that the rain has stopped, I'll be out in the morning to see how much hay I was able to keep dry. I promise not to stay long."

"Do you want some pie?" Naomi sat taller. "I have apple and coconut." Maybe if she kept feeding him and filling up his coffee cup, he wouldn't leave. She was safe with him, in all the ways that counted.

"Apple would be great."

She returned with two slices, but Naomi only got about halfway through with hers when she set the plate on the table and touched her stomach. Her baby was unusually active this evening.

"The baby is moving?" Brock set his plate down beside her and twisted to face her. His eyes stayed on her hand, rubbing her tummy.

"Ya, he—or she—has been busy all evening." She took her hand away and looked at Brock, but his eyes were still on her stomach.

"That must be amazing to feel a life like that, I mean—moving and alive."

As instinctively as breathing, she took his hand and placed it on her stomach. It was an uncommon practice among their people, and with her other pregnancies, she'd only allowed Stephen to touch her stomach. She placed her hand on top of Brock's.

They sat quietly for a while, the baby kicking and pushing against her new friend's hand.

"Thank you," he whispered in the dimly lit room as his eyes met hers. "It *is* amazing."

Naomi reached into her pocket to rub a hand over the purple packet, and her heart skipped a beat. She jumped to her feet and picked up the lantern, went to the kitchen, back across the living room, into her bedroom, then back again.

Brock stood up. "Can I help you find something?"

Naomi stopped in the middle of the living room and stomped one foot. "I cannot believe this is happening again!"

"What?"

She sat down on the couch and put her face in her hands. Brock sat down beside her, and she finally looked at him, fighting tears. Visions of burying her child—Adam—spilled into her mind. It was illogical to think a packet of spices controlled God's will, since it surely didn't, but before she knew it, she was babbling on and crying. When she was done, she waited for Brock's reaction.

His face was red as a freshly painted barn, his hands clenched at his sides from beside her on the couch. Naomi had never seen him like this.

It scared her.

Anger scared her.

Chapter Eight

Brock forced himself to remain calm by taking some deep breaths. He reached for Naomi's hand and held it tightly as her bottom lip trembled.

"Sweetheart, listen to me." Brock wasn't sure if he'd just crossed a line by using the endearment, but he was so mad at the moment, and she was so upset . . . "That purple packet of herbs doesn't hold *any* power at all. None." He huffed. "Nothing is going to happen on the night of the harvest moon except that the moon will be bigger and brighter. That's it."

"I know in my mind that you're right." Naomi eased her hand from his, then pulled a tissue from her pocket and dabbed at her eyes. "But I couldn't bear it if I lost another baby. I just couldn't." She shook her head so hard that her prayer covering slid to one side.

"Just remember, that packet holds no power. Only God holds the power, and everything that happens is His will." He'd heard that his entire life and could remember his Amish grandparents drilling that into his head even though his parents had chosen to leave the Old Order district and to raise him *Englisch*.

"I know." She sniffled and seemed to be catching her breath.

Brock didn't think it could be good for the baby for her to

get this upset. "God's in control," he repeated. He'd been praying for Naomi and her children. And as he listened to himself, he couldn't help but wonder why he continually questioned God's will for his own life.

Brock was still concerned about what Abby had told him, about the hitting. But now wasn't the time to bring it up. He waited awhile longer, until Naomi had completely stopped crying, then he stood up. "I should go. But only if you promise me that you'll forget everything that old woman said."

Naomi followed him to the front door. She nodded, then without warning, she put her arms around his waist and laid her head against his chest. He wrapped his arms around her, and when she looked up at him, he kissed her on the forehead. "Everything is going to be fine, and you'll deliver a healthy baby in a few months. And all that stuff about the moon is just stupid superstitions."

Brock believed everything he was telling Naomi to be the truth. She and her baby would be fine. But he was starting to wonder if he would be okay. When did he start to care so much about Naomi and her children? He might struggle with God's plan for his life, but he'd learned to live with it. Was God tempting him, goading Brock, to fall for a woman he couldn't have? He eased her away, and quickly left.

⁓☙⁓

Friday morning, Brock's emotions were all over the place, but there was something he needed to take care of before he went to Naomi's. Glancing at the ominous clouds overhead, he wondered if the weather forecast was correct. It wasn't supposed to rain the next few days, so he planned to take advantage and work over the weekend. But gray clouds rolled in as he walked to Pearl King's door. She hadn't been hard to find.

Brock had a faint memory of her. He'd seen her briefly at Naomi's but hadn't been able to place her. Now he remembered her from his childhood.

On the porch were two black cats curled up inside a small red suitcase. They both meowed when he knocked on the door.

"Are you Pearl King?" he asked when an elderly woman answered the door, even though he knew she was.

"Yes, I am. How can I help you?" The old woman smiled, but Brock's anger from the night before struck him anew.

"You're taking advantage of a friend of mine, and I'm here to make sure it doesn't happen again." Brock stuffed his hands in his pockets when Pearl's eyes widened, knowing his size often intimidated people.

"Who are you?" Pearl's eyes dropped into a squint. "And who are you talking about?"

"I'm Brock Mulligan, and I'm a friend of Naomi Dienner."

Pearl put a finger to her chin as her eyebrows drew into a frown, deepening the lines slithering across her forehead. "You're Andrew and Katie's boy."

Brock started to tell her that his mother had passed a few years after his father, but he didn't want to say more than he needed to. "Yeah, I am. And I remember you from when I was a kid, mostly when I was visiting my grandparents."

Brock's grandparents lived on the next block, and his grandmother would repeatedly warn him and his brother not to go near Pearl's house. Some of the elders still sought out respected powwowers, but Brock's grandparents believed that Pearl practiced a form of powwowing that resembled witchcraft. And it certainly sounded like she'd taken advantage of Naomi. "I know you were shunned by the Amish, and I also know that you're a powwower."

"My shunning had nothing to do with being a powwower. I needed electricity because I have health issues that require the use of an oxygen tank at times." Pearl raised her chin. "Now, what is your business here today?"

"Stop feeding Naomi's head with your nonsense. You've got her scared to death with all your talk about the phases of the moon and the harvest moon that will be here soon. It's all a bunch of baloney. She lost some packets of herbs you gave her, and it brought her to tears."

"Good grief. She lost a second packet?" Pearl frowned. "I'm not giving her another one."

"You mean *selling* her another one. You've already conned her out of a hundred and sixty dollars." Brock considered Naomi's misplacement of both packets divine intervention, so she wouldn't be taken in by such nonsense.

"I didn't con her out of anything," Pearl spat back at him. "Those packets have been prayed over, and—"

Brock pulled his hands from his pockets, and just the movement itself was enough to cause her to stop talking and step back from the other side of the screen door.

"Prayers are free. What you're doing is wrong, and I'm just here to tell you to leave Naomi alone. I'm sure it's no coincidence that you just happened to get confused and stumble upon Naomi's place." Brock suspected Pearl had done her research and knew all about Naomi losing a baby. "This is called targeting a vulnerable person and preying on their fears as a way for you to make a profit. Please, just stay away from her."

Brock turned his back to her, and as he walked to his truck, he could hear her rambling on in *Pennsylvania Deitsch*, but Brock ignored her. He was anxious to get to work. And to make sure that Naomi was okay. Ten minutes later, he was on her porch.

"You missed breakfast," she said as she pulled the door open.

"Yeah, I know. Sorry about that." Brock fought the awkward feeling, shifting his weight from one side to the other and avoiding her eyes. Things had probably gotten a little too intimate the night before. Maybe sharing every meal with Naomi and the girls wasn't such a good idea. "I brought my lunch today."

"Why?" She put a hand across her stomach.

"I-I just felt like chicken salad, and I . . . had some at home."

"Too bad. I'm slow cooking another roast with potatoes and carrots, since you said you liked it so much before." She shrugged, grinning. "But I'm sure your chicken salad is better."

Brock had grabbed an energy bar on the way to Pearl's house, and that wasn't enough to sustain him through midmorning. His stomach was already growling, and his mouth watered at the thought of eating roast. Naomi didn't look like she felt awkward at all. In fact, her bright eyes shone in a way that almost resembled flirting. "Okay, then. I'll see you at dinnertime." He tipped the rim of the baseball cap, then smiled and left.

***

Naomi knew good and well that she was venturing into a dangerous place with Brock. She never dreamed that a man could be such a gentle giant, so kind and protective. But she should have known that her father wouldn't be good friends with Brock unless he trusted him completely. And trust and safety were particularly appealing to Naomi, even though she'd vowed not to become involved with anyone. But when she recalled the intimacy of him feeling her baby move, the hug, the kiss on the forehead . . . she felt warm all over, the way she did when she'd first met Stephen.

She took a deep breath and opened the oven to check the roast, then went back to kneading her bread, her thoughts drifting to various places, but with each passing moment, she talked herself out of the possibility of anything romantic with Brock. He wasn't Amish, he was considerably older than her, and Naomi was fat, pregnant, and had two sassy, but wonderful, little girls.

I will pray that Brock finds someone suited to him, an Englisch *woman who will love him and give him a family. What a wonderful father he would be.*

Brock devoured the roast, potatoes, and carrots on his plate and reached for his third slice of buttered bread. So much for chicken salad.

They'd been quiet for most of the meal. When Brock was done, he swiped at his mouth with his napkin, and when Naomi got up to clear the table, he said, "Hey, I need to talk to you about something." He wanted to take advantage of the girls being out of the house so they wouldn't overhear.

Her face turned pale as her expression fell. "If it's about last night . . . um, we don't need to talk about it. I was upset and you comforted me." She smiled. "And that's what friends do. I'm overly emotional when I'm pregnant. I apologize for getting so upset."

Brock cleared his throat, feeling silly for thinking she may have romantic feelings for him. *Of course, she doesn't.* "No, I need to talk to you about Abby."

"About what?" She eased her plate forward, put her elbows on the table, and rested her chin on her hands.

"When we were at the carnival . . ." He hadn't realized until now how hard it would be to tell her this. It was most likely going to upset and embarrass her. "Was Stephen abusive to you?"

Naomi dropped her hands and laid her palms flat on the table as she sat taller. She blinked her eyes a few times. "What? Why would you ask such a thing?"

Brock was certain by her reaction that it was true. "I just think maybe you should talk to the girls about it, Abby at least. She told me that she knows Stephen hit you, but that you didn't know she knew."

Naomi stood up, paced her kitchen, then turned to face him, slamming her hands to her hips. "Well, it's not true."

"I think it may be, Naomi." Brock stayed seated even though she started pacing again. "And I think maybe you need to talk to Abby."

"I said it isn't true."

Naomi wouldn't look at him now, and she started to clear the table. Brock latched onto her wrist when she got close enough to him, and she jumped, pulled away, and backed into the kitchen counter, her eyes fearful and watery.

Brock held up both his hands. "Naomi, I would never lay a hand on you in anger. Never. Real men don't hit." He slowly stood up and walked toward her, close enough to cup her cheek. "Men *shouldn't* hit."

She eased around him and went back to cleaning the table.

"Did he—did he hurt the girls ever?" Brock was sure

Naomi would say no, since she wouldn't even confirm that he'd abused her.

She set the two plates back on the table and hung her head. "Never."

"How do you know?" Brock moved closer to her.

"Because I would have known. He was a *gut* father. *I* was the problem." She looked up at him as a tear trailed down her cheek. "I was a bad wife."

Brock sighed, his heart heavy. "Naomi, it was not you. There is nothing a person can do that warrants getting hit." He felt relieved that Naomi believed that Stephen hadn't harmed the girls.

"I didn't always do my chores in a satisfactory way," she said as her lip trembled. "And sometimes I didn't finish the laundry. Sometimes supper was late. And once I broke a serving platter that his grandmother had given us as a wedding present." She stepped back from him, her hands clenched at her sides. "And once I spit in his food when he wasn't looking . . . because . . ." Tears trailed down both cheeks as her face grew redder. "Because he was mean! Because he hit me! Because I couldn't do anything right." She covered her face with her hands.

Brock covered the short space between them quickly, pulling her into his arms, realizing that she probably thought of him as more of a father figure, a protector. But it didn't matter. His need to protect her was strong, even if it would have to be as her friend. He kissed her on the forehead again, something that felt as natural as breathing. "You're okay now. And it's okay to feel this way. I think it's normal to be angry."

"But he's dead," she said in a tiny voice.

Brock stepped back and slid his hands to her arms. "Yes, he is. But that's God's will, and it's not your fault. You're a good person, Naomi. You deserve to be happy. I've had a hard time accepting God's plans for me. For a long time, I couldn't wrap my mind around the fact that He took Patty from me, that her life ended, and in a way, mine did, too, for a while. I have trouble just blindly putting my faith in God these days. So, I continue to rebuild my relationship with the Lord, struggling to get back to where I once was. But Naomi, I've been praying for you to find a good man to take care of you, Abby, and Esther Rose. And through doing that, praying for you, I feel closer to Him."

Naomi stifled a gasp. *You've been praying for me too?* She wanted to tell him, but her mind was still reeling as she worried about her girls. How much did they know? Was that the reason they appeared to get over Stephen's death so quickly, or were they just young and resilient?

"Do you think Abby is okay?" She put a hand to her chest.

"Yes, I do. But maybe you should talk to her about it, let her know that not all men hit. I don't know if Esther Rose knows anything. Abby doesn't seem to think so. And Naomi, it might not be a bad idea for you to get some counseling. I know that's allowed by the bishop. And if it's a financial issue for you, or if you don't feel comfortable going into the community funds for that, I'd understand you wanting to keep your business private. But I have plenty of money to help you with this if you want to go talk to someone."

She shook her head. "*Nee.* I would never let you do that."

"Why not? It's just money." He smiled, winking at her. "And a little birdie told me that you've been giving yours to a retired, shunned powwower."

Naomi stepped back. She knew he was trying to lighten the moment, but . . . "How do you know Pearl is a powwower?" She held up a finger to indicate she wasn't done speaking so she could organize her thoughts. "And how do you know so much about the Amish in general? Just by living here all your life?"

"Partly." He shrugged. "And because my grandparents were Amish. I spent a lot of time with them growing up."

Naomi was quiet, but when Brock rattled off a string of sentences in *Pennsylvania Deitsch*, mostly about the weather, she felt her cheeks grow hot. "Uh . . ."

"Yep." Brock chuckled, then stood taller, if that was possible. "I know all about shopping for husbands."

Naomi lowered her head, shaking it, then looked up at him, smiling. "Oh dear."

"It's fine. Your girls just love you very much and want you to be happy and safe. They must feel safe with me."

I feel safe with you. "I think it's *you* my girls love," she whispered.

"Well, I'd be lying if I said that they hadn't stolen a part of my heart already."

"I will talk to Abby." She stared at the man before her, wishing things could be different. Wishing she'd always feel safe the way she did in this moment.

⁓

It was nearing the supper hour, and Naomi had just finished frying some chicken when her mother showed up with the girls. *Mamm* had wanted to take them with her to buy some fabric for more school clothes, so she'd asked to pick them up after school.

Naomi walked onto the porch as Abby and Esther Rose

81

helped Naomi's mother unload their scooters from the back of the buggy.

"You girls go put these scooters in the barn and tend to the animals. Then you can play out here for a little while. I need to talk to your *mudder.*" Naomi's mother marched across the yard, scowling. "Inside," she demanded. "You and I need to have a little chat."

Naomi couldn't recall *Mamm* speaking to her in that tone of voice since she was a little girl. "What? What's wrong?" She followed her mother into the living room.

Mamm untied the strings of her black cape, shrugged it off her shoulders, caught it, and tossed it on the couch. "When were you going to tell your father and me that you're pregnant?"

Uh-oh. Naomi placed her hands on her stomach. "I wanted everyone to be done mourning Stephen. I was waiting so that it would be a joyful occasion."

"Sweetheart . . ." Her mother walked toward her and held both her arms. Naomi thought of Brock instantly. "A baby is always a joyful occasion. A blessing. You know that."

Naomi nodded, but her mother let go of her arms, walked to the couch, and practically fell onto the cushions. "But we have another issue."

"What?" Naomi sat down beside her mother.

Mamm squinted her eyes until they were almost closed. "I don't know what you think you're doing playing hanky-panky with Brock Mulligan, but it needs to stop."

"What?" Naomi needed to buy a little time to sort through her jumbled thoughts. "And how did you know I was pregnant?"

Her mother rolled her eyes. "Goodness me, child. Do you think Abby misses anything?"

Apparently not. "What did she say?"

She got up to go to the bathroom last night while your . . . guest . . . was still here. And when she heard voices, she tiptoed halfway down the stairs and sat down. So, *ya*, she saw Brock with his hand on your tummy, feeling the baby move." Her mother shook her head, frowning. "Really, Naomi? How inappropriate."

"*Ach, Mamm.* It's not a concern, and we weren't playing hanky-panky. We've become friends, that's all."

"Well, your daughter told me that you are having a baby, that you and Brock kissed and made a baby!"

Naomi brought a hand to her mouth as her eyes grew round, but she couldn't stop the laughter from erupting. "What?" she asked again.

The corner of her mother's mouth lifted up a little as she raised an eyebrow. "It is rather funny, but you need to straighten that child out. I tried, but gave up." Now her mother laughed along with her, but quickly stopped. "What are you doing kissing that man anyway?"

"I didn't kiss him. He kissed me on the forehead before he left last night."

"Your father said it was awfully late for him to be here last night, and I think the hair on the back of his neck was still standing on end when he got back home."

"We're friends, *Mamm.*"

"*Ach*, and you need to keep it that way. Don't let those girls . . . or yourself . . . get attached to someone who isn't Amish."

Naomi was waiting for her mother to add something about Brock's age, but she didn't. She stood up. "He's a handsome man, but proceed with caution." Then she smiled. "So, how far along are you?"

"Five months."

"Goodness, Naomi. I can't believe you kept this blessing from us."

"I tried to tell you when I last visited the house, but you seemed so disappointed that I wasn't still wearing my mourning clothes, so I just decided to wait."

Naomi's mother stared at her long and hard. "Do you really feel like you are done mourning Stephen?"

It didn't take long for Naomi to find the answer to this question. "*Ya, Mamm.* I do."

Chapter Nine

Brock was just about to head to the water pump to wash up before supper when a buggy turned into the driveway. A young Amish man crossed the yard carrying a bouquet of flowers, and Naomi let him in after he knocked. Even in the distance, the fellow looked like a handsome guy, tall and lean, his shoulders back as he waved. Brock should feel good that someone was calling on Naomi. But would this fellow understand how fragile she was? Would he treat her right and always cherish her? Would he be good to her daughters?

He stuffed the thoughts. Maybe it was just a friend. *But bringing flowers?*

Brock looked at his watch and made his way to the water pump. Abby and Esther Rose were in the chicken coop gathering eggs, but he decided to go on in, to get a feel for Naomi's admirer. He tapped on the door that led to the living room twice, then opened it and walked in. "Hi."

Naomi was sitting on the couch next to the guy, which set Brock's skin on fire. He scratched nervously at his arm as Naomi made introductions. *This kid isn't handsome, he's goofy looking.*

"Supper won't be ready for about thirty more minutes," Naomi said from her seat next to Goofy Kid.

"Okay. I'll, uh . . . go check on the girls." Brock took a couple of steps backward until he bumped against the door and turned around. *This is what I wanted, for her to find a good Amish man. I prayed for this.*

Brock's heart was beating at what felt like an unhealthy rate. *What would Naomi want with a guy like me anyway?* Brock had noticed earlier in the day that Naomi wasn't wearing black anymore, and neither were Abby and Esther Rose. Life was as it should be, he supposed.

Abby and Esther Rose came out of the coop just as Brock got there, each of the girls toting a basket of eggs. He allowed himself a brief vision of what it would be like to have a role in their lives, as more than just a friend. It was a beautiful picture filled with giggles, bedtime stories, and even some nights playing Life on the Farm. But Brock figured the Lord was answering his prayer, thus the arrival of an Amish man who was more age appropriate showing up with a bouquet of flowers. *Even if he is goofy looking.*

"There were lots of eggs today!" Esther Rose held her basket up for Brock to see.

After inspecting the eggs in both their baskets, the girls rushed to the house, anxious to see who was visiting.

Brock walked toward the barn to make sure the horse's feed bowl was full, and for the first time in a long time, he'd lost his appetite.

Naomi accepted a supper date with Samuel for Saturday night. It seemed like the right thing to do. She couldn't imagine why anyone would want to date her when she was five months pregnant and starting to waddle like a penguin. But her people weren't prideful and focused more on what was on the inside of a person. Or that was how it was supposed to be. Naomi tried to ignore Samuel's protruding two front teeth. She'd known him all her life, and he was a good person. He hadn't deserved what his wife did to him, leaving in the middle of the night the way she had.

Up came the recollections about Stephen, reminding her that you never completely know a person. She'd invited Samuel to stay for supper, and when Brock came into the kitchen, everyone was already seated. Naomi had been busy slicing a loaf of bread, and she hadn't seen Samuel slip into the seat at the head of the table.

"That's where Mr. Brock sits." Esther Rose spoke loud enough that everyone heard. Naomi glanced back and forth between Samuel and Brock, but when Samuel started to stand up, Brock put a gentle hand on his shoulder.

"Keep your seat, Samuel." He looked at Naomi. "I just came in to tell you that I can't stay for supper tonight. I've got . . . plans."

"Oh." Naomi stared at his back when he went out through the kitchen door, then she tried to smile at Samuel when he flashed his big teeth.

She reached into the pocket of her apron, searching for the purple packet of herbs, but remembered she'd lost it. There were too many things happening around her, and the waxing moon seemed as easy to blame as anything else.

Naomi was glad when Samuel left after supper, promising to pick her up the following afternoon at four o'clock.

Once she had Esther Rose tucked in bed, Naomi glanced at Abby, then back at Esther Rose. "I need to talk with Abby for a few minutes downstairs. We won't be long." Her baby girl clutched her blanket like a lifeline. Although her youngest wasn't a baby anymore, Naomi wouldn't make her give up her lovey just yet. She'd been through enough lately. She held out her hand for Abby to take.

"You are in trouble." Esther Rose sat up in bed. "*Mamm*, what did she do?"

"She's not in trouble." Naomi held Abby's hand until they were downstairs, then Naomi went to the couch and sat down. She patted the spot beside her. "Come and sit, Abby."

Her daughter hung her head. "It's about what I told *Mammi*, isn't it?"

Naomi silently prayed for the right words. "*Ya*, partly." She took Abby's hand and placed it on her stomach. "I have a baby growing inside me. But it's not there because Mr. Brock kissed me on the forehead. It's there because *Daed* helped make the baby before he went to heaven. It takes a long time before a baby is ready to be born."

"I know."

Naomi bit her bottom lip for a few moments. "What do you mean, you know?"

"I know it takes nine months after kissing before the baby comes."

Naomi decided to leave the kissing part alone for now. "Then why would you say that Mr. Brock made the baby?"

Abby shrugged. "I want him to stay with us and be our

daed." She looked up at her mother with wide eyes. "*Not* Samuel. His teeth are funny."

"Abigail, we do *not* say things like that. You know better. We are not vain or prideful." Naomi cringed, knowing she'd have to say extra prayers tonight.

"But they are," Abby said in a whisper.

Naomi recalled a phrase she'd heard her mother say. *Choose your battles.*

"I need to talk to you about something else too." Naomi placed her hands on her stomach when her son or daughter started to twist and turn. "You told Mr. Brock something that concerns me."

"Now I'm in trouble, huh?" Abby's chin went down again, but Naomi cupped it in her hand and lifted Abby's face.

"*Nee*, you are not in trouble. But did you tell Mr. Brock that *Daed* used to hit me?"

Abby nodded. "He did . . . didn't he?"

A big part of Naomi wanted to lie, convince Abby that nothing like that had ever gone on in this house. But what kind of example would she be setting if Abby knew for sure?

"Your *daed* was a *gut* man." Naomi prayed for the words again. "*Most* of the time." She waited for Abby to respond, but when she didn't, Naomi went on. "Violence is not our way. So hurting people by hitting is not our way either."

"But you hit us."

Naomi brought a hand to her chest. "What?"

"You spank us if we're bad."

Naomi took a deep breath. "*Ya*, that's true. But that's different. Abby, did *Daed* . . . did *Daed* ever hit you anywhere besides on your bottom with a switch?"

Waves of relief washed over Naomi when Abby shook her

head. "Does Esther Rose know about . . . about your *daed* sometimes hitting *Mamm* in a bad way?"

Abby shook her head again. Naomi cupped her daughter's cheeks with both hands. "It is never okay to hit. Light spankings are okay for children, but we never hit with the intent to hurt someone."

"Then why did *Daed* hit you?"

Please, God. Help me. "*Daed* was sick. He didn't mean to hurt me. But he still did a bad thing that the sickness made him do. Do you understand?"

Abby nodded.

"And we don't have to talk about this anymore unless you want to."

"*Nee.* I don't."

Naomi picked up Abby's hand, brought it to her lips, and kissed her fingers. "Does Esther Rose understand that I'm having a baby? She must have heard you and *Mamm* talking today after school."

"*Nee.* We stopped to get chocolate shakes on the way back from the park, and Esther Rose was playing on the slide in the courtyard." Abby tapped her finger to her chin. "I didn't know if I was supposed to tell her. That's why I talked to *Mammi.*"

Naomi smiled. "Well, I say we go share this news, this blessing, with Esther Rose right now."

Abby's eyes lit up as she jumped from the couch and sprinted up the stairs. Naomi followed as fast as she could, looking up. *Thank You.*

Brock started to work at sunrise on Saturday morning, and it was midmorning when little Esther Rose caught his eye on the other side of the fence. She waved to him, so he shut down the engine on the plow and walked to where she was standing. He was thirsty anyway, and his cooler was there.

"*Mamm* is going to have a baby," she said as he neared the fence.

He pulled a bottled water from his cooler as Esther Rose peered through the slats of the fence.

Brock wasn't sure if he should let on that he already knew. "That's great. Are you excited?"

She nodded, but scowled. "I hope it's a boy. I don't want another sister."

"I think we just hope for a healthy baby, boy or girl."

Esther Rose was wrapped in the pink blanket. There were loose threads hanging in every direction, and it looked like maybe she'd spilled orange juice on it. Sighing, she said, "*Ya*, I guess."

Brock took another big swig of water as Esther Rose narrowed her eyebrows and puckered her lips. "Everything okay?" he finally asked as Naomi's youngest twirled the string of her prayer covering around her finger.

The girl nodded.

Brock waited since she seemed to have something on her mind.

"*Mamm* has a date with Samuel tonight." She frowned, and Brock felt his expression drop along with hers. This shouldn't be surprising, but it was like a kick in the gut just the same. His gaze finally met Esther Rose's. He needed to tread carefully.

"Uh . . . that's great, right?" He showed her the best smile he could muster, but she scowled even more.

"*Nee.* Samuel has big teeth, and Abby and I don't want him as a *daed.*"

"It doesn't matter what a person looks like. It's what's inside that matters." Brock wanted to rush into the house and beg Naomi not to go out with anyone, but he'd prayed for this. He was having some sort of physical reaction to this news, in a way he hadn't expected. His need to protect Naomi and her children had grown over the short time he'd gotten to know them, but something else was causing his heart to throb. "I-I guess I better get back to work." He tried to smile, unsuccessfully—his emotions swirling like a tornado in his stomach.

Esther Rose stared at him for a minute. "You look like Abby does before she is going to cry."

Brock wasn't a man who cried. But at this moment, he felt like he could. It wasn't just Naomi he cared for. What would happen to his relationship with her girls once she became involved with someone? "Nah." He tried again to smile, but another failed attempt brought an even more serious expression from Esther Rose.

She took the blanket from her shoulders and laid it across the fence slats that separated them. Blinking her eyes a few times, she kissed the blanket, then started to walk away.

That child had carted that blanket everywhere since the day Brock met her. "Esther Rose, you forgot your blanket."

Slowly, she turned around to face him. "Keep it," she said softly before she turned and walked toward the house.

Brock touched the worn fabric, damp from a spill, with its fraying and faded threads. No tangible item had ever felt more precious, and in that moment . . . he became a man who apparently did cry.

He worked through lunch. Around one o'clock, Naomi came to the fence between the front yard and the hay field, carrying something in a bag. He'd tucked Esther Rose's blanket inside a backpack he kept next to the cooler. Maybe Naomi was coming to reclaim it for her daughter. He got off the plow and went to where she was waiting.

"It's a ham and cheese sandwich and some chips." She handed the brown sack to Brock. "I figured you would be hungry since you didn't come in for breakfast and missed dinner." She pulled her black sweater snug around her, even though it didn't come together across her stomach.

Brock thanked her, though he still didn't have much of an appetite.

"I talked to Abby, and I'm hoping she understands that her *daed* loved her, that he wasn't a bad person, but that hitting is wrong. It was a hard conversation." She chuckled. "But there is kind of a funny story about how this baby came to be."

In an animated way, Naomi recited the conversation Abby had with Naomi's mother. It was nice to hear her laughing, though Brock could feel his face turning red. "If she knows it takes nine months for a baby to come, then why did she think, uh . . . that I made the baby?"

Naomi continued to look at him, still smiling. "My daughters have grown very fond of you. I think it was wishful thinking on her part."

Brock wanted to tell her it was a beautiful wish, one that he shared as well. But instead, he thanked her for the sandwich again and went back to work.

He had wanted to be done with work before Samuel showed up, but it didn't work out that way. The kid had arrived around three thirty, but Brock was pretty sure they were waiting on a babysitter now. Brock loved spending the time with the girls, though he'd intentionally missed today's meals. But staying with them while Naomi went out with Samuel seemed too much to handle right now.

When he heard the distant *clip-clop* of horse hooves, he looked over to see who it was, and he saw Gideon. Naomi's father parked the buggy and headed Brock's way.

"Almost done?" Gideon sidled up to the fence, opposite where Brock was on the other side.

"I think I'll finish tomorrow."

"*Gut.*" Gideon put his hands in the pockets of his black jacket. "Brock, we've been friends for a long time, so I hope that you will understand what I'm about to say, and follow my wishes."

Somewhere deep inside, Brock knew where this conversation was about to go, but he waited quietly, in case he was wrong.

"*Mei dochder* is a *gut* woman who lost her husband much too young. And I just can't help but wonder if you are having romantic feelings for her. All you'll do is hurt her."

"I'd never hurt her."

Gideon took a step closer to the fence, scowling now. "Are you involved with my daughter? Because I won't have that!"

Brock was tired. Naomi was inside with her date. And he wasn't up for this right now. "Gideon, it's not your choice to make."

"You will not court Naomi. You are supposed to be my friend. I trusted you to bring in the harvest. Not force yourself into my daughter's life."

"Force myself? Really, Gideon? Exactly how have I forced

myself into her life? You offered me the job and even insisted I eat three meals a day with them."

"That did not include outside activities like trips to Walmart, going to carnivals, and late-night board games! Carolyn says the two of you are quite close." He threw his hands in the air. "*Mei* sweet Abby thought you gave Naomi a baby!"

"No, she didn't. You're getting the story wrong."

"*Ach*, it doesn't matter. You'll be done tomorrow, and that will be that."

"Gideon, I do care about Naomi. A lot. And I'm crazy about those two little ones. But we are friends, and that's all."

Gideon stared at him for a while. "And it better stay that way. You are not *gut* for her."

Brock felt the pressure of the situation bearing down on him. "Maybe you should ask her how good Stephen was for her." He turned to walk away, but Gideon came through the gate and followed him.

"What are you talking about? You didn't even know Stephen, and I know you're a better person than to talk badly about a dead man. Don't take out your frustrations on the memory of a decent man who died too young."

Brock spun around and faced his friend. "A decent man? I don't think so. Decent men don't beat their wives." He held his breath, knowing he'd gone too far. But he couldn't help but wonder if Gideon knew about Stephen's abuse and had overlooked it.

Gideon squinted his eyes. "What did you just say?"

"You heard me. Stephen laid hands on Naomi when he was mad. You're telling me you didn't know?"

Gideon's eyes watered up right away and he blinked several times. "Are you certain?"

Brock nodded. Gideon slumped over like he was broken in two. "I'm sorry. I probably shouldn't have said anything, and—"

Gideon looked at the ground, still blinking, and held a palm toward Brock. Then he raised his head, turned, and walked toward the house without saying another word.

Chapter Ten

Naomi thanked Samuel for supper for the second time after they left the pizza restaurant Saturday night. Her date was as nice a fellow as ever, polite and even entertaining. Samuel was a storyteller, someone who had a tale to tell about most everything. Naomi had laughed more than usual, but aside from that, there was nothing special about the evening, and she'd known there wouldn't be. She supposed she'd only agreed to go so that her parents wouldn't think she was somehow involved with Brock.

Following a quick hug at the door, Naomi waved to Samuel and quietly opened the door into the living room. Her father was on the couch with his socked feet propped up on the coffee table, and he was reading a book. He took off his reading glasses and laid the opened book across his chest, then he yawned.

"Did I stay out too late?" She looked at the clock on the mantel. It was only seven thirty. "Where are the girls?"

"I sent them upstairs early. I just checked on them. They are coloring pictures." *Daed* yawned again. "I love those *maed*, but this babysitting stuff is a job for your mother. She has more energy than I do."

"I hate that *Mamm* wasn't feeling well this evening."

"Just a stomach bug, she said, but she didn't want to give it to you or the girls. And it's just as well I came instead. You and I need to talk."

Naomi sat down in the rocking chair across from the couch. "If this is about Brock . . ."

Her father raised his eyebrows. "*Ach*, well, it isn't. But I guess it can be, if you'd like."

"Is it too soon for me to date?" She laid her hands on her tummy. "Because I really don't want to anyway."

"Then why did you go?"

Naomi shrugged. "I don't know. I guess I thought . . ." She raised her shoulders and lowered them again, then repeated herself. "I don't know."

"You are with child, and this makes me very happy." Her father smiled, but his eyes said something was wrong. Rubbing his forehead, he blew out a long breath. "I don't even know how to ask this, *mei maedel*. But I need to know the truth about something."

Naomi swallowed back a knot forming in her throat. "What, *Daed*?"

"Did Stephen ever cause harm to you when he was alive? Did he ever . . . hit you?"

Naomi wished the rocking chair could take flight and carry her away from this conversation. Avoiding her father's eyes, she nodded. When she looked back at him, he dabbed at his eyes, and she quickly moved to sit by him on the couch. She grabbed his hand and squeezed. "*Daed*, please . . . I'm okay. I'm fine."

"How could I have not known?" he said in a shaky voice. "Why did you not come to your *mamm* or me? Why, Naomi?"

"I thought I wasn't a *gut* enough *frau*. And I was ashamed."

They sat quietly just holding hands for a while.

"I'm the one who is ashamed, my child. From the day you were born, I've tried to keep you safe."

There was that word again. "I am safe. Now."

They quieted again as embers from the fire sparked and crackled. Then her father gave her hand a final squeeze and eased his from hers.

"How was your date?" He closed the book still open in his lap and set it on the couch next to his glasses before he turned toward Naomi and rolled his eyes.

"What was that for?"

"I was just thinking about you dating Samuel Troyer."

Naomi smiled. "*Ya*, he is probably not the one for me. He is very nice, but . . ."

"He's too young for you."

"He's twenty-seven, my age, *Daed*."

"But you are older in mind and spirit. *Kinner* have a way of doing that to you." He winked at her, and she was glad to see him returning to his old self. "And you've always been wise beyond your years." He paused. "So, do you love him?"

"Samuel? *Nee!* I do not."

Her father shook his head. "*Nee*, of course not Samuel. You know exactly who I'm talking about. I'm old, *mei maedel*, not stupid. I recognize when two people care about each other. I saw it the night I came over when you were all playing that board game at the coffee table."

Naomi pulled her eyes away from him. "Is it wrong to care about him?" When her father didn't answer, she turned to him. "He's not Amish. And he's older than me."

Her father sighed. "*Ya*, he's not Amish, and he's older than you."

Naomi's chest hurt as her heart hammered away. "I wouldn't have your blessing, would I?"

Daed scratched his cheek, then stroked his beard, something he did when he was heavy in thought. "I keep running a few things over in my mind." He held up a finger, then went back to running his hand the length of his beard. "First of all, you shared news with this man that you didn't share with your parents. Pretty important news. You told him you were with child, and you told him about Stephen."

Not exactly. Abby told him about Stephen. She decided to sit on that information for now. Her father's plate seemed full at the moment.

"Has he behaved inappropriately in any way with you?"

Naomi shook her head. *"Nee."*

"I didn't think so." He paused, kept stroking his beard, but finally looked her in the eye. "There is danger in being involved with an *Englisch* person. Your heart leads the way, no matter what your mind might tell you. You will leave your community and your faith for this man."

"Nee, I don't think I could do that."

"Oh, *ya,* you could. But that's not my biggest fear. It used to be. But that was before I found out the type of danger you were living in without my knowledge. I'm more fearful now of someone hurting you, I think, than anything else. It sickens me to think—"

"*Daed,* Brock would never do anything like that. He's the only man I've ever felt completely safe with." She nudged him with her shoulder. "Except you."

"Security isn't love, *mei maedel.* Love him for the right reasons or don't love him at all. He has loved and lost greatly in his life."

"You mean his wife dying?"

"*Ya, ya.* And his parents and grandparents have passed. I think I told you that he has a *bruder* out of state, but no other family."

"*Ya,* his *bruder* has two children and lives in Oklahoma. And did you know his grandparents were Amish?"

Her father laughed. "*Ya,* I did. I see you two have covered a lot of territory in the short time you've known each other."

"I suppose we have."

Daed laughed lightly again. "Your *mamm* thinks he is a handsome man, and we've been married long enough that she can say things like that." *Daed* shrugged. "To me, he just looks like an average beau, but what do I know about such things?"

Naomi quietly waited to see if her father was going to approve of Naomi seeing where things went with Brock. She was old enough that she didn't need his approval, but his blessing meant a great deal to her.

"So, are there any more skeletons in your closet that your *mamm* and I should know about?" He glanced at her stomach. "You wouldn't have been able to wait much longer on that little secret."

"I know." She smiled as her father stood up.

Naomi lifted herself from the couch and walked her father to the door.

"*Mei maedel* . . ." He kissed her on the forehead, which had become a magnet for everyone's lips lately. "Give much thought and consideration to a life with Brock. Security and safety are not enough reasons to build a home with someone."

"Esther Rose gave Brock her blankie," Naomi said as her father stepped over the threshold, pausing his stride as he turned to her and ran his hand the length of his beard again. "Hmm . . . that's big for that little one."

"*Ya*, it is." Naomi had been shocked when Esther Rose told her the news, and when she'd questioned her, Esther Rose had simply said, "He needs it more than me." "Try not to worry, *Daed*. I'm not going to get hurt."

He offered a weak smile. "It's not just you I'm worried about. I don't want to see Brock or your girls hurt either."

Brock flipped the channels on the television, finally landing on the weather channel. He didn't think he would miss TV if he didn't have it. It was simply a sound to fill the emptiness around him. He reached for a book he'd been trying to read, but staying focused on a book about World War II only made him think about how unfair life was. He glanced at the tattered pink blanket on the couch. He'd prayed for Naomi to find a good man, and it only made sense for her to be with one of her people—and someone younger. If it wasn't Samuel Troyer, there would be others in her district who would come calling.

He had talked to her twice over the past week, but he made sure to keep any emotion at bay. She'd tried to ease him into deeper conversations beyond the weather, the harvest being done, and him missing her cooking, but he'd reverted back to those topics each time. His heart hurt, and it wasn't just her he missed. Brock missed Abby and Esther Rose too.

God, I have one more thing to ask You. Whoever Naomi ends up with, please, I pray that he will be good to her and Abby and Esther Rose for all of their days.

Then his ears perked up when something on television caught his attention.

Tonight is the harvest moon.

Naomi walked outside, forcing one foot in front of the other in the bright light of the harvest moon. *Face your fear.*

As she stood in the middle of her front yard, the moist blades of grass twinkled like stars that had fallen from the sky, illuminated by the big orb of light in the sky. And gazing up at it now, she knew that there was nothing to be afraid of.

Fear had controlled her life for years. But not anymore. God had brought her to this time and place for a reason, and Naomi would have to trust His plan for her.

She turned her attention to the road that led to her house. As bright lights lit her driveway, she wondered who would be visiting at eight o'clock at night. When the headlights went dark, Brock stepped out of his truck and walked toward her. Naomi's heart began to thud in her chest. *Something must be wrong.*

Brock stopped in front of her, his large frame blocking the light of the moon, casting a protective shadow on Naomi.

"I felt compelled to come check on you." One side of his mouth crooked up a little bit, and for the hundredth time, Naomi thought about how much she'd missed him. "I wanted to make sure the harvest moon hadn't swallowed you up or something," he added.

"I'm pretty sure I can take care of myself these days." Naomi smiled a little, realizing that she had grown stronger over the past month. She kept her gaze on him, her heart still pounding, wondering why he was really here.

Brock took off his coat and put it over Naomi's shoulders. "You're shivering."

Naomi pulled the collar of the huge garment snug around her neck as Brock's bottom lip quivered. "Now it's you who is cold," she said.

He stuffed his hands in the pockets of his jeans. "I'm okay."

Naomi stared at him for several long moments. "Do you remember telling me that you were praying for me to find a *gut* man to take care of me and my children?"

"Yes. Has that happened?" Brock looked away, seeming to examine the fields.

Naomi waited until he looked back at her, then she nodded. "*Ya*, I have found a *gut* man who will take care of me and the girls, someone I care deeply for. But I'm not sure how he feels about me."

Brock looked down. "You deserve to be happy. So do the girls."

When he didn't look back at her, Naomi said, "Brock . . ." She paused, knowing she could wish him well, go back inside, and stay in the comfort of her protected heart. Or she could take a large step forward and embrace the life God had given her a pre-view of. "I prayed for you too," she said when he finally looked at her, the light of the moon forming a halo around Brock's head. "I prayed for you to find a good woman, maybe even someone who could give you a family."

Brock didn't say anything, but his bottom lip quivered again. *From the cold or something else?*

Naomi took a step closer to him, her eyes still raised to his. "Have you found that person? A good woman to love you, some-one to give you a family?"

Brock took his hands from his pockets and dropped them to his sides. "Yes. I have. I want to love and cherish this woman and her children for the rest of my life, but I'm not sure I'm the best man for her."

"Why is that?" Naomi held her breath as her lip trembled now too.

"I'm a bit older than her, and the woman I've fallen for is Amish."

Naomi's heart warmed her in a way that she'd never known, so much so that she pulled the coat from around her neck, then reaching up, she draped it across Brock's shoulders. She wrapped her arms around him and laid her head against his chest. He pulled the oversized coat around Naomi and held her close.

Naomi heard her father's words loud and clear. *There is danger in being involved with an* Englisch *person. Your heart leads the way, no matter what your mind might tell you. You will leave your community and your faith for this man.*

Her father was a wise man, and he'd been correct. Naomi was allowing her heart to lead the way, and she would leave her community for this man. But her father had been wrong also. Naomi would never leave her faith. It would go with her wherever she went.

"I think this Amish woman you speak of would be very lucky and blessed to have you in her life." She eased away from him, still unbothered by the frigid temperatures that had crept up on them the past few days. Her heart was providing enough heat to keep her warm for the rest of her life. "Do you want to come in and have some coffee? Maybe we can talk about the opportunities God has placed before us."

"I'd like that." Brock took Naomi's hand and they started across the yard, but Naomi stopped and looked over her shoulder. Then she turned completely and faced the light in the sky. There wasn't magic in the moon's glow like Pearl had spoken of. Instead, it was a bright reminder of the miraculous ways that God provides for His children.

Brock turned around also, and they both stood quietly

under the harvest moon. When they started toward the house again, Brock chuckled.

They stopped on the front porch and faced each other. "What's so funny?" Naomi smiled back at him.

He stared over her shoulder and into the sky. "I was just wondering what my parents and grandparents would think right now. When I was a kid, I begged my parents to let me be Amish, even though they'd chosen not to themselves. They said when I was grown, I could make that choice." He looked back at Naomi. "But then I met Patty in high school, and she was Lutheran, so it didn't work out that way." Brock turned toward the sky again. "I think that my grandparents are smiling from heaven, knowing that there's a strong chance I'll finally have my wish."

When Brock turned to face her again, they were quiet. But Naomi's heart spoke to Brock in a language she knew he understood. *I lieb you.*

And when Brock smiled at her, she knew he'd heard her silent declaration in his own heart, and she heard his heart speaking back to her. *I lieb you too.*

DISCUSSION QUESTIONS

1. Naomi felt like the abuse she suffered at the hands of her husband was her fault. Have you or anyone you've known been in this situation and felt the same way as Naomi?

2. There is fourteen years difference between Naomi and Brock, but Brock is young at heart. Do you think this is too much of an age difference? What if the situation had been reversed and Naomi was fourteen years older than Brock? Does it make a difference?

3. There are a lot of superstitions attached to the phases of the moon. Is there any truth to them?

4. At the end of the story, we see Naomi and Brock moving toward a romantic relationship, along with Brock's willingness to convert to the Amish way of life. Where do you see Brock and Naomi in ten years? Twenty years?

5. Powwowing is a controversial practice with varying degrees of acceptance or rejection within certain Amish communities. This author's source said she believes powwowing to be an evil practice, while others seek

out powwowers in secret—for healing, help conceiving a child, or other wants/needs. Have you heard of this practice before? If so, what is your opinion?

6. Who was your favorite character in the story? Why?

ACKNOWLEDGMENTS

A huge thanks to my family and friends for your continued love and support throughout this amazing journey. A special thank you to my husband, Patrick, for your patience with a wife who always has a deadline for something, lol.

To my agent, Natasha Kern, I'm grateful for your keen insight about all things publishing and for guiding my career in ways that help me to grow as a writer and a person. In a world where publishing is changing almost daily, you continue to educate yourself (and me!) by staying on top of everything. I'm also incredibly blessed to have you as a friend.

Janet Murphy, as we rock and roll along, always know that I appreciate you very much. The title of "assistant" no longer works. You are so much more than that! And you are a blessing in my life both professionally and personally.

Thank you to my entire team at HarperCollins Christian Publishing. You are all unique and wonderful and brilliant and creative and in love with books as much as I am. You are fabulous. ☺

To Sharon Hanners. It is with love and thanks that I dedicate this story to you. Thank you for reaching out to me at a confusing time in my life when I longed to love a child who wasn't even born yet. How blessed we are to share in a life that was gifted to us through our children and God. Grandmas Unite! We love you CJ. XO

ABOUT THE AUTHOR

Beth Wiseman is the award-winning and bestselling author of the Daughters of the Promise, Land of Canaan, and Amish Secrets series. While she is best known for her Amish novels, Beth has also written contemporary novels including *Need You Now*, *The House that Love Built*, and *The Promise*.

You can read the first chapter of all of Beth's books at:
www.bethwiseman.com

Love and Buggy Rides

Amy Clipston

For Eric Goebelbecker, the coolest big brother on the planet.

GLOSSARY

ach—oh
aenti—aunt
appeditlich—delicious
bedauerlich—sad
boppli—baby
bruder—brother
bu / buwe—boy / boys
daadi—granddad
daadihaus—grandparents' house
daed—dad
danki—thank you
dat—dad
dochder—daughter
Englisher—a non-Amish person
fraa—wife
freind / freinden—friend(s)
froh—happy
gern gschehne—you're welcome
gude mariye—good morning
gut—good
gut nacht—good night

haus—house

Ich liebe dich—I love you

kaffi—coffee

kapp—prayer covering or cap

kichli / kichlin—cookie(s)

kind—child

kinner—children

liewe—love, a term of endearment

maed—young women, girls

maedel—young woman, girl

mamm—mom

mammi—grandma

mei—my

naerfich—nervous

onkel—uncle

schee—pretty

schweschder—sister

Was iss letz?—What's wrong?

Wie geht's—How do you do? or Good day!

wunderbaar—wonderful

ya—yes

FEATURED AMISH HEIRLOOM SERIES CHARACTERS

Timothy m. Sylvia Lantz

Samuel (m. Mandy)
Marie
Janie

Samuel m. Mandy Lantz

Becky

Martha "Mattie" m. Leroy Fisher

Veronica
Rachel
Emily

Vera (deceased) m. Raymond Lantz (deceased)

Michael ("Mike") (mother—Esther—deceased)
John

Chapter One

J anie Lantz sank down onto a wooden picnic table bench at the far end of the parking lot, next to Old Philadelphia Pike. The fresh, cool September breeze held a hint of the autumn weather on its way to Lancaster County as she opened her lunch bag and unwrapped her turkey sandwich. Before taking a bite, she glanced back at the Lancaster Buggy Rides and Souvenirs shop. Rows of pumpkins lined up in front of the store and orange and brown wreaths hung on the door and windows.

So far her first day as a cashier at the shop had gone well. But though she enjoyed talking with the tourists, her aching feet made her thankful for the opportunity to sit down while she enjoyed her lunch.

The *clip-clop* of hooves drew her attention to the highway. She recognized the long gray buggy full of tourists as one of the buggies her boss owned. Throughout the day, the buggies took tourists on rides around the Bird-in-Hand area. She hadn't met the three buggy drivers yet, but she'd seen the Amish men from a distance earlier in the day when they were standing by the stable next to the store.

Janie took a bite of her sandwich and watched the driver

start to guide the buggy into the driveway leading to the parking lot.

Suddenly a silver sedan sped up behind the buggy. The car's driver appeared to be looking down at something in his hand— just before he looked up and hit his brakes.

Then, almost as if in slow motion, the car slammed into the back side of the buggy, shattering the right rear wheel and causing the buggy to teeter. The buggy shifted awkwardly and then fell on the right rear corner, sending the driver and a few passengers on that side tumbling onto the ground. The car behind the buggy had come to a stop.

Janie gasped in horror as she jumped up from the bench, dropping her sandwich and knocking over her bottle of water. She rushed across the parking lot to the store's main entrance, reaching the door just as two customers were coming out.

"Excuse me!" Janie yelled. "Do you have a cell phone?"

One of the women nodded as she stared at Janie with confusion on her face.

"Would you please call nine-one-one? There's been an accident." Janie pointed toward the driveway, and both women turned, taking in the scene.

The woman who had nodded pulled out her phone and started punching in the numbers.

Janie burst through the front door and spotted her boss, Craig Warner, talking to her coworker, Eva, near the cash register in the center of the large store.

Janie ran to them, beckoning for Craig to follow her. "Craig! Craig! You need to come quickly! A car hit one of our buggies while it was turning into the driveway. It just happened. I'm sure people are hurt."

"Eva, call nine-one-one," Craig instructed as he started walking. "Tell Bianca to find the first-aid kit and get the ice packs from the freezer."

"Okay." Eva's brown eyes widened as she nodded and grabbed the store phone to make the call.

Craig hustled toward the door and Janie trailed behind him. "I asked a customer to call nine-one-one too."

"That was a good idea."

In his midforties, Craig was tall and fit. Janie was nearly jogging to keep up with his long strides. She knew his brown eyes, which matched his hair and goatee, had to be filled with worry for his driver and customers.

Once outside, Craig groaned as the accident came into view. "Oh no. This is much worse than I hoped."

A shiver raced up Janie's spine as she took in the scene playing out in the driveway and parking lot. A crowd had gathered around the broken buggy and car, which had a smashed front bumper and headlights. Sirens already blared in the distance, announcing the approach of first responders.

Craig rushed over to the buggy and joined someone helping an older woman sitting on the ground with a bloody gash on her forehead. A middle-aged man and woman sat on the ground as well, looking bewildered as the customer who had called nine-one-one for Janie knelt beside them. One young man was already helping some of the passengers to nearby benches. The horse looked spooked, but not injured, and two men were doing their best to soothe it.

The driver of the car still sat behind the wheel, looking stunned as a man leaned in, no doubt asking if he was all right. She guessed the driver was around nineteen.

At first glance, Janie thought most of the passengers' injuries seemed to be minor, but no one could be sure until EMTs arrived. As Janie wrung her hands, wondering what else she could do to help until then, she turned and nearly walked right into a man who towered over her by several inches. She immediately recognized him as one of the buggy drivers she'd seen that morning.

He was helping the remaining two passengers climb out of the buggy, but Janie could see he was favoring his left arm. Blood seeped from a cut on his head as well, streaming down the side of his face, a stark contrast to his paled face and dark brown hair.

"Take your time," he told a woman as she climbed down to the ground. He grasped her arm with his right hand and grimaced as she leaned on him.

Once the woman was safely out, he swayed slightly, closing his eyes for a moment as if trying to regain his balance.

Janie came closer. "Are you all right?"

He gave her a brief sideways glance. "*Ya*, I'll be fine."

"Your head is really bleeding," Janie warned. "I think you need to sit down."

"I'm okay," he insisted before turning toward the last passenger. "Give me your hand, and I'll help you down."

When the woman hesitated, he offered her a shaky smile. He was clearly trying to ignore his injuries. He swayed again, and Janie held up her hand to grab him. But then she stopped, not wanting to appear forward.

"I won't let you fall," he promised his passenger. "We need to get you out of this buggy before the other back wheel collapses."

The woman took his hand, and again he grimaced as he helped her down. He let a young man who had been leading the passengers to the benches take over, then placed a shaky hand on the side of the buggy for support as the blood continued to trickle down his cheek and drip onto his gray shirt.

"Please listen to me," Janie pleaded, her voice thick with worry. "You need medical attention. Look." She pointed at the red spots dotting his shirt.

He glanced down at his chest and then met her gaze. His eyes were honey brown. "I'll be okay. I need to take care of my passengers."

"I don't think you should—" Before Janie could finish, the man took a step and then staggered. Janie grabbed his arm, steadying him. "Lean on me, and I'll get you to that picnic table over there," she instructed, nodding toward the table where she'd been eating lunch. "I'm Janie Lantz. This is my first day working here."

"Jonathan Stoltzfus."

The man followed her instructions, and she slowly led him to the picnic table. He sank down onto the bench and slouched back against the table.

"*Danki,*" he muttered, squeezing the bridge of his nose. "I don't know what happened."

"You need medical attention," she repeated, taking a clean handkerchief from her apron pocket. "Now, sit here before you fall and hurt yourself worse, and press this against that cut to stop the bleeding."

Before Jonathan could take the handkerchief, Craig rushed over. "Jonathan! What happened?"

"I'm not sure." Jonathan shook his head and rubbed his left arm. "I thought I signaled before I turned into the driveway, but the driver hit us out of nowhere."

"Janie, Jonathan needs a bandage for his head," Craig said. "Would you please go find Bianca?"

"*Ya.*" Janie turned to Jonathan and handed him the handkerchief. "Wait for me here, okay?"

"I can't just sit here." Jonathan shook his head. "I need to take care of my passengers."

"I'll check on everyone," Craig promised. "And the EMTs should be here any minute. Let Janie take care of you."

Jonathan hesitated, then blew out a deep sigh. "All right."

Janie touched Jonathan's shoulder. "I'll be right back."

The sirens became deafeningly loud as two ambulances, a state police cruiser, and a fire engine steered into the parking lot. The firemen and EMTs began assisting the injured passengers and the two state policemen approached the driver of the car.

Janie saw Bianca rushing toward the chaos, her auburn ponytail bouncing behind her. Janie raced over to her.

"Bianca, Jonathan fell out of the buggy and has a gash on his head. We need some supplies for him."

"Sure. Take what you need while I distribute these ice packs. Just leave my kit on that bench there."

Janie gathered an alcohol wipe, antibiotic ointment, gauze pads, and a large bandage. When she returned to the picnic table, Jonathan looked up at her. His bright brown eyes stunned her. She'd never before seen eyes that resembled the honey she purchased at the Bird-in-Hand Farmers' Market.

"Let me look at that wound," she said, taking away the bloodied handkerchief and examining Jonathan's forehead. "I'm going to clean it with alcohol and then put on some ointment and a bandage. Are you allergic to antibiotic ointment?"

Jonathan gave her a blank look. "I don't think so. Are you a nurse or something?"

She looked incredulous. "No, of course I'm not a nurse, but

I helped take care of *mei onkel* Raymond until he passed away in the spring. He was weak from dialysis, and I took care of his wounds a few times when he fell." She cleaned the gash with the alcohol wipe, and he sucked in a breath. "I'm sorry."

"It's all right," he said softly, his eyes squeezed shut.

She cleaned the blood off his face, applied ointment to the wound, and covered it with the bandage.

"I did the best I could, and it doesn't look too bad despite so much blood. But you should still have a doctor look at it in case you need stitches," Janie said.

"*Danki,*" he said, again softly, absently rubbing his left arm.

"Do you think your arm is broken?" she asked as she slipped the wrappers from the bandage, alcohol wipe, and ointment into her apron pocket.

Jonathan glanced down at his arm. "The impact threw me out of the buggy, and I landed on it. I don't think it's broken, but it hurts. It might be sprained."

"I saw you fall." She pointed at her abandoned lunch bag behind him. "I was sitting here eating lunch when it happened."

"You saw it?"

"*Ya.*"

"I thought I signaled before I started guiding the horse into the driveway. Did you happen to notice if I did?"

"You did." She nodded. "I saw your blinker." She started to tell him the driver wasn't paying attention when his face contorted with anguish.

"I can't believe it. I was so careful." He seemed to be talking to himself instead of to her.

Maybe she should wait to tell him the rest until after he had calmed down a little. Besides, she'd already confirmed he signaled his turn, and that alone made him completely innocent.

"Can I get you anything else?" Janie asked, stepping closer to him. "Do you want me to see if I can find some ice for your arm?"

"No, *danki*. I'll be fine." Jonathan glanced around the parking lot. "I hope everyone is all right. I thought it was safe when I slowed to turn. I never expected that car behind us to hit the buggy."

Janie sank down onto the bench beside him, determined to ease his obvious distress. The man was shaking. "From what I saw, it wasn't your fault. You did signal before you turned." She pointed at his arm. "I really think you need to get your arm examined before you think much more about this." She spotted an EMT talking to one of the passengers nearby. "Do you want me to get an EMT to look at it?"

Jonathan shook his head again. "No, there are people who need help more than I do."

"Jonathan." Craig appeared in front of them. "One of the police officers would like to get your perspective on what happened. He's on his way over."

"Sure." Jonathan cleared his throat.

Janie stood. "I'll see if I can help anyone else." She stepped away and headed toward Bianca. She hoped she'd have a better opportunity to tell Jonathan and Craig what else she saw later.

⌒⌒⌒

Jonathan tried in vain to will his body to stop shaking, but he continued to tremble like a leaf caught in a windstorm. His arm throbbed, and the wound on his forehead stung. He took in the tumultuous scene around him and it all felt surreal. His passengers were receiving medical attention from a group of firefighters and EMTs. One of the passengers was lying on a stretcher, and others had bandages on their heads or arms.

His stomach pitched as trepidation seized him. How could he have allowed this to happen? How could he put his passengers' lives at risk?

Less than thirty minutes ago, he was enjoying giving another tour around the Bird-in-Hand area. For nearly a month, he'd been working as a buggy tour driver and relishing every minute of it.

He'd originally come to Bird-in-Hand for a short visit with his grandparents, but when Craig Warner, his grandparents' next-door neighbor, had offered him the job, Jonathan decided to stay through the end of November. He was not only making money to help his grandparents, but avoiding going home to Mechanicsville, Maryland, for a while longer.

"Jonathan?" A police officer—a balding, portly, middle-aged man with graying brown hair and dark eyes—broke through his thoughts. "Would you please state your full name?" Pen poised, he was ready to take notes.

"It's Jonathan Omar Stoltzfus," he said, then spelled his last name.

"What do you remember from before the crash?" the officer asked.

Jonathan ran his hand down his face. It was all a blur. Why couldn't he think straight?

"Just take your time," Craig said as he sat down next to Jonathan on the bench.

"We were coming back from the tour," Jonathan began, his voice shaky. "I thought I had signaled to turn into the parking lot. As I started to turn, I felt the jolt of the car hitting the rear right wheel, and then the back of the buggy collapsed and I was thrown to the ground. As soon as I got my bearings, I jumped up and started helping the passengers."

The officer was silent as he wrote frantically in his notebook, then asked his next question. "What is the route you take for the tour?"

Jonathan explained the route and the officer wrote that all down too.

"How long have you worked here?"

"Almost a month."

"Had you ever given buggy tours before you started working here?"

"No, but I'm a cautious driver. I always put my passengers' safety first."

The officer nodded and then fired off a few more questions.

"I'll be in touch," he said when he was finished. "I'm going to talk to a few of the passengers and find out what they saw." He pointed toward Jonathan's arm, the one he hadn't realized he was still rubbing. "You should get that looked at."

"He's right," Craig said as the officer left. "I want you to go to the hospital and get an X-ray. I'll get someone to drive you."

"Thanks." Jonathan glanced around the parking lot, and his eyes found Janie.

Jonathan studied her as she leaned down and said something to a man before placing an ice pack on his knee. Jonathan had never met an Amish girl with red hair before. Janie had been so attentive when she'd tended to his head wound. Craig mentioned last week that he had a new employee starting today, but Jonathan hadn't seen Janie until she approached him after the accident. Something about her intrigued him, but he pushed those thoughts away as Bianca came up to him and Craig.

"Jonathan, Janie told me you took a hard fall from the buggy. How are you?"

"I'm fine." Jonathan tried to shrug off his injuries even as his arm continued to throb.

"I think he should go to the hospital for an X-ray," Craig said. "I need to stay here. Would you take him?"

"Of course I will." Bianca's brow furrowed with concern. "You look like you're in a lot of pain, Jonathan. We should get going."

Jonathan followed Bianca to her SUV. As he walked past Janie, she gave him a concerned smile, and he nodded before climbing into the car.

Jonathan couldn't get the picture of the damaged buggy and injured passengers out of his mind. Later that evening, as he sat at the small kitchen table in his grandparents' modest two-bedroom cottage on his uncle's farm, the feeling of dread that had taken hold of him earlier that day continued to consume him. He kept wondering what he could've done to prevent the accident.

His tour had seemed so typical, but then it turned into a horrible nightmare. What had he done wrong? Janie said he signaled, but was she right? Witnessing the accident must have been upsetting for her, maybe enough to think she saw him signal when he hadn't.

He stared down at his plate filled with food, but his stomach remained tied in knots. The thought of eating made him feel nauseated.

"You need to eat," *Mammi* said from the other side of the table. "You're much too skinny, Jonathan. Isn't your *mamm* feeding you enough?"

Jonathan shook his head. "I usually make my own meals now that I have my own *haus*."

Mammi blotted her mouth with a napkin. "Your *mamm* should cook for you since you don't have a *fraa*. I'll have to discuss that with her the next time I speak with her."

"*Mammi*, I'm going to be thirty in February," Jonathan gently reminded her. "I'm capable of cooking my meals."

"You're obviously not cooking enough," she grumbled as she scooped more mashed potatoes onto her own fork.

"Now, Mary," *Daadi* chimed in, "how is Jonathan going to find a *fraa* if he's fat?"

Jonathan nearly choked on his water. "I'm not planning on getting fat, and I've all but given up on finding a *fraa* to marry. At this point, I think I'm too old to date."

"If you're not dead yet, then you're not too old," *Daadi* said with a wink.

Jonathan smiled a little despite the guilt that had settled on his shoulders, tightening his already-sore muscles. He'd always enjoyed visiting his father's parents. It was a shame they lived nearly 160 miles away from his home in Maryland. Jonathan's parents met while his mother was in Pennsylvania visiting her cousins one summer, when they were both in their early twenties. After Jonathan's father married his mother, they moved to Maryland to live near her family. From the time he was a young child, Jonathan always looked forward to visiting his grandparents.

A knock on the back door startled him. Before either of his

grandparents could stand, he jumped up and hustled to open the door. Craig was standing on the back porch.

"I'm sorry to bother you at suppertime. But I wanted to check on you."

"Come in." Jonathan opened the door wide and led him into the kitchen.

Craig greeted the older couple and then turned to Jonathan. "How are you feeling?"

"Sore, but I'm okay. I didn't need any stitches in my fore-head, and I just have to ice my arm later. The doctor said it's a sprain, but it's really nothing." He wasn't exactly truthful. His arm hurt, but he was more worried about the tour group that had been in his buggy.

"Jonathan, could I talk to you outside for a minute?" Craig asked.

"Of course."

Craig said good-bye to Jonathan's grandparents, then stepped out onto the small porch as Jonathan followed him.

"How are all the passengers doing?" Jonathan held his breath, afraid of what Craig might say.

"They're doing all right." Craig nodded and rested his hand on one of the pillars that held up the porch roof. "One man suffered a minor concussion after hitting his head on one of the posts in the buggy. Another woman broke her arm, but the rest only have minor bumps, bruises, and cuts."

Jonathan nodded as more remorse plagued him. He should have prevented the accident . . . somehow.

"It could have been much worse." Craig sighed, and his look of concern for the passengers turned to . . . was it regret?

"Jonathan, I spoke to my lawyer, and he thinks it would be

a good idea if we took you off driving duty for a while. Things may get messy if anyone in the tour group decides to sue us. The driver of the car insists you didn't signal. He will only admit to possibly following too closely, but he says he didn't have time to brake fast enough to avoid hitting the buggy."

He shook his head. "I have a difficult time believing you were careless, but when I spoke to the passengers, they all said they weren't paying attention to you. They were just enjoying the end of the ride." Craig sighed again. "Jonathan, I still want you to work for me, but I'd like you to work in the stable for a while until we get this cleared up. How do you feel about that?"

Jonathan rubbed his chin as disappointment mixed with guilt. He didn't want to give up his job as a buggy tour guide, but he understood Craig's reasons. "That's fine. I enjoy working with the horses."

"Great." Craig shook Jonathan's hand. "I'll see you tomorrow then?"

"*Ya*, I'll be there."

"Good night." Craig descended the porch steps and headed toward his large farmhouse next door.

Jonathan suddenly remembered something he'd wanted to ask his boss. "Craig!" he called, causing the man to turn and face him. "Did you pick up my straw hat by any chance? I lost it when I fell out of the buggy."

Craig shook his head. "I'm sorry, but I didn't see it."

"Well, maybe someone else picked it up, but I have a spare. Thanks." Jonathan stepped back into the kitchen and sat down at the table.

"What did Craig have to say?" *Daadi* asked as he cut up a piece of chicken on his plate.

"Did he have any more news about the tourists who were in the accident?" *Mammi* chimed in.

Jonathan shared what Craig had reported about the passengers.

"Thank the Lord their injuries weren't worse." *Mammi's* eyes were sympathetic.

Jonathan ran his fingers over his glass of water. "Craig said he needs me to stop driving the buggies for a while. His lawyer thinks it would be a *gut* idea in case any of the passengers sue. He wants me to work in the stables."

"Oh." *Daadi* leaned back in his seat. "Did he say how long he needs you to work in the stables?"

Jonathan shook his head and his throat dried. "I just feel so terrible about the accident. I never meant to put those people in harm's way." He cleared his throat, fighting back his raw emotion. "Craig said the driver of the car insists I didn't signal before I started to turn into the driveway, but I thought I did. One of the store's employees told me she saw me signal. I'm always cautious."

"We know you are." *Mammi* rested her hand on his. "It was an accident."

"You've never been reckless." *Daadi* spooned peas from his plate. "I'd have a difficult time believing you didn't signal."

"Everyone who was in the accident is going to be okay." *Mammi* pointed to his plate, still filled with chicken, potatoes, and peas. "You need to eat. Your food is getting cold."

Jonathan glanced down and tried to will his stomach to relax, but all he could think about was the sound of the buggy wheel shattering and the passengers' screams when the car struck.

Chapter Two

"It's a miracle no one was killed," *Dat* said before sipping his coffee.

Janie had spent most of supper telling her parents and her older sister, Marie, about the accident and the events that took place afterward when the emergency responders arrived to help. Her family had listened with interest as she described the scene in detail.

"*Ya*, I agree," Marie said as she cut a slice of their mother's homemade apple pie. She placed it on a plate and handed it to *Dat* before tucking a strand of her brown hair behind her ear. "It sounds like it was bad." Janie could see the concern in her sister's brown eyes, the ones that matched *Dat*'s. Janie, two years younger than Marie's twenty-two years, had inherited their mother's blue eyes. But *Mamm*'s hair was light brown and Janie was the only person in the family with red hair.

"You must have been so scared," *Mamm* chimed in as she stirred her coffee. "I can't believe it happened right in front of your eyes."

"It was scary," Janie insisted as Marie handed her pie. "I was just sitting there eating my lunch when it all happened."

She lifted her fork and frowned. "I overheard one of the police officers tell Craig the driver said the accident was Jonathan's fault. He said Jonathan didn't signal, but he did. I saw it."

Marie handed *Mamm* pie and then cut a piece for herself. "It sounds like the driver lied. That's a sin."

"That's not the worst of it." Janie took a deep breath. She'd had to hold the secret in all day. "The driver was texting on his phone."

Marie's eyes widened. "Are you sure?"

Janie nodded with emphasis. "I saw him looking down at something in his hand, and I'm sure it had to be a cell phone. He definitely was not watching the road. I was going to tell that police officer, but I never had the opportunity. Bianca ended up really needing my help, and before I knew it, the officers and medical personnel were leaving.

"Then as soon as all the passengers were on their way and Craig had talked to his lawyer on the phone, he had Eva and me call our drivers, closed the shop early, and drove off to join Bianca at the hospital. I'm going to tell him what I saw tomorrow."

Dat frowned and pushed his fork through the flaky piecrust. "No, Janie. Don't get involved. Let the authorities handle the case."

"But it's not fair that Jonathan is being blamed for something that's not his fault. I heard Craig talking on the phone to his lawyer." Janie set her fork next to her plate. "What if Jonathan gets fired over this? I can't let that happen when I know the truth."

"You need to stay out of it, Janie," *Dat* warned again. "You just need to worry about your job. Let Craig handle the accident."

Janie nodded, then looked down at her uneaten piece of apple pie.

"My day at the schoolhouse wasn't nearly as exciting," Marie said. "In fact, the *kinner* all behaved quite well."

While Marie talked on about her job working as a teacher's assistant at the nearby schoolhouse, Janie pushed her fork through the pie. She couldn't stop herself from recalling the anguish in Jonathan's brown eyes as she took care of the gash on his head. She was certain Jonathan blamed himself for the accident even though he had signaled, but if no one else saw what really happened, only she knew the truth. How could she allow Jonathan to be charged with an accident that was not his fault?

The question continued to swirl through her mind after her father went out to the barn to care for the animals. As Janie cleared and wiped down the table, her mother started washing the dishes.

"I really like teaching," Marie said as she dried a pot. "I'm so thankful the assistant position opened up this fall. Maybe I can become a full-time teacher next year."

"That would be really nice," *Mamm* said, smiling at Marie. "You'd make a very *gut* teacher."

Janie's focus moved to the end of the counter where Jonathan's straw hat sat. She'd picked it up at the scene of the accident after he and Bianca left, and she planned to give it back to him tomorrow. She gnawed her lower lip as she listened to her mother and Marie talk. She wanted to discuss the accident and the information she had about the driver, but she didn't want to go against her father's instructions.

"*Mamm*, do you think *Dat* is right about the accident?" The question burst from Janie's lips before she could stop it.

Mamm spun to face her. "What do you mean?"

"Do you think I should keep the information about the driver to myself?" Janie fingered the washrag she still held in her hands. "I feel as if I need to share what I saw so Jonathan can clear his name."

Mamm frowned as she turned toward Janie, wiping her

hands on a dish towel. "I know you want to help Jonathan, but you need to listen to your *dat*. Besides, you know it's not our way to get involved in legal issues. Leave that to the *Englishers*." She gave Janie a little smile and turned back to the sink.

Janie finished cleaning the table and then swept the kitchen floor as Marie talked on about her students. Janie tried to concentrate on her sister's words, but her thoughts were still stuck on the accident and Jonathan's innocence.

After her chores were done, Janie headed upstairs to her room. She chose a book off her shelf, sat on her bed, and began to read, hoping to take her mind off the day's events. She had just started the second chapter when a knock sounded on her doorframe. She looked up and found Marie watching her with concern in her milk-chocolate brown eyes.

"Are you all right?" Marie asked, stepping into the room.

"*Ya*, I'm fine. Why?" Janie closed the book and set it on the bed beside her.

"You seemed so concerned at supper." Marie crossed the room and sat down on the corner of the bed. "I'm worried about you."

Janie fingered her dress. "I can't stop thinking about the accident."

"Do you want to talk about it?"

"*Ya*, I do." Janie shared how she'd taken care of Jonathan's wound. "I can't stop thinking about how upset Jonathan was. He blames himself for the accident, even though I told him I saw him signal. I know it wasn't his fault. And I want to help him with the rest of the information I have."

Marie ran her fingers over Janie's maple-leaf-pattern quilt. "You know it's not a *gut* idea to go against *Dat*, so why are you even still thinking about this?"

"If you had only seen Jonathan's eyes, Marie, then you

would understand." Janie sighed, removed her prayer covering, and started to pull the bobby pins out of her hair. "I just can't stop thinking about him and the accident. It was all so . . ."

"Traumatic?" her sister finished her thought.

"*Ya.*" Janie released her bun, and her red hair fell in waves past her shoulders. "All those people were hurt. And I didn't mean to eavesdrop, but Craig had his door open when he was talking on the phone to his lawyer. I heard Craig say he didn't want to fire Jonathan, but he understood what the lawyer was saying about liability. He said he and Bianca have put all their savings into the business, and they could lose everything they've worked for.

"The driver should be the one taking the blame, Marie. How can I stand by and let Jonathan take the blame?"

Marie gave her a sad smile. "I know you want to help. It's your nature to step in and take care of everyone, but *Dat* doesn't want you to get involved. You told Jonathan you saw him signal, and now you need to leave everything to him and Craig. It will be fine."

Janie nodded, but she wasn't convinced keeping quiet was the best way to handle this situation.

Marie stood. "I'm going to take a shower. I'll let you know when I'm out so you can take yours."

"All right." Janie placed the handful of bobby pins on her nightstand.

As Marie walked to the door, she looked back over her shoulder. "You have that look in your eye like you're planning something. Promise me you won't do anything that will get you in trouble with *Dat.*"

Janie sighed. "I promise."

"*Danki.*" Marie hurried out the door and disappeared into the hallway.

Janie stared down at the book beside her on the bed as she contemplated her sister's words. Marie was right. Janie needed to be an obedient daughter. Yet she still couldn't stop the feeling that she needed to tell Jonathan and Craig what else she'd witnessed.

After thanking her driver the following morning, Janie hefted her tote bag onto her shoulder, gripped Jonathan's straw hat in her hand, and climbed out of the van.

As she walked past the stables, Janie spotted Jonathan standing by one of the stalls. He must have worn his spare hat today. Since her driver had dropped her off fifteen minutes early, she had time to talk to him for a moment. She'd spent most of last night worrying about him, and she longed to check on him as well as return his hat.

The scent of animals and wet hay filled her senses as she stood by the entrance to the stable. She watched Jonathan gently rubbing a horse's forehead and muzzle as he quietly talked to the animal. She recognized the chestnut-colored Belgian from the accident. She was drawn to Jonathan's concern for the horse as she took in the sight of the man in front of her. Jonathan was tall and slender, but muscular. He was handsome with chiseled cheekbones and a perfectly proportioned nose. He looked older than she was.

Janie had never seen him before yesterday, and she wondered where he lived. Jonathan's strong jaw was clean-shaven, so he wasn't married.

Janie stepped into the stable. Her shoes crunched on the hay, causing Jonathan to turn toward her. Her cheeks burned with embarrassment, and she hoped her thoughts weren't written all over her face.

"*Gude mariye,*" she said as she walked over to him. "How are you feeling today?"

"I'm fine. *Danki.*" He smiled, but the happiness didn't reach his eyes. He still seemed upset.

"How's your arm?"

Jonathan glanced down and rubbed it. "It's sore, but the doctor said it's only a sprain. He gave me a sling, but I don't need it. I iced my arm for a while last night, and it seemed to help." His attention moved to the straw hat in her hand. "Is that mine?"

"*Ya,* it is." She'd been so busy admiring Jonathan that she almost forgot she was holding his hat. "I picked it up yesterday."

"*Danki.*" He took the hat from her hand and examined it. "I was wondering if it had been damaged in the accident."

"No, it seems like it's still perfect." She smiled up at him.

"I appreciate that you picked it up for me. I asked Craig about it last night when he stopped by my grandparents' *haus* to see me, and he said he hadn't seen it." He gave her another tentative smile and then hung the hat on a hook beside the stall door. He pointed to his forehead, where a fresh bandage covered his wound. "Thanks also for taking care of me yesterday. You'd make a *wunderbaar* nurse."

Janie chuckled and fingered the strap of her tote bag. "No, I don't think so. I just know how to apply ointment and bandages."

"You do a *gut* job." Jonathan leaned against the stall, and the horse sniffed his hat and then his shoulder.

"How is he?" she asked, pointing to the horse.

"Bucky is fine." Jonathan turned toward the horse and rubbed his chin. "He was a little spooked but he's okay."

Janie's thoughts turned to the accident, and her father's words of warning echoed through her mind.

"I'm going to be working in the stables now," Jonathan said while keeping his eyes focused on the horse.

"What do you mean?" She stepped closer to him and inhaled his scent of earth mixed with sunshine.

"Craig doesn't want me doing the buggy tours anymore. Well, at least for now." He shrugged, but she found disappointment in his eyes. "He asked me to work in the stables instead."

"Why doesn't he want you to give tours?" Janie knew the answer, but she wanted to hear what Craig had told Jonathan.

"He said his lawyer felt I should step down from giving the tours in case anyone in the tour group sues." He faced her and gestured around the stable. "I enjoy taking care of the horses, and mucking stalls isn't so bad."

"But the accident wasn't your fault." The words slipped from her lips before she could stop them. "I saw you signal before you guided the horse into the parking lot. And the driver was—"

"I appreciate your concern, but it doesn't matter." Something flickered in his brown eyes, but he shook off her words. "I'm *froh* to have the job. I'm just trying to help out my grandparents while I visit them for the fall. And we don't have much interaction with tourists in Maryland, so this is like a treat for me."

Janie let his words soak through her. Jonathan was only visiting his grandparents for the fall and then he'd return to Maryland. Why did this information bother her so much? She didn't even know him.

And maybe she should stay out of this, just as her father

asked, and not even tell Jonathan she saw the driver distracted. Surely she wasn't the only one who saw him signal, so just as Marie said, he would be okay. She'd have to keep that information to herself to obey her father.

"Thanks again for retrieving my hat. It's my favorite one," Jonathan said, changing the subject. He nodded toward the hat, still hanging on the hook beside the stall despite Bucky's interest.

"*Gern gschehne.*" She pointed toward the building that housed the souvenir shop and the offices. "I'd better get to work. I'm going to eat at the picnic table where we sat yesterday if you'd like to join me for lunch." She wasn't planning on asking him to eat lunch with her, but again, the words seemed to escape her lips without forethought. She held her breath, hoping he wouldn't reject her.

"I'd love to." His smile was genuine this time, lighting up his handsome face.

"Great," she said. "I'll see you around noon."

"I look forward to it."

Janie hurried toward the main building as excitement rushed through her. She couldn't wait to see Jonathan again at lunchtime. Not only was he handsome, but he was nice and easy to talk to. She felt as if she'd made a new friend, and she couldn't wait to get to know him better.

Jonathan watched Janie head toward the souvenir shop. She was several inches shorter than his six-foot stature and stunningly beautiful. Her green dress complemented the red hair peeking out from under her prayer covering. Her hair resembled the deep

orange hues of the summer sunset. Her eyes were bright blue, like
the cloudless summer sky, and her skin was pale, reminding him
of the porcelain dolls he'd once seen in a gift shop in Baltimore.

Jonathan surmised Janie was in her early twenties, which
was much too young for him, but there was something about
her that captivated him. Was it her sweet spirit? He shook the
thoughts away, reminding himself that he was going to return
to Maryland in a couple of months. It was silly to think about a
maedel he'd never see again.

Jonathan grabbed a shovel as he contemplated his conversation with Janie. She seemed determined to defend his innocence
in the accident even though he told her he was fine with working
in the stable. It warmed his heart that she would insist on supporting him even though she barely knew him.

As Jonathan mucked out a stall, he realized how much he
was looking forward to eating lunch with Janie and learning
more about her. All he knew was that she used to take care of her
sick uncle until he passed away. He wondered where she lived.
Did she have a boyfriend?

Jonathan stopped shoveling and grimaced. Why was he tor-
turing himself by thinking about Janie that way? He was leaving
soon, and he didn't know when he'd be back to Pennsylvania.
Besides, relationships never turned out the way he planned.
After having his heart broken twice, he'd given up on love. He
was better off alone.

Jonathan swiped the back of his hand across his brow and
returned to the task at hand. He would put Janie out of his mind
for now and not think about her until lunchtime.

Janie retrieved her lunch bag from the refrigerator in the break room, plucked her sweater from a closet, and hurried out through the front of the store, waving to Eva as she headed outside. She'd spent all morning thinking about Jonathan. She found herself watching the clock, impatiently awaiting noon. She couldn't wait to find out more about his life in Maryland.

Her excitement dissipated when she found the picnic table empty. Where was Jonathan? Maybe he had gotten too busy in the stables to break for lunch, or even forgotten about their plan to eat together.

Janie sat facing Old Philadelphia Pike and opened her lunch bag. She pulled out her chicken breast sandwich and bottle of water and then bowed her head in silent prayer. When she opened her eyes, she turned around and saw Jonathan crossing the parking lot, holding a brown paper bag in one hand and waving to her with the other. She smiled and waved back as happiness rang anew inside her.

"Sorry I'm late," he said as he sat down across from her. "I lost track of time."

"It's fine," she said. "I'm glad you could make it."

After a prayer, Jonathan pulled a sandwich and bottle of water out of his bag. "How was your morning?"

"*Gut.*" She opened her bottle of water. "The store has been busy today."

"I noticed," he said, glancing around the parking lot. "The horses and buggies have been going all morning too." He seemed to be in a much better mood.

"*Ya*, they have." She took a sip of water as she considered her curiosity. Would she seem too forward if she began firing off questions about his life?

"Do you live far from here?" Jonathan asked before biting into his sandwich.

"No, not very far at all," Janie said with a smile, relieved that he started the conversation. "I live in Ronks."

"Oh," he said with recognition twinkling in his eyes. "I know where that is. My grandparents live close by. They're near the bakery. Do you know where the bakery is in Bird-in-Hand?"

Janie nodded while chewing.

"They're only a few blocks from here, and they're right next door to Craig and Bianca. My grandparents live in a *daadihaus* on *mei onkel*'s farm." He took another bite of his sandwich.

"How long are you going to visit them?" she asked, hoping she didn't sound as eager as she felt.

Jonathan shrugged. "I'll probably be here through November."

"Oh." She pulled a plastic zippered bag of peanut butter cookies from her lunch bag and held it out to him. "Do you like peanut butter *kichlin*?"

He grinned. "Are you kidding? I love them."

Janie laughed. "Take a few. *Mei schweschder* makes the best *kichlin*."

"*Danki*." Jonathan bit into one and nodded. "They are fantastic."

"I'll tell her you said that."

"Is your *schweschder* older or younger than you?" he asked before taking another bite of the cookie.

"She's two years older. She's twenty-two." Janie took a sip of her water.

"Do you have any brothers?"

"*Ya, mei bruder*, Samuel, is married. He and his *fraa*, Mandy, have a *boppli* named Becky." She smiled. "Becky is the sweetest little *boppli*. How about you?"

"Two *bruders*. I'm the middle *kind*." Jonathan broke another cookie in half. "*Mei bruder* Daniel is thirty-two, and *mei bruder* Peter is twenty-seven. I'm the middle one and the shortest."

Her eyes widened. "You're the shortest?"

Jonathan chuckled, and she enjoyed the rich warmth of his laugh. "That's the truth. Daniel is six-foot-two, and my baby brother, Peter, is six-foot-four."

"Oh goodness." Janie gasped. "They're very tall."

"*Ya*, they are, and they like to remind me I'm shorter than they are." He opened his bottle of water and fingered the cap. "They're both married and have *kinner*. I'm the outcast who isn't married and doesn't have a family. *Mei mamm* keeps telling me she's worried about me because I'll be thirty in four months and I haven't found a *fraa*." He shrugged as if it didn't bother him, but she saw vulnerability in his eyes.

"Oh." Janie studied his face. "What kind of business do your *bruders* run?"

"Peter is a dairy farmer, and Daniel is a carpenter. Daniel went into business with *mei dat*." He spun the cap with his fingers and watched it turn. "I work with *mei dat* and Daniel, but I came up here to get away for a little while. I wanted to visit my grandparents and help them out. *Mei onkel* takes care of them, but he's so busy during harvest time." He looked sheepish. "I'm sure you're bored with hearing about my life. Tell me about yours."

"Well, there's not much to tell." Janie placed her sandwich on her napkin. "I live with my parents and *schweschder*, Marie. *Mei dat* and *bruder* work at Bird-in-Hand Builders, the shop *Dat* and *mei onkel* Raymond owned together, but they don't need *mei schweschder* and me to work there. *Mei bruder* and cousin help *Dat* run things just fine.

"Marie and I used to take care of our *onkel* Raymond. He was on dialysis, and our *aenti* had died several years ago. Marie and I took turns caring for him while our cousin Mike worked. After *Onkel* Raymond passed away, I babysat for my neighbor for a few months. *Mei freind* Eva also works here. We grew up together, and we're in the same youth group. When she told me Craig had an opening, I jumped at the chance to work here."

"And you had an exciting first day." Jonathan held up his bottle of water toward her as if to toast her.

"That is true." She took another bite of her sandwich. Again, she was amazed at how Jonathan's outlook had improved since just that morning. Maybe he had begun to really believe the accident wasn't his fault.

They were both silent for a few moments as they chewed. The *clip-clop* of hooves filled the air as a horse and buggy returned to the parking lot after a tour. They both looked over toward the buggy, and Jonathan's smile faded.

"Craig told me the passengers who were in the crash are going to be okay," Jonathan said. "The worst injuries were a broken arm and a mild concussion."

"I'm *froh* to hear they will all be okay." She studied his handsome face and once again saw guilt there. "I'm glad you're okay too. When I saw you fall, I was afraid you were badly hurt."

"You were worried about me?" He looked stunned.

"Of course I was. Why wouldn't I be?" Janie handed him another cookie, and his hand brushed hers. Her skin tingled at the contact. Had he felt that too?

"*Danki,*" Jonathan said, his intense eyes studying hers. "I always loved coming to see my grandparents when I was little. Bird-in-Hand is one of my favorite places."

"What sort of things did you do when you visited?"

"*Mei daadi* always took *mei bruders* and me fishing," Jonathan said with a smile. "One time, *mei bruders* and I all wound up in the water."

Soon they were both laughing at his funny fishing stories, and when they finished eating, they walked across the parking lot, side by side.

"I enjoyed lunch," Jonathan said as they approached the stables. "May I join you again tomorrow?"

"Absolutely," Janie said, thrilled that he would ask.

Jonathan grinned and tipped his hat to her, and Janie's heart fluttered as she smiled. She watched him amble into the stable, and she knew she was already falling for Jonathan Stoltzfus.

Chapter Three

Janie hummed to herself while organizing the postcards for sale in the souvenir shop. The store had opened thirty minutes earlier and a group had already come in and bought tickets for the first round of buggy rides. After the group left, Janie and Eva busied themselves with straightening the displays and preparing for the next rush of customers.

She'd thought about Jonathan all weekend and couldn't wait to see him again. She hoped he'd thought of her during the weekend too. And, most of all, she hoped he would eat lunch with her again this week as he had every day last week. She looked forward to the one hour each day they spent talking and laughing together.

After the postcard display was straightened, she moved to the T-shirts on display and began folding and organizing them by size.

"*Gude mariye*, Janie."

Startled, Janie spun and saw Jonathan grinning at her. "Jonathan," she said with surprise. "Hi. *Wie geht's?*"

"How was your weekend?" he asked, crossing his arms over his wide chest. His blue shirt complemented his tan skin and dark hair.

"It was *gut*," she said, trying her best not to stare at him. "How was yours?"

"*Gut*." He paused for a moment. "Lunch today?"

"*Ya,*" she said, hoping she didn't sound too eager. "Of course."

"Great." Jonathan held up a paper sack. "I brought some of *mei mammi's kichlin* to share with you. You can tell me if they are as *gut* as Marie's *kichlin*."

"I can't wait." And she couldn't.

"I have to get out to the stable, but I'll see you later." He gave her another electric smile and headed toward the back of the store.

"Janie," Eva gushed, sidling up to her. "Jonathan likes you!"

"Shh," Janie hissed. "Keep your voice down or he'll hear you."

"He's in the break room," Eva said, waving off Janie's worry. "So what's going on with you two?" Her grin was wide.

"Nothing. We're just *freinden*." Janie picked up another stack of T-shirts and began absently folding them to avoid her friend's questioning stare. "We ate lunch together last week."

"Every day?" Eva asked.

"Every day except for Monday. It's not a big deal, Eva. We only talk about our families and share funny stories." Janie saw Jonathan walking back through the store, and she gave Eva a warning look.

"See you later," Jonathan said as he moved past them. "Have a *gut* morning."

"You too," Janie and Eva sang in unison.

"That's so sweet that you ate together," Eva commented once Jonathan was gone. "I'm sure he's grateful for your friendship."

"What do you mean?" Janie asked.

"His *mammi* told Bianca that Jonathan had his heart broken

twice. He dated two *maed*, each for a long time, and they both broke up with him. His last girlfriend is going to marry one of his *freinden*." Eva shook her head. "He was so heartbroken he decided to come up here and spend the fall with his grandparents. He didn't want to be in town for their wedding."

"That's so *bedauerlich*." Janie clicked her tongue. Now she understood the vulnerability she'd seen in his eyes when he said he was the only son in his family who wasn't yet married.

Eva suddenly smiled. "You're just what he needs."

"Don't be ridiculous," Janie said. "I'm sure he's not interested in me." *But I wish he was.*

"Why wouldn't he be interested?" Eva pointed toward Janie's hair. "You're so *schee*. All of our *freinden* are envious of your hair."

"*Danki*." Janie frowned, not convinced. She considered herself ordinary, which was why she'd never had a boyfriend. What was she thinking? "He's so handsome, and I can't see why he would be interested in me. Besides, he's going back to Maryland before Christmas."

Eva touched Janie's arm and looked hopeful. "Maybe he'll stay."

"I doubt it," Janie said.

The bell above the door rang, and a group of tourists entered.

"We'd better get back to work," Janie said.

"We'll talk more later. I'll help the customers so you can finish what you're doing." Eva headed toward the tourists. "May I help you?"

While Janie finished folding the last stack of shirts, her thoughts were stuck on Jonathan and his heartaches. Would Jonathan ever share that story with her? She hoped someday he would tell her the truth about what happened to bring him to Bird-in-Hand for the harvest season.

Janie stood in her sister's bedroom doorway that evening and found Marie sitting on the edge of her bed, brushing her waist-length brown hair.

"Hi, Janie." Marie looked up at her. "Did you need something?"

"*Ya*, I was wondering if you had a minute to talk." Janie fingered the long braid dangling over her shoulder.

"Of course I do." Marie gestured for Janie to enter the room.

"*Danki*." Janie stepped into her room and sat on the cedar chest at the foot of Marie's double bed. She took a deep breath and looked up into Marie's concerned eyes. "I think I'm falling in love with Jonathan."

Marie gaped. "Jonathan? The man who had the buggy accident?"

"*Ya*." Janie crossed her arms over the front of her pink nightgown. "We've had lunch together every day since last Tuesday. We enjoy talking to each other. And he's so handsome, Marie. He's tall and has *schee* brown eyes. He's so sweet and charming." She sighed. "I don't know what to do."

"Janie." Marie leaned forward and touched her arm. "I don't understand what the problem is."

"He's going to be thirty in three months. Do you think *Dat* would approve?"

Marie frowned, and Janie dropped her hands into her lap.

"I'm sorry, but I'm not sure if *Dat* would approve," Marie said gently. "You might want to discuss it with *Mamm* first and get her thoughts. Do you want me to go with you?"

"No, I'm not ready to tell them yet." Janie touched the hem of her nightgown. "He's from Maryland. He's only here to visit his grandparents for a few months before he goes back home."

Marie looked concerned. "If you were to marry him, would you move to Maryland with him?"

"I don't know." The question had occurred to Janie earlier today as she'd eaten the cookies Jonathan had brought to share during lunch. If she were to marry Jonathan, would he expect her to move to Maryland? Janie shoved away the question. She was getting ahead of herself by already thinking about marriage.

Marie's face brightened. "I have an idea! Why don't you invite Jonathan over for supper one night? That would be the best way for *Mamm* and *Dat* to meet him. You've already mentioned Jonathan is charming, so I'm certain *Mamm* and *Dat* would like him too."

"That's a great idea!" Janie popped up from the cedar chest and hugged Marie. "*Danki*. I knew you could help me." She started for the door, her long braid bouncing off her back.

"Janie, wait."

Janie looked over her shoulder at Marie. "What?"

"Just be careful, okay?" Marie's face was full of caution. "I don't want to see you get hurt. Don't forget he's leaving in a few months, and things might not work out."

"Okay." Janie's smile faded. Her sister was right. Janie was risking her heart, but somewhere deep in her soul she had a feeling Jonathan cared for her as much as she cared for him.

⁓⁓⁓

Jonathan hummed to himself as he finished caring for the horses in his grandfather's barn Wednesday evening. The week had gone well so far. He'd cherished the one hour each day he and Janie spent together, sharing stories along with their lunches. She was sweet, funny, and beautiful. He thought about her constantly, and he couldn't wait to see her tomorrow.

Once he finished caring for the animals, Jonathan stepped outside and closed the barn door. When he turned, he found his grandfather smiling at him.

"Were you just humming?" *Daadi* asked with a sly grin.

Jonathan shrugged. "*Ya*, I guess I was."

"What's gotten into you?" *Daadi* raised an eyebrow. "Have you met a *maedel*?"

Jonathan shoved his hands in his pockets. "*Ya*, I suppose I have."

"Let's go sit on the porch and talk. I want to hear all about this *maedel* who has stolen my grandson's heart." *Daadi* climbed the back steps, sank into the swing, and grinned with enthusiasm. "Well?"

Jonathan chuckled to himself as he climbed the steps and then leaned back against the railing across from *Daadi*. "Her name is Janie Lantz, and she works in the souvenir shop."

"What does she look like?" *Daadi* asked, resting his hands on his rotund middle.

"She's beautiful." Jonathan smiled. "She has red hair and blue eyes. She's very sweet." He shook his head. "It will never work out though."

Daadi squinted at him through his glasses. "Why not?"

"She's only twenty. I'm a decade older than she is."

"So?" *Daadi* shrugged. "Your *mammi* is nine years younger than I am."

"She is?" Jonathan was stunned to hear this fact.

"*Ya*, she is." *Daadi* shrugged. "When I met her, I was thirty, and she was twenty-one. What matters is how you feel about this young woman and how she feels about you, Jonathan."

Jonathan nodded. "*Danki, Daadi*."

"Are you going to tell her how you feel?" *Daadi* asked with a hopeful look on his wrinkly face.

"I will eventually," Jonathan said as he sat on the railing.

"Eventually?" *Daadi* scrunched his nose. "What are you waiting for?"

"The right time." Jonathan frowned. "I have a history of sharing my feelings too soon and winding up alone after the *maedel* changes her mind. I don't need to go through that again. Twice was already too many times."

"I can understand that, but don't wait too long either." *Daadi* shivered as a cold breeze wafted over them. "Fall is here." He stood. "Let's go inside before it gets any colder."

As Jonathan followed *Daadi* into the house, he wondered if his grandfather was right. Could a relationship work out between Janie and him despite their age difference? But more important could Janie be the *maedel* who would truly love him and not break his heart? The thought took hold of him and a renewed hope settled deep in his soul. Before he shared his feelings, Jonathan had to make sure Janie felt the same way about him that he felt about her.

Janie smiled at Jonathan as they sat at the picnic table and shared a bag filled with the chocolate chip cookies she and Marie had made the night before.

"I can't believe tomorrow is Friday already," she quipped, snatching another cookie from the bag. "The week has flown by."

"It has gone by quickly." He took a cookie and then met her eyes. "Janie, I want to ask you something."

Janie's stomach tightened at the seriousness in his eyes. "Okay."

"Do you have a boyfriend?" He looked worried.

Janie had to bite her lip to stop a laugh from escaping her mouth. "No, I don't."

"Oh." Relief relaxed his features.

"Do you have a girlfriend?" Even though Eva had told her the answer, she wanted to hear Jonathan confirm it.

"No." Jonathan looked down at his napkin covered with cookie crumbs. "I haven't told you the real reason I came to visit my grandparents."

Janie's stomach clenched again, this time with anticipation. Was he finally going to share his story of heartaches?

"I was dating someone," he began with a melancholy look in his eyes. "I was so sure she was the one for me. In fact, I was trying to work up the courage to ask her to marry me, but I never got the chance to ask. She broke up with me, and she's marrying one of *mei freinden* in November."

"I'm so sorry," Janie whispered, her voice thin with sympathy.

"Thanks." He gave her a bleak smile. "I couldn't stand the idea of being there for their wedding. I would be expected to go since it's in my church district. I came up with the idea of spending the fall with my grandparents to get away from the situation." He grimaced. "I'm a coward."

"No, you're not." Janie resisted the urge to reach across the table and touch his hand. "I can understand why you wanted to get away. My cousin's girlfriend, Rachel, went through the same thing. Her ex-boyfriend is dating her former best friend. She told me it was difficult to see them at every youth gathering and every church service. You can only take so much."

"*Danki* for understanding. *Mei bruders* think I overreacted by leaving the way I did, but I don't regret my decision. I'm helping my grandparents too." A smile found his lips. "And I met you."

Butterflies danced in Janie's stomach. She suddenly remembered her sister's advice. "Would you like to come to supper one night to meet my family?"

He smiled. "I'd love to."

"*Wunderbaar.*"

He looked hesitant. "Do you think your family will like me?"

"Absolutely." Janie started a mental list of what she and Marie could make for supper the night he came.

She also said a silent prayer, asking God to help her parents approve of her friendship with Jonathan.

Chapter Four

Jonathan guided the last horse toward the stable the following evening. A brisk breeze whipped over him as he glanced up at the fluffy clouds dotting the late-afternoon sky. He halted the horse and climbed down from the buggy. As he started to unhitch the horse, he saw movement in his peripheral vision. Looking up, he found Janie standing in front of him, hugging a black sweater over her blue dress and black apron. Her tote bag was slung over her shoulder.

"Jonathan." She smiled. "I'm glad you're still here. My driver is running a little late, so I thought I'd stop by to say hi."

"How long is your driver going to be?"

"He said he had to make a run to Philadelphia and is stuck in traffic. It's going to be at least another forty-five minutes." She shook her head. "Craig and Bianca had to leave; they usually visit some relatives on Friday evenings. Since I don't have anyone else to call for a ride, I told my driver I would wait. I hope you don't mind if I wait out here."

An idea flashed in Jonathan's mind. He pointed toward the buggy. "Would you like to go for a ride? I can take you on the route I normally take the tourists."

She hesitated. "How long is the ride?"

"It's about thirty minutes, but I can shorten it."

"I don't know." She shivered and hugged her sweater closer to her body.

"I'll grab a quilt," he offered.

"Okay," Janie said, finally agreeing. But then she held up her hand to stop him. "Wait. Are you allowed to take the buggy out? I don't want to get you in trouble."

"I can still drive a buggy," he explained, "but I can't take any tourists out. You're *mei freind*, not a paying passenger."

"Okay."

Jonathan got a quilt from the stable and then took Janie's hand and helped her climb up into the buggy. He enjoyed the warm, soft feel of her skin and resisted the urge to not release her hand. Once she was settled in the seat, he walked around the buggy, climbed up on the seat beside her, and took the reins.

"Are you cold?" she asked, moving closer to him. "Would you like to share the quilt?"

Jonathan nodded. "Sure." How could he say no to her request? He savored the thought of sitting close to her.

Janie tossed the blanket over his lap and slid closer to him. He breathed in the scent of her shampoo—apple.

"When is your driver coming to get you?" she asked.

"I walk to work since it's only a few blocks," he explained, guiding the horse toward the road. "Sometimes I get a ride from Craig and Bianca, but I don't mind the walk. It gives me time to think and enjoy the fresh air. I love being outdoors."

"Oh." Janie's lips turned up in a sweet smile, and his pulse galloped.

Janie was so pretty with her warm smile and bright blue

eyes. The sun was starting to set, and the deep orange hues in the sky nearly matched her hair. She scooted closer to him, and his leg brushed hers under the blanket.

"I'm *froh* my driver was late so I can spend more time with you today," she said, breaking through his thoughts.

"I'm enjoying it too," he said as he slowed the horse at a red light.

"I love autumn," Janie continued with her eyes fixed on the road ahead. "I enjoy seeing the leaves change and the cooler nights." She looked over at him. "What's your favorite season?"

Jonathan looked over at her face and all his worries melted away. *Any season with you is my favorite.* "I think it's autumn."

"You think it's autumn?" She laughed, and he relished the sweet sound. "Don't you have a favorite season?"

"I'm not fussy." He guided the buggy down a quiet residential street and the aroma of the smoke from a fireplace permeated the air.

"October will be here soon," she said. "It will be much colder then." Her smile faded. "But I don't want October to come."

"Why not?" he asked.

"October is closer to November, and you're leaving in November." Janie's big blue eyes misted over. Was she going to cry?

Jonathan halted the horse at a stop sign and angled his body toward Janie. He cupped her cheek with his hand, and she turned her face toward it. The air around them sparked with electricity. He felt the overwhelming urge to kiss her, but he knew it would be inappropriate.

"I really like you, Janie," he said, his voice husky with emotion.

"I like you too," she whispered in response, her voice sounding equally sentimental.

Jonathan moved his thumb over her cheek, and she closed her eyes. A horn blasted behind him, and he quickly grabbed the reins and guided the horse down the road. The scent of rain saturated the air as their trip wore on.

"Do you think it's going to rain?" Janie asked.

"It might," Jonathan said. He looked up at the sky.

"Do you like the rain?" she asked, scooting even closer to him.

"I do when I'm not working outside."

"I love falling asleep to the sound of rain tapping on the roof."

For the remainder of the ride, they sat in contented silence, peppered with moments of conversation about the sights they passed. When they returned to the parking lot, she helped him stow the buggy and horse.

As they walked out of the stable, Janie took Jonathan's hand in hers. He glanced down at her, and she smiled up at him.

"I had a *wunderbaar* time tonight," she said. *"Danki."*

"Gern gschehne." Jonathan squeezed her hand. "I hope you have a nice weekend." He couldn't stand the thought of saying good-bye to her and not seeing her for two whole days.

"I hope you do too." Janie opened her mouth to say something but stopped when headlights gleamed in their faces. She released his hand and hefted her tote bag farther up on her shoulder. "That's my ride. I'll see you Monday."

"Take care," he said as she hurried toward the van and climbed into the front passenger seat.

Jonathan waved as the white van steered through the parking lot, then started his journey on foot to his grandparents' house. His mind swirled with thoughts of Janie and their buggy ride. He had enjoyed every moment he'd spent with her, snuggled close under the blanket as they rode under the beautiful sky. Janie had worked her way into his heart, and he wanted to spend as much time with her as possible. He dreaded the thought of going back to Maryland and not seeing her again.

A cool mist of rain sprayed over him, and he shivered. He crossed his arms over his middle and picked up speed. He hurried down the street and smiled despite the damp weather. For the first time in nearly a year, he felt himself falling in love, and he prayed somehow he and Janie could find a way to make their relationship work.

⁕

"You went on a buggy ride with him after work?" Marie asked with a gasp as she washed the dishes later that evening.

"*Ya*, I did," Janie said, smiling so widely her cheeks hurt. She lifted a dish from the drain board and began to dry it. "It was really romantic. We went on the route he takes passengers, and it was nice and cold. He gave me a quilt to stay warm. He's so sweet." She sighed as sadness threatened to squelch her euphoria. "I just can't stand the thought that he's going to go back to Maryland."

"Who's going back to Maryland?"

Janie glanced over her shoulder to where her mother stood watching as she leaned on a broom. Janie hadn't heard her mother come in after sweeping the porch.

"Jonathan," Janie explained, her cheeks burning. "He's the one who was in the buggy accident."

"He's still working at the buggy rides?" *Mamm* tilted her head with surprise.

"He's working in the stable." Janie frowned. "It's not fair. The accident wasn't his fault at all, but he said he's *froh* to have the job. His *onkel* cares for his grandparents, but this is a chance for Jonathan to help them too."

"He's supporting his grandparents?" *Mamm* asked, and Janie nodded. "But you said he's from Maryland? He's only visiting them?"

"*Ya*, that's right. He said his *daed* is from here, but his *mamm* is from Maryland. After his parents married, they moved to Maryland to be by her family." Janie began drying another dish. "He came to spend some time with his grandparents. He said he loves coming here and working since they don't have much contact with tourists in Maryland." She considered sharing the story about his ex-girlfriend, but she felt it wasn't her place to share something so personal.

Mamm studied her for a moment. "Did I hear you say you took a romantic buggy ride with him?"

The tips of Janie's ears blazed with embarrassment. "We did. He took me on the route where he used to take the tourists. He's very respectful and friendly. I want you to meet him."

"When is he going back to Maryland?" *Mamm* frowned.

"In late November." Janie placed the dish on the counter and grabbed a handful of utensils to dry.

"You know you shouldn't get attached to him, Janie." *Mamm's* voice held a hint of warning. "He's already planning to go back to Maryland, and you don't know when you'll see him again."

"But what if he decides to stay?" Marie suddenly chimed in. "He may fall in love with Janie and decide to stay here. He could build a *haus* near his grandparents and ask Janie to marry him."

Janie's pulse fluttered at the thought, but her mother's skeptical look brought her back to reality.

"I think you should take it one step at a time," *Mamm* said gently. "Jonathan might decide to stay, but you should prepare yourself in case he doesn't. Just enjoy being his *freind* for now and see what the future brings."

"*Ya.*" Janie nodded. "I'd like to have him over for supper one night so you all can meet him. He already said he'd like to come sometime."

Mamm began to sweep the kitchen floor. "*Ya,* we'll see. Maybe when things slow down some at the shop. You know orders at the shop pick up again during the harvest season. Between that and the farm, your *dat* is very busy right now. Maybe in a couple of weeks we can have him over."

"All right." Janie couldn't wait for her family to meet Jonathan, but her mother's warning echoed in the back of her mind. Would Jonathan return to Maryland and forget all about her?

⁓

The next two weeks flew by as quickly as the autumn leaves blew from the trees. Janie and Jonathan ate lunch together every day and discussed everything from the cooler temperatures to their favorite foods. When Janie finally invited him over for supper, he accepted her invitation, and she almost jumped with joy.

Janie rushed home from work on Wednesday evening during the last week in September. The day had finally come for Jonathan to come over, and excitement skittered through her as she fluttered around the kitchen.

Marie appeared in the doorway. "Need some help?"

"*Ya,*" Janie said as she mixed the meat loaf. "Would you please set the table and then mix up the brownies?"

"*Ya,*" Marie said with a grin. "You're awfully *naerfich*. You really like him, don't you?"

"You already know the answer to that question." Janie frowned. "I just hope *Dat* likes him."

"What are you worried about? The age difference?"

Janie nodded and looked down at the meat-loaf mix. "I'm worried he won't approve and won't let me date Jonathan. He's the first man who has ever shown an interest in me, and I'll just be devastated if *Dat* doesn't approve."

Marie placed her hand on Janie's shoulder. "Have faith that it will work out well tonight."

"*Danki.*" Janie prayed Marie was right.

At six o'clock, the warm aromas of meat loaf and brownies permeated the kitchen and the table was set. Janie smoothed her hands down her favorite green dress and black apron and touched her prayer covering, hoping it was straight.

"You look *schee,*" Marie whispered. "Everything will be fine."

"*Danki,*" Janie whispered in return as she stared out the window above the kitchen sink and watched for Jonathan's driver.

When the crunch of tires sounded on the rock driveway, Janie's stomach lurched. A combination of joy and anxiety rioted inside of her.

"I think he's here," *Mamm* said, entering the kitchen from the family room. "What can I do to help?"

"We're all set," Marie announced. "Janie is very *naerfich*."

"No, I'm not," Janie said, clearly fibbing. "I'm fine. Where's *Dat*?"

"He's in the barn. Do you want me to go get him?" Marie offered.

"He'll come in when he hears the car," *Mamm* said, patting Janie's shoulder. "Relax, *mei liewe*. Dinner will be *appeditlich*. Your meat loaf is always *wunderbaar.*"

"That's not what I'm worried about." Janie turned to face her mother. "What if you and *Dat* don't like Jonathan?"

Mamm touched Janie's cheek. "If you like him, then we will like him too."

Janie turned her attention back to the window and saw Jonathan climbing from the burgundy van. He looked handsome clad in clean black trousers, a tan shirt, and black suspenders. He said something to his driver and then waved as the van drove away.

Janie held her breath as her father appeared from the barn and walked over to Jonathan. When they both smiled, Janie's shoulders relaxed and a smile spread across her face. *Mamm and Marie are right; everything is going to be fine.*

After talking for a few minutes, Jonathan and *Dat* walked up the short path toward the house. Janie crossed the kitchen to the doorway leading to the mudroom. The back door opened, and *Dat* stepped into the mudroom with Jonathan close behind him.

"Hi, Jonathan," Janie said, her voice a little higher and more excited than she'd hoped.

Jonathan gave her a breathtaking smile, and her pulse raced. "Hi, Janie."

Her father washed his hands at the sink as Jonathan stepped into the kitchen.

"*Mamm*, Marie, this is Jonathan." Janie gestured between Jonathan and her sister and mother.

"It's nice to meet you," *Mamm* said. "I'm Sylvia, and I see you've met Timothy. Please have a seat."

"We're so *froh* you could come today," Marie said. "We've heard a lot about you." Janie swallowed a gasp.

"Danki." Jonathan met Janie's stare. "I'm glad to meet you all too. Where would you like me to sit?"

"Sit here," Marie said, putting her hand on the back of a chair. "You'll be next to Janie."

Jonathan sat down on the chair, and *Dat* sat to his right at the head of the table.

"So," *Dat* began, "what kind of business do you have in Maryland?"

"I'm a carpenter," Jonathan said. "I work with *mei dat* and *bruder*. We make furniture. We fill a lot of custom orders for bedroom suites and dining room sets."

"Oh." *Dat* nodded and fingered his beard. "So you're only here to visit your grandparents?"

"That's right," Jonathan said, running his finger over the gray tablecloth.

"How long are you planning to stay?" *Dat* asked.

While *Dat* and Jonathan got acquainted, Janie, Marie, and *Mamm* began placing the platters and bowls of food on the table. Once the meal was delivered, they took their seats and bowed their heads in silent prayer.

After the prayer the sound of utensils scraping the dishes overtook the kitchen. They filled their plates with meat loaf, mashed potatoes, and green beans.

"Everything smells *appeditlich*," Jonathan said, dropping a spoonful of mashed potatoes onto his plate.

"Janie did the cooking," Marie announced. "I helped a little."

Janie gave Jonathan a shy smile. "It wasn't difficult. Meat loaf is easy to make."

"How do you like working at Lancaster Buggy Rides and Souvenirs?" Marie asked.

"I like it," Jonathan said. "I miss giving the buggy rides, but I enjoy working in the stables. I love visiting Lancaster." Then he took a bite of meat loaf.

"Is it much different from where you live in Maryland?" *Mamm* asked.

Jonathan nodded and swallowed. "We're more conservative in Maryland and don't have much contact with *Englishers*."

All through supper, Janie's parents and sister peppered Jonathan with questions, including as they ate brownies and drank coffee. But Jonathan didn't seem to mind sharing stories about his life in Maryland.

Once they finished dessert, Janie carried mugs to the sink and Marie collected the rest of the dishes. Now *Dat* was talking to Jonathan about his work at Bird-in-Hand Builders too.

Mamm stepped over to the counter and touched Janie's arm. "Marie and I will clean up. Why don't you go sit on the porch with Jonathan?"

Janie glanced over her shoulder to where *Dat* was telling Jonathan about his business. Jonathan nodded politely as if he was hanging on his every word.

"Save him," *Mamm* said with a smile. "I'm sure he'd rather talk to you than hear your *dat* talk about our store."

"Go on," Marie chimed in as she filled the sink with frothy water. "We'll handle this. Go enjoy your guest until his driver comes to pick him up."

Janie smiled. *"Danki."* She stepped over toward Jonathan

and he gave her a sideways glance as her father continued talking about the items they created and sold at the store. He was detailing the wishing wells, planters, swings, lighthouses, and other lawn ornaments. When *Dat* paused to take a breath, she grabbed the opportunity to jump in.

"Jonathan," she began, "would you like to sit on the porch and talk while you wait for your driver to come for you?"

"That would be nice." Jonathan looked at her father as if awaiting his permission.

Dat nodded. "That's a *gut* idea. Go and enjoy the night. I don't think it's too cold out there yet, but the cold weather is coming soon."

Jonathan stood. "*Danki* for supper. I had a great time."

After saying good-bye, Jonathan followed Janie into the mudroom, where he retrieved his hat and jacket, and she grabbed her wrap.

"Do you need to call your driver?" Janie asked as they stepped onto the back porch. She hugged her wrap around her.

"*Ya*, I do." Jonathan jammed his thumb toward the small shed next to the barn. "Is that your phone shanty?"

"*Ya*," Janie said. "Go right ahead and use it."

As Jonathan hustled down the porch steps, Janie sank onto the porch swing and glanced up at the sunset, which sent streaks of yellow, orange, purple, and pink across the sky. She hugged her wrap closer and smiled, recalling how Jonathan had fit in with her family during supper. Her parents and sister seemed to like him, and her heart warmed at the thought.

Jonathan's footsteps startled Janie back to the present.

"I didn't mean to scare you," he said as he crossed the porch. "You looked as if you were lost in thought."

"It's fine." She scooted to the other side of the swing and patted the bench beside her. "Have a seat." Looking up at his face, she saw the gash on his forehead was healing and barely noticeable.

"Thanks." He sank down beside her, his long legs stretched out in front of him. "Your family is great."

"*Danki.*" She gave the swing a little push, and it gently moved them back and forth. "I think they liked you."

"I hope so." He turned toward her. "I just have a question for you."

"What's that?"

"Your *mamm*'s hair is light brown, and your *dat* and *schweschder* are brunettes." A smile played at the corners of his mouth. "Where did you get that *schee* hair of yours?"

Janie's cheeks heated as his warm eyes remained focused on her. "*Mei mamm* told me her *mammi* had red hair. She thinks I inherited it from her."

He looked up at the sky. "Your hair reminds me of the sunset." He pointed. "See that orange there? That's almost the same color."

Janie gaped. No one had ever described her hair that way. "*Danki,*" she said softly, marveling inside at the unexpected compliment.

"That was what I thought the first time I saw you." His fingers brushed her shoulders, sending chills dancing up her spine as he rested his arm on the back of the swing. "I immediately thought your hair was the color of a sunset. I'd never seen a *maedel* with hair like yours. It's unique and *schee.*"

"*Danki,*" she repeated, not knowing what else to say.

"September is flying by quickly." Jonathan turned his attention back to the sky. "I can't believe it will be October next week."

"I know." Janie wanted to ask him to stay in Pennsylvania, but she didn't want to be too forward.

"We'll have to make the most of the next two months." He turned back toward her. "It's nice to spend time together."

"I agree."

"Great," he said.

It seemed as though the rest of their conversation had barely begun when the hum of an engine and the reflection of headlights on the side of her father's large barn drew Janie's focus to the driveway. Her smile faded. She dreaded the idea of saying good night to Jonathan.

"I guess it's time for me to go." Jonathan's frown mirrored her mood. "But I'll see you tomorrow."

They both stood and he held out his hand. She took it, and warmth zipped through her body. As they walked toward the waiting van, Janie relished the feeling of walking by his side. She felt as if she belonged there. Did he feel it too?

"Thank you for supper," Jonathan said when they reached the passenger side door. "I had a great time."

"I did too." Janie smiled up at him. "I'm glad you came."

Jonathan was silent as he gazed down into her face. She longed to know what he was thinking. He brushed his fingers over her cheek, and she sucked in a breath.

"*Gut nacht,*" he finally said.

"*Gut nacht.*"

He climbed into the passenger seat, and Janie waved as the van backed down the driveway. As it disappeared down the road, Janie closed her eyes and silently asked God to help Jonathan decide to stay in Pennsylvania.

Chapter Five

Jonathan paid the driver and then walked past his uncle's house and down the path to his grandparents' cottage. His gait was as light as if he were walking on clouds after spending the evening with Janie and her family. Her father had asked a lot of questions, but it didn't bother Jonathan. Her mother and sister had made him feel welcome.

The best part of the evening, however, had been sitting on the porch with Janie. Jonathan was so comfortable with her. It was as if he could tell her anything. She was attentive, much more attentive than his ex-girlfriend Grace had ever been. Janie was the *maedel* he'd waited for his whole life.

But this is wrong! You have to go back to Maryland in November!

The warning rang out from deep in his soul, and it choked the happiness that had been brewing inside of him all evening.

With a sigh, Jonathan climbed the front steps and entered the cottage, stepping into the small family room. As he hung up his coat, he saw his grandmother sitting in her favorite chair, reading a devotional by the light of the propane lamp. His grandfather snored quietly in his wing chair on the other side of the room.

"How was your supper?" *Mammi* asked softly.

"It was *gut*." Jonathan smiled over at his grandfather, shaking his head.

Mammi stood and took Jonathan's hand in hers. "Let's go talk in the other room." She steered him into the kitchen.

"Sit," she instructed, then brought a plate of oatmeal raisin cookies to the table. "I made your favorite this afternoon."

"*Danki*." He didn't have the heart to tell her he was full. Instead, he swiped a cookie from the plate.

"Tell me all about your evening." *Mammi's* brown eyes sparkled with curiosity. "How was her family?"

"They were great. I had a *gut* time." Jonathan bit into the cookie as his worries continued to nip at him.

"*Was iss letz?*" *Mammi* seemed to sense his hesitation.

"I really care about her," Jonathan admitted. "I just don't see how it can work."

"Why not?" *Mammi* picked up a cookie. "You both seem to like each other and that's probably the most important part of a relationship. If you don't like each other, you won't make it through the tough times." She bit into the cookie while seeming to ponder something. "Is it the distance? You know you're always welcome here. You don't have to rush back home unless your *dat* is tired of taking care of your *haus* and animals."

Jonathan couldn't lie. The distance was part of his hesitation. "It's not only that." He took another cookie from the plate. "I just don't see how it can work with our age difference."

"Why not?" *Mammi* lifted her eyebrows. "Your *daadi* and I have made it work." She grinned. "In fact, we still like each other after all these years."

Jonathan chuckled. "That is fantastic, *Mammi*, but I'm not

sure her *dat* will give me his permission to date her. He seemed to be grilling me from the moment I stepped out of the van."

Mammi waved off his comment. "*Mei dat* did the same thing to Omar, but he came around. They got along wonderfully. It's a *dat*'s job to make sure his *boppli* marries a *gut* man. If you ever have a *dochder*, you'll do the same thing to her boyfriends."

Jonathan nodded and took another bite of the cookie. He wanted to believe his grandmother's encouraging words, but he knew in the back of his mind—in his heart—he was afraid to trust another woman after the way Grace had hurt him. Janie was too sweet to mean to hurt him, but maybe she wouldn't care about him enough to look past their age difference, even if he could.

"Are you worried she'll break your heart the way Grace did?" *Mammi* asked gently. Had she been reading his mind? "Janie is a different *maedel*."

"I know." Jonathan stared down at the table. "But I'm just not sure."

"It's late," *Mammi* said after a few moments of silence between them. "I need to get your *daadi* out of his chair and into his bed. I go through this every night."

"I'll help you." Jonathan popped the last of his cookie into his mouth and headed into the family room. As he tried to coax his snoring grandfather awake, he wondered if his grandmother was right. Maybe he and Janie could somehow make their relationship work.

Janie's smile was wide as she climbed the porch steps after saying good-bye to Jonathan. The dinner had gone better than she'd ever imagined it would. Her parents were welcoming, and Jonathan seemed comfortable getting to know them and Marie.

She stopped walking when she reached the porch swing. Their visit on the porch had been even more romantic than the buggy ride. She was still stunned by the way he'd described her hair. No one had ever said her hair was as beautiful as the sunset. When she was in school, the boys used to make fun of her, saying her hair was the color of orange crayons. She always felt different and strange because she was the only redhead in the school.

When she was with Jonathan, however, she felt beautiful and special. He wasn't like any other man she'd met. None of the boys in her youth group were interested in her, but Marie never had any trouble getting the boys' attention. Janie always assumed it was due to her strange hair, but Jonathan told her he noticed her hair when they first met. He felt like a gift sent to her by God, and she was so very thankful!

Her feelings for him were growing deeper and deeper with each passing day. She wondered if this was how true love felt. If Jonathan felt the same way about her, he could possibly be the man who would love her for the rest of her life. Her spirit soared at the thought of settling down and raising a family together.

Janie stepped into the house and hung up her wrap. Then she found her parents sitting at the kitchen table. She smiled as she greeted them. Her cheeks ached from smiling so much.

"*Danki* for allowing me to invite Jonathan over tonight. He said he had a very nice time." She started toward the stairs. "I'm going to go get ready for bed."

"Janie, wait," her mother said. "Please sit down for a moment. We'd like to talk to you."

Janie spun, and their dismal expressions sent dread pooling in her belly. "Is something wrong?"

"No, but we'd like to speak with you." *Dat* cleared his throat and rested his elbows on the table.

"Did I do something wrong?" Janie asked, her voice squeaking like a young child's. She sat down across from her parents and felt as if she were facing the congregation after she'd been caught committing a sin. But she hadn't deliberately done anything sinful.

"No, of course not. We'd just like to discuss Jonathan with you." Her mother glanced at her father, and he nodded. "He's a very nice young man, but we have some concerns."

"Concerns? I don't understand." Janie's throat suddenly became dry, and she tried in vain to swallow.

"I spoke to him outside when he arrived," *Dat* began, his eyes somber. "I asked him what his intentions are with you, and he said he would like to get to know you better. He said he cares about you."

A glimmer of hope ignited inside of Janie, but her father's serious face quickly extinguished it.

"He's planning to go back to Maryland in early December," *Dat* said. "Your *mamm* and I don't want you to get involved with him and then decide to move away. We'd like all three of our *kinner* to stay in our community."

"He could decide to stay here," Janie offered. "He hasn't left yet." Janie looked at her mother, hoping for her support, but instead, her mother continued to frown.

"Your *dat* is right," *Mamm* said. "We don't want you to move away, but we also don't want to see you hurt when he leaves. You need to keep going to youth group, and you'll find the right *bu* for you in our community."

"No," Janie said, her voice now trembling with emotion. "I'm not interested in the *buwe* in my youth group. I want to get to know Jonathan better. Why can't you give him a chance? You'll see why I like him."

Her parents exchanged bleak looks.

"Do you realize he'll be thirty in a few months?" *Dat* asked her.

Janie nodded. "*Ya*, he told me, and I'll be twenty-one in June."

Dat shook his head. "I'm not comfortable with you dating a man who is nearly a decade older than you. It's not right."

Mamm nodded. "I agree."

Janie gasped and tears stung her eyes as she looked back and forth between her parents. "But, *Mamm*, you said he's a nice man. Why does his age matter if he's a *gut* Christian man?"

"I would like you to find someone your age or at least closer to your age," *Mamm* said. "You have shared life experiences with your *freinden* from your youth group."

"Shared life experiences?" Janie wiped away an errant tear with the back of her hand. "What does that even mean? We're both Amish and we have a special connection I've never felt with any other *bu*. We enjoy each other's company. What more do we need?"

"I don't want to see you get hurt, Janie." *Mamm's* eyes were sympathetic as she leaned forward to hold Janie's hand, but Janie moved her hands out of her mother's reach. "As your *dat* said, Jonathan is going to go back to Maryland and leave you here with a broken heart."

"You don't know that," Janie retorted with more resentment than she'd meant to share. She turned her focus to her father. "You said he told you he cared about me. Please give him a chance."

Dat shook his head, looking unconvinced. "I don't think he's right for you. If he asks for permission to date you, I'm going to tell him no."

Speechless, Janie turned to her mother again, but her mother only shook her head.

"I don't understand you," Janie said, her voice radiating with anguish. "You want Marie and me to get married and have a family like Sam, but you won't approve of the man I want to see. It doesn't make sense."

"There will be other *buwe*," Mamm said, her eyes warming. "I promise you, Janie." She glanced at *Dat*. "I had my heart broken before I met your *dat*. Jonathan won't be the last man you care about."

"Your *mamm* is right," *Dat* said. "We're only doing this for your own *gut*. We know what's best for our *kinner*."

"You can be his *freind*, but we can't allow you to date him," Mamm clarified. "I know you enjoy talking to him at work, and there's nothing wrong with that, right, Timothy?"

Dat gave a quick nod. "There's nothing wrong with being his *freind*, but that's all."

Janie bit back angry words as she wiped away more tears. She would never speak belligerently to her parents, but she was crushed by their decision. She'd never known her parents to be so unreasonable. Why couldn't they see how special Jonathan was? Why couldn't they support Janie's choice in a suitor?

"I'm going to bed," Janie finally said, softly. *"Gut nacht."* She stood and rushed up the stairs, throwing herself onto her bed and letting her tears flow into her pillow.

Janie heard her door click shut, followed by light footsteps crossing her room. She squeezed her eyes shut and hoped it wasn't her mother who had come to see her. She couldn't stand the idea of hearing more negative words about Jonathan.

The bed shifted and a gentle hand touched her shoulder.

"Janie?" Marie's sweet voice asked. "Are you all right?"

Janie shook her head, still facing the wall. "No, I'm not."

"I heard everything," Marie admitted as she rubbed Janie's back. "I'm sorry for eavesdropping, but I couldn't help it. I'm so sorry *Mamm* and *Dat* don't approve of Jonathan. I think he's perfect for you." She sighed. "I was hoping *Dat* and *Mamm* would see past his age."

Janie rolled over and sniffed as she looked up at her sister. "I was hoping too." She hugged her arms around her middle as if to stop her heart from breaking. "They said I can be his *freind*, but *Dat* will never permit him to date me. I just don't understand. I thought they would see how wonderful Jonathan is and be *froh* that I found him. You've never had a problem finding *buwe* who like you, but they never like me. What if I never find anyone else who likes me?"

Marie clicked her tongue. "You can't possibly believe that, Janie. You'll find someone. For now, you can enjoy being Jonathan's *freind*. At least *Dat* will allow you to do that."

Janie nodded. "You're right." The tiny flicker of hope took root inside of Janie. She would cherish Jonathan's friendship for as long as she could.

⁓⁓⁓

Janie lifted a tray of peanut butter spread and stepped out from the Riehls' kitchen the following Sunday. This week's church service was hosted by the Riehl family on their farm only a mile away from where her family lived, and now the noon meal was being served in their barn.

She shivered as the October breeze caused her black sweater and purple dress to flutter in the wind. Her thoughts had been stuck on her conversation with her parents Wednesday night. She hadn't told Jonathan what her parents had said about him, and she tried to hide her disappointment from him. She was grateful she could still enjoy lunch with him every weekday, but she longed for their relationship to progress.

"Janie!" Marie called behind her. "Janie, wait!"

Janie turned as her sister hurried toward her, carrying a coffeepot. *"Was iss letz?"*

"Nothing is wrong." Marie grinned. "You'll never guess who is here."

Janie shrugged. "I have no idea."

"Jonathan!" Marie pointed toward the barn. "I saw him sitting near Samuel and Mike."

"He is?" Janie asked with surprise. "I didn't see him during the service."

"I didn't either, but we were sitting all the way in the back." Marie held out the coffeepot. "You take this and go fill his mug. I'll handle the peanut butter spread."

"Danki." Janie took the pot and headed into the barn. She found the table where Jonathan sat next to a man, who must be his grandfather, and was surprised to see her brother sitting across from them. Excitement overtook her at the prospect of introducing Jonathan to Samuel. Perhaps Samuel could help her convince her parents that Jonathan was an acceptable choice for a boyfriend.

She began filling coffee mugs and worked her way down the table toward Jonathan. When she reached him, her smile broadened and happiness surged through her.

"*Kaffi?*" she asked.

Jonathan looked up and his eyes widened in surprise. "Janie. I saw your *dat* earlier, but I didn't see you." He touched the arm of the elderly man beside him. "*Daadi*, this is *mei freind* Janie. Janie, this is Omar."

"It's nice to meet you." Janie shook Omar's hand and then looked at her brother and cousin, who were sitting across from Jonathan. "Have you met *mei bruder*, Samuel, and my cousin Mike? Sam and Mike, this is Jonathan and his grandfather, Omar."

Samuel leaned over the table and shook Jonathan's hand. "We were talking earlier, but I didn't realize you were *freinden* with *mei schweschder*."

"Hi, Jonathan," Mike said.

"It's great to meet you," Jonathan said, shaking Mike's hand. Then he looked up at Janie. "I didn't realize we were visiting your district, but I should have known since we're not far from your *haus*."

"I'm glad you could come today." She pointed toward the end of the table. "I need to go now."

"Maybe we can talk later?" he asked, his brown eyes hopeful.

"*Ya*," she said with a nod. "I'd like that."

⁓∽∼

After lunch, Jonathan smiled and nodded as his grandparents introduced him to a few of their friends. While he tried his best to be friendly to their acquaintances, he couldn't stop scanning the knot of people for Janie. His grandparents had suggested they visit another church district since it was an off Sunday in their home district, but Jonathan hadn't realized he was going to Janie's district.

He was surprised when she appeared at his table with the coffeepot. He was thankful to see her beautiful smile this morning. She'd been on his mind nonstop since he'd had supper at her parents' house. The hour they spent together at lunch every day at work was never enough to satisfy his growing desire to be with her.

As he glanced around, he saw Janie's parents standing on the other side of the barn, talking to another couple. Her mother met his gaze and raised her hand in greeting, and he returned the gesture. He'd seen Janie's father earlier, and Timothy had been pleasant as well. He hoped that meant they approved of him. Janie hadn't indicated they didn't like him, but he still worried.

Jonathan looked through the barn door and spotted Janie standing near the pasture fence, talking with a petite and pretty woman with light brown hair. The young woman was holding a baby, and he assumed she was Janie's sister-in-law. He excused himself from his grandparents' conversation and made his way toward the two women.

When Janie saw him, her pretty face lit up with a warm smile. "Jonathan, this is my sister-in-law, Mandy, and my niece, Becky."

"Hi, Jonathan," Mandy said with a nod. "I've heard a lot about you."

Janie's cheeks turned pink, and she was even more adorable.

Samuel and Mike sidled up to them, along with a little blond boy, who resembled Mike, and a pretty brunette, who was holding Mike's hand.

"Are you ready to go?" Samuel asked Mandy, and she nodded.

"Jonathan," Janie said, "you met Mike earlier. This is Mike's girlfriend, Rachel, and his younger *bruder*, John. This is *mei freind* Jonathan. We work together."

Jonathan greeted them and then they said good-bye before heading to the buggies, leaving Jonathan and Janie standing by the fence alone.

"I'm so glad I got to meet more members of your family today," he said, silently admiring how the sunlight made her hair resemble fire. She was so beautiful he couldn't take his eyes off her.

"I am too." She watched her family walk toward a buggy. "Marie and I used to take care of Mike and John's *dat*. He was our *onkel* Raymond."

"He was the one on dialysis?"

"That's right. We miss him." As she turned toward him, he saw her face brighten. "I talked to your *mammi* in the kitchen earlier. She's very nice." She peered up at him, and her eyes somehow seemed a deeper shade of blue. "Did you have a *gut* day yesterday?"

"*Ya*, I did." He leaned against the split rail fence. "I helped *mei daadi* and *onkel* with a few projects around the farm. I always have a *gut* time when I'm with them. How about you?"

"I had a *gut* day too. I did some baking and cleaning." She rested her hand on the rail beside him. "The weekends go by too fast."

"They do, but I look forward to our time together at work during the week."

"I do too." Janie looked pensive, as if she was mentally debating. She opened her mouth to speak but was interrupted by someone calling her name.

"Janie!" Marie called from across the driveway. "It's time to go."

Janie stepped away from the fence. "I'm so sorry. My family is ready to go. It was *gut* seeing you."

"*Ya*, it was." Jonathan smiled. "I'll see you tomorrow."

"Good-bye," she said, then rushed off to meet her family.

Jonathan's smile faded. He wondered what she was going to say before her sister interrupted their conversation.

Chapter Six

Janie handed the *Englisher* her change and bag of souvenirs with a smile. "Thank you for shopping here. Please come back soon."

"Thank you, sweetie," the woman said, then turned for the door.

Eva rushed over, looked around the room, and then leaned in close to Janie. "I've been waiting until we had a lull in the store. It's finally empty," she said softly. "I need to tell you a secret."

"What secret?" Janie asked, bewildered.

"I heard Bianca and Craig talking in the office this morning when I put my lunch in the refrigerator." Eva craned her neck to look toward the back of the store where the staff offices were. "Bianca said the driver of the car and some of the passengers in the buggy accident are blaming Jonathan and they're going to sue the store."

Janie gasped. "No!"

"Shh," Eva said, hissing her warning with a frown. "Keep your voice down. I don't want Bianca or Craig to hear me. Craig said if they sue them, they could lose everything. Bianca said their lawyer told them they have to fire Jonathan now so they eliminate the liability or something."

Janie's stomach plummeted. "They're going to fire Jonathan?"

Eva nodded solemnly. "That's what Bianca said."

"*Ach* no." Janie gnawed her bottom lip as an urgency to tell Craig or Bianca what she'd witnessed the day of the accident took hold of her. Her father's warning for Janie to steer clear of any of the business associated with the accident echoed through her mind. She had to obey her father, but how could she not tell Craig and Bianca what she saw when Jonathan was not only wrongfully accused but would now lose his job?

Worst of all, if they fire him, I'll never see him again.

That was the final straw. Janie couldn't stand by and watch Jonathan get fired when she held the key to his exoneration.

"Eva, I need to go talk to Craig. I have to tell him I know the accident wasn't Jonathan's fault."

"You know for certain?" Eva asked, raising her eyebrows.

Janie nodded. "I witnessed it."

"Go," Eva said as a line of customers filed into the store. "I can handle things up here."

"*Danki,*" Janie said.

She wove past the displays of wooden signs, magnets, and cloth dolls as she made her way to the back of the store. When she reached a door with a sign that read Employees Only, she pushed it open and entered the hallway leading to the storeroom, offices, and break room.

She approached Craig's office and found him working on his computer. She knocked on the doorframe, and he looked up at her and smiled.

"Hi, Janie," he said. "Is everything all right in the store?"

"Everything is fine." She folded her hands over her apron. "May I speak with you for a moment?"

"Of course. Come in." Craig gestured toward a chair in front of his desk. "Have a seat."

"Thank you." Janie sank into the chair.

"Well, what's on your mind this fine Monday afternoon?" Craig leaned forward on his large wooden desk and steepled his fingers.

"I want to tell you something about the accident." Although her father's warning to not get involved still echoed through her mind, she pushed on. "I was eating lunch at a picnic table near the entrance to the parking lot, so I saw everything. That's when I ran into the store to get you."

Craig gasped, his eyes widening. "The police asked me for possible witnesses, and I completely forgot you were outside and might have seen the whole thing. Please tell me what you remember."

Janie paused and breathed in a deep, shuddering breath.

"Take your time," Craig said.

"The accident wasn't Jonathan's fault," she said, her heart pounding with anxiety. "Not only did Jonathan signal before he turned into the parking lot, but the driver of the car was distracted."

"What do you mean?" Craig asked.

"He was looking down at something in his hand instead of watching the road. I think he was texting on his cell phone." An invisible load lifted from Janie's shoulders as she said the words aloud.

"He was texting?" Craig asked, and she nodded. "Are you sure?"

"It looked like a cell phone. But the point is, he was look-ing down, not at the road to see Jonathan's signal. He didn't brake until he looked up to see he was about to crash into the buggy." Her words came in a rush now. "Craig, it has bothered me that Jonathan was blamed when the accident wasn't his fault. Jonathan wasn't reckless. He did nothing to endanger those passengers. I'm so sorry I didn't tell you before. I was hoping someone else saw Jonathan signal too."

Craig blew out a puff of air. "I'm glad you told me now." He raked his hands through his dark hair. "You have no idea what a relief this is. Would you be willing to talk to a police officer if he needs more information?"

Janie nodded, but her father's instructions to stay out of the investigation reverberated through her mind once again. She hoped she wouldn't have to recount the story numerous times.

"Thank you, Janie," Craig said. "I appreciate your help."

"You're welcome." As Janie walked back into the store, she hoped she'd helped save Jonathan's job.

Jonathan's boots crunched on dry leaves as he led Bucky toward the stable. He hummed to himself as he contemplated the conversation he'd shared with Janie at lunch. He cherished every moment he spent with her and tried not to think about how November was just around the corner.

"Jonathan!" Craig called as he ambled from the store toward the stable. "I need to talk with you for a moment."

"Okay." Jonathan stopped the horse and began rubbing his neck while waiting for Craig. "You're a *gut bu*, Bucky," he murmured to the horse. "*Ya*, you are."

"I'm glad I caught you before you left for the day," Craig said as he walked over to him.

"Is everything all right?"

"Yes." Craig smiled. "In fact, I have fantastic news. The driver of the car admitted fault."

"What?" Jonathan tried to process what Craig had said. "He admitted he caused the accident?"

"That's right." Craig folded his arms across his chest. "I just spoke to my lawyer, and the driver admitted he was distracted because he was texting his girlfriend. You're off the hook, and you can return to giving buggy rides tomorrow if you want. You're completely cleared of any wrongdoing."

Craig held out his hand, and Jonathan shook it as questions swirled through his mind.

"I'm still a little confused," Jonathan said. "Why did he suddenly admit guilt? I thought he blamed me for the accident."

"Janie came to see me on Monday. She not only saw you signal, but she insisted she witnessed the driver looking down at what seemed to be a cell phone, probably texting. I called my lawyer right away, and he contacted the driver's lawyer. Apparently the driver was caught in a lie. He said he wasn't texting, but the police looked into his cell phone records and found the evidence. He sent a text just as the car hit the buggy, and his lawyer told him he had to admit fault. You can thank Janie. She got the process started."

"Janie did that for me?" Jonathan asked with surprise.

"That's right. I'm not sure what made her tell me now, but it's a good thing. Our lawyer said the driver and some passengers were going to sue, and he was pressuring us to fire you, Jonathan. And that's the last thing we wanted to do."

"So do you want to go back to giving tours tomorrow?" Craig asked, rubbing his hands together.

"I'd love to," Jonathan said. "Thank you."

"You're welcome," Craig patted Jonathan's back. "I'll see you tomorrow."

Jonathan silently marveled at the great news as he led Bucky into the stable. He was astonished Janie had gone out on a limb to make things right for him, and he hoped she wasn't in any trouble for it. The Amish didn't like to get involved in legal matters. Had she suspected he really might lose his job if she didn't step forward? She was a truly special *maedel*. He had to thank her. But a question lingered in his mind—why hadn't she told him she'd spoken to Craig on Monday?

Jonathan finished his chores in the stable and then stepped out into the parking lot. When he spotted Janie walking toward the white van idling nearby, he took off running.

"Janie!" he called. "Janie, wait!"

Janie spun toward him, her eyes wide with question. "Jonathan?"

"Janie," he said, trying to catch his breath. "I need to talk to you."

"What's wrong?" Her eyes searched his.

"Nothing is wrong. In fact, everything is right."

"I don't understand." Janie tipped her head in question, and she looked even more adorable than usual.

"I need to thank you," he said, taking a step closer to her and breathing in the sweet apple scent of her shampoo. "I know you said you saw me signal, but *danki* for telling Craig not only that, but that the driver wasn't paying attention."

"Oh." She waved off the words. "It wasn't anything."

"It was something," he insisted. "Because of you, the driver admitted he caused the accident, and I'm cleared of any wrongdoing. And I got my driving job back."

"Oh, that's fantastic!" Janie gasped. "I'm so *froh* for you!" She dropped her tote bag and threw her arms around him, pulling him into a warm hug.

Stunned, Jonathan held her in his arms, and he felt something spark between them. A small flame ignited inside of him and then settled deep in his soul.

I love her.

The feeling was so intense that his pulse accelerated. Janie had somehow broken through the wall he'd built around his heart after Grace left him. He closed his eyes and longed to freeze this moment in time. He wanted to hold her close to him forever.

"Oh." Janie suddenly stepped away from him. She smoothed her hands down her sweater, and her cheeks were the color of a red delicious apple. "I'm so sorry. I didn't mean to be so—"

"It's fine." Jonathan touched her cheek. "And *danki* again."

Janie nodded, her cheeks still flaming. *"Gern gschehne."* She glanced back at the van and then turned toward him again. "I need to go, but I will see you tomorrow."

"Gut nacht," he said.

"Gut nacht," she repeated before climbing into the van.

As the van drove away, Jonathan said a silent prayer, thanking God for sending him to Bird-in-Hand to meet Janie.

~~~

"Jonathan was cleared of all wrongdoing today," Janie finally blurted as she cut up her piece of pork later that evening. "The driver of the car admitted he was distracted and was texting when he hit the buggy."

"Really?" Marie asked, her brown eyes wide with interest. "That's *wunderbaar.*"

"*Ya*, I'm so *froh* for him," Janie said, hoping her cheeks wouldn't burn with embarrassment as she remembered how she'd hugged Jonathan earlier. What had possessed her to be so forward? She had never done anything that forward or impulsive before. Why did she feel so comfortable with him? It felt natural to hug him.

Janie suddenly realized her family was studying her. Had she missed part of the conversation?

"I asked you a question," *Dat* said.

"Oh, I'm sorry." Janie did her best not to look guilty even though she knew her parents would have been furious if they'd seen her behavior earlier. "What did you say, *Dat*?"

"I asked you why the driver suddenly confessed," *Dat* said, placing his glass of water on the table. "Did you hear what made him change his mind and tell the truth?"

With her father's brown eyes watching her, Janie realized she'd shared too much. Now she had to admit she went against her parents' wishes. But maybe her father would go easy on her when he realized she helped Jonathan keep his job.

"Janie?" *Dat*'s voice was laced with irritation. "Why are you acting so strangely tonight? Are you not feeling well?"

"I'm fine," Janie said softly, placing her fork and knife on her plate.

"Then what is it?" *Dat* demanded. "You've been distracted all evening."

Janie took a deep breath. It was time for her to tell the truth. "I'm the reason the driver admitted the truth. I told Craig I saw the driver texting. Craig spoke to his lawyer, and then—"

"You disobeyed me?" *Dat*'s voice boomed throughout the kitchen.

Janie nodded as tears stung her eyes. "I did, but I only wanted to help Jonathan. I found out he was going to be fired because some of the passengers in the buggy and the driver were going to sue Craig—"

Dat's face turned bright red as he wagged a finger at her. "I told you to stay out of it, Janie Lynn. The last thing I want is for you to be dragged into court as a witness. The Englishers love to sue each other, and it's against our beliefs to get involved in that." He fisted his hands. "You are not to see Jonathan any longer. I don't want you to have any contact with him."

"Why?" Janie asked. "This isn't Jonathan's fault. It was my choice to talk to Craig. Jonathan didn't know anything about it."

"I don't care," Dat continued, his voice full of anger. "You are not to see him at all. I don't want you to eat lunch with him or talk to him. You don't make logical decisions when he's around. Steer clear of him. He'll be back in Maryland in a month and then we can forget all about this mess."

"But, Dat," Janie began, her voice trembling with both grief and regret. "I care about him. I can't pretend I don't know him."

"You can and you will," Dat ordered. He turned his attention to his plate and speared a piece of his pork.

Janie looked at her mother for help, but Mamm merely shook her head and frowned. Janie knew her mother would never go against her father, but she'd hoped somehow her mother could help. Janie looked at Marie, who seemed nearly as upset as she was.

Janie trained her eyes on her plate and willed herself not to cry. She'd prayed she and Jonathan could make their relationship work, but in a matter of a few minutes, all her hopes and dreams had dissolved. All she had left was a hole in her heart.

Jonathan sipped his cup of coffee and looked across the table at his grandmother. "I still can't believe Janie came forward for me," he said after explaining what had happened that afternoon. "I've never known a *maedel* like her."

Mammi gave him a knowing smile. "She's special to you."

"She is." Jonathan took a deep breath. "I think I'm in love with her."

Mammi patted his hand. "Oh, Jonathan, I'm so *froh* to hear you say that. I know Grace hurt you deeply."

"Grace did," Jonathan admitted as he cradled the warm cup in his hands. "But I don't think I felt this way about Grace. It's different this time. I've been thinking all evening that I want to stay here in Lancaster. I think I want to sell *mei haus* back in Maryland and move here. I'll find a job and—"

"Oh, that's *wunderbaar!*" *Mammi* clapped her hands. "We'd love to have you, right, Omar?"

"Absolutely," *Daadi* said. "You can stay with us until you build a *haus*. You can get a job working for your *onkel* or one of your cousins."

"That would be great." Jonathan's heart raced with the possibility of starting a new life in Pennsylvania, a new life with the beautiful Janie Lantz. He couldn't wait to tell her.

Chapter Seven

Jonathan hurried into the souvenir shop the following morning. He was bursting with excitement. He couldn't wait to see Janie and tell her he loved her. He couldn't wait to start their future together.

He entered the store, and when he saw her standing in front of the cash register, he stopped in his tracks. Janie was ringing up T-shirts for a customer, but Jonathan could tell her smile wasn't genuine. Her eyes were dull, and he could see purple circles under them. Alarm surged through him. Where was the happy *maedel* who had hugged him last night?

He padded up toward the counter and stood close by until she handed the customer her change and told her to have a nice day.

"Janie?" he asked. "How are you?"

"Jonathan," she said, her smile gone, her voice flat and devoid of emotion. *"Wie geht's?"*

Jonathan's heart splintered over the sadness in her eyes. What had happened to her? He glanced around the store and saw only a few customers. He reached for her arm and then stopped himself.

"May I speak with you for a moment?" he asked.

She hesitated, but then gave a curt nod. "Let me go find Eva."

Worry washed over him as she hustled to the back of the store. She whispered something to Eva, who looked over at Jonathan and smiled. Then Janie gestured for Jonathan to follow her into the Employees Only area. They entered the break room, and Janie closed the door behind them.

She fingered the hem on her black apron and studied her shoes, seemingly to purposely avert her eyes. Anticipation and worry were eating away at his soul.

"*Was iss letz?*" he finally asked. "Janie, I can't take this silence between us."

When Janie looked up, her eyes glistened with tears. "I can't be your *freind* anymore." Her voice trembled with raw emotion as tears trickled down her pink cheeks.

"What?" He took a step toward her, the grief on her face stabbing at his heart. "I don't understand. Is it your parents?"

"It's *mei dat.*" She wiped her tears with the back of her hand. "He instructed me not to get involved with the accident, but then I admitted to telling Craig what I saw. He was furious I disobeyed him. I tried to explain I only did it so you wouldn't get fired, but he still wouldn't listen to me."

"You thought I was going to get fired?"

Janie nodded. "Eva overheard Bianca and Craig talking. Some of the passengers and the other driver were going to sue, so they were going to have to fire you to help save their business. I couldn't let that happen."

Jonathan was speechless.

"So now I have to steer clear of you, and I can't even have lunch with you anymore." She sniffed as more tears escaped her eyes. "I'm sorry."

"No, Janie," he said. "I'm sorry this happened to you." He

longed to touch her arm and hug her the way she'd hugged him last night, but he couldn't disobey her father. He didn't want to make things more difficult for her, but the thought of not having her in his life was so painful it stole his breath.

"I have to go," she said, her voice hitching on the last word.

Before he could respond, Janie rushed out of the break room and into the staff restroom, the door lock clicking behind her.

Jonathan leaned his back against the wall and squeezed his eyes shut. His life had changed dramatically within the past twelve hours. He'd gone from realizing he was in love and wanting to start a new life in Pennsylvania to losing that love before he even had a chance to share his feelings with her. Disappointment, anger, and guilt warred within him. If only he could convince her father that he loved her.

Pushing off the wall, he ambled through the store and tried to think of a way to convince Janie's father his feelings for her were pure, and that he would love Janie and take care of her for the rest of his life.

※

Janie sat alone in the break room and tried to eat her lunch. Her turkey sandwich tasted like sand as she slowly chewed it. She wasn't hungry even though she couldn't stomach her breakfast either. Last night, she'd tossed and turned all night long and cried until she was convinced she had no tears left to shed. The thought of losing Jonathan's friendship had cut her to the core, and the anguish on his face when she told him the news had jammed the knife even further into her heart.

Janie had tried to talk to her mother last night, begging her to convince *Dat* to change his mind about Jonathan. Despite Janie's best efforts, *Mamm* had refused, explaining she couldn't go against his decisions. Janie knew she was out of options. There was nothing she could do except try to avoid Jonathan and pray her heart would someday heal.

The door opened, and Eva entered the break room. She tilted her head in question.

"What are you doing in here?" Eva asked as she crossed the room and opened the refrigerator. "Is it too cold to eat outside?"

"I decided to eat in here."

"Where's Jonathan?" Eva retrieved her lunch bag and sat down across from Janie. "Don't you two eat together every day? Is he out on a buggy run?"

"No." Janie studied her half-eaten sandwich. "I can't eat with him anymore."

"You can't eat with him?" Eva pulled out her sandwich. "I don't understand."

Janie met her friend's curious eyes and shared her father's reaction to the news that she had told Craig the truth about the other driver.

"So now I can't see him." Janie cleared her throat in hopes of dissolving the lump that swelled there.

Eva gave a sympathetic frown. "Janie, I am so sorry. Just give your *dat* time to calm down and maybe he'll change his mind."

"He won't." Janie heaved a deep sigh. "I don't regret helping Jonathan. I couldn't keep the truth to myself, but I couldn't lie to *mei dat* either. I thought Jonathan and I might someday be more than *freinden*, but now I just have to find a way to get over my broken heart." Tears flooded her eyes, but she willed them not to fall. She'd already cried too much since last night.

"Don't give up hope, Janie." Eva leaned across the table and touched Janie's hand. "Jonathan obviously cares about you, and I have a feeling he won't let you go so easily. Maybe he can find a way to show your *dat* you belong together."

"I doubt it," Janie muttered as more heartache drowned her.

Craig came out of his office one afternoon in late October as Janie straightened the T-shirt display and Eva arranged the shelves of cloth dolls.

"Could one of you possibly lock up tonight?" Craig asked. "I meant to ask you earlier in the week, but I forgot. Bianca and I are having a Halloween party tonight, and she needs me to run a few errands." He rested his elbow on the counter. "I'm sorry this is last minute, but the party is a big deal to Bianca. She loves Halloween and invites all her friends."

Eva grimaced. "I'm sorry, but I can't stay tonight. I promised *mei mamm* and *dat* we'd go see *mei* cousin Esther's new *boppli* tonight."

Janie shrugged and looked at Eva. "I can stay."

"Are you sure?" Craig asked with concern. "Are you comfortable locking up alone?"

"*Ya.*" Janie nodded with emphasis. "I helped Eva lock up last week, and she showed me what to do. I have my own set of keys. I'll just call my parents and my driver. It's no problem."

"And you remember how to make the deposit?" Eva asked. "Can your driver take you by the bank?"

"Oh *ya.*" Janie waved off the question. "It's not a problem at all."

"Thank you so much, Janie." Craig smiled with relief. "You just saved me from getting in trouble with Bianca. I'll see you both tomorrow."

The remainder of the afternoon flew by as Janie and Eva helped customers and restocked shelves.

After Eva left for the day, Janie vacuumed, dusted a few shelves, and then closed out the register, pushing the stacks of bills into the zippered bank bag for the nightly deposit. She put the bank bag into her tote bag, put on her sweater, and then gathered her purse, tote bag, and lunch bag before turning off the lights and walking to the front door. The keys jingled as she pulled them out of her apron pocket. She flipped the electronic Open sign to Closed, made sure the front door was still locked, and then stood there, listening.

An eerie feeling prickled Janie's spine as she looked out at the deserted parking lot. Only a little moonlight and a couple of lampposts from neighboring businesses illuminated the grounds outside the shop. She couldn't stop the feeling that someone was watching her. She tried to push the ridiculous thought away. *Of course there's no one there.*

Janie moved to the side door to wait for her driver. She looked toward the stable and saw a light burning inside. She wondered if one of the buggy drivers had forgotten to turn off the lights before leaving. Had Jonathan been the last one to close up tonight? Her heart kicked at the thought of his handsome face. Oh, how she'd missed him the past two weeks.

Janie had tried her best to avoid him, but he seemed to appear when she least expected it. She ran into him in the break room one afternoon last week, and although he offered her a kind greeting and smile, she quickly excused herself. The following morning he arrived at the store at the same moment she did, and they shared an awkward greeting before parting ways like two mere acquaintances.

When Janie walked past the stable a few days later, she saw him talking to two pretty *Englisher* girls, who giggled and smiled at him. She gritted her teeth at the sight, and something that felt a whole lot like jealousy bubbled up inside of her. Jonathan looked over at her and gave her a cordial smile and wave, and she hurried past the stable toward the store. She'd tried to put on a brave face, but every time she saw Jonathan, her heart seemed to shatter a little more.

Now as Janie stood gazing out over the dark parking lot at the side of the building, she longed for the warmth of Jonathan's protective hand to calm her nerves. She'd never been afraid of the dark, but something felt wrong tonight—she just couldn't put her finger on what was amiss. When she saw headlights reflecting off the side of the stable, she looked up at a clock over the door that read seven fifteen. Frank, her driver, was early, but Frank was often early.

Janie stepped outside, and the cold October air seeped in through her dress, sending goose bumps up her arms. She longed for a warmer sweater. The door clicked shut behind her.

As Janie pushed the key into the lock and turned it, she thought she heard footsteps. The hair on the back of her neck stood as she turned around. She had to be hearing things. The headlights were gone and there was no van in sight. The driver of the vehicle must have been turning around in the parking lot. Frank wasn't there.

Janie heard the sound again. Her hands shook and her mouth dried. Perhaps it was an animal, maybe a stray cat. She'd seen a mother cat and kittens near the stable the other day.

"Hello?" Janie's voice shook. "Is someone there?" she tried to shout, but her voice was thin, and her hands trembled as she gripped the strap of her bag. "Hello?"

Suddenly, out of the darkness, a man rounded the corner of the building and came at her. Janie's heart hammered as her eyes focused. Under the dim light mounted over the door, she could see he was dressed in black from head to toe, with a black knit cap over his dark hair. His face and lips were covered with sores and blemishes, and when he flashed a menacing smile, he was missing a few teeth. He pointed something metal at her, and it gleamed in the light above her.

Janie gasped as her eyes focused on the metal object.

A gun.

Icy fear slithered up her back, and panic tightened her throat.

"Give me the money," he said, stepping closer to her. He smelled like sweat and onions, and she willed herself not to gag.

Her mind raced with confusion and terror. Was she dreaming?

"Don't play dumb with me! I saw you put the money bag in there through the window," the man bellowed, training the gun on her tote bag. "You have two choices. You either give it to me willingly or I will take it by force. What's it gonna be?"

The gun clicked, and Janie stood frozen with fear. She opened her mouth to scream, but no sound came. A tear trickled down her cheek.

This is it. I'm going to die.

⸺⁓⁓⸺

Jonathan rubbed Bucky's neck. "Want some fresh water, *bu*?"

Bucky nodded his head in response.

"All right, then." He walked toward the back of the stable to get a bucket of water.

Jonathan had told Craig he was going to stay late tonight to fix the stall doors, but the truth was he had to stay busy in a lame attempt to keep his mind off Janie. He'd nearly gone crazy with regret and heartache since she'd stopped talking to him. Seeing her at work every day was sweet torture. Staying busy was the only thing that kept him sane.

As Jonathan approached the sink near the stable door, he thought he heard a voice outside. He cracked the door open and listened. It sounded as if he'd heard a man's voice, but it was after seven o'clock. Everyone should've gone home by now. He stepped into the doorway, looked toward the store, and was surprised to find two figures standing by the side entrance to the store.

Suddenly the scene came into focus. A tall man was standing in front of Janie and had a gun pointed at her face.

Jonathan's stomach plummeted, and adrenaline surged through him. He spun, grabbed a two-by-four piece of wood, and dashed toward the store.

As Jonathan approached, the man spun and trained the gun on him. Jonathan swung the piece of wood, knocking the gun from the man's hand. The gun flew through the air and skidded across the parking lot. The thief's eyes widened and he lunged for Jonathan as Janie screamed. Jonathan held the piece of wood up, preparing to hit the man with it.

Bright beams of light danced around the parking lot and blinded Jonathan for a split second. When his eyes focused again, he saw a white van speeding toward them.

The man spun to face the van and then sprinted across the

parking lot toward the road. Jonathan blew out a puff of air and dropped the piece of wood with a clatter, his hands shaking.

"Jonathan!" Janie cried before rushing over and throwing herself into his arms. *"Danki."* Her voice was shaking. "I thought he was going to kill me. Thank you so much." She wrapped her arms around his waist and held on to him.

He rubbed her back and tried to will himself to stop shaking. "I'm just glad I was here," he whispered.

"What happened?" Frank, Janie's driver, had rushed from his van.

Without letting go of Janie, Jonathan explained.

"We need to call the police and give them a description," Frank said. "We can use my phone."

Janie looked up at Jonathan. "Will you stay with me?" Her eyes pleaded with him to say yes.

He stared into her blue eyes and found fear mixed with relief. "Of course I will."

—⁂—

Nearly two hours later, Janie sat in the backseat and held Jonathan's hand as Frank's van steered down her street. Her mind kept replaying the scene at the store, and she shuddered at the memory of the man's face. She'd never been so terrified in her life. She couldn't stop wondering what would've happened if Jonathan hadn't been working late in the stable. Would the man have shot her just to get the money?

She squeezed Jonathan's hand and looked up into his brown eyes. He gave her an encouraging smile, and her eyes misted over again. She loved him deeply.

"I've missed you," she whispered.

"I've missed you too," he echoed, his finger gently pushing an errant lock of her hair back from her face.

"Thank you so much for saving me."

Jonathan smiled. "I think that's the hundredth time you've thanked me. You don't have to keep saying that."

Janie leaned her head against his shoulder and closed her eyes while still holding his hand. Warmth and security replaced her earlier panic and fear. She didn't want to ever let go of Jonathan.

The van came to a stop at the back door of her house, and her parents rushed out, followed by Marie.

"Janie!" *Mamm* hollered as Janie climbed out of the van. "We got Frank's message that a man tried to rob you. Are you hurt?" Her eyes were wild with worry.

"Are you all right?" *Dat* asked, looking equally concerned.

Marie's eyes were red as if she'd been crying. "What happened?"

Janie took a shaky breath and then felt Jonathan's calming hand on her shoulder. She glanced up at him.

"Do you want me to tell them?" he asked.

Janie nodded, knowing she'd start to cry if she spoke.

Jonathan slowly explained what happened while her family gaped as they listened. "The man ran when Frank drove up. It was perfect timing."

Frank shook his head and scowled. "I'm just so sorry I didn't come early tonight." He turned to Janie. "I'm so sorry."

Janie opened her mouth to say it wasn't his fault when her mother interrupted.

"*Ach!* Jonathan," *Mamm* said, tears glistening in her eyes, "you saved *mei dochder*." She hugged him. "*Danki.* That man could have killed her."

"I'm so *froh* you were there," Marie said, her voice thick. "I don't want to think about what could have happened."

Dat approached Jonathan and shook his hand, then gently slapped his shoulder. "*Danki*, Jonathan. I can't thank you enough."

A tear trickled down Janie's cheek. She sniffed and tried to hold back her emotions.

"Timothy," Jonathan began, his voice trembling, "I love your *dochder.* I've decided to sell *mei haus* in Maryland and move here. I'm going to talk to *mei onkel* and cousin about going into business with them. I want to make a life here, and I would be honored if I could date Janie." He turned toward her. "I would do anything in my power to take care of her and keep her safe."

Janie's eyes widened. For the second time tonight, she was speechless.

Jonathan looked back at her father. "I know I'm quite a bit older than Janie, but age doesn't mean anything to me. My grandparents are nine years apart, and they've built a wonderful life together. They both told me their ages never mattered. What mattered to them was how they felt about each other." He paused as if to gather his thoughts. "All I know is I care about Janie, and I would be honored to have your blessing."

To Janie's surprise, her father smiled. He turned toward her mother, and she nodded. Janie gasped with surprise.

"Jonathan, you have our blessing," *Dat* said. "Come back tomorrow for supper and we'll talk more. I think we all need some sleep after this stressful night."

For the second time tonight, Janie wondered if she were dreaming. Renewed hope and happiness blossomed inside of her.

Jonathan nodded. "*Danki* so much, Timothy."

Dat's smile suddenly faded as he looked back and forth between Janie and Jonathan, and worry shoved away Janie's happiness. She held her breath in anticipation of what her father was going to say.

"I owe you both an apology," he began. "I never should have told Janie to keep the truth about the accident from Craig. Telling the truth is always the right thing to do, and I was completely wrong. I'm sorry it took something like this for me to realize my mistake." His focus settled on Jonathan. "I also was wrong to instruct her to stay away from you, Jonathan. I'm grateful you've come into Janie's life. You're a blessing."

"*Danki, Dat.*" Tears clouded Janie's vision as she gave her father a quick hug.

"Let's go inside," *Dat* said to Janie.

"Would you give me just a minute?" she asked.

"Five minutes."

Her parents and Marie said good night to Jonathan and Frank and then headed into the house. Frank climbed into the van and left Janie and Jonathan standing together on the rock driveway.

Jonathan cupped Janie's cheek with his hand and smiled down at her. "I meant what I said to your father. I love you and I want to build a life with you."

Janie's heart thudded as warmth flooded her body. "*Ich liebe dich*, Jonathan."

He leaned down and his lips brushed hers, sending electric pulses singing through her veins. She closed her eyes, savoring the feel of his lips against hers.

"I'll see you tomorrow," Jonathan whispered, his breath warm against her cheek.

Janie opened her eyes and nodded. "*Danki* again for saving me."

Jonathan shook his head and smiled. "Janie, you've saved me, so we're even. When I came here, I'd given up on love. You showed me I could love again."

As he kissed her again, Janie silently thanked God for sending Jonathan to her.

DISCUSSION QUESTIONS

1. Janie is determined to clear Jonathan's name despite her father's warning to stay out of the legal issues surrounding the buggy accident. She feels torn between her yearning for justice for Jonathan and her obedience to her father. Have you ever felt compelled to go against your family in order to do something you believed was important?

2. At the beginning of the story, Jonathan is convinced he's too old for Janie; however, his feelings about that change throughout the story. What do you think causes his feelings to change?

3. Jonathan came to Pennsylvania for a long visit with his grandparents after his girlfriend betrayed him. Were you ever betrayed by a close friend or loved one? How did you come to grips with that betrayal? Were you able to forgive that person and move on? If so, where did you find the strength to forgive?

4. Timothy, Janie's father, does not approve of Janie and Jonathan's friendship becoming something more. He's

concerned Jonathan will return to Maryland and break Janie's heart, and he is convinced Jonathan is too old for her. He changes his opinion, however, near the end of the story. What do you think is the catalyst for Timothy's change of heart?

5. Which character can you identify with the most? Which character seemed to carry the most emotional stake in the story? Was it Janie, Jonathan, Timothy, or someone else?

6. Janie's heart is broken when her father forbids her from spending any time with Jonathan. She was certain she'd finally found her soul mate, and then she lost him. Think of a time when you felt lost and alone. Where did you find your strength? What Bible verses would help with this?

7. Jonathan realizes that he longs to move to Pennsylvania and start a new life with Janie. Have you ever longed to make a huge change in your life? If so, did you follow through with that change? How did your family and friends react? What Bible verses helped you with your choice?

8. What did you know about the Amish before reading this book? What did you learn?

ACKNOWLEDGMENTS

As always, I'm thankful for my loving family. Special thanks to my Amish friends, who patiently answer my endless stream of questions. You're a blessing in my life.

To my agent, Natasha Kern, I can't thank you enough for your guidance, advice, and friendship. You are a tremendous blessing in my life.

Thank you to my amazing editor, Becky Philpott, for your friendship and guidance. I'm grateful to Jean Bloom, who helped me polish and refine the story. Thank you also for connecting the dots between my books. I'm grateful to each and every person at HarperCollins Christian Publishing who helped make this book a reality.

Thank you most of all to God—for giving me the inspiration and the words to glorify You. I'm grateful and humbled You've chosen this path for me.

ABOUT THE AUTHOR

Photo by Dan Davis Photography

Amy Clipston is the award-winning and bestselling author of more than a dozen novels, including the Kauffman Amish Bakery series and the Hearts of the Lancaster Grand Hotel series. Her novels have hit multiple bestseller lists including CBD, CBA, and ECPA. Amy holds a degree in communication from Virginia Wesleyan College and works full-time for the City of Charlotte, North Carolina. Amy lives in North Carolina with her husband, two sons, and three spoiled rotten cats.

Visit her website: amyclipston.com
Facebook: Amy Clipston
Twitter: @AmyClipston

A Quiet Love

Kathleen Fuller

For all the special, unique, and quirky people in the world. You are loved.

GLOSSARY

aenti—aunt
bruder—brother
daed—dad
danki—thank you
dummkopf—a stupid person
familye—family
geh—go
grossmutter—grandmother
gut—good
haus—house
kaffee—coffee
kapp—prayer cap
kinner—children
lieb—love
maedel—girl
mamm—mom
mann—husband
mei—my
mudder—mother
nee—no
nix—nothing

schee—pretty
sohn—son
vatter—father
ya—yes

Chapter One

"Do you, Jeremiah Mullet, take Anna Mae Shetler as your lawful wedded wife?"

Amos Mullet grinned as he looked at his brother. It was strange, standing here in a Yankee church for the first time, watching his brother and his best friend get married. Anna Mae looked so pretty. She was always pretty, but today she was prettier than usual. She was wearing a fancy white dress and her blond hair was still short. She said it was easier to have short hair because of her work as a nurse. At first Amos wasn't used to it, just like he wasn't used to Jeremiah's mustache and beard, and that he was wearing a suit with a short black tie instead of his Sunday Amish clothes. But Jeremiah and Anna Mae were Yankees now. They hadn't joined the Amish church like Amos had.

"I do," Jeremiah said with the biggest smile Amos had ever seen.

The man at the front of the church—the pastor, Jeremiah had called him—turned to Anna Mae. "Do you, Anna Mae Shetler, take Jeremiah Mullet as your lawful wedded husband?"

Amos glanced around the church. He'd never been inside a Yankee church before. A huge cross hung at the front. Behind it were white curtains, and behind the curtains were white lights, which made the cross look like it was glowing. The long bench Amos was sitting on had dark blue padding, which was a lot softer than the hard benches he sat on in Amish church.

"I do," Anna Mae said, her smile making her look even prettier. He wished he had a pad and pencil so he could sketch her and Jeremiah.

As the pastor said a few more words, Amos watched Jeremiah and Anna Mae, trying to remember details. It was hard to remember things. He squinted and studied them carefully.

The tears in his brother's eyes.

Anna Mae's lacy dress.

The exact shade of pink and white in the bunch of flowers she was holding in front of her. The flowers shook a little, as if her hands weren't steady. Maybe he would draw that detail too.

"Jeremiah, you may kiss your bride."

Jeremiah took a step toward Anna Mae. His smile widened. So did hers. When Jeremiah kissed her, Amos looked away. He and Jeremiah and Anna Mae were best friends. Growing up, they did everything together. Then Jeremiah decided to become a veterinarian. Everything changed after that. Several years later, Jeremiah and Anna Mae fell in love. That made everything change again.

Judith sniffed next to him. She was his neighbor and she had come to the ceremony with Amos and *Daed* in a taxi they hired to bring them to this church. There weren't many people here. If this was an Amish wedding, their whole district would have come. But Jeremiah and Anna Mae said they wanted only family and close friends: Anna Mae's parents, her siblings, and Doc Miller and his wife, who had traveled all the way from Arizona to see Jeremiah get married.

"Jeremiah's like a son to me," Doc had said. Amos thought *Daed* would be mad about that, since Doc Miller wasn't Jeremiah's dad. But *Daed* had just nodded, then swallowed so hard Amos saw his throat move up and down.

"Ladies and gentlemen," the pastor said, "I present to you Mr. and Mrs. Jeremiah Mullet."

Amos saw everyone else stand, and he made sure to do the same. He didn't want to mess up Jeremiah's special day. A warm feeling filled his heart as Jeremiah grinned at him. Amos smiled back. He was happy for his brother and Anna Mae. His father and Judith were happy too. Everyone in the church was happy because Jeremiah and Anna Mae were now married.

Then Amos saw a flash of light glint off his brother's wide silver wedding band. Amos stopped smiling and the nice feeling went away. Would he ever get married? Would he know happiness like Jeremiah and Anna Mae? Would he ever have a family of his own?

Jeremiah and Anna Mae walked down the aisle, her arm looped through his. They disappeared through the sanctuary doors. Amos remembered what Jeremiah had told him would happen after the ceremony.

"We'll have a reception in the church hall," Jeremiah had said. He'd met with Amos privately before the wedding. Amos had noticed his tie looked like a bow and that it was a little crooked. But he didn't say anything so he could focus on what Jeremiah was telling him.

"There will be food, like at an Amish wedding." Jeremiah smiled. "After a while Anna Mae and I will leave. We have a plane to catch."

Amos had frowned. "How do you catch a plane?"

Jeremiah chuckled. "You don't. Not literally. We're going to Florida for our honeymoon, and we're traveling by plane. We're leaving tonight." He put his arm around Amos's shoulders. "That's why I wanted to talk to you now. After the wedding, things will be busy. I might not get a chance to say good-bye."

"Good-bye?" That had scared Amos. Jeremiah had left once before, when he had gone away to veterinarian school. "You're leaving again?" he asked, his chest feeling tight.

"Just for a week." Jeremiah squeezed Amos's shoulders. "Only a week. Then we'll be back and Anna Mae and I will come see you."

Amos relaxed. "I'm glad you're not leaving for *gut* again."

Jeremiah pulled Amos in for a hug. "I'll always be here for you, Amos. I promise." His brother's voice sounded thick, like he had peanut butter stuck in his throat.

"Wasn't that a lovely wedding, Amos?"

Judith's question brought Amos back to the present. She was his *daed*'s age, and she and *Daed* were close friends. Just like Jeremiah and Anna Mae had been. Would Judith and *Daed* ever get married? For some reason he thought so. "*Ya.*" Amos nodded. "It was nice."

"We should *geh* congratulate the happy couple." Judith glanced at *Daed*. His eyes were bright and shiny, like Jeremiah's had been before he kissed Anna Mae.

Daed's throat made a funny sound. "*Ya.* We should."

Judith and *Daed* left the bench and walked down the aisle together. Amos decided he would like Judith to be his step-mother. He'd spent most of his life without a mother. It would be nice to have one now, even though he was an adult.

Amos hung back as everyone left the church. He was alone

in the sanctuary and he knew he needed to join his family. But he couldn't leave. Not yet.

He turned and looked at the glowing cross, wondering again if he would ever find love. Until now he'd never thought about it. He'd never had a girlfriend. He'd never even met a girl he liked, not the way Jeremiah liked Anna Mae. No one in his district liked him, either. Not enough to marry. He was different. Jeremiah and Anna Mae said he was "special," but he didn't believe that. There was nothing special about being different, about being called a *dummkopf* while growing up, about not understanding a lot of things everyone else easily understood. He looked down at his hands as they gripped the back of the bench in front of him. A pew, he'd heard Judith call it. He didn't even know what a pew was.

No, he wouldn't find love. Or a wife. That was impossible.

Then he heard the words as clearly as if God were standing next to him, whispering in his ear.

Nothing is impossible, my son.

Amos looked at the cross again and smiled.

Chapter Two

Two years later

"I-I d-don't understand w-why I have to l-leave t-today." Dinah watched her mother fold one of Dinah's long-sleeved dresses and put it into the suitcase. Long sleeves? It was only the end of August. How long would she be gone?

"I don't see any reason for you to wait." *Mamm* smoothed out one of the wrinkles in the dress before closing the case. "Your *aenti* Judith will be happy to see you."

Dinah had to fight the urge to open the suitcase back up, snatch out the neatly packed clothes, and hang them up in her closet. She didn't want to leave New York, even if she was going to visit her favorite aunt. "S-she's n-not e-expecting m-me u-until tomorrow."

"I know she won't mind if you come a little early."

"But i-it's nearly h-harvest t-time." She was grasping at straws, but she couldn't help herself. "Y-you n-need m-me here."

"Dinah," *Mamm* said as she moved the suitcase and sat beside her on the bed, "you and I both know I have plenty of help."

Dinah glanced away. Of course *Mamm* had enough help. All five of her brothers were married, the last one marrying earlier this year. *Mamm* had five daughters-in-law to pitch in with harvesting the garden. It wasn't as large this year as it had been in the past. After all, it was only her and her parents living in this house now. *And* Mamm *seems eager to get rid of me.*

When *Mamm* received the letter from *Aenti* Judith last week suggesting Dinah come for a visit, *Mamm* jumped at the opportunity. "Just think, you'll get to visit Ohio again," she'd said before running to the phone shanty to call her sister and make arrangements. Before Dinah knew it, she was scheduled to leave the following week.

Dinah loved her aunt and wanted to see her again. The last time she had was at her aunt's wedding to David Mullet. But she hadn't wanted to go so soon. She picked up Jasper, one of several stray pets she'd adopted over the years. "Who's going to help you can the tomato sauce?" she asked, stroking the tabby's soft head. He purred his appreciation. At least her cat was happy.

"Joanna wants *mei* recipe." *Mamm* beamed. "She also wants me to show her how I make Chow Chow."

Resisting a sigh, Dinah put Jasper down. Making tomato sauce and Chow Chow were things she and her *mamm* did together. *I guess* Mamm *and Samson's wife will be doing it from now on.*

Mamm took Dinah's hand. "Look at me, Dinah." When she did, *Mamm* said, "Don't be upset about this. You're spending too much time at home. You're becoming more insulated. I'm worried about you."

"I c-can *geh* to M-Middlefield later." Much later. Or maybe not at all.

"Later will never come."

Dinah had heard all this before. So what if she'd rather spend time in her room with her poetry books and journals? When she wrote, she didn't stutter. She didn't get nervous. She didn't feel judged.

She also, as *Mamm* had been pointing out lately, would never meet her future husband.

But her family didn't understand how nervous she became in front of other people. How she hated the fact that she stuttered and her face turned red every time she talked. Dinah was content to be home, to take care of the myriad of pets she had collected over the years, along with writing her poetry. Which reminded her that she had one more excuse left to use. "W-who's g-going to t-take care of S-Skipper?"

"*Yer daed* said he'd keep an eye on him for you."

"B-but his leg—"

"Is healing nicely, according to the vet. He said you did a fine job taking care of his sore foot. *Yer* horse is in *gut* hands. So are the rest of *yer* pets." *Mamm* bent and scratched Jasper behind his ears. "I want you to enjoy *yer* time with *yer aenti*, Dinah. Hopefully this will also give you the chance to meet new people."

"I-I d-don't w-want to m-meet anyone n-new," she whispered.

Mamm either didn't hear her or decided to ignore Dinah's words. She released Dinah's hand and stood. "I'll let you finish getting dressed. The taxi will be here soon to take you to the bus station." She smiled. "You'll be fine, Dinah. I promise."

"W-when c-can I c-come b-back?"

"Two weeks. Unless you want to stay longer. You can always extend *yer* ticket."

Dinah was positive she wouldn't do that. She watched her mother leave her room, and her shoulders slumped as she heaved a pent-up sigh. Two weeks? That was an eternity. She said a small prayer, asking for courage, but her heart wasn't in it. This was her first trip alone, and she felt foolish for being so nervous. She was twenty-five, not five, and she should be able to go on a trip without feeling like her stomach was turning inside out.

She sat on the edge of the bed and took a deep breath. She could do this. *Aenti* Judith had married a stern man, but Dinah had seen the way he looked at her aunt at the wedding—with love. Love that a secret part of her wished she could have. But who would want a stuttering wife who was afraid of her own shadow?

"Dinah!" her mother called from downstairs. "The taxi is here!"

Dinah jumped up from the bed. She still hadn't put on her shoes. She scrambled for her black sneakers, yanked them on, then grabbed her suitcase. She flew down the stairs, fighting her fear.

"I love you," *Mamm* said, giving her a quick hug. "This will be a *gut* trip for you, Dinah. You'll see."

But Dinah could only nod, unable to speak. She walked outside and went to the taxi. As she got in, she hoped her mother was right.

⁓⁓⁓

"Amos! Amos!"

Amos's body stiffened with fear. "Whoa!" he shouted at Penny and Nickel, his two draft horses. He yanked on their reins as hard as he could. They halted and the hay mower behind him stopped rotating.

"Amos!"

Daed sounded hurt. And scared, which scared Amos too. He

dropped the reins and ran to the other side of the hayfield. He found his father on the ground, his left knee pulled up to his chest. He was also grabbing the front part of his leg under his knee.

Blood flowed from between his father's fingers. The old scythe he'd used to cut down the patch of hay was lying beside him.

"Have to be strong . . . Have to be strong." He repeated the words over and over as he made himself kneel beside his dad. The sight of blood always made him sick, and he had a bitter taste in his mouth, as if he'd eaten an orange peel. *Daed*'s face looked dark red, like beets. Sweat poured down *Daed*'s face and he sounded like his shirt collar was too tight around his neck. He tried to speak but all he did was groan.

"Don't get scared . . . Don't get scared." Spots showed up in front of Amos, but he knew they weren't real. His brother, Jeremiah, had explained that his eyes were playing tricks on him when he felt like he might pass out. "Don't get scared . . . Don't get scared." But Amos was scared. He wished Jeremiah were here. Jeremiah was a vet, and he would know what to do.

But his younger brother was at work and Anna Mae was at the hospital doing her job. Amos rubbed a grubby hand over his face, then did what he always did when he was upset. He closed his eyes and prayed.

"Amos . . ."

His father's voice sounded a little louder than a whisper. Yet Amos didn't open his eyes. He couldn't until he knew what to do. *Stop the bleeding.*

He opened his eyes, then yanked off his shirt. He moved his father's hands away from his leg.

"Don't," his *daed* said. "It's bad, *sohn*."

But Amos ignored him as he looked down at the ripped fabric of his father's work pants. His thoughts were clear now, his movements automatic. The blood had soaked through his father's pants, and Amos saw part of an open wound through the torn material. His stomach steadied as he wrapped his shirt around *Daed*'s shin, then tied the fabric tightly. "Stop the bleeding . . . Stop the bleeding." He didn't understand how tying the shirt over his father's leg would work; he only knew that it would. He swooped *Daed* up into his arms and hurried across the field, through the backyard, and into the house.

"Judith!" Amos cried out for his stepmother as he ran into the kitchen.

Judith was mopping the floor and she looked up from her work. "Goodness, Amos, what's—" Her face turned the color of new fallen snow. "Dear *Gott*." She dropped the mop and went to Amos. "What happened?"

"Accident," was all Amos could say.

"Lay him on the table," she said, her voice calmer than Amos thought possible.

Amos did as he was told. He always tried to follow directions the best he could. He set his father on the polished oak table, then stepped back and let his stepmother take over. Amos's chest moved up and down as he tried to catch his breath. Sweat fell into his eyes, but he couldn't stop looking at his father. Judith untied Amos's shirt from around *Daed*'s leg.

"You don't want to be here, Amos." Judith sounded different now. Worried. Afraid. Judith was never afraid. Amos's thoughts became jumbled and confused again. She sounded like Amos felt inside.

"I'm okay . . . I'm okay." Amos lifted his chin and refused to move. He was twenty-eight years old. Time for him to be a man and not a scared *kin*. "I can help."

"Grab some towels out of the drawer." Judith winced at the sound of *Daed*'s moan. "And a bowl. Fill it with water."

Amos did what Judith told him to do, then he heard her speak to *Daed* in that soft voice that always made his father smile.

"I'm here, David," she said. "Everything will be all right."

When Amos turned around, the bowl of water in his hands and the kitchen towels over his shoulder, he saw Judith brush his father's damp hair off his forehead. She wouldn't let anything happen to *Daed*. She loved him too much.

He handed the bowl to her and she set it on the table. "I need scissors," she said. "I've got to cut off the leg of his pants."

Amos took the edge of his father's pants leg and ripped it up the seam. That would be faster than getting scissors. But when he saw his father's bleeding leg, Amos's head felt like air again.

"Amos?"

The room turned like a merry-go-round. He used to ride those at the park when he was younger. It had been fun. But the spinning wasn't fun now.

"It's all right, Amos," Judith said. "You did a *gut* job. I don't need *yer* help anymore."

"Will *Daed* be okay?"

Judith nodded. "*Ya*. But why don't you *geh* outside and pray for him anyway?"

"Okay. I'll pray for him . . . I'll pray for him." He hurried out of the kitchen and into the driveway. His stomach hurt and he felt like he had the flu. He bent over and put his hands on his legs. "Don't throw up . . . Don't throw up . . ."

"A-are y-you o-okay?"

Surprised, he lifted his head at the nice voice. A girl's voice. No, a woman's voice. And although he was always forgetting things, he recognized her right away. She was Judith's niece. He had met her at his *daed*'s wedding. She must be here for her visit. Judith had said she was coming. Suddenly his stomach didn't hurt as much. "Hello," he said, standing up. "Hello, Dinah Keim."

Chapter Three

Dinah's breath caught when she saw Amos Mullet in the driveway of her aunt and uncle's house. She remembered meeting him at the wedding. But she had been so self-conscious that she spent most of that day hiding upstairs in *Aenti* Judith's old house, which was next door. She met his gaze. He'd said hello, and while the words were normal, she could see something wasn't right.

"Uh-oh." He bent over again.

Forgetting herself, she went to his side. "A-Amos?"

He held up his hand. Swallowed. Then straightened. She noticed the color coming back into his cheeks. She also noticed he wasn't wearing a shirt.

Under normal circumstances she had trouble finding her voice. But even if she were the smoothest talker alive, she wouldn't have been able to speak. He was at least half a foot taller than her, with wild-looking, longish brown hair, and rich, mahogany-colored eyes. She couldn't stop her gaze from sweeping across the expanse of his muscular torso before she turned her head away. She shouldn't be staring at him.

Then she felt his hand on her shoulder and she couldn't stop herself from looking at him again. His eyes were warm and not as bewildered as they had been before. "Don't move, Dinah Keim."

Her brow furrowed as he sprinted inside, moving swiftly for a man of his size. Then she heard an agonized cry from inside the house.

Without thinking, she opened the door and dashed inside. Another harrowing moan came from the back of the house, and she followed it until she was in the kitchen. There she saw David, Judith's husband, lying on the table, writhing in pain. Her aunt was tending to his leg. When Dinah saw the gash and the blood-soaked towels, she went to her aunt's side. A sudden calm went through her, the way it did when she saw one of her beloved pets injured.

"What can I do?"

Aenti Judith glanced at her. Her eyes rounded with surprise behind her wire-rimmed glasses, then returned to their former concentration. "He needs stitches. Lots of them. We're too far from a hospital."

"I can do it," Dinah said. It wouldn't be the first time she had stitched up a wound, although the patient had been another one of her cats, Fido, and the wound had been short and not as deep. Still, Dinah knew she could handle David's injury. "Do you have a first-aid kit?"

Judith nodded.

"I'll keep pressure on this while you *geh* get it." Completely engrossed in her task, she took over and pressed the blood-soaked compress on David's leg as her aunt left the kitchen.

Aenti Judith came back moments later with a large kit. Her mother also had a huge first-aid kit at home. Raising six children, five of them boys, it had come in handy more than a few times.

"I need to wash *mei* hands before I start stitching," Dinah said. As she passed David on her way to the sink, she saw his eyes close. He was on the verge of becoming unconscious, which might be a blessing considering how much pain he was in. Or he could be going into shock. Dinah quickly washed her hands and went back to the table. "He needs blankets," she said. "And something for the pain."

While her aunt was gone, Dinah went to work. She had finished irrigating the wound when Amos burst into the room, a shirt untucked from his dark blue broadfall pants and hanging a little crookedly over his wide shoulders.

"Amos," *Aenti* Judith said as she came in carrying the blankets, "call Jeremiah."

"I did. Before I came in here. But I put a shirt on first. Then I went to the phone box. A nice lady answered the phone."

Dinah kept her focus on the wound, but she also noticed the simplistic way Amos was speaking.

"What did she say, Amos?" *Aenti* Judith's normally placid voice was edged with impatience.

"She said Jeremiah is out. But she's gonna call him."

"Did you tell her it was an emergency?"

"*Ya.* I told her *Daed* was hurt bad." He paused. "He's hurt real bad, *ya*?"

Her aunt laid the blankets over David's torso. "*Ya.* He is."

Amos moved to stand next to Dinah. "Can you fix him?"

"I-I c-can . . ." Oh no. A moment ago she felt in complete control of the situation. With one earnest question, she was faltering. She glanced up at Amos and saw tears shining in his eyes. She had to get her wits about her. "I-I will try *m-mei* b-best."

"Okay. Trying is *gut*. I'm always trying."

He was so open and honest that she almost smiled. Then she put all her concentration into stitching up David.

Nearly an hour later, Dinah cleaned the blood off David's skin. She wiped the back of her hand over her damp forehead and checked her work. The stitches were neat and even. David was still unconscious, and Judith tucked the old, faded quilt around his chin.

"You saved his life," *Aenti* Judith whispered.

Dinah looked at her uncle. His eyes were closed and his skin looked gray. But at least he wasn't bleeding anymore. She started to say something to her aunt, only to see Amos staring at her hands. Dinah glanced down at her palms. They were covered in blood. When she looked up at Amos, she noticed he was turning green again.

"You can *geh* outside, Amos." *Aenti* Judith put her hand on his shoulder. "*Yer vatter* is going to be okay, and Jeremiah will be here soon."

"I can't," Amos said, his hand covering his stomach. "I can't leave him."

"Amos." Judith's voice turned soft. "If you pass out, how are we going to get you back up? You're too big for me and Dinah to lift."

Amos nodded. "Okay. I'll *geh*."

After Amos left, Dinah went to the sink and washed her hands. She remembered that Amos's brother, Jeremiah, was a vet, and she breathed out a sigh of relief. At least there was someone here who could make sure she had done a good enough job stitching David's leg.

She dried her hands and turned around to see David stirring. By the time she reached the table he was trying to get up, only to fall back against the table with a growl of pain.

"Stay still," *Aenti* Judith said. "You don't want to break *yer* stitches."

"Need . . . to check on Amos."

"He's fine. He's outside waiting on Jeremiah. And as soon as he arrives you're going to the hospital."

David shook his head. "*Nee. Nee* hospitals. I'll be fine. Just a little cut—"

"That took almost two dozen stitches." *Aenti* Judith's lower lip trembled. "You will not argue with me, David Mullet."

Glowering, David turned his head away. With a sigh, *Aenti* Judith said, "Dinah, do you mind checking on Amos? I'm sure he's fine, but it might help if he wasn't alone."

Dinah nodded, eager to leave the tension of the kitchen. Although it was warm outside, she welcomed the fresh air. Amos was pacing along the driveway, muttering to himself. As she neared, she could make out what he was saying.

"Where is Jeremiah? Where is Jeremiah?" He shoved a beefy hand through his hair. "Should have called an ambulance . . . Should have called an ambulance . . . Should have called Anna Mae . . . Should have called Anna Mae . . ."

She went to his side. He was working himself up and she had to calm him down. He was already halfway down the driveway.

"Messed everything up . . . Messed everything up . . ."

Then before she reached him he stopped and closed his eyes. He was perfectly still, even while a faint breeze kicked up around him. His lips started to move and she realized he was praying. She started to back away when he opened his eyes and turned toward her.

"Hello, Dinah Keim."

"I-I'm s-sorry," she said. "I shouldn't h-have interrupted y-you."

"It's okay." He faced her fully. "Is *Daed* okay?"

"H-he's in a l-lot of p-pain. I st-stitched up the w-wound the b-best I c-could."

"That's *gut, ya?*"

She wanted to take the worry out of his eyes. "*Y-ya.* It's g-*gut.*"

He blew out a long breath. "I didn't mess everything up."

Glad to see the relief on his handsome face, she took a step toward him. "*Nee*, Amos. You didn't mess anything up."

His eyes met hers. "You're brave, Dinah Keim. And smart. You knew what to do to help *Daed.*"

She blushed at his compliment, which took her off guard and made her nervous again. "I-I had s-some practice. I-I didn't d-do that m-much."

"I'm not smart. I mess up a lot."

"I'm sure that's n-not true."

"It is." He tilted his head and frowned, but his gaze didn't flinch. "You talk funny."

That wasn't the first time she'd heard those words, especially when she was a child. And each time someone pointed out her stutter, it made it worse, made her feel more like a failure. Like she was broken. But for some reason, Amos's words didn't hurt. Maybe it was the kindness mixed with respect she saw in his gaze. Or the fact that there was no malice behind the simple statement. "*Y-ya.* I s-stutter. A l-lot."

"Like tripping over *yer* tongue?"

She couldn't help but chuckle. She'd never heard it put that way. "I g-guess s-so." Then she looked away, her mirth evaporating.

"I'm sorry," Amos said.

Dinah looked at him. "For what?"

"I hurt *yer* feelings." He pulled on his earlobe. "I didn't mean to. Sometimes I use wrong words. Say the wrong thing."

"You s-said th-the t-truth." She smiled at him. "Y-you d-didn't hurt *mei* feelings."

"You have pretty eyes. They look like the sky does in the summer. When there aren't any clouds."

An intense feeling came over her as he continued to gaze at her, as if he were memorizing not only her eyes but her entire face. The sharp switch in topic threw her a bit.

A car pulled in the driveway, then came to an abrupt stop near the house. Amos turned from Dinah and she heard him sigh with relief. "Jeremiah is here. He'll know what to do."

A wiry man with a beard jumped out of the car. He rushed to Amos. "What happened to *Daed*?" Jeremiah asked. "I got a message from my tech and she said it was an emergency."

"We were out cutting hay," Amos said. "He cut his leg. He cut it real bad."

Jeremiah groaned. "He was using that old scythe, wasn't he?"

Amos nodded. "But Dinah Keim stitched his leg."

Jeremiah gave her an odd look. "Thanks," he said, sounding confused. Then he dashed into the house.

Dinah saw that Amos was about to follow him. Knowing how squeamish he was, she knew that wouldn't be a good idea. She put her hand on his arm and he stilled. He stared at her hand as if he'd never seen one before. Then he looked at her, his brown eyes darkening and filling with confusion at the same time. She snatched her hand away. She shouldn't have touched him. And although the gesture was innocent and meant to get his attention, something had passed between them. Something both unsettling and pleasant.

"W-we sh-should stay o-out here," she said. Then she clamped her lips together. She needed to get her stutter under control. "I think the kitchen is c-crowded enough." There. That was better.

"Okay. Jeremiah is a *gut* vet."

She had remembered that from her aunt's wedding. Jeremiah and his wife, who was a nurse, had never joined the church but were still close with their families. They were Yankees, which is what the Amish in Middlefield called the non-Amish.

"A vet can take care of people too," Amos said.

"In c-certain s-situations, *ya*."

"I remember you. From the wedding."

There he went, switching topics faster than a flapping hummingbird's wings. "I-I know you d-do."

"Judith is *yer aenti*."

Dinah nodded. "I'm here for a v-visit." She frowned. "You d-didn't k-know I w-was c-coming?"

"I must have forgotten you were coming today. I forget a lot of things."

"It's o-okay, Amos. I forget things t-too. And I was s-supposed to be here t-tomorrow. So you didn't forget anything."

He grinned. "I didn't?" Then his brow scrunched in concentration. "We're friends, *ya*? I mean, we can be friends? Like me and Anna Mae are? Even though you're a *maedel* and I'm a *bu*?"

He was far from a boy, despite his simple speech. "*Ya*, Amos. I would like to be friends."

Jeremiah came out of the house and Dinah was glad to see he didn't look as upset as he had when he arrived.

"How is *Daed*?" Amos asked, turning from Dinah.

"Judith and I got him to the couch. I wanted to take him to the doctor but he refused." Jeremiah shrugged. "You know how *Daed* is. At least he keeps up with his tetanus shots. He did agree to let Anna Mae look at him when she gets off work." Jeremiah turned to Dinah. "You did a mighty fine job with those stitches. Where did you learn how to suture like that?"

"I-I h-have a c-cat." Her explanation sounded stupid. "A-and I-I've r-read a l-lot of b-books." Irritated with herself, she looked away.

"You're very skilled," he said in a patient tone.

Dinah knew he was being nice, but she didn't appreciate his coddling. She nodded and kept her gaze from him.

If he was bothered by her rudeness, he didn't let on. Instead he turned to Amos. "*Daed* won't be able to do much work for a while. I know it's harvest season and there's a lot to be done. I can come over and help you after I get off work."

Amos shook his head. "I can do it."

"Amos, the hay needs cutting and stacking. The corn needs to be picked. So do the beans, peas, zucchini, carrots—"

"I *know*, Jeremiah."

Dinah jerked up her head at the frustration in Amos's voice. She saw his cheeks redden and caught the quick glance he sent her way. She immediately understood. Jeremiah was coddling him, too, and Amos didn't like it any more than she did. "I c-can h-help," she piped up.

Amos looked at her. "But you're our . . ." He scratched his head and frowned. "Our . . ."

"Guest," Jeremiah supplied. "And Amos is right. You're a guest here. You don't need to be doing so much work."

"I d-don't m-mind." And she really didn't. Her aunt would

be busy tending to David. At least if she was helping Amos, she wouldn't be alone in a strange house. That defeated the purpose of her coming here. Keeping busy would make the time pass faster until she could go back home.

Home. Odd, she hadn't thought about home since she'd arrived.

"I said I could do it!" Amos stalked off toward the barn.

Dinah flinched. She should have kept her mouth shut. She should have realized that Amos wouldn't appreciate the offer. He didn't even want his brother helping him. It was as if he had something to prove. She understood exactly how that felt.

"Don't worry about Amos," Jeremiah said, moving to stand next to her. They watched as he disappeared into the barn. "He'll be okay. He's worried about *Daed*."

Dinah nodded and bit her lower lip.

"He'll come around." Jeremiah smiled at her. "Let's go in the house and check on the curmudgeon. I'm sure he's giving Judith a hard time. Not that she can't handle it."

Dinah nodded. *Aenti* Judith could handle anything. She had been widowed for several years and didn't have any children of her own. She'd moved to Middlefield from New York by herself, against everyone's wishes, saying she wanted a new start. And she had made one. Now she was married and had stepchildren. Knowing *Aenti* Judith, Dinah was sure she loved them as if they were her own. She followed Jeremiah into the house, but paused at the doorway and looked at the barn again, hoping Amos was okay.

Chapter Four

Later that evening Dinah prepared supper while *Aenti* Judith, Jeremiah, and his wife, Anna Mae, were in the living room with David. As Dinah made a fresh salad to go along with the roasted chicken, green beans, and mashed potatoes, she thought about her conversation a few hours earlier with her aunt. They had spent several moments talking after David finally fell asleep. Jeremiah had left to go back to work, and Amos returned to the hayfield.

"I'm surprised you're here a day early," *Aenti* Judith had said as Dinah handed her a cup of chamomile tea in the kitchen.

"M-*Mamm*'s idea." Dinah joined her at the table, clasping her hands on her lap as she sat down.

"Not that I'm complaining." Her aunt took a sip of the tea. "Thank the Lord you were here to take care of David's leg. I had *nee* idea you were so skilled."

Dinah hadn't either. But now that she had time to process what had happened, she wasn't sure where she had gotten the strength or the confidence to stitch David's leg. *Wait. I do know. Thank You, Lord, for guiding mei hand.*

"Amos brought in *yer* suitcase. You can stay in Jeremiah's

old bedroom." *Aenti* Judith let out a long breath. "I'm glad you're here, and not just because of David. I've been looking forward to *yer* visit."

"M-me too." She relaxed the tight grip she had on her interlocked fingers. She was comfortable around her aunt, who had never made her feel like she was less because of her stutter and shyness. *Aenti* Judith had understood, unlike her mother who was always pushing her to go to singings and to think about marriage. The idea of marrying someone frightened her. What if he was impatient with her? What if he lost his temper? Her fingers tightened their grip again.

"I can hear David stirring in the other room, probably trying to get up again." *Aenti* Judith rose. "Please, make yourself at home. I want you to feel welcome, despite the rough day we had."

"*Danki, Aenti* Judith."

Dinah had made herself at home in the kitchen, and now she sliced a ripe tomato into small pieces, then sprinkled them on the salad. She wondered if Amos liked tomatoes. She probably should have put them in a little bowl on the side just in case he didn't.

Thinking about Amos made her smile. There was something about him. He was more appealing than any man she'd ever met. He was a gentle giant. She wasn't even bothered by his earlier outburst. She understood his frustration.

Then the image of him without a shirt on entered her mind. *He's a handsome* mann, *for sure. And I'm only human.* But there was more to Amos than his looks, or even his simple demeanor. He was special.

Anna Mae walked into the kitchen, *Aenti* Judith behind her. Anna Mae smiled at Dinah. "David's going to be fine," she said. "He lost a lot of blood, but not enough to need a transfusion. His color is good and he's not in shock. The stitching job you did, Dinah, was excellent. I know some of my fellow surgical nurses would be jealous of such fine work."

Dinah reddened and moved to put the salad bowl on the table. She'd never received so many compliments in one day. Her father and brothers were never big on sentimentality, and her mother seemed more concerned with pushing Dinah into doing things she didn't want to do than recognizing what she could do. "I-I'm g-glad I c-could h-help." Dinah forced her voice to be as steady as possible. When she failed, she tried not to frown.

"If you hadn't helped," *Aenti* Judith said, "David might have . . ." She brought her trembling fingers to her lips.

Anna Mae put her hand on *Aenti* Judith's shoulder. "David would have been fine. God was watching out for him." She pushed a strand of her short hair behind her ear. "Jeremiah's talking to David, trying to convince him he needs to take it easy. He could pop the stitches if he tries to do too much."

"I'll make sure he rests," *Aenti* Judith said.

At that moment Jeremiah came into the kitchen, looking grumpy. "The ogre is hungry," he said.

Anna Mae went to stand by her husband. They were a striking couple, she with her blond hair and he with the darker hair and a full beard. They both wore wedding rings, and if Dinah hadn't known their history, she wouldn't have assumed they had once been Amish. She'd always wondered what made people decide to leave their faith, although in this case she knew neither of them had joined the church, choosing instead to pursue their careers. They couldn't have done that if they were Amish. As for herself, she had no desire to be anything but Amish. She was content with her life—at least where her faith was concerned. The rest she wasn't so sure of.

"Did David agree to take it easy?" her aunt asked.

Jeremiah nodded. "Yeah, but it took some convincing. My *daed* is nothing if not stubborn."

Aenti Judith chuckled. "That's one of his charms." She picked up a plate, but then lifted the spoon from the pot of mashed potatoes when Anna Mae shook her head.

"After what he's been through," she said, "something light would be better. Maybe a piece of bread and butter to start?"

Aenti Judith nodded and went to the table. She picked up a fresh slice of bread and spread a thin layer of butter on top.

Dinah finished setting the table. Without being asked, Anna Mae went to the stove to check on the pot of green beans simmering on the burner. She seemed comfortable in this house. Jeremiah poured himself a glass of tea. He was about to take a sip when he stopped, the glass halfway to his mouth. "Where's Amos?"

Her aunt put another slice of bread on top of the one she had buttered. "He must still be outside working." She frowned. "He's usually not late for a meal."

Jeremiah put down his glass. "I'll get him."

"I-I c-can d-do it," Dinah said without thinking.

"It's all right," Jeremiah said. "I don't mind getting him—"

"Help me with these green beans," Anna Mae interrupted.

Jeremiah frowned and looked at his wife. "You can't stir a pot of beans by yourself?"

Anna Mae's eyes narrowed. "No, I can't."

Jeremiah paused, still looking confused. Then he nodded. "Oh. Right. I'll help you, then." He turned to Dinah. "It would be great if you could get my brother. He's probably in the hayfield or maybe the cornfield right beside it. That way I can help my wife, uh, stir the beans."

Clearly Anna Mae didn't need any help with the beans. Maybe she wanted to talk to Jeremiah privately about David. It wasn't Dinah's business, so she left the kitchen to find Amos.

When she was outside, she looked around the property. She hadn't paid much attention to it before. Last time she was here there were so many people and too much commotion. But now she had a moment to appreciate the small, neatly kept farm.

She started walking again, and a few minutes later she found Amos working at the opposite end of the hayfield. He was raking a row of hay into a roll, then with light strokes he gathered it up into a loose, cylindrical pile. There were many piles at the edge of the field. She'd seen haystacks before, but she didn't know the process of cutting and drying hay. *Guess I'll find out tomorrow.*

She yelled out to him as loud as she could, pleased she didn't stumble over his name. Amos stopped raking and lifted his head. Dinah shielded her eyes from the setting sun and yelled, "S-supper's r-ready!" So much for not tripping over her tongue.

He nodded and raked for a few more minutes. When he finished, she watched him head for the barn, which was in front of the field and several yards from the house.

Amos motioned with his head for her to follow him to the barn. She did, but remained outside. He hadn't invited her inside, and she didn't want to overstep her bounds. When he came back out, he said, "I'm late."

"N-not too late. We haven't s-started eating. But everyone was w-wondering where you w-were." Her nerves weren't jangled like they usually were around people, especially those she didn't know very well. And especially men. Of course, Amos was different.

"I'm sorry," he said in that simple yet appealing way he had. "I know better. I'm not supposed to be late for supper." He headed for the house, his broad shoulders straight, his posture tall. He carried himself well. She began to follow him, only to skid to a stop when he stopped in his tracks.

"Put the horses up . . . Put the horses up . . ." He turned. "I almost forgot to put the horses up. I would be in big trouble if I forgot to do that. They're in the pasture." He brushed past her and started for the grassy field when he sharply spun around. "Will you wait for me, Dinah Keim?"

An unexpected flow of warmth went through her and she nodded. "*Ya.* I w-will wait for you."

"I won't be long." Then he paused, frowning. "Or maybe I will." He spun on his booted heel and jogged to the pasture.

Dinah couldn't help but chuckle. "It's okay, Amos," she said, even though he was too far away for her to hear. "I'll wait for you as long as it takes."

When Dinah and Amos entered the kitchen, Judith wasn't there. "She wanted to stay with David," Anna Mae explained. Dinah nodded, not surprised at her aunt's devotion to her injured husband.

"Amos, don't forget to wash up," Jeremiah said as he sat down at the table.

Dinah saw Amos frown. But he didn't say anything as he went to the sink and washed his hands. Then he sat next to Jeremiah and across from Dinah.

She bowed her head and silently prayed with the Mullet family. When prayer was over, both Jeremiah and Amos handed Anna Mae their plates and she filled them up, giving Amos a little more food than Jeremiah. Dinah could see why. Jeremiah was leaner than Amos, and as she had seen earlier, Amos was all muscle. She averted her gaze and focused on her empty plate.

"How much hay is left to cut?" Jeremiah asked Amos as he took his plate from his wife.

"I got half the field done. Tomorrow I'll do the other half. Right, the other half." Amos's eyes moved from left to right.

Dinah watched as he paused, as if he was searching his mind.

"Then you'll dry and stack the hay," Jeremiah said.

Amos's eyes widened. "Okay. Dry and stack the hay." He stabbed several green beans with his fork, then shoved them into his mouth.

"My offer to help still stands," Jeremiah said.

"So d-does m-mine." Dinah froze as Amos, Jeremiah, and Anna Mae all looked at her. This was why she never volunteered to do anything. Her stutter never failed to draw unwanted attention. But she couldn't stop herself from making sure Amos knew she was here to help. That she wanted to help.

Amos finished chewing and swallowed. "You know how to stack hay?" he asked Dinah.

She shook her head. Her father and brothers were carpenters, not farmers. "B-but I c-can l-learn. I want t-to learn. I-it sounds l-like f-fun."

Jeremiah and Anna Mae started to laugh. Amos looked at them both, a bewildered expression on his face. Then he laughed too.

Dinah shrank in her chair. Had she misjudged this family? Were they making fun of her?

Anna Mae touched Dinah's arm. "You have no idea what you're in for."

"Yeah," Jeremiah said, grinning. But his smile was kind. "Amos and *Daed* have several acres of hay. It's a lot of work."

She lifted her chin. "I-I d-don't m-mind w-working." Now she sounded defensive. She shouldn't have said anything at all. She tried to look away, but sensed Amos's gaze on her. When she met his eyes, the soft kindness she saw there comforted her. He seemed to understand her sensitivity to criticism. Overly sensitive, her mother would say. And in this case, it was true. She could see that Jeremiah and Anna Mae weren't laughing at her. But knowing that didn't make her feel totally at ease, either.

Jeremiah and Anna Mae turned the topic to their jobs, and Dinah was grateful. She didn't know much about veterinary medicine, so she paid attention to Jeremiah's story about how he had helped deliver a breeched calf. But when Anna Mae started discussing her job, Dinah's attention waned. She could stitch up a wound, but she wasn't interested in the ins and outs of working at a hospital. Neither Jeremiah nor Anna Mae mentioned any names during their discussion, and Dinah could appreciate their attention to privacy. Still, her mind wandered as she helped herself to a slice of bread.

Amos was also quiet, engrossed in finishing his meal. Jeremiah tried to bring him into the conversation, but Amos gave one word answers. He wasn't being rude, but like Dinah, he clearly wasn't interested in participating in the discussion. Jeremiah seemed fine with that, and Dinah could feel the easy camaraderie between the three of them. She wished her family was this tight-knit. She wasn't close with any of her siblings. She had little in common with her older brothers, who all worked in the family carpentry business and were busy with their own families. While Dinah enjoyed being an aunt and loved her nieces and nephews, her brothers were too busy to talk to her about poetry or books or pets, the three things she loved. They also didn't have the patience for her stuttering. She knew they loved her, but she wasn't sure they truly accepted her. *Because I'm different.*

"Dinah?"

She lifted her gaze and looked at Amos. He was staring at her. She should feel put off by his open perusal, but she didn't. There was no guile with this man. After today's events she also knew he was earnest and hardworking, and that he loved his family.

"You don't like supper?" he asked, glancing at her almost-full plate.

"Amos." Jeremiah's tone held a bit of warning. And a touch of condescension, which Dinah found irritating.

"I'm sorry." He bent his head and stared at his food. "I was rude."

"You weren't," Dinah said, indignant on his behalf. "You simply asked me a question."

"I'm not supposed to be nosy."

"You're not nosy." She smiled when he looked at her again. "I was lost in *mei* thoughts."

"I get lost in mine too." He tapped on the side of his head and grinned.

She laughed, then noticed that Jeremiah had relaxed. He and Anna Mae exchanged a smile.

For the rest of the meal, Dinah made sure to eat her food. She'd made it, after all, and it was delicious. She had to admit she was a decent cook. And she liked seeing Amos thoroughly enjoy the meal. When he finished, there was a small drop of mashed potatoes on the corner of his mouth. She had a strange urge to reach out and wipe it off with the tip of her finger.

Amos pushed back against the table. "Time to take care of the animals."

Jeremiah jumped up from his chair. "I'll help you."

This time Amos didn't protest. Dinah started clearing the table while Anna Mae filled the sink with water. "Do you mind drying the dishes?" she asked when Dinah had brought the last of the plates to her.

"*Nee*, n-not at a-all."

"The kitchen towels are there." She pointed to a drawer near the sink. "Unless Judith moved them. I used to know where everything was in this house. I practically grew up here when I was kid."

"H-how long have y-you and J-Jeremiah been married?" Dinah found the dish towels and pulled one out of the drawer.

Anna Mae rinsed off a glass and handed it to Dinah. "A little more than a year. But we've been together much longer than that. We were best friends as kids. Me, Jeremiah, and Amos." She paused from washing the dishes and looked at Dinah. "I guess you can tell Amos is . . . special."

Dinah nodded. *He definitely is.*

"How long are you planning to visit?" Anna Mae asked.

Dinah dried a serving spoon. "T-two weeks."

Plunging her hands back into the soapy water, Anna Mae said, "Since you'll be here for a while, I think it's okay to tell you about Amos. If you're going to help him with the hay, there are a few things you should know about him. You are *familye*, after all."

Dinah was surprised when Anna Mae slipped into *Dietsch*.

"Amos is a sweet *mann*. The kindest soul you'll ever meet." Anna Mae paused. "People tend to take advantage of that."

She could see how that would be possible. She imagined he'd been ostracized for his differences more than she had for her own.

251

"While he's never been formally diagnosed," Anna Mae continued, adding a little more water to the soapy sink, "Jeremiah and I think he is autistic. Have you heard of that before?"

"*Nee.*"

"It's complicated, but basically it's a developmental disorder. Amos gets confused in social situations and when he has to interact with other people, even one-on-one. He's forgetful and gets very focused on certain things. He also has some learning problems. But he's gifted in so many other ways." She smiled. "You'll see as you get to know him better."

Dinah dipped her head, scrubbing the towel over an already-dried plate. She was glad Anna Mae was sharing information about Amos.

"It's important that we all be patient with him." Any trace of Anna Mae's smile disappeared. "He's been through so much."

Dinah's heart squeezed at the break in Anna Mae's voice. It was clear she loved her brother-in-law. "I u-understand," Dinah said.

Anna Mae's smile returned. "*Danki.* Somehow I knew you would."

They finished washing the rest of the dishes, and as Dinah put the last plate on the counter, *Aenti* Judith walked into the kitchen and sat down. Her aunt's shoulders drooped as she took off her glasses and rubbed her eyes.

Dinah went to her and put her hand on her shoulder. "H-how's D-David?"

"Sleeping, finally. He's still on the couch. Tomorrow I'll have to talk him into moving into the bedroom and staying there for a couple of days. He still thinks he's going to help Amos with the hay in the morning." She put her glasses back on, then pushed back a stray lock of brownish-gray hair that had escaped from her *kapp*. "I'm not finding his stubbornness charming at the moment."

"Do you want Jeremiah to talk to him again?" Anna Mae asked, joining her at the table.

Aenti Judith shook her head. "I can handle *mei* husband. Even if he is being ridiculous." She looked up at Dinah with a weary smile. "*Danki* again for all you've done."

"I-I'm glad I c-could be here." She was no longer upset with her mother for forcing her to visit *Aenti* Judith, even a day early. And now that she was here, the fear and longing for home she'd expected to feel weren't nearly as bad as she thought they'd be. That didn't mean she wouldn't wish to go home soon, especially by the end of her visit. But for now, she felt needed and accepted. That would be enough to get her through the next two weeks.

Chapter Five

A mos liked having Jeremiah help him settle the animals down for the night. His father sometimes helped him, but other times he stayed in the house with Judith. Amos didn't mind. His father was happy now that he was married, and Amos was happy for him. If *Daed* wanted to spend more time with his wife than with the animals, Amos understood.

When the chickens were nested, the pigs were fed, and the horses were in their stalls chomping on their nightly feeding of hay, he sat down on a square bale of hay against the back wall of the barn. Almost every evening he would take a little time to sit and look at the walls, trying to decide what to draw next on the few blank spaces left on the oak slats.

He'd been drawing in here for years with his pastels. Some of the drawings were faded. Others were bright and new. Tonight he was too tired to think about drawing, but as always, his gaze landed on the portrait he and Jeremiah had drawn of their mother the day they'd found out she'd died of cancer. She had left them for the Yankee world when Jeremiah was eight and Amos was nine. They hadn't seen her since. But before her death she had written to them. This drawing was how they remembered her—young, pretty, and smiling. Jeremiah didn't know how to color very well, and Amos had to help him with that. The finished portrait was Amos's favorite artwork.

Jeremiah sat down next to Amos. "How are you doing?" he said, clapping his brother on the back.

Amos shrugged. He was tired. A little sad, too, for some reason. Usually he could look at his mother's picture without feeling sad, but not today.

Jeremiah looked at the portrait. "Missing her?" he asked, his tone gentle.

Amos nodded. It was strange, because he hadn't seen her in almost twenty years. She had left—or abandoned, as his father and Jeremiah had said—the family, and now she was gone forever. "*Ya*. I miss her."

"Me too."

He and Jeremiah didn't say anything else. It wasn't long before Amos started to think about Dinah. He had to try very hard not to stare at her during the meal because she was so pretty and nice. When she caught him, he thought she'd be mad. But she wasn't and that made him glad. He was never sure how people would react to him.

"So what do you think of Dinah?" Jeremiah asked.

Amos felt his cheeks get hot. He wasn't surprised his brother knew what he was thinking. Jeremiah was very smart. "She's pretty." His voice sounded weird and low.

"You think all women are pretty, Amos."

"Because they are." Old or young, thin or fat, it didn't matter. "Dinah is different. Not different like me. She's *gut* different."

Jeremiah opened his mouth, but no sound came out. Then

he closed his mouth and stood. "Anna Mae and I should be getting home. She's working a double tomorrow."

Amos didn't know what that meant, but he nodded as if he did. He stood up next to his brother. "Okay."

"I'll check on *Daed* before I leave." Jeremiah looked up at him. "He's going to be fine, Amos, thanks to *yer* quick thinking."

"Dinah Keim helped."

Jeremiah smiled. "*Ya*, she did."

"And she said she would keep helping."

"I know. Don't make her work too hard, Amos."

"I won't."

"I'll stop by tomorrow and check on *Daed* again." Jeremiah paused. "If you need anything, you let me know."

"Okay." But Amos knew he would be all right. *Daed* would be better soon. Dinah was here to help. And Judith too. God was taking care of all of them, like he always did.

"*Gute nacht*, Amos."

"*Gute nacht*."

After Jeremiah left, Amos sat back down on the hay bale. He stared at his drawings again. Then he closed his eyes and prayed, thanking God that *Daed* was okay and that Dinah had helped save him. Then he stopped thinking in words. Words were hard for him sometimes. It was better to let his heart speak. He knew God was listening.

⁓

Dinah sat at the edge of the bed in Jeremiah's old room. It was a simple space, similar to her brothers' bedrooms when they lived at home. They never had the luxury of their own rooms like

Amos and Jeremiah had. Her family lived in a small house and had to share everything, including sleeping quarters. She was the only one who had her own room, and it was little more than a closet. But it was hers.

She glanced at the bedroom door. How was she going to sleep tonight when she knew Amos was a few feet down the hall? Earlier she had read a few pages of the poetry notebook she'd brought with her. She'd been copying poems since she was a teenager and had written some of her own. She didn't know why she was so drawn to poetry. Perhaps it was the lyrical smoothness of the words that contrasted to her own halting speech. Poems also gave her peace, but tonight she couldn't concentrate. For some reason she was excited to be working with Amos tomorrow.

Heavy footsteps sounded out in the hall, and she assumed Amos was heading to his bedroom for the night. She waited until everything was quiet and then stood. She took off her *kapp* and brushed out her hair, then realized she needed to use the bathroom before she went to bed. She should put on a kerchief before leaving the room. But she was only going down the hall. No one would see her. Dinah opened the door and looked out into the hallway. When she saw it was empty, she started for the bathroom.

As she stepped on the cold floor of the bathroom, a door opened behind her. She whirled around and saw Amos standing in the doorway of his room.

"I-I'm sorry," he said.

This time he was stuttering instead of her. He was also staring at her again, like he had during supper. "I w-was just going to, uh, brush *mei* teeth," she said. "You don't have to a-apologize."

His gaze didn't move from her long hair. It was if he'd never seen a woman's hair before. Realization dawned. He probably hadn't. She knew about David's first wife, how she'd left the family when the boys were young, and that she'd died of cancer several years ago. Of course *Aenti* Judith would never be seen outside her bedroom without her hair bound up. Dinah regretted not taking the time to put her kerchief on. It wasn't proper for Amos to see her without a head covering. Yet she couldn't make herself move. His unabashed curiosity kept her feet planted in place.

Truth be told, she couldn't stop looking at him, either. He wore the same light green shirt he had on earlier, again untucked, and his broadfall pants were covered in pale brown dust and a smattering of straw. Just before his gaze dropped to his bare feet, she saw a flash of uncertainty in his eyes that tugged at her, as if he'd been caught stealing candy from the candy dish. She didn't want him to take responsibility for something that was her fault.

Unable to stop herself, she went to him. *This is wrong. This is so wrong.* A woman's hair was for her husband's eyes only. She knew that. From the way he kept his eyes from her, she could tell he somehow knew it too. Still, that didn't stop her from taking his hand and placing it on the thick lock of hair covering her shoulder. At the confused doubt in his eyes when he looked up, she said, "It's okay, Amos."

His gaze moved back to her hair, his fingers barely brushing against the strands as he moved his hand downward, stopping above her elbow. "Beautiful," he whispered, sounding like a man and not a confused boy. Then he pulled his hand away. *"Danki,"* he said, as if he understood what she had done and why. He gave her a small smile and went back to his room.

She stood in the hallway for a moment, looking at his closed bedroom door. He was so sweet. So gentle. She'd never met a man like Amos Mullet. He was one of a kind.

⁓⁓

"W-wow. That's a l-lot of hay." Dinah surveyed the field in front of her and Amos. She'd been up since before the sunrise, and after breakfast she and Amos had headed for the field, leaving her aunt to reassure David that Dinah and Amos could take care of the work themselves. Dinah was starting to see what everyone meant by David's stubbornness. Although he was limping and in pain, he still tried to get out the door until *Aenti* Judith had raised her voice, something she rarely did. That had gotten David's attention, and he'd started back to his bedroom, muttering to himself that he didn't need to be coddled like a child.

"Then stop acting like one," *Aenti* Judith had said as she followed him out of the kitchen.

Dinah couldn't help but chuckle. David couldn't be more different from *Aenti* Judith's first husband, Samuel. Dinah had always thought they were a good match. But she could see David and *Aenti* Judith were too.

She glanced at Amos. He was also smiling. "I-is it t-time t-to s-start—"

But before she could finish, he opened the back door and left.

She stood there for a moment, expecting to feel dismissed by his abruptness. Or at least a little put out. She felt neither, knowing he wasn't being rude on purpose. And he had answered her question. Clearly he was ready to start working.

Now she could see why. "We have a big field," he said.

Dinah stared at it again. It wasn't wide, but it was long. Very long. Before her stretched acres of hay grass. Amos had overestimated how much work he had accomplished yesterday. She was starting to understand David's concern. But she was also determined to get as much work done as she could.

She looked up at Amos. "W-we better get started, *y-ya?* Y-you'll have to show m-me what t-to d-do."

His brow lifted. "Like a teacher?"

"Exactly like a t-teacher."

"I've never been a teacher before." A small smile curled his lips, and he seemed pleased with the comparison. "First I have to hitch up Penny and Nickel."

Dinah waited while he brought the horses from the barn. He quickly hitched them to the hay mower, then turned to Dinah. "They are *gut* workers."

"They look like fine h-horses."

"I like to give them treats." He stroked one horse's long nose. "They like treats." He picked up a long rake that was lying on the ground. "I forgot to put this up last night." He frowned and handed the rake to Dinah.

She studied the rake in her hand. It was taller than she was. "What do I d-do?"

"Use the rake. Like this." He took the tool from her and started to untangle a pile of hay. "Spread the hay." He spread out the hay in a flat row the width of the field. When he was finished, he was at the opposite side of the field. He brought the rake back and handed it to her. "*Yer* turn."

She took the rake and started to stab at the next hay pile.

"That's not right."

His words stopped her, but his voice was calm and kind. He definitely liked to get to the point.

"I used to do it like that. *Daed* said it was the wrong way. He said . . ." Amos frowned, his eyes moving the way they did when he was thinking. "He said to be gentle. *Ya*, be gentle."

To her surprise he moved behind her, put his hands over hers, and showed her how.

Chapter Six

Dinah's skin tingled at the touch of Amos's hands over hers. She tried to focus on their movements and what he was showing her. Spreading hay was a simple task, and all he'd had to do was tell her to spread it with less force and she would have understood. But she liked his way of showing her a lot better.

"See?" He spoke above her ear. The top of her head reached just below his chin, and he was bending over slightly. The sweet scent of hay, the warmth of the morning sun, the cows lowing from a field far away, and the birds singing their lovely songs . . . all while Amos almost had her in an embrace as they spread the hay. She couldn't think of a better place to be.

"Try it by yourself." He released her hands and moved away.

She couldn't help being disappointed when he stepped away, and a stab of guilt passed through her. She remembered what Anna Mae had said about Amos having difficulty with social situations. He probably didn't think there was anything unusual being this close to her. Yet she was sure his father wouldn't appreciate seeing them together like this. He might even think Dinah was taking advantage of him, or that Amos was doing something wrong. Which he wasn't, of course. For Amos, everything was innocent. She'd have to remember that and keep her own thoughts from making something as mundane as raking hay into a romantic moment.

A few moments later she was spreading hay with ease. When she finished the row, Amos jogged toward her. "*Gut* job," he said, grinning.

"You're a *gut* t-teacher." Dinah beamed at him, enjoying the way his smile widened at her compliment.

"I am?"

"Definitely."

His chest puffed out a bit and she hid a chuckle. She'd never had so much fun complimenting someone before.

"Okay. You finish the piles. I'll cut the hay. Then we can have lunch. I'm getting hungry."

Breakfast had been less than an hour ago. And it had been a big one too. Before David and Amos had woken up, Dinah and *Aenti* Judith made a huge spread—pancakes, bacon, sausage, eggs, bread, butter, jam, and even banana muffins. Dinah had been stuffed by the time she was finished cleaning her plate, but Amos had filled his plate again. "We just ate."

"I know," he said with complete seriousness. Then he turned and went back to the hay mower.

She smiled and shook her head. Before long the whirl of the mower drowned out the birds and cows. As she usually did when she tackled a task, she focused her concentration. By the time the sun was straight above her in the sky she was thirsty and sweating, and she had raked several rows of cut hay. Although there was much more work to be done, she was satisfied with her progress.

The hay mower stopped and she turned to see Amos unhitch

the team. He led them toward her, then looked at the work she'd accomplished. "You did a lot," he said. "*Daed* will be glad."

She glanced away, but his plain-spoken compliment had warmed her more than the bright sun. "Are you r-ready for lunch?" she asked, even though she knew he was.

He rubbed his flat stomach. "*Ya.* I have to put Penny and Nickel to pasture. Will you wait for me?"

Did he really think she would walk into his house without him? That she even wanted to? She nodded. "Of course I will, Amos."

After he took care of Penny and Nickel, she and Amos walked together into the house, both of them covered in perspiration from the exertion and the heat of the day. As Amos put his hat on a peg near the back door, Dinah heard his stomach growl. "You *are* h-hungry," she whispered to him.

"*Ya.* I'm always hungry."

"I made plenty for lunch, Amos," *Aenti* Judith said as she set down a plate of deviled eggs among the rest of the food. Dinah and Amos took turns washing their hands at the sink. Dinah was about to sit down when David arrived, limping.

"I told you I would bring you *yer* lunch," *Aenti* Judith admonished.

"I can eat here." He scowled as he took his seat at the head of the table. Dinah was struck by the resemblance between him and Amos. David's hair was streaked with silver and his beard, which was short and looked like it was still growing in, was completely gray. He was lean like Jeremiah, but Amos had his facial features—the square jaw and slightly sloped nose. She imagined that when David was younger he'd been as handsome as his sons. Right now he looked grouchy and intimidating.

But her aunt didn't back down. "Scowl at me all you want, David Mullet, but I'm going to make sure you heal properly."

He looked at her, still frowning, but there was a softness in his eyes. Love. He loved her aunt, and from the way she gazed at him, that love was returned just as deeply.

After prayer Amos grabbed the platter of deviled eggs. He was about to put one on his plate when he looked at her. "Would you like one, Dinah?"

She saw David and Judith exchange a puzzled glance, as if they were surprised he'd thought of her first. "Y-ya," she said, not even able to say a proper thank-you. David was making her nervous. She took an egg from the plate, then Amos took two and set them on his dish.

When everyone had the food they wanted, they began to eat. "Amos," David said, taking a swig from his glass of tea. "Getting that field mowed?"

"Ya," Amos said over a mouthful of food. He wiped his mouth with the back of his hand, only to stop halfway and pick up the napkin next to his plate. He finished cleaning his mouth. "I'll be almost done by tonight."

"Almost?"

"There's a lot of hay."

"I know exactly how much hay there is, Amos. That's why you need help."

"Dinah Keim is helping me. She did a *gut* job this morning."

David looked at Dinah, his stern features relaxing a bit. "I, uh, appreciate it."

She nodded, too intimidated to respond. She was also getting angry. Amos was working hard. David should acknowledge that instead of berating him.

He turned back to Amos. "After you finish eating you need to rake the hay and spread it."

"Okay."

"Don't tarry. You know the hay has to dry on the top before you rake it into a stack."

"*Ya, Daed.* I know."

"What about the animals? They get fed?"

"*Ya.*" Amos's good-natured expression disappeared. "I always feed them."

"Sometimes you forget."

Amos kept his head down as David continued to talk. "Can't let anything happen to the pigs, so make sure they get enough feed. Did you collect the eggs this morning?"

"David," *Aenti* Judith said, her soft voice holding a bit of an edge. "I get the eggs, remember?"

"Oh." He glanced down at his plate. "That's right. Reminding Amos is a force of habit. He doesn't remember very much."

Dinah met Amos's gaze. It hurt her heart to see the shame and defeat in his eyes. Amos had nothing to be ashamed of. His father, on the other hand, was a different story. She couldn't believe he was talking to Amos as though his son was stupid.

Suddenly Amos pushed his half-eaten plate away, stood, and walked out of the kitchen without saying a word.

"A-Amos, w-wait." Dinah pushed away from the table.

"Dinah," her aunt said. "Maybe you should give him some time alone."

"I-I c-can't." Dinah couldn't help but look at David. His grayish-brown eyebrows flattened above his eyes with disapproval. Of her or Amos, she had no idea. And she didn't care. She lifted her chin and spoke directly to him. "L-like y-you s-said, there's w-work t-to do." She stormed out of the kitchen, clenching her teeth. No one should feel belittled by family. Especially someone as wonderful as Amos.

⁓⸜⸍⁓

Amos stomped to the field, feeling anger growing inside his chest. His face was hot and not only from the sun beating on top of his head. He frowned. He'd forgotten his hat. *Daed* was right about him being forgetful. That just made Amos angrier.

"Amos!"

Dinah's voice brought him to a stop. Why did *Daed* have to treat him like a stupid little kid in front of Dinah? *She probably thinks I'm stupid too.* But it was the truth. He was dumb. He could barely read. He laughed at the wrong times. He was a messy eater. He didn't know how to talk the right way to girls—or to anyone else.

"Amos?" Dinah came up beside him. She sounded like she needed more air, the way he did after he'd been running for a while. "Here."

He looked down and saw his hat in her hand. He snatched it from her, then felt bad. He wasn't mad at her. He was ashamed . . . ashamed of who he was. "I'm sorry."

"For what?"

Amos looked out over the freshly mowed hayfield. There was still a lot of hay to mow. He might not be able to mow all of it like he'd told *Daed*. That would make *Daed* mad all over again. "For being me."

Dinah stood in front of him. Her light brown brows looked like two arches above her pretty eyes. "You have *nix* to be sorry for, so stop apologizing."

He couldn't look at her. "I wish I was normal," he whispered. He'd never admitted that out loud before.

"You're exactly how God made you." Dinah moved a step closer to him. "But I know what you mean. I wish I didn't stutter."

"You're not stuttering now."

Her eyes grew big. "*Nee* . . . I'm not. But I think that's because I'm with you. I feel safe when we're together, Amos. I don't have to worry that you'll make fun of me."

"I would *never* make fun of you."

"I know. And that's why I like you."

The tops of her cheeks turned pink. He really wished he could draw her portrait. He studied her. He knew she would be leaving in two weeks and he wanted to remember. Her sunny smile. Her warm face. The bright blue sky behind her. His anger disappeared. "You make me feel *gut*, Dinah Keim. *Very gut*." He stared at her and she stared back. He could see sparks of light in her eyes. He wanted to draw those too.

She didn't say anything. His stomach turned. He'd said the wrong thing again.

Then she looked up at him with a smile. "You make me feel *gut* too, Amos." Then she backed away. "We should get to work, *ya*?"

She was right. *Daed* would be mad if he saw Amos talking instead of working. He watched her pick up the hayfork. He would draw her tonight, he decided. And he knew exactly where to put her portrait.

Chapter Seven

Dinah spent the rest of the afternoon raking hay. Jeremiah and Anna Mae had been right—it was a lot of work. Amos continued to mow the hay while she was still getting the hang of how to make a loose roll that also stuck together. She was getting tired. She was also thinking about Amos. She'd been surprised by what he'd said, and she was more surprised that she admitted her own feelings. But then again, why wouldn't she like Amos? He was so easy to like.

What she didn't understand was why he liked her.

She finished one more roll of hay as the sun started to set. They had put in more than a full day. Her back hurt. Her whole body was damp with perspiration. Her arms ached from the repetitive motion of moving the hay rake. When she was done, she leaned on the rake. She should probably help *Aenti* Judith with supper since they were eating late tonight, but right now all she wanted to do was rest for a minute.

"You're tired, Dinah Keim. You need to *geh* inside."

"I can wait for you."

He took the hay rake from her. "I'll be finished in a little while."

She didn't argue and went back to the house. When she went

inside, *Aenti* Judith was making supper. David wasn't in the kitchen and Dinah was relieved. She was too tired to face him right now.

"Dinah," her aunt said, "*geh* upstairs and take a shower."

"I-I c-can h-help w-with s-supper." Her stutter always worsened when she was tired.

"It's almost done. *Geh* on," she said, ushering Dinah out of the kitchen. "A shower will help those sore muscles."

Her aunt was right. Dinah took a long, hot shower—probably longer than she should have. But the water had felt so good. She was still tired, but she wasn't as sore. She dressed quickly, combed and pinned up her damp hair, and put on a light yellow kerchief before going downstairs for supper.

Amos and David weren't in the kitchen, and Dinah saw that they had eaten already. "I took too long," she lamented.

"*Nee* worries. You've had a busy couple of days. We all have. I saved a plate for you." Her aunt gestured to a foil-covered plate on the table among the other dishes.

When Dinah sat down to eat, she noticed her aunt didn't get up to clear the table. She looked tired, and Dinah could see the toll David's injury had taken on her. "I'll clean up after I'm finished," Dinah said.

"Nonsense. I just need a few minutes of rest. You're our guest and you've been working harder than me."

Dinah knew she hadn't, but she didn't argue. She was hungry and she dug into the food, not caring that it was slightly cold.

"You're different."

Looking up from her plate, Dinah met her aunt's eyes. "What?"

"You have been since you arrived. First you stitch up David's leg like you've been doing it all *yer* life, and then you stand up to him." *Aenti* Judith smiled. "I like the new sense of confidence."

Dinah brushed a few crumbs off the table. "I'm not sure where it's c-coming f-from."

"That's because you don't give *yerself* enough credit."

It was just like her aunt to be so supportive, but Dinah couldn't take the compliment seriously. "I'm sorry if I-I was rude to D-David."

"I know. And believe it or not, he understands. David's not usually like this. He's worried about the crops. He and Amos have always worked the harvest together." Judith glanced at the top of the table. "He has trouble seeing Amos as an adult."

Dinah took a bite of the cooked, buttered cabbage, silently agreeing.

"Once David's leg heals up enough for him to work, he won't be so crabby. He doesn't like to sit still. He's always worked hard, and he's always had a heavy burden on his shoulders."

"Amos isn't a burden."

Aenti Judith shook her head. "*Nee*, not Amos. Although at times they have a complicated relationship." She sighed. "I need you to know that David is a *gut mann*. He loves his sons very much. He sometimes has a strange way of showing it."

Dinah nodded. Who was she to judge David Mullet? Perhaps that was her aunt's point.

"I'm glad you and Amos are getting along," *Aenti* Judith said. Then she grew serious. "It's *gut* for him to have a friend."

Friends. Somehow her relationship with Amos was becoming more complex than friendship.

"How is *yer mamm*?"

"She's f-fine."

"I wasn't expecting you to respond to *mei* invitation so soon." After a pause she added, "That was *yer mamm*'s decision, *ya*?"

"*Ya*. She said I needed to g-get out m-more. I w-wish she understood that I l-like being a-alone."

"Do you? Or is it just easier?"

Dinah put down her fork. "Both."

"There's *nix* wrong with spending time alone. But you need to be with people too." She squeezed Dinah's hand. "People who enjoy *yer* company. Like me. And like Amos." She let go of Dinah's hand. "As soon as David's back to full strength I'll start harvesting the garden."

"I c-can h-help you with the c-canning."

"I'd like that. It will be nice to have another woman in the kitchen. Plus you and *yer mamm* always make the best tomato sauce. Will you share *yer* recipe with me?"

"Of course." She'd be making tomato sauce after all.

"We have church this Sunday. I'd like to introduce you to our friends. But only if you feel comfortable."

"I'd like to meet th-them," she said, meaning it.

"I better check on David." *Aenti* Judith got up. "I'll be back to do the kitchen."

"*Nee,* I'll get it. I've got a second wind."

"Are you sure?"

"Positive. *Geh* be with David."

Her aunt gave Dinah a grateful look. "And you get plenty of sleep."

Dinah finished her meal, then cleaned up the kitchen. She was wiping off the table when Amos walked in. "Where's Judith?" he asked. "She always cleans the kitchen."

"She's t-tired." Dinah took the damp dishcloth to the sink and shook out the crumbs.

"I'm tired too." But he didn't tell her good night or leave the kitchen.

She hung up the cloth to dry, then turned to him. She

wanted to ask him where he'd been for the last few hours, but she wouldn't pry. "I should *g-geh* upstairs. I h-had some reading I planned to do t-tonight."

"Oh." His tone was wistful.

"Is everything all r-right?" she asked. "Do you need s-something, Amos?"

He met her eyes. "Do you like reading?"

"*Ya*. I like it very much."

He paused, but continued to hold her gaze. "I wish I could read."

Dinah was stunned. "You don't know how to read?"

He shook his head. "I can read a little. But not much."

"What if I taught you to read?"

"You can't. *Mei* teacher couldn't and she was a *gut* teacher. Jeremiah tried and he couldn't do it. Anna Mae tried too."

"But I haven't. I love to read, Amos. Especially poetry. Have you ever read poems?"

"I don't think so."

"Then we can start with those." She was warming up to the idea. How wonderful it would be to share something she loved with him. "We can have lessons after s-supper each night."

"Tomorrow night?"

"*Ya*. We can s-start tomorrow night."

Amos grinned. "*Danki*, Dinah Keim." Then he left.

Dinah smiled as she turned off the battery-powered lamp in the kitchen, then went upstairs. She closed the bedroom door and eagerly opened her book of poems. Which one should she use to teach Amos? The poems were her personal collection and she had read them over and over until she had them memorized. She'd started copying poems when she was fifteen, and now had over three notebooks full. But this volume held her favorites. She flipped through the pages. "Annabel Lee" by Edgar Allan Poe? No. Not only was it a love poem, but it was also sad. The last thing she wanted was for Amos to equate reading with sadness.

The middle of her notebook contained several of Shakespeare's sonnets. She glanced at "Sonnet LIV".

> *O! how much more doth beauty beauteous seem.*
> *By that sweet ornament which truth doth give.*

That wouldn't work either. Too complicated, and she didn't want him to get frustrated.

Then she found the perfect one. "The Autumn" by Elizabeth Barrett Browning:

> *Go, sit upon the lofty hill,*
> *And turn your eyes around,*
> *Where waving woods and waters wild*
> *Do hymn an autumn sound.*
> *The summer sun is faint on them—*
> *The summer flowers depart—*
> *Sit still—as all transform'd to stone,*
> *Except your musing heart.*

He might not understand the meaning of the poem, but the words weren't too challenging or too easy. Afterward she could tell him what the poem meant. They would work on one stanza each night, she decided. Smiling, she closed her notebook, eager for tomorrow night to arrive.

Chapter Eight

A mos was avoiding her.

Sure, they worked together the next few mornings, Amos mowing the hay while she raked it. The hay would need a few days to dry, which meant spreading it out with the hay rakes so it would be exposed to the sun, then raking it back up into hay piles. Fortunately it hadn't rained, so the hay was drying fairly quickly. The green grass was now the color of typical hay, a light brown with green undertones. In the afternoon she picked tomatoes from the garden and helped *Aenti* Judith can. Amos spent the afternoons raking and turning the rest of the hay, then harvesting the corn. She didn't see him until suppertime, and even then he wolfed down his food and then went back outside. She waited for him to return for two nights in a row, but when he didn't, she'd gone upstairs, tired and dejected.

By Saturday morning she and *Aenti* Judith had canned forty jars of tomato sauce. "More than we need," her aunt said. "God has blessed us with enough to share."

But there was more work to be done, and Dinah settled herself on the front porch that afternoon and husked corn, trying not to be irritated with Amos. What was he doing after supper that was so important? Barn chores didn't take that long. Then again, he was a farmer, so maybe there were some chores he had to do that she didn't know about. She wanted to follow him and offer her help. *If he wanted* yer *help, he'd ask for it.*

Maybe it had been a mistake to offer to teach him to read. Maybe he didn't want to learn and had only agreed out of politeness. But that didn't explain why he had initially said he wished he could read.

There was another reason he could be avoiding her. Perhaps he didn't want to spend time with her anymore.

She tried to focus on the corn, but the thought stung. She'd read too much into their friendship. He was a busy farmer, and although David had gotten the go-ahead from Anna Mae to go outside, he still wasn't allowed to do any work. Dinah was sure David was barking out plenty of instructions, though.

For the first time since she'd arrived, she felt a pang of homesickness. She'd accomplished what her mother wanted her to do. She'd spent time with other people. Tomorrow she would actually be meeting strangers at church. She'd had fun canning tomato sauce and Chow Chow with her aunt. But now that David was on his feet, Amos didn't need her anymore.

Neither did anyone else here. She yanked on the tough corn husk. She wanted to go home. She wanted the sanctuary of her room, the comfort of her pets. Her mother said she could change her ticket. *Extend her trip* were the exact words, but Dinah didn't see why she couldn't shorten it too. She'd pay the extra money if she had to.

The next morning Dinah woke up early, her stomach a bundle of nerves. Her mouth was already turning dry at the thought of meeting strangers. She'd been truthful when she told her aunt she wanted to meet the people in this community, but that had been when she felt more confident. Now that she would be facing them soon, she wished she hadn't seemed so eager.

She put on her best Sunday dress, a light blue one that she had sewn this past spring. She also took time with her hair, even though no one would see it under her *kapp*. But Amos had seen it. She shivered, remembering the way he touched it. Then she shook her head. She should be thinking about worship, not about Amos.

After she dressed, she went downstairs to get a muffin for breakfast. She froze as she stood in the doorway of the kitchen. Amos was there, drinking milk from a large glass. His black pants, crisp white shirt, and black vest enhanced his good looks. He drained the glass and put it down on the table, then looked up. His hair was neatly combed, the neatest she'd seen it since she'd met him.

He also had a milk mustache.

Despite her nerves, she had the urge to smile. She went to him and handed him a napkin. "Y-you've g-got m-milk o-on y-yer l-lip."

"Oh." His eyes widened and he took the napkin from her. "I'm always doing that." He wiped off the milk. "Did I get it all?"

He didn't. There was one spot right above the right corner of his mouth. Without thinking, she reached up and wiped it away with her thumb. Then she drew back quickly, her face blazing with embarrassment.

"Are you two ready to *geh*?" *Aenti* Judith walked into the kitchen, tying her black bonnet on her head. David was right behind her, still limping, but looking much better than he had when she'd arrived. Last night he'd been talking about helping stack the hay tomorrow, and *Aenti* Judith hadn't protested. Life was getting back to normal for the Mullet family.

Which meant it was time for her to get back to her life in New York. *A lonely life.*

Amos moved away from her and walked out of the kitchen. He didn't look at her while they sat next to each other in David's buggy on the way to church. In fact, he was turned from her, looking outside.

Dinah wanted to jump out and walk back to the Mullets. She'd definitely offended Amos. Maybe he didn't even understand exactly why he didn't want to talk to Dinah or even look at her. But being ignored by him hurt, more than she thought possible.

Aenti Judith had said it was a ten-minute buggy ride to Bekah and Caleb Mullet's house, Amos and Jeremiah's cousins. Finally they pulled into the driveway of a large, beautiful farm, which caused her nerves to go into overdrive. There were two houses on the property, along with several white-fenced corrals, two large barns, and one smaller barn.

"Caleb and his brother, Johnny, own this farm," Judith said as David parked the buggy next to another one, adding to the long line of black buggies already there. "They have both their houses on the property. We'll have church in the smaller barn, but lunch is at Bekah's *haus.*"

Dinah barely heard her aunt's explanation. She saw men and women greeting one another and visiting while younger kids stayed nearby and older kids congregated together. There weren't as many people as she feared, but as Judith and David stepped out of the buggy, she realized the number didn't matter. Whether it was five or fifty new people, she was still anxious. She would still stutter. She would still be judged.

Then she felt Amos's warm hand cover hers. She looked at him, stunned, seeing understanding in his eyes. "It will be okay," he said.

As usual, his words were simple, but filled with deep meaning. A flood of emotion washed over her. His simple reassurance was what she needed to hear. He released her hand. Taking in a deep breath, she exited the buggy.

Aenti Judith was immediately at her side. "There are so many lovely people here," she said. "They will make you feel right at home."

Her aunt was right. While Amos visited with a small group of men who looked about his age, *Aenti* Judith introduced her to several women. She met Bekah Mullet, whose bright eyes and animated way of speaking put Dinah more at ease. Her sister Katherine, who was married to Johnny, Caleb's brother, was a contrast to Bekah—quiet, graceful, with pretty reddish-blond hair and freckles. She also met Laura Thompson, and noticed the thin scars on the woman's face. They didn't detract from her beauty or her confidence.

"N-nice to m-meet y-you," Dinah said, wishing she could be as confident as Laura.

"You are planning to stay for lunch, *ya?*" Laura said. She glanced at Bekah, who was standing next to her. "We'll make sure to point out the pies Bekah made."

Bekah arched her eyebrow. "*Mei* pies aren't that bad." Then she looked from Katherine to Laura and laughed. "Katherine made the pies this time."

"Bekah's famous for her cooking skills," Laura added with a wink. "Her poor cooking skills, that is. We're all surprised Caleb isn't starving to death."

"I'll have you know that while I haven't mastered baking, I make a decent supper." She pointed her thumb at a well-built man who looked to be in his early thirties talking to Amos. "As you can see, *mei* husband is definitely *not* wasting away."

The women burst into laughter. Dinah was a little bewildered that Bekah was taking the teasing so well. Clearly her feelings weren't hurt.

Bekah's laughter faded. "Dinah, I'm a terrible cook. I know it. Caleb knows it. He married me anyway." She grinned and gestured at Laura and Katherine with a tilt of her head. "These two and their husbands never miss a chance to tease me about it."

"That's part of the fun of being *familye*," Katherine said.

"I'm not actually *familye*," Laura added.

Katherine shook her head. "You are *familye*. Not by marriage or blood, but by friendship."

"Which is why you get a pass for teasing me." Bekah let out an exaggerated sigh. "See what I put up with?"

Dinah started to relax and returned the smile. Before she could say anything, people began heading for the barn. "Service is starting," *Aenti* Judith said.

As Dinah tried to focus on the sermon, she thought about her own family. The way her brothers had teased her about being shy and stuttering. How they had made her cry. Her reaction had been so different from Bekah's. What if she hadn't let the teasing get to her? What if she hadn't been so sensitive to it? What if she hadn't hidden away with her books and her poetry, afraid she was going to be made fun of at any moment?

But she wasn't Bekah. She was Dinah. Stuttering wasn't the same as not being able to cook.

She forced herself to focus on the rest of the service. When it was over, she filed out of the barn with the other women. She searched for Amos, but he had disappeared.

"Are you sure it's okay if we stay for lunch?" *Aenti* Judith asked.

She wasn't going to say no. "Sure." She would do what she normally did at large gatherings—observe. Stay in the shadows. Make herself invisible.

It was a beautiful afternoon and Bekah and Caleb had long tables set up in their backyard, along with another table filled with cold food that didn't need to be cooked. Dinah held back while everyone filled their plates, then she took a few pickles, a slice of Swiss cheese, a piece of bread, and a cookie. She avoided the pies, not because she didn't trust them but because her stomach was still upside down. She went to sit by *Aenti* Judith, who was with several other women. David was at the next table with a few of the men. There was no sign of Amos.

Then she found him a few yards away, playing with several of the younger children. The oldest looked no more than seven. They were tossing and kicking a volleyball back and forth. Amos had taken off his vest and his shoes and socks.

"Watch this, Amos!" The oldest boy tossed the volleyball in the air and pounded it with his fist. It flew a few inches before landing with a thud on the ground.

Amos smiled and picked up the ball. "Let's play hot potato!"

The children shouted their agreement and arranged themselves into a circle, Amos towering over them. He bounced the ball back and forth in his hands as if it really were hot, then gently tossed it to the child next to him. They continued to move the ball around the circle until it came back to Amos. "Oh *nee!*" he said, juggling the ball in his hands. "It's so hot!" Then he dropped the ball and collapsed on the grass. The boys ran over and piled on top of him.

Dinah started to laugh. Amos playing with the children was the most charming thing she'd ever seen. They loved him, she could tell. "Let's do it again," Amos said, squirming from underneath the kids and jumping to his feet.

"Amos!" David shouted. "That's enough!"

Amos and the children froze, as if they were all in trouble. Then Amos looked at them, crouching down as he spoke. "I have to mind *mei daed*. Just like you have to mind *yer daeds*."

The children nodded solemnly and dispersed. Amos put on his shoes, socks, and vest, then went to his father's table and sat down, not saying a word.

Aenti Judith remained silent, but she did give David a pointed look. The rest of the women and men had picked up their previous conversation as if nothing happened.

David looked at Judith. "He was behaving like a little *kinn*."

"He was behaving like a father," Dinah said, furious that Amos was humiliated like that. "A father playing with his *kinner*."

That brought another round of silence, a frown from both David and *Aenti* Judith, and no response from Amos. Oh *nee*. She'd overstepped her bounds this time. "E-excuse m-me," she said and fled from the table. She went to David's buggy and hid behind it, burying her face in her hands. She embarrassed not only herself, but *Aenti* Judith and David, and most of all, Amos.

As tears welled in her eyes, she heard the sound of footsteps approaching. Figuring it was Judith either coming to chastise her or see if she was okay, she wiped away the one tear that had escaped. She turned around and stilled.

Amos could tell Dinah had been crying. Not a lot, but he saw how wet her eyes were. That made him feel worse than he had when she had run from the table. This was his fault. If he hadn't been playing with Caleb and Johnny's sons and a couple of other boys, his father wouldn't have said anything and Dinah wouldn't be upset right now. He loved his little cousins and enjoyed playing games with them. This was the first time his father had said anything, and Amos hadn't realized he'd been acting like a child when he was playing with them. He thought they were all having fun. Once again, he was wrong.

"A-Amos, I'm so s-sorry." Dinah went to him. "I-I d-didn't mean to embarrass y-you."

"I'm not embarrassed." At least not by what she said.

"I shouldn't have . . . I-I d-didn't w-w-want t-t-t-to . . ."

Shaking his head, he went to her. She was fighting to speak. She didn't have to do that around him. He put his hands on her shoulders, not understanding why he did it, but knowing he needed to touch her, to let her know he wasn't upset with her. "Dinah."

She took in a big breath, like he did right before he put his head underwater when he went swimming. "I-I'm g-going t-to g-*geh* back to N-New Y-York."

Chapter Nine

Dinah felt Amos's hands tighten on her shoulders. The movement wasn't painful, but it did get her attention. She looked up at him, seeing his expression change to panicked confusion. He seemed genuinely upset. "Why are you leaving?" he asked.

"I-it's t-time f-for m-me t-to *geh* home."

"But you have another week here."

He'd kept track of her visit? She tried not to think about how good Amos's touch felt. How right it felt. "Y-you are v-very busy. D-David is b-better, and y-you need t-to finish th-the harvest."

"Aren't you going to help?" His brow furrowed. "You said you were going to teach me to read."

"You still want to learn?" she said, her surprise causing her to forget about her nerves and her stammer.

"*Ya.*"

"I-I thought you changed *y-yer* mind."

"Why would I do that?"

"Because every n-night you've left r-right after supper."

"I know."

She waited for him to elaborate. Then she realized she needed to be specific with him. "You've been busy, *ya*?"

284

"*Ya.* Very busy. But I finished what I was doing. It took longer than I thought. So now I'm ready to learn to read." He paused. "Why are you running away?"

"I-I'm n-not r-running . . ." But wasn't that exactly what she was doing? Running away because she was uncomfortable. Because she was embarrassed. Because she'd been afraid that Amos didn't feel the same way she did. At the first sign of difficulty she did what she always had—she fled.

He shook his head. "You can't *geh*. Everyone leaves me. Jeremiah left." He paused. "Jeremiah also came back. But *Mamm* left and didn't come back. I don't want you to do that. Please, Dinah Keim. I want you to stay."

Her heart squeezed in her chest as she saw the pleading in his eyes. He wasn't trying to guilt her into changing her mind. He was telling the truth. And because of her selfish fear, she would be another person who hurt him. She couldn't bear that.

And if he could be honest with her, she had to be honest with him. "I-I w-want . . ." She cleared her throat and tried again. *This is Amos, remember?* "I want to stay. But that will be hard because I like you so much."

"I like you too."

She shook her head. "Amos, I'm not talking about being friends."

He tilted his head to the side. "I'm not talking about being friends either."

It amazed her how he did this, going from sounding like a sweet, innocent guy to a strong, determined man. But she knew she had to be clear. She had to make him understand how she truly felt. "I like you like a girl likes a boyfriend. A *mann* she wants to date."

"You like me like Anna Mae likes Jeremiah?"

Biting her bottom lip, she nodded.

He grinned. "Then everything is okay, because I like you like Jeremiah likes Anna Mae."

"Dinah? Amos?"

Amos dropped his hands from her shoulders at the sound of Judith calling their names. He peered into her eyes, his gaze intense. "You're staying."

"*Ya,*" she whispered, locked into place by what she saw in his eyes, what she felt from the tone of his words. It wasn't a request, or even a demand. It was a fact. "I'm staying."

"There you are." *Aenti* Judith looked from Dinah to Amos. Her forehead creased so slightly that Dinah almost didn't catch it. "Are you ready to *geh* home?"

"*Ya,*" Amos said. "We're ready."

No one said anything on the ride home. David tucked his chin and stared straight ahead as he guided the horse and buggy. *Aenti* Judith remained silent. Amos looked out the side of the buggy, much like he had when they had driven to Bekah's this morning.

Dinah placed her hand on the space between her and Amos, her mind whirring. Amos liked her. Knowing that made her feel like she was tucked in a warm cocoon. They had feelings for each other. But what did that mean?

She also had to figure out how to apologize to David. She didn't regret what she said, yet she shouldn't have made a public outburst. But even that couldn't diminish the peace she felt.

Feeling a light brush against her hand, she looked down. She smiled as Amos linked her pinky finger with his.

After a cold supper, Amos told Dinah to meet him out in the barn. Dinah hesitated. *Aenti* Judith and David were in the living room napping. After what she and Amos had admitted to each other, she didn't think it would be a good idea to be alone with him. It wasn't that she didn't trust him. She wasn't sure she trusted herself.

He stood in the kitchen, waiting for her to answer. Then she remembered the reading lessons. She needed to focus on something other than being alone with him. "I need to run upstairs," she said. "Will you wait for me?"

"*Ya.* I will wait for you, Dinah Keim."

Dinah hurried upstairs, grabbed her poetry notebook, then ran downstairs, slowing her steps near the bottom when she saw *Aenti* Judith shift in her chair. David was snoring on the couch. She softened her footsteps and crept to the kitchen. Amos was already holding the back door open for her and they went outside.

She followed him to the barn, stopping when he did before walking in. He turned to her. "This is a secret. No one knows about this except *mei familye.* You can't tell anyone, okay?"

"I promise I won't." She couldn't imagine what he was going to show her that could be so secret. She also couldn't imagine Amos having a secret David would be willing to keep. But when she stepped inside, she understood.

"Oh, Amos." She looked around the barn. Amos was lighting the lanterns that hung on the wall. As he lit each one, light shone on magnificent artwork. She nearly dropped her notebook as she looked at the variety of drawings—livestock, family members, the hayfield, a golden sunset, a lavender sunrise . . . the stunning creations were everywhere.

Amos blew out the long match he'd used to light the lanterns and turned to her. "Do you like it?"

"I—" She wasn't stuttering. She was speechless. "You drew all of these?"

"*Ya.*" He went to her and took her hand. He held it as he took her around the barn, telling her about the drawings, speaking with the surety of an artist who was a master at his craft.

Then he took her to the corner of the barn. "This is *mei* favorite."

Her eyes widened as she knelt in front of the two portraits. One was clearly her. A better, prettier version of her. *Is this how he sees me?* Next to her much-improved face was another woman a little older than Dinah. She looked at the portrait . . . and saw Amos's eyes. "*Yer mamm,*" she said.

"*Ya.*" He crouched beside her. "Jeremiah and I drew it after she died."

Tears pooled in Dinah's eyes. "She's beautiful."

"She's pretty," Amos said. He ran his fingers over Dinah's portrait, touching the top of her cheek. "You're beautiful."

Now how was she supposed to focus on reading after that? She wiped her eyes and stood. "*Danki,* Amos."

He rose and faced her. "That's what I was busy doing. Drawing you. I wanted the picture to be perfect. Like you are."

"I'm not perfect, Amos."

"You are to me."

Her heart drank in his compliments. Pride was discouraged in their faith. But were they being prideful? Or was Amos being honest? She knew he wasn't stroking her ego or giving her empty flattery. This was how he saw her. *Perfect.*

Knowing she needed to start the reading lesson before she

lost all reason, she moved away from the portrait. She saw a square hay bale on the opposite side of the barn against the wall. That would be a good place for them to sit. She walked over there, hearing Amos behind her. She sat down on the hay bale, and he sat down next to her. Close quarters, but not as close as they had been moments before. She blew out a breath and opened her notebook. "This poem is called 'The Autumn.'" She pointed to the word *autumn*, thinking it would be tricky for him. "The *n* is silent."

"Why?"

She chuckled. "Because English is a strange language. It helps not to think about it too much. Just try to remember what the words look and sound like."

"Okay." He reached over and touched the word. "Autumn."

"*The* is the word in front of it."

"The Autumn."

"Right."

He grinned. "It's almost autumn now."

They worked through the first stanza of the poem. Dinah thought Amos did rather well, even though he was slow and she had to remind him about certain words when he repeated reading the stanza. By the time they went through it a third time, he read almost every word.

"*Sehr gut*, Amos!" Dinah's heart swelled at the happy excitement in his eyes. "Now I'll explain what the verse is about."

"I already know. It's about autumn." When Dinah was about to interrupt him, he continued. "It's about taking time to notice the change in nature. Like when the color of the grass fades to a light green and the oak tree leaves look like they're on fire."

Dinah's mouth dropped open. "*Ya.* That's what the whole

poem is about." Well, some of it. She didn't want to get into the other verses, which were a metaphor for the changing seasons of life.

"Reading was a lot harder when I was in school."

"Sometimes things become easier when we get older," Dinah said. "And sometimes things just click."

"Click?"

The man understood poetry but not an idiom. *Amos, you are full of surprises.* "Like when you hitch the horses to the hay mower. When you hear the clicking sound, you know it's in place and working."

"So my brain is working now?"

"*Yer* brain is always working." She was out of her depth. She wasn't a teacher. Maybe she should have started with something simpler. Like *roses are red, violets are blue.* But she didn't want to insult him. Amos was anything but a simple man.

He took the notebook from her and looked through it. She didn't mind. "You wrote all these words?" he asked.

"I copied them from other books."

Amos continued to turn pages. "Is it wrong to do that?"

"Only if I sell them." At his frown she said, "It's okay since I'm the only one who reads this notebook."

"I'm reading it." He barely glanced at the words as he went through the notebook. He stopped at one page. Studied it for a minute. Then handed the notebook back to her. "Will you read this one to me?"

She read the title. *Oh nee.* "Are you sure?"

"*Ya.*" He stretched out his long legs and clasped his hands loosely together. "I want to hear that one."

Dinah took a deep breath and began to read.

How do I love thee? Let me count the ways.
I love thee to the depth and breadth and height
My soul can reach, when feeling out of sight
For the ends of Being and ideal Grace.

She cleared her throat. "Do you want me to keep reading?"
He was staring down at his lap as he nodded.

I love thee to the level of everyday's
Most quiet need, by sun and candlelight.
I love thee freely, as men strive for Right;
I love thee purely, as they turn from Praise.

She swallowed and finished the rest of the poem.

In my old griefs, and with my childhood's faith.
I love thee with a love I seemed to lose
With my lost saints,—I love thee with the breath,
Smiles, tears, of all my life!—and, if God choose,
I shall but love thee better after death.

Dinah closed the notebook and shut her eyes. Amos had chosen her favorite poem and she hadn't fumbled a single word. She remembered the day her brother Job had caught her reading this poem out loud in her room. She had been fourteen and had been reading to her pillow, which was embarrassing enough. She had also been reading with as much earnest emotion as a young teenage girl could muster. She couldn't remember if she'd even stuttered.

Just as she'd finished reading the third line, Job burst into her room, laughing hysterically. She threw the poetry book at him—this was before she had started writing them down—but he ducked and said, "*Yer* fault for not closing *yer* door." He put his hand over his chest. "'How do I love thee?'" he said in a falsetto. "'Let me count the ways.'"

At that point she'd jumped off the bed and slammed the door in his seventeen-year-old face. The experience had been mortifying and she hadn't read a poem out loud since.

"That was nice." Amos turned to her. "The words are pretty."

"They are." She pressed the notebook against her chest, and neither of them said anything for a while. She looked around at the drawings again, softly lit in the low lantern light. Anna Mae had said Amos was gifted, and now Dinah knew what his most precious gift was. He had the gift of seeing beauty in everything. Not only with his eyes, but also with his heart.

She turned to him. He was so close to her, his handsome face inches from hers. When it came to Amos, she couldn't think straight. That's why she leaned forward and kissed him.

His lips didn't move. They stayed on hers like they were frozen. She'd never kissed anyone before, and she wasn't sure what to do. But this didn't seem normal. Her eyes opened, and she saw him staring at her with surprise.

He lifted his mouth from hers, and her heart sank. He hadn't understood her feelings after all. This was her first kiss and it was awkward and emotionless.

Then his gaze darkened. His hair, tamed for church that morning, was now back to an unruly, thick mass. "Was that a kiss, Dinah?"

"*Ya.*" She could barely get the word out.

"I . . . liked it." A smile spread across his face. "Can we do it again?"

She laughed, her doubts dispelled once and for all. They would figure this out together. She nodded and lifted her face to his.

This time his lips lightly touched hers, pulled away, then touched hers again with such sweetness she thought her heart would burst.

~~~~~

The next morning after breakfast Dinah went to the phone shanty and called her mother.

"Dinah?" *Mamm* said, a note of concern in her voice. "Is everything all right?"

"*Ya.*" Dinah smiled and touched the dial of the rotary phone.

She heard her *mamm* sigh with relief. "I thought you were calling to tell me you were coming home early."

"Actually . . . I-I'm c-calling to t-tell you I-I'm s-staying a l-little longer."

"That's wonderful news. Then you're having a *gut* time with *yer aenti?*"

"I am." She went on to explain about David's accident and how she was helping with the harvest. "So I thought I-I'd s-stay a f-few more weeks, if that's o-okay."

"Weeks?" Her mother paused. "Are you sure?"

"Very sure, *Mamm.*"

"Then stay as long as you need to. I'll miss you, of course."

"I'll miss y-you too."

"Dinah . . . you sound happy."

"I am," she said. "I'm very happy."

Chapter Ten

For the next month Dinah helped the Mullets with the harvest. She and Amos spent their evenings together reading, and Amos even showed her how to draw. But she was terrible at it. She and *Aenti* Judith had canned enough vegetables to fill three pantries, and her aunt had shared the bounty with several families at church. Dinah had become more comfortable at church services, and had even gone to Bekah Mullet's house a few times to visit.

When October rolled over into November and the harvest was finished, Dinah realized she didn't want to leave Middlefield, her aunt and uncle—and especially Amos. She had fallen in love with him. For the past week they had worked on his handwriting so he wouldn't have difficulty writing her letters when she returned to New York. But what would happen to their relationship then? She could come visit more often, of course, but it wasn't the same as being here with the family she had grown so close to.

One evening she and Amos were in the barn. They were supposed to be working on more letter writing, but Amos had something else in mind. They were sitting close to each other on the hay bale. The weather had turned cold at night, and even though the barn was warmer than the outside air, Dinah was still a little chilly in her light jacket. She hadn't packed a coat. She hadn't planned to be here this long.

Amos put his arm around her and drew her next to him. "Better?"

"Better." She snuggled against his shirt, which smelled of firewood smoke, hay, and Amos. He rubbed his hand over her shoulder and she glanced up at him. He was staring straight ahead, as if deep in thought. He did this sometimes, and usually when he turned his attention back to her he didn't seem to realize he had mentally left. This time when he looked down at her, he appeared fully present. And when he kissed her, she knew something had changed. His kiss was deep, loving, and full of promise.

When they stopped kissing, he touched her cheek. "I had a dream last night, Dinah. I had a dream that we were married."

Her breath caught.

"Do you think we could be married? Like Jeremiah and Anna Mae?"

Dinah put her hand over her pounding heart. Then she settled her pulse. "Amos, do you know what it means to be m-married?"

"I know you live together. Like Jeremiah and Anna Mae. Like *mei daed* and *yer aenti*."

"And what about . . ." She swallowed. Oh, this was hard. She tried not to blush, but she couldn't help herself. "What about *kinner*?"

He thought for a moment, rubbing his chin. "We should have some."

She laughed and realized that she didn't want to live her life without this man. She'd have to explain some things to him—okay, a lot of things—but that didn't matter. All the important things did. Their faith, their ease with each other, how right things felt between them. That's what mattered. "Amos, I need to know one thing."

"*Ya?*"

"Do you l-love me?"

Without hesitation he took her hand in his. "*Ya.* I love you, Dinah. I think *mei* dream was a promise from God. A promise that we will be together forever."

"Then *ya*, Amos. I will marry you."

He grinned. "Okay."

She threw her arms around his neck and hugged him tight.

Dinah took Amos's hand as they stood in the backyard.

"I'm worried," he said, looking at Dinah.

She looked up at her husband-to-be. "Don't be worried," she said.

"What if *mei daed* gets mad? What if he doesn't think I'll be a *gut* husband?"

Dinah squeezed Amos's hand. "I know what your father thinks is important to you, and it should be. But I think you will be the perfect husband. That's all that matters."

That brought a smile to Amos's face and he let out a deep breath. "Okay."

Although on the outside she sounded confident, inside butterflies were crashing together in her stomach. Not because she doubted what she felt for Amos, but she did have the same fear he had. What if his father didn't accept her? What if *Aenti* Judith disapproved? She was almost positive her parents and brothers would think this was a terrible idea. But hadn't her *mamm* been eager for Dinah to find someone? She'd said herself that this trip would be good for Dinah. She was right.

And Dinah knew what she felt for Amos was right. It didn't matter that they'd only known each other for a couple of months. They knew their hearts. There would be obstacles ahead, but she was prepared to face them. Amos was worth it.

They walked inside to the kitchen where David was sitting at the table with Judith. They were both sipping hot cups of tea, as if they had been waiting for Dinah and Amos to appear.

"Where have you two been?" David asked. "It's late, Amos."

Dinah could already feel her hackles rise, but Amos didn't seem bothered. "*Ya, Daed*. I know."

David looked up at Amos, his expression contrite. "I'm sorry. Of course you do. Sometimes I forget that you don't need much reminding anymore."

Dinah couldn't believe it. David was apologizing? She remembered what her aunt said about David loving his family. *Loving someone means admitting when you're wrong.* Her mother had told her that. Dinah had been ten and Samson eleven. Samson had poured glue into her shoes when she was asleep. When she stuck her bare feet inside the shoes, her feet got covered in the sticky, thick glue. Instead of telling her mother, she had retaliated by cutting the hems off all Samson's pants legs. Neither of them had thought about the cost of replacing the clothes. Both of them were grounded. And both of them had to apologize.

Loving someone means apologizing when you need to. She hadn't loved Samson that day. Not even close. But she had apologized. She'd also worked extra chores to pay for her brother's new pants, and he had bought her a new pair of shoes.

She swallowed, missing home again. Suddenly she wished her parents were here and her brothers and their wives. That she could announce to everyone that she was getting married, and so they could celebrate with her. Instead she'd have to call her *mamm* and break the news over the phone. Right now they needed to share the news with David and *Aenti* Judith. "W-we . . ." She felt Amos squeeze her hand. "We have something to t-tell you."

"We're getting married," Amos blurted.

Dinah would have preferred to ease into the conversation, but she couldn't help but smile. That was so like Amos to get to the point. She would always know where she stood with him.

Aenti Judith's brows shot up while David's mouth dropped open. "What?" he said, his teacup rattling against the table.

"David," *Aenti* Judith said with calm sternness.

"Did you hear what he just said?" David's brows knit together.

"I heard." *Aenti* Judith looked at Amos and Dinah.

So much for good news. She should have known it would be like this. There would be no celebrating. Even her aunt, who she had thought would be the one person who would unconditionally understand, looked baffled.

"Amos, what have you done?" David gripped the teacup so tightly Dinah thought it would shatter in his hand.

Dinah felt Amos shrink into himself. This time she took his hand and squeezed. She also asked God to put her stammer on hold for a little while. "He hasn't done anything. *We* have decided to get married."

"You've only known each other for a few weeks," *Aenti* Judith said. "You can't possibly be in love in that short period of time."

"Why not?" Amos asked.

The question was asked so earnestly and with such serious-ness that it left everyone in the room speechless.

"Because you don't know what love *is!*" David exclaimed after the long pause. Then he hesitated, looking apologetic again. Dinah gave him credit for at least knowing he hurt his son's feel-ings. "Amos, I know you know what love is," David said. "You know you love Jeremiah, and me, and Anna Mae, and Judith. But you don't know what romantic love means."

"Dinah's been teaching me." Amos lifted his chin.

Aenti Judith's brow nearly lifted to her scalp. "I thought you were teaching him how to read."

Oh, this was going badly. She wished she could converse easily enough to speak clearly. *Lord, help me—help us—make them understand.*

Her aunt let out a breath. "Why don't we all sit down and discuss this calmly."

Leave it to her aunt to be the voice of reason. Dinah sat down, Amos joining her. They were both opposite Judith and David, the large wood table between them. But it might as well have been a chasm separating them.

Aenti Judith folded her hands together, her brow still creased, but at least she seemed willing to listen. "Now, exactly what plans have you two made?"

"Plans to get married." Amos rubbed his large palms on his thighs. "And after we get married we are going to have lots of *kinner.*"

David's face fell into his hands. "This can't be happening," he muttered.

"David." *Aenti* Judith touched his arm. "Let's hear them out."

Dinah said another quick prayer for her stutter to settle.

"Amos is very special to me. He understands me, and I understand him. We have had some talks, and I did tell him what marriage was about. That's how we knew we loved each other."

"Like a husband and wife," Amos added.

"And exactly how are you going to handle a household and *kinner*?" David's gaze pinned both of them. "How will you raise them?"

"Like any other husband and *daed*," Amos said.

Didn't David see that Amos was so much more capable than he gave his son credit for?

"I don't think you two need to be hasty about this," *Aenti* Judith said. "Why don't you take some time and get to know each other better? Then you can revisit this subject at a later date."

"Or never," David grumbled.

Dinah tried not to lose hope. If she couldn't convince her aunt that she and Amos belonged together, how was she going to convince her family?

Amos stood. "We don't have to revisit anything, whatever that means." His square jaw was set with determination. "*Daed*, you're married. Jeremiah is married." He didn't sound like Amos usually did. He sounded sure of himself. Like he completely understood everything. "Why can't I do the same? Why can't I have a wife?" He looked at Dinah. "Why can't I marry the woman I love?"

Judith and David exchanged a look. The kitchen grew silent. Dinah had never been more impressed with Amos than at this moment. If he hadn't shown the kind of man he was with this small speech, she didn't think his father would ever understand.

"Amos," David said, this time his tone subdued. "Why don't you and I *geh* outside and talk? Judith and Dinah can talk alone too."

"I think that's a *gut* idea." *Aenti* Judith rose. "I'll cut some of that coffee cake Dinah made yesterday."

"I'm not hungry," Amos said.

"That's a first." Judith's chuckle disappeared quickly. "Amos. Talk to *yer daed*. We'll be waiting here for you."

—⁂—

Amos didn't want to have this conversation. He'd already said his piece back in the kitchen, and he meant it. He was happy, like his brother and father were. He wasn't stupid. He wasn't incapable. He was different, and for once that was fine by him.

"Amos." *Daed* looked over at him as they stood on the patio. He pulled out a chair. "Have a seat."

"I don't want to sit. I don't want to talk. I want to get married."

His father sat down. "*Mei* leg is bothering me, so do you mind if I sit?"

Amos felt bad. He sat down next to him.

"I think I might have handled this wrong." *Daed* looked at Amos. It was dark outside, but the gas lamplight from the kitchen shone enough light on the patio that Amos could see his father's face. "You surprised me, *sohn*. That's all." He shook his head. "You always surprise me."

"I'm getting married." Amos wasn't going to budge.

"I know that's what you want to do. You've made that clear." He ran his hand over his face. "Now I need to make myself clear. Marriage isn't easy. The love you feel at first, it's special. Exciting. But after a while, when the newness wears off, you're only left with each other."

"Right."

Daed frowned. "What do you mean, 'right'?"

"I don't want to be with anyone else. I want to be with Dinah."

His father didn't say anything, and Amos could tell he was thinking. He was also rubbing his palm across the back of his neck, something he did when he was upset. But for once *Daed* stayed calm. "Amos, you've never been on *yer* own. You don't know what it's like to pay bills, to keep a bank account . . ." He sighed. "You can learn that stuff. What will be the hardest thing for you to learn is how to understand *yer* wife."

Amos frowned. "I understand Dinah."

"You don't know Dinah. She's been here only two months."

"How long did you know *Mamm* before you loved her?"

Daed sat back in his chair. "That's not a *gut* example. *Yer mamm* left. I loved her, but she didn't love me enough to stay."

"Dinah won't leave me." Amos couldn't explain how he knew this was true. He just did. "And I won't leave her."

"Amos . . ." His father's shoulders slumped, and he gave Amos a crooked smile. "Why don't you at least sleep on it?"

"But I sleep on *mei* bed."

"I mean think about it overnight. We can talk again in the morning."

His mind wouldn't be changed by morning. He knew he wouldn't have any trouble falling asleep tonight. And if he was lucky, he would dream about Dinah again.

⁓⁓⁓

"Dinah, this isn't like you." Judith leaned over the table, genuine worry on her face.

Dinah hoped Amos and David's conversation was going better than this one. Her aunt was definitely trying to talk her out of marrying Amos.

"You don't do things impulsively," her aunt continued.

"I-I don't do much of anything."

"And now you want to take care of Amos?"

She crossed her arms over her chest. "*Nee.* I want to m-marry him. That's not the same thing."

"Dinah, Amos is—"

"I k-know how A-Amos i-is! And I love him for it. There's a lot he doesn't know. I understand that. B-but I want to teach him. I w-want us to learn about l-life and each other t-together." Her lower lip trembled. "I've been so sheltered, *Aenti* Judith. By *mei* own choice. Amos has shown me that I don't have to be a-afraid anymore."

Aenti Judith didn't say anything for a long while. Then she touched Dinah's elbow. Dinah unfolded her arms and clasped Judith's hand. "I don't want either of you to get hurt."

"Neither do I. God never p-promised us life would be easy. But it will be easier facing it with Amos."

Her aunt closed her eyes. "What will *yer mutter* say?"

"She's always wanted me to get married."

Aenti Judith looked at her. "That's true. She has." Tears shined in her eyes. "I've prayed for Amos from the moment I met him. That he would be happy. Safe. And loved." She wiped away her tears from beneath her glasses. "I don't know why I was surprised that you want to marry him. You're both special. I can't think of a better woman to be Amos's wife."

Dinah started to cry, and she and Judith hugged each other. Amos and David walked into the kitchen just as the two women were drying their tears on a dish towel. Amos went to Dinah and knelt by her side. "You're crying," he said.

"Happy tears." Dinah smiled. She touched Amos's face. "They're happy tears."

"Does this mean we're getting married?"

She looked at her aunt, who nodded, then at David, who was frowning. Finally, he gave a small nod. Dinah would take it. "*Ya*, Amos," she said, grinning. "We're getting married."

Epilogue

Two months later

Amos yanked on the collar of his white shirt as he stood in the living room. Despite it being January, the room felt hot. Stifling. That was a new word he learned from Dinah last week. He liked that word. Stifling.

Dinah called her *mamm* and told her they were getting married. Then Dinah went back to New York. She was gone for two weeks. That was hard, not seeing her for that long. Then she came back with her belongings, including a cat named Fido. "I couldn't leave him behind." She and Fido now lived in Judith's old house. After today it would be his house too. A wedding present from Judith.

He looked around the room, which was filled with people. Dinah's brothers and their families took up most of the space. He liked her brothers, even though they teased Dinah. But Dinah didn't seem to mind anymore. She barely stuttered in front of people now. Her father and mother had said she had changed, and he was glad. Last night her *daed* had thanked Amos for making his daughter happy.

Amos didn't need to be thanked. He wanted to make Dinah happy. God knew she made him happy. She had taught him so much in the past few months. He was reading a lot better now, and not just poetry, although poetry was his favorite. She helped him learn how to budget money. How to pay bills. He found out that she knew everything there was about running a household. She knew a lot of things, and he wanted to keep learning from her.

He looked at Jeremiah, who was standing next to him. His brother grinned. Both he and Anna Mae had come. Anna Mae was with Judith upstairs, helping Dinah. Jeremiah and Anna Mae had worn their Amish Sunday clothes. Amos didn't know they even had them anymore. He was glad they had decided to dress Amish today.

Jeremiah had talked to him right before bedtime. He had explained to Amos what happens after the wedding. How children came into the world. Amos didn't have the heart to tell him he already knew. Dinah had explained all that to him too.

He heard movement on the top of the stairs, and a few moments later Dinah showed up. She was beautiful. So beautiful. None of the poetry he'd read or artwork he drew could compare with how she looked right now, wearing a dark blue dress, black stockings, and a black bonnet. She smiled, and he stopped breathing. At one time he had wondered if he would ever find love. If he would ever marry. It had seemed impossible. He should have known better. *Nothing is impossible with God.*

He and Dinah proved that.

DISCUSSION QUESTIONS

1. Dinah held some resentment toward her mother for pushing her into doing something uncomfortable—leaving home and visiting her aunt. Sometimes God makes us uncomfortable so we can grow and change. Discuss a time where God wanted you to do something out of your comfort zone.

2. Amos's special gift is his ability to see beauty in everything. What gifts has God given you and how do you share them with others?

3. Dinah's confidence grows as she feels appreciated and accepted by Amos. How does Amos's total acceptance of Dinah mirror God's acceptance of us?

4. Amos wishes he were normal, but Dinah says he's exactly the way God wants him to be. What would you tell Amos?

5. Amos's family underestimates him and are overprotective, but they love him deeply. What lessons did they have to learn from Amos and Dinah's relationship?

6. Do you think Amos and Dinah will have a good and strong marriage? Why? What advice would you give them?

ACKNOWLEDGMENTS

Amos and Dinah's story is extremely significant to me. As a special education teacher I've had the privilege of meeting and working with so many extraordinary students and their parents. They have touched my life and my soul, and I thank them for the many lessons they have taught me over the years. Thank you also to my editors, Becky Monds and Jean Bloom. I keep repeating myself but they are fantastic, and I appreciate their insight and encouragement. A special thank-you to Kelly Long for her critique and support of this story. And as always, thank you readers, for going on another journey with me. Blessings to you all!

ABOUT THE AUTHOR

Kathleen Fuller is the author of several bestselling novels, including *A Man of His Word* and *Treasuring Emma*, as well as a middle-grade Amish series, the Mysteries of Middlefield.

Visit her website at www.kathleenfuller.com.
Twitter: @TheKatJam
Facebook: Kathleen Fuller

Mischief in the Autumn Air

Vannetta Chapman

For Kris Stutzman

GLOSSARY

aenti—aunt

dawdi haus—a smaller dwelling for aging parents, usually connected to an Amish home

danki—thank you

dat—dad, father

Englischer—non-Amish person

freind—friend

Gotte's wille—God's will

gut—good

haus—house

kapp—prayer covering

kinner—children

nein—no

Ordnung—set of rules for Amish living

wunderbaar—wonderful

youngie—teenaged to young adult

ya—yes

The LORD will indeed give what is good, and our land will yield its harvest.
                                    —PSALM 85:12

Come, ye thankful people, come,
Raise the song of harvest home;
All is safely gathered in,
Ere the winter storms begin.
—HENRY ALFORD, "COME, YE THANKFUL PEOPLE, COME," 1844

Prologue

Sugar Creek, Ohio

April

Martha Beiler stared out across her porch and yard, oblivious to the cold rain splashing against the porch rail, wetting her shoes and apron.

"What does it say, Martha? And why are you standing there in the cold? Land sakes, dear. I thought something terrible had happened." Fannie had hurried across the small pasture that separated their two farms. Carrying an umbrella and wearing sensible shoes, she was dryer than Martha. Though twenty-two years older than Martha's forty, they'd long ago become fast friends.

"Let's go inside. You can put on dry clothes while I heat some water for tea."

That's the way things were between them—the other's kitchen felt as familiar as their own. When Fannie tugged on her arm, Martha nodded in agreement, folded the letter, and slipped it back into the envelope. She stopped only to scoop up the barn cat and set it in the basket away from the rain. Twenty

317

minutes later, Martha and Fannie were at the old oak table, hot cups of tea in front of them.

Fannie read the letter again and then passed it back to Martha. "Your *aenti* wants you to come."

"There are conditions."

"Attend church, help around the house, plant a spring garden." Fannie's finger ran down the page. "Oh, and no pets. Well it's not as if you would have taken Bandit with you."

"I suppose whoever buys this place might allow him to live in the barn—he is a good mouser."

"He spends at least half his time on my back porch. You know I will continue to feed him."

Martha nodded, one problem resolved. What of the dozen or so others? How would she ever find the strength to sell all they owned and move two hundred and fifty miles west?

"You're blessed to have family who will provide you a place to live."

"I have a place to live." Martha sipped the tea, though she'd rather have been out walking in the rain, trying to make sense of what her life had become.

"Ack. You have your husband's farm, which should fetch you a goodly amount. You'll be able to pay off the bank loan and have some left over to live on." She tapped the letter that sat between them. "Especially if you stay at your *aenti*'s and accept the job she mentions."

"At an auction house? I know nothing of auctions."

"We have them every year for the school."

"That is different and you know it. The auctions in Shipshewana, they are famous. Tourists come from all around. Life there is nothing like our quiet life here in Sugar Creek, Fannie."

"Perhaps not, but it seems to be where *Gotte* is directing you."

"Do you really think so?" Martha swiped at her hair and pushed the tea aside. Crossing her arms on the table, she leaned forward and studied her best friend. "Do you think I should go?"

"I think that Melvin would like to know that you are taken care of and that you are with family."

"But you're my family." The words were an ache in Martha's heart. How could she leave the life she and Melvin had built together, the only true home she had ever known, and the dear woman sitting across from her?

"I will always be your *freind*." Fannie reached forward and covered Martha's hands with her own. "We can't understand why *Gotte* chose to call Melvin home when He did, or what His intentions are for sending you to Shipshewana. But this?"

She gestured again toward the letter. "This is a blessing for sure and for certain. It will solve all of your financial problems."

Martha nodded, pulled her hands away, and picked up the letter. "But working at the auction? I can't imagine—"

"You've always been *gut* with numbers. Remember when my Stephen couldn't fathom the math in his textbook?"

"We had that Mennonite teacher from Millersburg."

"Who thought he should be able to read his books while the children learned on their own."

Martha smiled for the first time since the mailman had dropped off the letter and changed the course of her life. "Stephen was so worried. He used to rub at his forehead when something troubled him."

"Still does. I'm certain it's why his hair has receded there." Fannie touched the right side of her own forehead, indicating the spot where Stephen's hair had fled. "But my point is that you helped him then and in fact, helped all of my children with their math. I was never good at it, and Leroy certainly didn't have time, what with trying to pull a living from this place.

"We managed though. We've made a *gut* living and a *gut* life." Martha felt as if she could not sustain one more loss. Leaving this woman and her church community would be like leaving a part of herself among the hills and valleys of Sugar Creek.

"That we did." Fannie stood, walked around the table, and pulled Martha to a standing position. "Be strong, dear. *Gotte* has a plan. He always has a plan for His children."

Martha knew that Fannie was right. The problem was that it wasn't a plan she understood or liked. Nonetheless, it would do no good to behave as a child and be pulled from her home kicking and screaming. She could either let it go voluntarily or wait for the bank to kick her out. Best to follow the path her *aenti* was providing. She understood that truth, but she didn't have to like it.

Chapter One

Shipshewana, Indiana

Eighteen months later

Martha stood with a ledger in one hand and a cup of coffee in the other. "Maybe you should call the police."

"Because people were seen inspecting our merchandise?" Eli Wittmer ran a hand along his jaw, something he tended to do when he was aggravated.

At six feet and thin as the coatrack he stood next to, Eli never failed to make Martha feel short and dumpy. She was short, and she tended toward chunky. Neither was Eli's fault, but still she liked him less for it. She realized the feeling was shallow and illogical. When he frowned at her so, she became shallow and illogical. That certainly *was* his fault.

Martha had no doubt that she had once again tried her boss's patience, which was an incredibly easy thing to do.

"Something's not right. I saw them early this morning when I walked through to make sure everything was set up for the opening."

"Our auction barn is open to buyers at seven a.m."

"But they're not supposed to touch the merchandise. They'd pulled out one of the dressers and were inspecting it."

"Buyers often do, in spite of our signs warning them to only look."

"And Joey Davis saw them last night, after we had already left. He came by to tell me about it earlier."

She'd finally caught his attention. Eli pulled off his hat and ran his hand through curls that were still ridiculously chestnut brown with no hint of gray. She'd suspect the man used hair dye if she didn't know him better. Not only was it not allowed by their *Ordnung*, but Eli was too tight with money to spend even a dime on something so superfluous.

"Maybe you're just nervous."

Martha stamped her foot. "I am not nervous. I've worked here long enough to understand—"

"This is the biggest auction we'll have this year. Lots of *Englisch* and Amish . . ."

"They're only people, Eli. More people. I will personally be happy when the Fall Festival is over—"

"Hasn't started yet," he muttered.

"I was only drawing your attention to this particular couple because the situation bothered Joey, and it seemed out of the ordinary to me. You keep your eyes peeled. The man, he is tall like you and wears a ball cap pulled low. The woman was wearing black jeans and a black T-shirt."

"I'll keep a watch for them. Now are you ready?"

Martha downed what remained of the cup of coffee and hurried after her boss. When she'd moved to Shipshewana, she'd expected her life to be different—to be difficult and full of new things and new people. What she hadn't expected was for her boss to be a crotchety old bachelor. She didn't mind the hours spent at the auction house, and she loved doing the books—numbers calmed her and helped her to forget the situation with her *aenti*. Martha was pragmatic about what she'd gained and what she'd lost. There was no turning back, and she'd determined to make the best of things, as Fannie had cautioned her many times since her move.

Hurrying from their office into the auction barn, she was a bit stunned at the size of the crowd. The barn was an eighty-by-two-hundred-foot facility, and today it seemed that every inch was covered with people. The doors at both ends had been opened to allow in the fall breeze. She caught a glimpse of trees, their leaves beginning to turn red and gold and brown. Beyond that was the outdoor flea market—one hundred acres, which boasted everything from fresh produce to hand-sewn quilts to homemade baskets.

"All nine hundred booths are full in the market," Eli said. "Even more people than usual are here because of the Fall Festival. We should fetch *gut* prices for today's items."

She hoped so. Perhaps once they had purchased the items they came for, some of these people would leave. It was entirely too crowded for her taste. Shipshewana itself was a small town—only six hundred residents, half of whom were Amish. During market days, that population often swelled to over thirty-five thousand.

The auction was set to begin at nine o'clock. They had lined up all ten of their auctioneers to work until closing at three. Most days Martha worked in the quiet of the office she and Eli shared, tallying up what each lot had gone for, being sure that each buyer paid for all of their merchandise, reconciling the day's total revenue with the items that had been sold. Once everything balanced, she wrote checks for the folks who had hired Eli to auction their items. The auction house kept between 10 or 15 percent, depending on the contract signed by Eli.

Each auctioneer had a scribe assigned to them—someone who would notate the item, buyer number, and amount of the sale. Today there weren't enough scribes to go around, which was how Martha found herself crossing the crowded floor of the auction barn in Eli's wake. She would be his scribe, which meant they'd be spending the day in each other's company. Her, Eli, and a few thousand visitors.

Though she didn't like the crowds, she couldn't help being affected by the atmosphere—a kind of cross between a carnival, fall outing, and shopping spree. Just on the way in from where she'd parked her buggy, she had passed one booth filled with pumpkins, another selling fresh apple pies, and a third with scarecrows on a stick. The scarecrows were more adorable than scary, and she'd thought about purchasing one for their garden. It was easy for Martha to become caught up in the excitement. Though the auctions ran fifty weeks of the year, this was the last weekend of the flea market.

Folks literally filled every square inch of the barn.

The weather was cool and crisp—a fine fall day.

Martha found herself relaxing as she enjoyed the call of the auctioneer, folks' laughter as they bid, and the occasional whoop of joy when someone purchased an item they'd set their heart on. She had a short break after Eli's noon auction.

Unable to resist the aroma of hamburgers, French fries, and fresh funnel cakes, she hurried to the snack bar. Best to keep her energy up. They still had two hours to go, followed by more work back in the office. Reason enough to purchase the funnel cake along with her burger. She swigged it all down with ice-cold lemonade and made it back to their auction square as Eli raised his hands and announced the opening bid for the items from Charity and Jacob Weaver's homestead.

The Weavers were a sweet elderly couple who lived not far from her *aenti*. Martha had been to their home several times in the last six months. Often she took them food that her *aenti* declared was unfit to eat because it wasn't prepared precisely to her liking. She hated that the Weavers would be moving to the old folks' home in Goshen, but she understood the need. Since Jacob's stroke, times had been hard for Charity.

Eli opened the auction with bids for an antique dresser, and that was when Martha knew that something was very wrong.

Chapter Two

Eli treated all of his auctions the same. His aim was to get the best return for the person selling their prized possessions, and at the same time make it an entertaining and worthwhile experience for the buyers and onlookers. He'd been an auctioneer for twenty-four years—a young man looking for his spot in the world when he first realized he had a talent for it. He'd learned, over those years, to keep a good emotional distance from the items on the auction block.

The one o'clock auction was different, and perhaps that was why he'd been more curt than usual with Martha. The woman was a fine bookkeeper, but she didn't understand the way things were done in Shipshe. She was stubborn and outspoken. For those two reasons alone, she wasn't the best employee he'd ever had. Frankly, she asked too many questions. Then there was her propensity to "brighten up" their office space. He didn't need a coatrack, even if it was made of a beautiful oak and she had purchased it herself. It was as ridiculous as the basket filled with candy, which she kept on her desk for any *kinner* that might wander into the office.

Martha Beiler was unlike anyone Eli had ever met before,

and he wasn't quite sure how to respond to her. So, too often, he responded with words that were abrupt. Like this morning. Plus his mind and heart had been filled with other things—specifically with his one o'clock auction. He'd known Charity and Jacob Weaver all of his life. It hurt his heart to see them suffer with Jacob's deteriorating health. And in spite of how much or how often their Plain community stepped in, the situation was still more than Charity could handle.

Which was why they were moving.

Why they were selling off the items from their home.

Why Eli was standing there, auctioning the items in Lot Number 28 and pointing to an antique dresser that he knew had been made by Jacob.

"Who'll give me two hundred dollars? Two-hundred-dollar bid, now three, now three, will ya give me three?"

He fell easily into the rhythm and cadence of his work. Though other auctioneers continued calling out their lots in various sections of the barn, the crowd around the Weavers' things grew.

"Four, give me four hundred dollars? Going once, going twice . . ." When no one answered, he raised his hand to declare the item sold.

Suddenly a man at the back, tall and wearing a ball cap, shouted, "Five hundred."

The crowd quieted. Occasionally someone would go over the auctioneer's bid—either due to the excitement of the moment or because they were tired of trying to outbid one another. This man had not bid at all until that very moment.

"Sold," Eli declared, glancing at Martha who nodded that she had written down the bid and the buyer's number. Her face was scrunched up in a concerned expression and she was nodding her head to the right as if she had a tic of some sort.

Eli shrugged and moved on to the dining room table. This too was made of northern red oak, as was most of Jacob's furniture. The man had been a fine woodworker, known throughout the state for the quality and simple beauty of his furniture. Eli had auctioned off the final pieces from Jacob's workshop six months ago. All that was left now were the personal items that wouldn't need to be moved to Goshen with Jacob and Charity.

The dining room table included six chairs, which wasn't particularly large, by Amish standards. Jacob and Charity had only had the one son, and he had died when he was but a small lad. The family was well liked, and they often had guests for dinner—he supposed that was why they'd kept it all these years. Eli himself had spent many a dinner with the two at the very table that he was now offering up for bid. Though it bore the scars of many years of use, it was worn to a smooth, beautiful shine.

Because it was a small piece of furniture, he started the bid lower than he normally would.

"One, give me one hundred dollars? One-hundred bid, now two, now two, who will give me two?"

An *Englisch* couple at the back offered two. Eli tried for three but no one was taking.

"Going once, going twice . . ."

This time a woman dressed in black shouted, "Four hundred."

Eli felt a rush of satisfaction. The Weavers needed the money from this auction. He had no idea why folks would be overbidding, but neither would he turn the money down.

Glancing again at Martha, he felt a spike of irritation. She was adamantly shaking her head and gesturing for him to walk over to where she stood. No way was he going to stop in the middle of an auction, especially one that was going so well.

Next he sold two of Charity's quilts, the dishes, and a well-used couch. The pieces went for about what he had expected. Then he stepped over to a sofa table, which was being sold with two end tables. Once again made of northern red oak, they were perhaps the nicest pieces in the lot. He prayed for *Gotte's wille*, even in this, and then he began his call.

"Five, give me five hundred dollars? Five-hundred bid, now six, now six, who will give me seven?" The bid worked its way up to a thousand dollars—a very good price.

Eli tried one more time to raise it a fraction more. "Eleven hundred dollars, give me twelve. Who will give me twelve?"

"Fifteen hundred." It was the tall man at the back again. He hadn't bid since the first piece, but Eli would have known it was him without looking. He'd once again waited almost too late and then jumped the current bid, stunning those around him. An *Englisch* couple shook their heads in disappointment. The price was more than they could or would pay. A furniture dealer Eli was quite familiar with marked the item off his list. It wasn't worth fifteen hundred—both the dealer and Eli knew that.

"Sold, fifteen hundred to the gentleman in the ball cap." And when he said those words, he suddenly remembered Martha and her warnings about a tall man wearing a ball cap and a woman dressed in black. He glanced over at his bookkeeper, who was frowning mightily and noting the sale in her book.

When he looked again toward the back, the gentleman in the ball cap was walking away.

And the woman in black? She was nowhere to be seen.

Chapter Three

M artha somehow made it through the one o'clock auction in spite of the fact that Eli ignored her. It was the last auction he was calling that day, so as soon as it was over, he left to help the other auctioneers. Martha checked her book to make sure she'd noted each sale, and then she set off to find the stranger in the ball cap or his sidekick dressed in black. She had no doubt the two were working in conjunction with each other.

The question was what were they up to?

The building was jam-packed with buyers and tourists, and Martha was too short to see more than a few feet in any direction.

"Want me to find you a ladder?"

She heard the laughter in Joey's voice before she turned and caught the sparkle in his eyes. Though he was 100 percent *Englisch*, Joey Davis reminded her of Fannie's youngest. Just because Martha had been unable to have children of her own, didn't mean that she was without a mothering gene. Fannie's sons and daughters had felt like her children—and Joey definitely reminded her of Fannie's son, Micah.

Medium height, brown hair, and an ever-present smile, Joey was a good worker. He'd often stop by after his shift and talk to

Martha about work, or the latest girl he was dating, or whether he should take more college classes in the fall. She'd listened to the first, rolled her eyes about the second, and told him to follow his heart on the third.

"You remind me of my mother's Chihuahua, the way you're bouncing trying to see over folks."

"It's too crowded in here."

"Yeah. All the auctions seem to be going well."

Eli referred to Joey as a *gopher*. "He *goes for* whatever I need," Eli had explained during her first week there.

Martha tugged on Joey's arm and pulled him over toward the water fountain, where there was a small measure of open space. "The two people you told me about—the ones you saw this morning . . ."

"Man and lady, checking out Lot Number 28."

"Yes. They're the ones. I need to find them."

"Did they do something wrong? I could call the police—" Joey was already reaching for his phone.

"*Nein*. I want to speak to them. Do you see them?"

Joey moved left and then right. "I don't. Are you sure they're still in the auction barn?"

"I doubt it. They didn't seem interested in most of the items Eli auctioned, only the big furniture."

"There's another furniture auction on the north side of the building."

"You go and check there. I'll head out to the vendor stalls."

"Don't get lost," he cautioned, the smile returning to his face.

"I know my way around the market stalls."

"I'll come out and join you if I don't spy them first." He started in the opposite direction and then turned back. "What do you want me to do if I find them?"

"Tell them . . . tell them the bookkeeper has a question about their bid. Take them to my office and then wait with them until I get there."

But she didn't see the man or woman at any of the outdoor booths, and when she reached her office, only Joey was waiting there. She shooed him away and tried to focus on the rest of the day's work.

It was nearing five o'clock when Eli walked in. Normally he would nod to her and head straight into his office. But this time he stopped at the door, removed his hat, and turned it in his hands.

"Tried to get over here earlier, but . . . seems everyone needed my help."

"So you did notice them?"

"Of course I noticed them. They bought three pieces and paid too much for each one."

"Those two are up to no good."

"Maybe. Or maybe they don't know the value of a piece of furniture. Some people have more money than common sense."

"There was a method though—to the way they worked. They alternated which pieces they bid on, so as not to draw attention to themselves."

"That could have been coincidence."

"And they didn't jump into the bid until the item was practically sold."

"I noticed that." Eli studied the chair across from her desk. Finally he trudged over to it and sat down with a *humph*.

"There's a possibility I'm getting too old for a full day on the auction floor."

"When your mind is filled with worry, each task becomes

more burdensome." When he looked at her in surprise, she said, "Something my neighbor used to remind me of."

He frowned at a potted fern sitting on the corner of her desk. Who frowned at a fern? She was quite happy with this one as it was responding well to the new spot on her desk. She'd found it in one of the vendor booths, at the back, nearly wilted into oblivion. Her fern was making a comeback, and there was no reason for Eli Wittmer to frown at it so.

"I suppose I was worried," he admitted. "Did they pay?"

"In a manner of speaking."

He cocked an eyebrow and waited. Just like Eli—never one to speak a word when silence would do.

"That is to say they sent someone with payment."

"Is there a phone number on the check?"

"Paid with a money order."

"Not unusual . . ."

"Not unusual for Amish who don't usually have checking accounts, but it's the first time I've had an *Englischer* pay that way."

Eli shifted in his chair. He glanced at the clock, frowned once more at her fern, and then said, "Perhaps we need to take a closer look at the things they purchased."

Chapter Four

M artha hurried to keep up with Eli. It was strange being in the auction barn with all the buyers and tourists gone. Their footsteps echoed across the floor. She could just make out the whistling of George, the cleaning guy. He was in his seventies and insisted that work—even work like sweeping and mopping and taking out the trash—kept him young.

"Do you need to call your *aenti*?" Eli asked. "I know she worries."

"*Worry* is a nice word for *Aenti* Irene's nagging."

Did she imagine it or did Eli smile at that?

Instead of responding to her comment, he said, "The items in question should be here. They're usually not moved until later in the evening."

"I barely noticed what they bought. I was so focused on how they bought it."

"And I should have responded to your crazy attempts to catch my attention."

"So you did notice?"

"I'm not blind, woman." Now Eli was laughing, a sound she wasn't sure she'd heard before. Maybe he was tired, and it was causing him to behave in an unusual manner. Maybe she didn't know her boss as well as she thought she did.

Once they were standing in front of the three pieces, Eli's somber disposition had returned.

"I don't see anything unusual," he said.

Martha tapped her pencil against her ledger. She wasn't sure why she'd brought them, but it felt good to hug something to her chest as she contemplated this strange mystery.

"We could start with what they have in common." She turned to the back of her ledger and wrote *Lot Number 28* at the top of the last page.

Eli was looking at her skeptically, but he didn't argue.

"So, what do they have in common?" she asked.

"I'm not sure."

"I certainly don't know. I'm not a furniture expert."

"They're all made of northern red oak."

She wrote *Northern red oak* in the ledger. "Were there any other pieces sold today made of the same type of wood?"

"Certainly. It's a common enough wood for furniture making."

"But Mr. and Mrs. Strange only bought these three pieces."

Eli smiled, but he didn't respond to her names for the oddly behaving couple. He rubbed a hand over his jawline, which was beginning to sport a five-o'clock shadow. Did he have to shave every day? Did he wish he'd married when he was younger? Did he iron his own clothes?

Why was she even wondering such things?

She returned her attention to the furniture. "They're all rather large."

"True."

"Lots of large furniture sold today, I suppose."

"Indeed."

"What are we missing?"

Eli shrugged. "They're all made by Jacob Weaver, obviously. It was his lot."

"Didn't you sell his shop items several months ago?"

"Nine months ago, I believe. Right before you moved here."

She was surprised he would remember that she'd been there six months. Some days she wondered if he even knew he had a bookkeeper. Some days he would walk past her desk with barely a word and they wouldn't speak to each other at all. It was strange that they spent so much time in close proximity but rarely talked. "So you sold his shop pieces earlier in the year, and these pieces—"

"Were from his home."

Martha wrote *Large items* and *Made by Jacob Weaver* in her ledger. They now had three clues. She couldn't see how they helped. This wasn't working out the way mysteries did in the books she had borrowed from the local library. Her love of reading was another thing that irritated her *aenti* Irene, though actually that list would have been quite long if she wrote it in the ledger. That idea bothered her less than it probably should have.

"It's an odd situation for certain," Eli said as he removed his hat and ran his hand through his hair. "However, I can't see that anything wrong or illegal has been done."

"*Ya*, but—"

"The items have been paid for."

"With a cashier's check," she reminded him.

"Which is still good money last I checked."

"I know it is. The point is that it's unusual—"

"We should pack everything up and ship it. We do have a

shipping address. Don't we? For . . ." He paused for a moment and then with an impish look in his eyes, continued. "For Mr. and Mrs. Strange?"

"That's another point. They didn't put a name on the shipping instructions—only an address."

"Which is really all we need. If we send these three pieces to the address you have, then we'll have fulfilled our part of the agreement." Eli slapped his hat on his head, looking quite pleased with himself.

"What about our mystery?" Martha asked.

"Some mysteries aren't meant to be solved." Eli gestured toward the outer door, and they both began walking in that direction.

Martha waited until they stepped outside. It was only a few minutes past six, but already the sun was seeking the horizon. The fall evening air was cool and crisp. Martha thought of Ohio and her husband and the life she had left behind. She was pierced momentarily by the sadness and loss of it.

Eli, misunderstanding her sudden melancholy, patted her shoulder in an offhanded, clumsy manner. "Don't let it bother you. We can't always know another person's reasons or intent."

She shook off her memories. "But mysteries should be solved."

"I suppose, though some, I'm afraid, are meant to remain a mystery. Don't look so troubled. Think of it this way—Mr. and Mrs. Strange have given us something to wonder about when we can't sleep at night."

Which might have been the most ridiculous line of reasoning Martha had ever heard. She hurried across the parking lot and found her horse and buggy, climbed in, and pulled out onto the two lane. Her *aenti*'s *haus* wasn't far. She almost wished it were a longer ride, as what she had to face back home would be much less peaceful than riding behind a black mare on an Indiana road as day turned to night.

Chapter Five

Eli watched Martha hurry toward her buggy. He had to admit, there was more to the woman than met the eye. Possibly, he'd been so overwhelmed by the potted ferns and coatracks and candy baskets that he'd failed to consider the person.

Martha was the rarity in an Amish community—no children and now no husband. He knew very little about her. Only that the bishop had asked that he give her a job. Her *aenti*, Irene King, was a member of their district. She was getting on in years and needed help around the house, though she'd leased out the acreage to one of the young men in their church. She could have sold the whole thing, pocketed the money, and gone to live with her husband's people in Sarasota.

He'd heard Irene's answer to that idea. "Can you see me riding a bicycle and playing shuffleboard? No *danki*. I was born here, and I plan to die here."

Irene was always quick to speak her mind, and it was true that she had a nagging tone. He wondered how the two women were getting along, not that it was any of his business. He'd done what the bishop asked, given Martha Beiler a job. He couldn't be expected to look after her beyond that.

She was a perceptive thing. He'd give her that. She missed very little, and she wasn't shy about voicing her opinion—perhaps that was a trait she'd inherited from her *aenti*. In every other way, Martha was the opposite from Irene.

Where Irene was painfully thin and fragile, Martha looked robustly healthy.

Irene wore a constant frown, but he'd rarely seen Martha when she wasn't smiling.

Irene stuck strictly to the *Ordnung*, seeming to revel in its most extreme interpretation. He'd heard Martha say, "I'm just going to plug my itty-bitty book light into the socket here so it will be charged when I get home."

For what it was worth, Eli shared Martha's perspective. The *Ordnung* was meant to guide them, not bind their hands and hearts.

Eli probably should have gone home, but in truth he wasn't very hungry yet, and there was plenty of paper work to be completed in his office. A part of him longed to be outside in the fresh fall air, but they'd just recorded their biggest auction day of the year. He could enjoy the festival during the weekend—with its candied apples, cloggers, and chain-saw sculptors. He'd relax better if he wasn't worried about a pile of paper work waiting on his desk.

He spent the next hour working through his in-box. Martha was good about separating things into folders—colored folders, of course. She'd decided on blue for new contracts that needed his approval. Red for any invoice that needed his signature—auctioneers, employee time sheets, or supplies. Green was for correspondence he had received. He would jot a few notes down on top of the letter, and she would handwrite a response. Her handwriting was certainly better than his.

The yellow folder was Martha's Employee Suggestions folder, another of her ideas. She would sometimes clip articles and put them inside. Occasionally another employee would stop by the office with a suggestion and she would fill out a suggestion form for them. He picked up the top sheet. Janie over in the food booth thought they should have fans mounted up high on the wall. That wasn't a bad idea. He'd seen something similar done in a few of the vendor booths. He scribbled *Remind me in May* at the top and placed it back into the folder.

Fortunately there were no clipped articles. The last one Martha had given him suggested having a company dog or cat that employees could stop by and dote on if they became stressed. The article claimed that employees who had access to an animal at work actually increased their productivity. Martha had even added a note that said animals adopted from their local shelter were free. Not that the shots, food, or care of the animal was free. Besides, most of his employees had plenty of pets at home, though they generally stayed in the barn.

Probably Martha didn't. Had she had animals at her home back in Ohio? Had Irene forbid her to bring them? Eli didn't know and besides, what difference did it make? He was her boss, not her buddy. That was an uncharitable thought, and it was possible that he was reading too much into her requests.

She was a person trying to find her way through a difficult time in her life. Would a kitten help? He honestly didn't know.

He closed the folder and walked back through her office, avoiding the coatrack and turning off lights. As was his custom, he exited through the auction barn. As he headed that direction, Martha's words tumbled round and round in his mind. *Mysteries should be solved.*

He supposed she was right.

He crossed the auction floor and stopped in front of Lot Number 28. Standing in front of the three pieces of furniture, studying them, he didn't hear George Hasley walk up beside him.

"Scared me, George. Make some noise next time."

"I was whistling, but I guess you didn't hear me."

"No. I was trying to figure out a mystery."

"Something wrong with the furniture?"

"Only that someone desperately wanted it, and they were willing to pay too much to get it."

"Doesn't sound like a problem exactly."

"I suppose it isn't."

George leaned against his broom and motioned toward the furniture. "You plan on shipping it out tomorrow?"

"Ya." Eli got down on his knees, which was no problem even though he'd recently turned fifty. No, the problem was getting back up. He ran his hand across the top of the coffee table and then down the sides.

"You looking for a secret panel?"

"I don't know what I'm looking for. Want to help me turn this over?"

"Sure thing."

Eli pushed himself up, using the table as leverage. Then he and George turned the table over.

"Huh. Looks like someone scratched on it," George said.

"Except those don't look like scratches to me."

"No. Looks more like a map."

Chapter Six

Martha sat reading her book, doing her best to ignore her aenti Irene's glare.

"Must be nice to have no darning that needs done." Irene stabbed a needle through the heel of a sock that had to be older than she was.

"You're right. It is."

"Though we are expecting three babies before Christmas."

"Real blessings."

"Blessings that will need blankets and booties and sweaters."

Martha doubted that. Babies born into an Amish church were showered with gifts—not to mention the items used by the previous newborn were often still in good condition. No, she didn't think any baby would be suffering because she chose to read instead of knit. But she kept that thought to herself. She was learning that it was an exercise in futility to try to change Irene's opinion about a thing.

Her aenti's attitude did continue to puzzle her. It was another one of those mysteries that she wondered about when she couldn't sleep at night. Remembering Eli's words made her smile. Obviously he had not read any Julianne Deering or

Lorena McCourtney or Mary Ellis—all fine Christian mystery authors whose books their local library carried. If he had, he would understand the importance of solving a mystery.

She laughed at something in her book and turned the page.

"*Humph.* I don't know how you can be laughing when there is so much hurt in the world." Irene carefully folded the darned socks and pulled out her knitting needles. The yarn she pulled from a basket was black and gray. Martha hoped she was not using it to make a baby gift.

Martha read.

Irene rocked and sighed dramatically from time to time. Finally she said, "When I think of poor Charity and Joseph, and how they have suffered."

Martha stared at the page in front of her, but rereading the words wasn't helping. She simply could not focus on the book in her hands. She'd completely lost the thread of the story, and to think that two pages ago she had thought she had the mystery figured out. Sighing, she carefully placed her marker into the book and set it aside.

"Would you like some herbal tea?"

"I suppose, not that I expect it to help any. My arthritis will be the death of me yet."

Martha had never read of someone dying from arthritis, but she didn't think saying so would cheer up Irene. Instead she went into the kitchen, made the tea, and arranged some of the cookies she'd bought on her way home onto a plate.

Irene accepted the tea, but sniffed when Martha set the plate of cookies between them.

"One would think that a woman with your figure would learn to resist sweets, especially at this hour."

Martha bit into the peanut-butter chocolate-chip cookie, closed her eyes, and relished the taste. When she opened her eyes, Irene was once again knitting.

The Mysterious Ways of Aenti *Irene.*

It might make a good book title. Irene was only twelve years older, being Martha's mother's youngest sister. She'd had five children, all of whom were scattered about the country— Colorado, Kentucky, and even Maine. No doubt they had invited Irene to come and live with them when her husband passed. But Irene was intent on staying put, or it was possible that she simply enjoyed being unhappy. Another letter had come the week before from her husband's family who were now living down in Sarasota.

She'd read it aloud, and the description of beaches, cottages, and ice-cream shops sounded quite pleasant to Martha. Irene's reply had been, "They will probably all suffer skin cancer, though I pray it isn't so."

She wasn't a bad-looking woman with a slim figure, good skin, and few wrinkles except for the frown lines around her mouth. It was her demeanor that was the problem.

While Martha had been studying her, she'd been complaining about the young man who was leasing her land. As far as Martha could tell, Simon Miller was hardworking and courteous.

Irene paused in her monologue to sip the nearly cold tea. Martha took advantage of the moment and jumped in with the question that had been on the tip of her tongue all night. "What do you know of Jacob's woodworking?"

"Jacob Weaver? God bless his soul. To think that man was churning out furniture this time last year and now he can't even speak."

"So his woodwork was well regarded?"

"My yes, though Jacob didn't let pride enter his heart. No, like many of my generation, we understand and abide by the ways of the *Ordnung* as well as the admonitions in Scripture . . . 'Pride goeth before destruction, a haughty spirit before a fall.' Those are words your generation would be wise to heed."

Martha knew that once Irene started quoting Scripture, she could become quite carried away with it. While she appreciated hearing a Good Word, she had specific questions she needed answered.

"Was any of your furniture made by Jacob?"

"Lands no. We were always careful with our money and never bought anything new. Used is good enough."

"Eli auctioned the last of Jacob and Charity's things today."

"A real shame."

"Someone purchased the large items, but paid more than they were worth."

"How people use their money is a mystery to me."

"They paid more than they needed to in order to win the bid. It was very strange."

"I'm not sure you should be working at that place. It was the bishop's idea more than mine. I suppose he was worried about the financial burden you would be on me."

Martha happened to know that Bishop Abram had been more concerned about her spending too much time cooped up with Irene. "*Gotte* makes all sorts—apples and plums and lemons. I can tell by your sunny attitude that you're an apple." It went without saying that he considered her *aenti* a lemon. Martha had thanked him for the job recommendation and gone down to apply that day. The next week she'd begun working at the auction house.

"But why would someone pay more than something is worth? What could it be about Jacob's furniture that would cause a man to do so?"

"*Englisch* or Amish?"

"Dressed like *Englisch*."

"Which means nothing. Children these days. Did I tell you that I saw the younger Miller boy texting while he was driving his buggy? Irresponsible if you ask me . . ."

Martha tuned out her *aenti* and tried to figure out how to get the conversation back on track, but what specifically did she think Irene could tell her? It wasn't like she had a picture to show her of the man in the ball cap or the woman in black. But there had to be something about those specific pieces of furniture, something that would cause a person to spend more than they were worth.

Irene continued to give examples of youth who had gone astray in their community, though she paused now and again to sample the cookies on the tray.

"Then after Peter had left, Jacob had all of these orders to fill and no one to help him. He was in a real pickle, I'll tell you that. And all because youth do not understand the consequence—"

Martha's mind belatedly caught up with what Irene had said.

"Who was Peter?"

"Jacob's apprentice." Her *aenti* paused in her knitting to shoot her a reproving look. "If you paid attention to me even half as well as you pay attention to those fairy-tale stories of yours, you wouldn't have to ask me to repeat myself."

It was a fair criticism. Martha silently vowed to do better.

"What can you tell me about Peter?"

"That depends. What would you like to know? Why he fought with Jacob? Or why he left the Amish?"

Chapter Seven

Generally Thursdays were quiet days, something that Eli looked forward to. His habit was to stop by Rise N' Roll Bakery for a cinnamon caramel donut. When he was a young man, he'd eat two or three, but he had recently realized that his metabolism was changing. One donut and a cup of coffee saw him through until lunch. Of course, he'd eaten a breakfast of oatmeal and fruit when he'd risen at six o'clock, after which he'd done the few chores around his small three-acre place—caring for his mare, making sure the hound dog had water and food, watering his small garden. By the time he hitched up the buggy and drove into town, he was ready for a snack.

He enjoyed the hour of having the office to himself. Martha never arrived before eight and the rest of the employees showed up at eight thirty. Thursdays were devoted to shipping out what was auctioned on Wednesdays and preparing for the horse auction on Friday. With the Fall Festival now in full swing, it was shaping up to be a busy week.

When Martha stepped through the office door at seven thirty, he still had most of the donut and half a cup of coffee left.

He heard her turn on the lamp on her desk, put her purse

in the bottom drawer, and start the coffeepot. Ten minutes later she was standing in his doorway, smiling at him, clutching her coffee cup, and wearing a very pretty dark green dress.

"I'm going to have to try one of those."

"Caramel cinnamon donut?"

"I think I could smell it from my buggy."

"Want what's left?"

"Yes, but you eat it. I'll save my first for a special occasion— like when we solve the mystery of Mr. and Mrs. Strange."

Eli popped the rest of the donut into his mouth, swigged it down with his nearly cold coffee, and nodded toward the chair across from his desk.

"I have an idea," she said. "But I'm not sure how it fits in."

"Tell me yours, and then I'll tell you what I found last night."

"All right. I was talking to *Aenti* Irene, and she mentioned that Jacob once had an apprentice. His name was Peter Fisher."

"I remember Peter."

"So you knew him?"

"Shipshe wasn't nearly as large twenty years ago. It's been some time since Peter lived here."

"Where did he go?"

"Last I heard he was living over in South Bend."

"South Bend? So he left the church?"

"He did. Took up with the Mennonites, but I don't know if it stuck."

"Oh."

Eli nearly laughed at the look of disappointment on her face—it was so childlike. Her expression reminded him of his nieces when they were told it was time for bed.

"Thought he was our man in the ball cap?"

"Possibly. Only because Irene said that the parting between Peter and Jacob was somewhat bitter. I thought—"

"That he'd want to return and pay too much for Jacob's furniture?"

"Okay. I admit it doesn't make much sense."

"No. Especially since Peter Fisher had quite the pronounced limp, and the man who bought the furniture yesterday didn't."

"You're sure?"

"I am, not to mention Peter would be at least fifty now. The man at the auction, he was younger."

Martha sighed and stared at his empty donut bag as if it might sprout more baked goods.

"What did you find last night?" she finally asked.

"Oh. Well, it doesn't make any more sense than yours, but I went back to look at the furniture before I left for the evening."

"And?"

"Didn't find anything out of the ordinary. Until I turned the furniture pieces over."

"Why would you do that?"

Eli shrugged. "George Hasley helped me. I guess we thought we might find something written there."

"Did you?"

"Not exactly."

"Then what did you find?" Martha was sitting on the edge of her seat now. She'd set the coffee cup on his desk and was clutching her hands in her lap.

"Something etched—looks to be a map."

For a moment she only stared at him, and then a grin spread across her face. "Just like in the mystery I read last night. It could be a map to a treasure."

Eli laughed. "Doubtful. I don't know of much treasure that has been buried around Shipshe."

"But it is a map?"

"Part of one."

"So what are we going to do?"

"I thought before I shipped the items off, I'd take a ride out to see Jacob and Charity."

"Let me get my purse."

"Hang on."

She was already at the door. She turned slowly and said, "Don't even think of going without me."

"Fair enough, but I have some horses to see to for tomorrow's auction. I thought I'd go at lunch."

"Even better. Solve this mystery, and we can celebrate with another caramel cinnamon donut."

Eli wasn't sure how good an idea that was. Had to be a thousand calories in the thing, and he'd already devoured one. But he wouldn't mind taking a ride down a country road with Martha Beiler, especially given the fall weather. There'd been a pleasant chill in the air when he'd been doing his morning chores.

As he left the office and headed over to the animal barn, he found himself whistling. It was turning into a *wunderbaar* day, and maybe they would even find some answers.

Chapter Eight

Martha sat next to Eli at the old red oak dining table. It was a smaller version of the one they'd sold and had only two chairs on each side. Across from them, Charity split her attention between her husband and her guests.

As for Jacob, he wore a bib like Martha had seen on some of the old folks at church suppers. Charity spooned what looked like vegetable broth into his mouth. The way Jacob gazed at Charity, it caused Martha's heart to ache. She understood that kind of love, a devotion that could withstand even the ravages of a stroke and an unclear mind. She'd had that kind of love, and seeing it again . . . it caused her to feel her loneliness more sharply than before.

"Jacob, he's not one to speak much anymore, but we always enjoy company. Don't we, Jacob?"

He continued to smile at her, giving no indication that he'd heard or understood the question.

"The auction went very well yesterday, Charity." Eli had stopped at the bakery and picked up a pie as well as fresh bread. He'd explained to Martha that although Charity was an excellent cook, she rarely had time to bake up fresh goods. The bulk of her time was now spent caring for Jacob.

"Glad to hear it. The Lord has been *gut* to us."

Eli cleared his throat. "We have a bit of a mystery though. The pieces made by Jacob, they went for a good deal more than I expected."

Charity reached forward and wiped broth off the corner of Jacob's mouth with a dish towel. Patting him on the hand, she rose, collected the lunch dishes, and set them in the sink. Martha understood that she was taking her time, gathering her thoughts. Rinsing the dishes, pouring another cup of coffee, offering it to her guests—all were ways to slow down the conversation. The question was why had it rattled her so?

When she returned to the table, she said, "Jacob enjoys sitting on the front porch after his lunch."

Eli stood, walked to the wheelchair, and released the brake. As he pushed the wheelchair through the house and out onto the covered porch, it occurred to Martha that he had done this many times before. He'd never mentioned that they were close friends, but within a Plain community it was often this way— neighbors and family helping without being asked to do so.

By the time Eli returned to the table, Martha had fixed them both a cup of coffee and Charity seemed prepared to talk. Before Martha or Eli could ask a question, she launched into an explanation.

"I'm sure you remember that Peter Fisher was once an apprentice to Jacob. Do you recall the disagreement between the two of them?"

"Only that there was one. I never knew what it was about."

"No one did. We saw no need to speak of it."

"You think this is related?"

"I do."

Eli cleared his throat. "Did you know about the map on the bottom of the furniture?"

"My, yes. It was my idea."

"I'm afraid I'm lost," Martha admitted.

Charity smiled, reached out, and patted her hand. "Peter came to work with my husband when he was nineteen years old. He'd tried a few other jobs, but none of them stuck. He was an excellent apprentice and would have turned into a *gut* furniture maker."

"So what happened?"

"Peter had been with us for six years and was becoming a fine craftsman in his own right. Jacob often worked with new material, but occasionally he'd buy old pieces and refurbish them. One such piece was a large wardrobe. He purchased it at auction—" She turned to Eli. "I don't remember now if the auction was held at your place or at the owner's farm."

Eli shrugged, indicating that he didn't recall the piece.

"When he got the wardrobe home, and Peter began to work on it, they discovered the map. It was inside the piece, etched into the back wall."

"What was it a map of?"

"We weren't sure, but Peter got it into his head that money was involved. He was a young man, still given to flights of fancy. Jacob wanted to sand over the map, but Peter wouldn't hear of it. They fought, and Peter became so angry that he left and vowed to never return."

"And he never did?" Martha asked.

"No. It broke Jacob's heart. Peter had become like a son to

him, and we . . . well, we had already lost one son. Jacob thought that Peter would come to his senses and find his way back to Shipshe, to his home, and to us." She paused and then smiled. "My husband couldn't bring himself to sell the wardrobe. For years, it sat in the back of his workshop."

"But then something changed . . ." Martha leaned forward, feeling the answers to their questions within reach.

"Five years ago, we began to receive letters from Peter. They revealed very little about himself, and asked nothing of how we were. He only wanted to know about the wardrobe—if we still had it. Apparently he had tried to memorize the map before he left, but over the years he'd had no luck finding whatever the map led to."

"Did you try to contact the original owners?" Eli asked.

"They'd died, which is how Jacob came by the piece in the auction."

"Did you answer Peter's letters?" Martha asked.

"At first, but when it became plain that Peter was only interested in the treasure, we stopped. Jacob vowed to destroy the wardrobe, but I had a better idea." Now her eyes twinkled, and Martha realized that somehow this woman had learned to overcome several tragedies in her life and retain her sense of humor. "I suggested that he cut up the map and use it in different pieces. That way it wouldn't be destroyed, but neither would someone be able to become obsessed with it."

"Which is why I have three pieces of furniture with parts of a map."

"There were seven in all because Jacob cut the map up into fairly small pieces. We sold three of those when we auctioned his workshop inventory."

"And three are sitting on my auction floor."

"Correct, but you don't have the final piece."

"I don't?"

"No." Charity's smile had widened.

"Where's the fourth piece?" Martha asked.

"Here." Charity tapped the table. "We knew that this would be the last thing we would ever sell. It holds too many memories, of our son, our friends, even of Peter. So Jacob glued the last piece of the map to the back of our table."

Chapter Nine

"I don't understand," Martha admitted.

They'd turned the table upside down and were studying the map etched there.

"This shows a number seven along a squiggly line."

"Plain enough." Eli leaned closer, as if he could make more sense by putting his nose right on the map.

"One through six were attached to other pieces of furniture." Charity sat in one of the kitchen chairs, plucking at her apron. "I suppose three of those numbers were on the pieces you sold, Eli."

"*Ya.* Numbers four, five, and six."

"But it doesn't make any sense." Martha worried her thumbnail with her front teeth. "Look, we can tell this spot is to the northwest of Shipshe, and we can tell that it has something to do with water if that's what the wavy line next to it means."

"Wavy lines do usually mean water."

Martha resisted the urge to give him her most serious look. He was plainly enjoying himself, or enjoying watching her struggle with the mystery of the map. She was already thinking of it that way. The Mystery of the Map. She could practically see the title on the spine of a book.

"But why bother with numbers one through six? Why not just look for number seven and find the supposed treasure? If that is a treasure chest next to it, which I rather doubt."

"Oh dear." Charity stood up quickly, nearly knocking over her chair.

"What is it?" Eli was beside her in a flash.

"The letter. I forgot to show you the letter."

She returned a few minutes later with a small envelope. "We found this in one of the drawers that was built into the bottom of the old wardrobe. We thought that perhaps the husband had etched the map into the wood and the wife had written the letter for whoever found it."

Charity pulled the piece of paper out from the envelope and handed it to Eli. It looked as if it would fall apart in his hands—old and fragile and capable of holding great secrets. Martha crowded in next to them in order to read the faded handwriting.

If you have found this, then you have probably also found the map. No doubt you are wondering why someone would go to so much trouble and whether there is a real treasure at the end. I'll attempt to answer the first and let you answer the second.

The people of this area—all of the people—are God's children, blessed by fertile land and bountiful harvests. We've had our share of trouble and tragedy, but when we pull together we find that the things we share outweigh our differences. The final destination will be revealed to the person who patiently and studiously follows the map through all seven markers. You will learn more than our history. You will receive a glimpse into the heart of the people of this region. May God bless your journey.

As soon as she reached the bottom of the page, Martha began rereading the letter. But it made no more sense the second time.

"The letter tells us to *patiently and studiously* follow the map through all the markers." Eli chuckled. "No rewards for taking shortcuts."

"Indeed," Charity agreed. "I don't think you would recognize the seventh spot, if you hadn't visited the first six."

Martha handed the letter back to Charity.

They turned the table back over and repositioned the chairs around it. Eli went to the porch and pushed Jacob back into the house, and then he helped Charity to settle him into his bed.

"I can tell that you two are going to follow this thing through." Charity walked between them back to Eli's buggy, her arms looped through theirs. "Be sure to keep me posted on what you find."

As they made their way back to the auction house, Martha's mind was scattered like the seeds from the harvested stalks of grain.

Who wrote the letter?

Why did they go to the trouble?

What was the person seeking the treasure supposed to learn?

And what—if anything—waited for them at the end?

Chapter Ten

Eli wanted to deliver the furniture himself. He planned to ride along with his delivery workers. Once at the house, he would ask the young man in the baseball cap to clarify his intentions. If worse came to worse, he would return the money order and refuse to sell him the pieces. The contract he had with buyers allowed him some leeway if the buyer misrepresented himself, and in this case, that just might be true.

"You need to stay here and oversee the horse auction."

Martha was standing on the shipping ramp with him. Her purse was strapped over her shoulder and she'd donned a sweater for what was turning out to be a beautiful, brisk October day. Outside the dock, the festival was in full swing. Though it was only nine in the morning, already the crowds were pouring in.

"I can go and you can stay here," she added.

"No."

"But—"

"The auction will be fine. That's what I hire auctioneers for."

"But what if they have a question or something they can't handle? What if someone overbids on a horse?"

"Martha, as you know, I'm not here for every auction. Stop worrying."

"Who said I was worrying?" She stuck her thumbnail in her mouth, realized what she was doing, and pulled it out—clasping her hands behind her back.

"It will be fine."

"What if he's dangerous? Or violent?"

"He won't be."

"Why don't we leave the furniture here?"

"Because there could be a very simple explanation."

"But the map!" She lowered her voice, as if suddenly aware that the delivery guys—Matt and Joshua—were within listening distance.

They continued to load auction items onto the truck, as Eli tried to think of a way to discourage Martha from coming along. He was her boss and he could tell her to get back to work. But he couldn't outright forbid it should she take it in her mind to follow them. Perhaps there was a little part of him that thought she might be handy to have along. She certainly seemed keen on solving the mystery.

In the end, it wasn't worth arguing with her. They rode in the front of the truck with Matt and Joshua. It was a tight fit in spite of the fact that the delivery truck had a large cab. The ride to South Bend was only forty-five minutes, but they stopped in Jamestown to deliver four rocking chairs that had sold in another of Wednesday's auction lots. Many of the fields they passed were harvested already. In others he saw farmers working hard to bring in their crops before the weekend's predicted rain. Both Amish and *Englisch* worked in the fields, sometimes side by side. For any who didn't believe the two groups could live peaceably beside each other they had only to drive down a country road during harvesting time.

By the time they turned onto the street listed on the buyer's form, it was ten in the morning. Matt pulled up in front of a country style house—small but meticulously maintained.

"Wait here," Eli said. "I'll let you know whether to unload."

Martha never hesitated. She popped out of the truck and hurried up the walk with him.

A small sedan sat in the driveway, originally black, but now desperately in need of paint.

Eli's finger was barely off the doorbell when the door opened. The young man in the baseball cap who answered was the same person who had overbid at the auction.

"Do you have my furniture?"

"I have the furniture, yes, but there's something we need to clear up first. My name is Eli Wittmer and this is my office manager, Martha Beiler."

"Duncan Fisher." He didn't offer his hand, but he did step out onto the front porch, closing the door behind him. He wore jeans and a plain black T-shirt. The ball cap sported a Cubs logo. He was probably five foot ten, approximately the same height as Eli, but he still had the too-thin look of a teenager. "What's the problem? What needs clearing up?"

"You overbid on the furniture that you purchased."

"So?"

"You're aware then, that you paid too much."

Duncan tugged on his ball cap and then settled for sticking his hands in his back pockets. "I guess."

"Why would you do such a thing?" Martha asked.

"That's my business. I bought the furniture. You've been

paid, and now you need to have those two guys haul it off the truck."

"Whoa, son. Not so quick. The sellers—Jacob and Charity Weaver—have the right not to sell if there's a problem with the bid price."

"Those rules are in case someone isn't paying what a thing is worth."

"Usually, yes. I see you understand auctions."

"I should. I've been to enough of them."

Eli let that pass. "Maybe we should speak with your parents about this."

"I'm nineteen." Duncan shook his head in disgust. "I need those pieces. If you want me to pay more, I will."

"No. That won't be necessary. What I need is for you to tell me why you're so interested in these pieces."

Duncan had been looking toward the truck, but now he turned his gaze on Eli and Martha, understanding dawning in his eyes.

"You know about the maps."

Eli nodded once.

Duncan stared off across the yard for a moment. When he once again focused on them, he said, "I guess you better come inside."

Chapter Eleven

Martha had been in *Englisch* homes before. This one looked a bit different. Although the outside had seemed well maintained, the inside had a disheveled appearance. An ivy struggled to survive next to the front window. Mail was stacked in a haphazard fashion on the coffee table. Clean clothes sat in a pile on the couch, with the laundry basket on the floor tipped on its side. Someone had begun folding the T-shirts, but never finished.

Duncan swept the clothes into the basket and sat on the edge of a leather recliner.

Martha wanted to jump straight into the interrogation phase of this visit. She'd read enough detective novels to know what questions to ask, or at least she thought she did. But Eli seemed content to wait out the boy.

Finally Duncan said, "How'd you find out about the map?"

Eli shrugged.

Martha took pity on the boy. "Someone saw you and a woman—"

"My sister, Beth."

"Saw you looking at the furniture before the auction."

"Everyone looks."

"But you moved the furniture around, as if you were looking *for* something."

Duncan flopped back into the recliner.

"Why don't you start at the beginning?" Eli suggested.

"I don't suppose I know the beginning." Duncan glanced around the room and then sat up straighter and dove in. "My pop, he told us about the maps, since we were young."

"Where is your pop?" Martha asked.

"Died, earlier this year."

Now Martha wanted to reach across and pat his hand. She was a terrible detective. She caved the first time her suspect showed his vulnerable side. "So it's just you and your sister?"

"Yeah. Mom, she passed a long time ago—cancer."

"We're sorry for your loss." Eli leaned forward now and looked the boy straight in the eye. "Was your father's name Peter?"

"How did you know that?"

"Because he once worked for Charity and Jacob, the owners of the furniture. You didn't know their connection?"

"No. He didn't mention how he knew about the maps. To tell you the truth, we always thought it was some kind of fairy tale. But then he got sick, and he showed us the first three sections of the map."

"Affixed to the back of the furniture?" Martha glanced around the room, wondering where the pieces were.

"Yes." Duncan hesitated, and then he said, "I'll be right back."

He hurried from the room, bounding strides that reminded Martha of a pup.

"What do you think?" she asked Eli.

"I think we're about to learn more about this mystery."

When Duncan returned, he wasn't carrying furniture. Instead he had three pieces of paper in his hand.

"I couldn't actually carry furniture around with me while I was searching, so I used a sheet of paper and a pencil and did a rubbing of each piece of the map. You know, like you would do with leaves when you're a kid." He placed the sheets on the coffee table, one beside the other, until they were lined up like buggies at a stop sign. "I'm fairly sure this is the first of the three pieces, and it seems to line up with the other two. I can't know for certain though. Not until I find all of the pieces."

Eli studied the maps and then sat back and ran his thumb up and down his suspender. Finally he asked, "Why are you so interested in the map . . . in finding the rest of it?"

"Because I promised my pop I would. I told him that I would solve this." Tears filled Duncan's eyes, but he blinked them away. "See, it ate away at him. He was like obsessed with it. And Beth and I thought that he was maybe losing his grip on things. Right before he died, he made me promise, and I did. I would have promised him anything."

He took off the cap, rubbed the back of a hand across his eyes, and replaced the cap on his head. "My sister, she's in college now—over at Ivy Tech community college. It's here in South Bend. She's working on an Imaging Science degree. Once she gets it she can work as an X-ray tech or maybe an ultrasound tech, and those jobs pay good money."

"Must be hard, if it's just the two of you." Martha's mothering urge was on full alert.

"We do all right. I'm sort of taking a few night classes, and I pick up some work on a landscaping crew here and there."

"So you need the money?" Eli asked.

"Beth could use the money. College isn't cheap."

"How did you afford the furniture?" Martha asked.

"Saved it up." Now Duncan looked proud of himself. "I'm supposed to use it for college this fall, but honestly I don't think college is where I want to be."

"So you're going to spend your college money to fulfill a promise to your dad." Martha liked this kid more every minute. In fact, she had a sudden urge to help him.

"I guess. If this map does lead to money, if that's what we're looking for, then yeah, we could use it. But honestly I just need to do what I promised, even if we end up finding that there is no treasure at the end."

Martha completely believed Duncan's story, but did Eli?

One, then two minutes ticked by, silence filling the room as Eli considered Duncan's story. Martha's hands itched to straighten the piles of mail, fold the laundry, even walk to the kitchen and fetch a cup of water for the poor dying ivy.

She didn't though. Like Duncan, she waited.

Finally Eli stood, nodded toward the truck, which they could see through the front window, and said, "Let's go and get your furniture."

Chapter Twelve

Martha stood at the stove, sweat running down her neck though a nice breeze came through the window.

"Perhaps next year we should have a smaller garden."

"Why would we do that?" Irene asked sharply.

Her *aenti* had been pleasant through breakfast, and Martha had hoped for a Saturday without argument. But now she was grumbling, a scowl etched on her face.

"I'm not sure we need this much canned food." Martha gestured toward the rows of canned tomatoes, okra, and green beans. "We'll never be able to eat this much."

"Be grateful that *Gotte* has blessed us with such a harvest."

"*Ya.* For certain, only I'm thinking we could reduce the garden next year. Even with a smaller garden, we'd be able to share with the neighbors and donate to auctions."

Irene muttered something under her breath and stomped out of the room.

Martha continued to can the remaining cucumbers and allowed her mind to slip over the events of the last twenty-four hours.

Matt and Joshua had unloaded the furniture and driven away to make another delivery in South Bend, promising to pick them up within the hour. Martha and Eli had watched as Duncan had once again used paper and a pencil to rub off images of the new map pieces. It had taken a few minutes to put the various sheets in the proper order, and when they were done, it was obvious that something was still missing.

"The piece that Charity showed us," Eli said.

Duncan had been kneeling in front of the coffee table. Now he sat back on his heels. "She still has a piece?"

"*Ya*, and I think we'll be needing it if we're to follow this map of yours."

So it was decided that Duncan would drive to the auction house the next day and meet Eli. Together they would go to Jacob and Charity's. Martha wasn't about to be left out. She'd refused to leave work the previous day until Eli had promised he'd pick her up. Now they were due at her house in under an hour and she was still standing in the kitchen canning cucumbers. On top of that, she'd managed to irritate Irene once again. But then whatever she did bothered her *aenti*. Perhaps she wouldn't worry too much over that one.

How she longed for the days she'd spent in Ohio with her best friend, Fannie. There was no task too burdensome with Fannie's laughter and positive attitude to lighten things. Well, she would have to be the encouraging one in this household. That much was obvious.

She quickly finished up the canning, cleaned the kitchen, and was pinning a fresh *kapp* on her head when she heard the clatter of hooves. Hurrying out the door, she assured her *aenti* that she would be home before dinner. Martha was forty years old, and although she appreciated Irene's willingness to give her a place to live, she couldn't abide being treated like a child much longer. It was time to have a talk with Irene, but she dreaded that moment.

Duncan had pulled in behind Eli.

She waved at him and then climbed into the buggy. The scenes they drove by would have made a perfect postcard. One neighbor raised a hand in greeting as he turned his team of Percheron work-horses. In another field, a wife and children stood on the back of a wagon, helping as the men tossed up large forkfuls of hay.

Ten minutes later the three of them were walking up to Charity and Jacob's front door.

Eli called out and tapped lightly on the door.

Duncan hung back. "What if they don't want to see me? It sounds as if Pops wasn't very nice to them."

"You will like Charity and Jacob. They're very kind people. Let's give them a chance."

Charity knew that Duncan was coming. Eli had stopped by the night before and asked if it would be all right. But when she walked out onto the porch, when she saw the young man, her hands flew to her cheeks and her eyes widened.

"Oh my. You look just like your *dat*. It's as if he were stand-ing here on my porch like he so often did all those years ago."

Duncan blushed, stepped forward, and said, "Pleased to meet you."

Charity grabbed his hand and pulled him into the house, calling out, "Jacob. Jacob, you have to see Peter's boy."

Eli smiled and held the door for Martha, and then they stepped into the house. At first she thought that her eyes hadn't yet adjusted to the darkness of inside. But then Eli placed his hand on her back, stepped closer to her, and she knew that she wasn't imagining this scene.

Martha had never seen Jacob responsive, not really. He would gaze in adoration at his wife, but he'd never spoken, and he'd never actually reacted to anyone else's presence in the room.

Perhaps they'd caught him on a good day.

Or maybe, God was allowing His grace and compassion to shine through Jacob's deteriorated state, like sunlight piercing through a cloud-covered sky.

Charity had pulled Duncan into the room and over in front of Jacob's wheelchair. Duncan stooped down to say hello, and when he made eye contact with Jacob, the old man's smile first trembled, faltered, and then grew. He clasped Duncan's hand, reached out, and touched his face. Whether he thought that Duncan was his father, Peter, Martha couldn't say. But there was no doubt that he recognized the young man, and that he was overjoyed to see him.

Martha had been quite focused on the map and the mystery. She couldn't imagine what would have caused the two men to fight over such a silly thing, or why Jacob would decide to carve up the map and then hide it. Men often remained a mystery to her, but this was above and beyond anything she'd seen before or even read about in a book.

Watching the reunion of a young man and an elderly couple, it occurred to her that Duncan and his sister, Beth, might be the grandchildren that Jacob and Charity never had. And perhaps the elderly Amish couple could fill the hole in Duncan's life.

The mystery of the map remained unsolved, but the mystery of God's ways? Well, those were unfathomable. It was almost as if God had a plan for bringing the prodigal home in the form of his son. It was almost as if God had found a way to bless them in spite of the foolishness with maps and treasures.

Chapter Thirteen

Two hours later they had left Duncan's car near the auction house. Martha and Eli rode in the front of the buggy. Duncan Fisher sat in the back. He'd wanted to drive his vehicle, but Eli had only said, "Simple is better," and walked off toward his buggy.

"Stubborn as my pop," Duncan had mumbled, hurrying to catch up.

Now Martha wondered what Duncan was thinking. He hadn't been raised Plain, hadn't known the joys of buggy travel or life without his cell phone. But he'd obviously heard about Shipshe.

"Have you been here before, Duncan?" Martha half turned around in the seat.

"A few times. My dad was Amish, I guess that's why he worked for Mr. Weaver. His family moved off to Ohio and we sort of lost touch. Mom, she was Mennonite and she had some distant relations who lived here, so we did come once in a while. It was never this busy though."

Now that she knew him, saw the man beneath the baseball cap up close, she realized he was little more than a kid. Yes, he was nineteen, but in many ways he reminded her of their local youth—still trying to find his way and decide what path he'd take in life.

The streets were crowded with tourists attending the Fall Festival, most wearing brightly covered sweaters and jackets. Eli had to slow his mare to a walk as throngs of folks crossed the road, not even bothering to walk down to the crosswalk. All of the parking lots were full, and though it was near sundown on a Saturday afternoon, more folks were still coming.

The booths would stay open until nine that evening—basket weavers, candlemakers, potters, painters, and many more. She could hear a band warming up their instruments, smell the candy apples and kettle corn, feel the arrival of fall. Though it was her first Fall Festival, she didn't mind missing the grand finale. Somehow she knew that Shipshe was where she belonged, and that there would be other festivals.

"I've never been here during a big event. It looks pretty . . . crowded."

"Apparently you do have some experience at an auction." Eli kept his eyes on the road.

"Yeah. Pop would take me during the summer, when he'd go in search of a great deal." He made quotation marks in the air to surround the last two words.

"So he stayed in the woodworking business?"

"He did. Worked at one of the factories for a few years, then saved enough to open his own business. He didn't bother with new stuff, but he could restore just about anything you brought him."

Eli had finally guided his horse through the bulk of the crowds. He allowed the mare to settle into a nice trot as they made their way to the west side of town. Martha didn't know where they were going, where the map would lead them. But Eli seemed to know. Occasionally he would glance at her and smile. As for Duncan, he sat in the back of the buggy, clutching the sheets of paper that he'd rubbed the map onto.

When they'd reached the outskirts of town, Eli pulled into a vacant lot, allowing the mare to come to a stop under the shade of a maple tree resplendent with leaves of red, yellow, and gold.

Eli got out of the buggy, and Martha and Duncan quickly followed.

"You and your father, you did a good job of following the map . . ."

"The portions we had."

"Exactly. Whoever created the map stayed true to the town directionally, but much has changed since that time. In addition, the person apparently wanted to make it a bit of a challenge, so the map includes clues but not specific locations."

"It wasn't too hard to figure out the first spot. *Chief* obviously referred to the statue of Shipshewana, but at first we thought it referred to the monument at Main and Morton."

"That monument was dedicated in 2000, many years after your father and Jacob came in possession of the map."

"But we were close, I guess."

"Indeed, the original crossroads of the town ran through that section, and so it makes sense that your mapmaker would mark the spot with Shipshewana, the chief, who helped those original settlers."

"I can't imagine what it could have to do with a treasure. Unless it's an Indian treasure."

"As the memorial explains, Shipshewana, chief of the local Potawatomi Indians, is where our town got its name."

"But . . ." Martha could tell that Eli was enjoying drawing this out. The question was how much did he know? Had he figured it out to the very end? She didn't think so.

"But it also speaks of Abraham Summey and Hezikia Davis," Eli said. "Those two men disagreed over where the town should be built. Amish folks were already settled here by the mid-1800s, so some of this history has been passed down from father to son and so forth."

"Your father?" Duncan asked.

"He was something of a history buff—a bit odd in an Amish man, but not unheard of." Eli nodded toward the remains of an old building that sat back from the road.

There wasn't much left of the structure from what Martha could see. Part of a foundation, a little bit of a brick wall, and a half-crumbled chimney. They began to walk toward it, shoulder to shoulder as leaves crunched beneath their feet, Eli in the middle.

"Not that I listened as much as I should have," Eli admitted. "But what I couldn't remember, I found at the local library."

"I wondered what you were doing there," Martha muttered.

"Mr. Summey and his wife, Rachel, owned this area on the west side of town. Mr. Davis owned the land to the east. The two men could not agree where to build, and so each proceeded to build on his own. In fact, the east side was once called Davis Town."

"So the first stop—the one to the statue or the original crossroads—was only to point us to history?" Duncan asked.

"I believe so. Whoever made this map, and we can't be sure who that was, enjoyed puzzles and knowledge. He, or she, wanted someone with a keen intellect and a curious spirit—" At the last two words he slanted his eyes toward Martha. "To find your treasure."

"The second stop—why was it so far away?"

"We can't know for certain, but the location on Detroit Street in La Grange, it's an important part of our history."

"Took us some time to figure that one out. The words *La Grange* and *knowledge* were rather vague. And a free reading room?" Duncan shook his head. "I'd never even heard of such a thing."

"Miss Ellison built that room in the late 1800s."

"Again pointing to the importance of knowledge," Martha said.

"I think so."

"We spent several hours there trying to figure where the third stop might be. For that the map only shows a bell . . ."

"Like is found on a school."

"The librarian was able to figure that out. She directed us back to Shipshe."

"Today's school sits on the same site as the original school. The school was built the same year that Miss Ellison opened the free reading room. The area was booming."

"So why are we here?" Martha stepped under the limbs of a red oak tree. Acorns crunched beneath her feet.

"This is the site of what was once Sunthimer's Corner."

"I didn't read about this when I looked in the archives at our library—maybe a general reference but not the exact location." Martha stared at the old brick wall, now crumbled. What had their lives been like over one hundred years ago? Certainly they had loved, rejoiced, lost, hurt, and prayed, just as people did now. And what was the point of the map?

"I had to ask a few old-timers," Eli admitted. "I couldn't

figure it out myself, until Duncan showed us his rubbings from the first three pieces of the map, specifically the last one."

"It pointed toward U.E. Mast." Duncan stared down at the sheets in his hand.

"A drug store that was built on this site."

"And the first mark on the map from the furniture that you auctioned." Martha brushed leaves and acorns off the wall and sat on it. She studied Eli and Duncan, two very different men who had found a common interest—a mystery. And what of Jacob back at home? And Charity? What would solving the mystery mean to them?

"I didn't even need the fourth piece then." Duncan stared around him in frustration. "I have a feeling that if I could just think clearly enough, I could skip all the spots in between and go to the end—to the treasure."

"Possibly you could have, but I imagine the mapmaker wanted you to follow these steps, to understand the history of Shipshe before you found the treasure. Anyone willing to go that far, to invest that much time and energy, would have earned it."

"Okay. But it's almost dark, and we still have your last two pieces, plus the final piece from Charity and Jacob."

"I think we can find one more tonight."

"And then?"

"Well, tomorrow is the Sabbath—we'll rest. And then we'll begin again Monday afternoon."

Chapter Fourteen

Rain pounded against the roof of Bishop Abram's buggy shop. Martha stood near the open bay doors, watching it drench the earth, trying to put some rhyme or reason to *Aenti* Irene's recent moods.

She'd seemed more bitter than usual as they'd prepared for church and had even thrown out a few disparaging remarks as they'd helped set out the Sunday luncheon. Try as Martha might to resist it, sometimes her own mood plummeted right alongside her *aenti*'s. Which was all the more reason for her to enjoy the few moments of solitude as she watched the storm and allowed her senses to focus on the sound and the smell of it. Reaching out her hand, water slicked down her palm, and she thought it felt clean.

"Playing in the rain?"

Martha smiled even before she turned to see Eli watching her. "It's been many years since I've enjoyed a walk in the rain, but I will admit, I adore a good downpour."

"I'm surprised you're not visiting with the women." Eli nodded toward the group of mothers and grandmothers and even great-grandmothers.

When she didn't answer right away, he motioned toward two rocking chairs that were sitting on the bishop's front porch. "We'll get wet, but those look inviting."

And indeed they did. Together they hurried across the yard and arrived on the porch, laughing and shaking water from their clothes. Eli didn't push her to speak or explain herself. She liked that about him. That he allowed her to just . . . be.

The sermons that morning had been what she needed to hear. The first focused on loving one's neighbor. She understood that her *aenti* was her neighbor in one sense and certainly that she should love her. It was liking her that Martha sometimes had trouble with. The second sermon had helped with that. "Be devoted to one another in love. Honor one another above yourselves."

That word *devoted*, it had snagged her conscience and wouldn't let go.

"I do care for her, you know." She didn't say her *aenti*'s name, and by Eli's nod, she knew she didn't have to. "It's the devotion that is difficult."

"In what way?"

"When I think of devotion, I think of a mother's abiding love for a child."

"Or a father's."

"Yes. I think of the way our *youngie* fall in love and become devoted to one another."

"Certainly that is another type of devotion."

"There are others?"

Eli rocked for a few minutes before answering. The rain continued to fall, soaking the ground and soothing the prickly points in Martha's soul.

"It's true the *youngie* are very devoted to one another," Eli said. With his thumb he traced the grain of the wood across the rocker's arm and finally looked up to meet her gaze. "And yet Charity is devoted to Jacob—that is an entirely different thing."

"I suppose."

"What they have is born of years of shared experiences, dreams, hurts, and hopes."

"I had that with my husband, Melvin," Martha said softly.

"It's a blessing that you did."

Martha pushed her foot against the porch's wooden floor, setting her chair into a rocking motion. As they watched, one of the young boys dashed out into the rain, and two others followed. She guessed their ages to be between eight and ten. They hurried over to squat under the limbs of a tree, and it was then that she saw they each held a small paper boat, which they attempted to float.

"With *Aenti*, I appreciate that she has offered me a home, but I don't understand her bitterness or why she is the way that she is."

"It's often difficult to understand one another."

"Perhaps it is arthritis or some other health issue, but she won't speak of it. She won't explain herself."

"Many times I've talked with *Englischers* who admire much of the Amish life, especially the way we treat our elders—with respect and courtesy."

"*Ya*. It's true that we do."

"But whether a person is *Englisch* or Amish, as they grow older they often begin to feel unimportant, disconnected in some ways, even afraid as to what lies ahead."

Martha considered Eli's words. Would she feel that way in another thirty years? It was hard to imagine.

"I know that I should be devoted to her." Now she turned

in her chair and studied Eli. She appreciated that he was not judging her. It said much about his character, and that possibly he had endured a similar situation. "I want to care about her. I want things between us to be less scratchy."

"I think that often devotion looks different in different relationships. It speaks of commitment to one another. There's no doubt that you are dedicated to Irene. Perhaps you should give it time."

"But I want our relationship to be better now." Martha laughed as soon as she said the words. She sounded like a child. Some days she felt like one.

"We can't always know what has injured a person in life, what has caused them to take the outlook they have."

Something in his voice caused Martha to think they'd changed the subject. Was Eli talking about himself?

"But if we wait, if we are patient, a time might come when a person will change their outlook. If we're devoted . . ." He smiled at her, hesitated, and then reached out and covered her hand with his. "Then we will be there on that day when they glance up and realize life isn't as dark as they had imagined."

Eli patted her hand, released it, and stood.

"Would you like me to walk you back?"

"I think I'll stay here awhile."

He nodded as if he understood.

Martha spent the next half hour watching the rain bless the fields, releasing the dozens of slights she'd committed to memory, and embracing her new life. It would be difficult to maintain a positive outlook—she understood that. In all honesty, life had never been particularly easy. Even with Melvin, each day had brought its share of challenges.

The rain lightened, and she walked back across to the barn.

As she did, she couldn't help thinking that perhaps in the midst of those challenges was where God often set His plan. Like the locations on Duncan's map, those times—the bad as well as the good—seemed to always point to God and His will for their lives. She could trust that it would continue to be so.

Chapter Fifteen

Monday dawned, bringing even cooler temps and a world washed anew. Martha realized as she dressed that she was looking forward to solving the mystery of Duncan's map. She didn't think they would find a treasure, but perhaps they would find some answers for the young man. Hurrying downstairs, she ate a quick breakfast and then gathered up her purse and lunch.

"I certainly hope you can pick up the items on our shopping list today." Irene frowned and fidgeted with her *kapp*. "Though I know you're busy with your job and chasing down that foolish map."

Martha heard her *aenti*'s harsh words, but this time she turned and watched the expression on her face. Her eyes were glancing around the room, and once she'd repinned the already perfectly pinned *kapp*, she plucked at the apron on her dress. What did Irene do all day when Martha was gone? How did she fill her hours? Was she lonely? Was she . . . Eli's words came back to her suddenly . . . was she afraid?

Martha piled her things on the counter near the back door, walked across the room, and sat down next to her *aenti*. "I could pick up our supplies or we could wait until tomorrow and go together."

Irene looked at her sharply. "You work tomorrow."

"That's true, but we'll be done with the map. Eli and I have agreed that we either find it today or we give up. Something like this—it can quickly become an obsession if you're not careful."

"*Humph.*"

"You and I both have sewing to do this winter. Let's look for fabric while we're out. Tomorrow I'll come back and pick you up at lunch. We'll grab a bite to eat and then stop by the fabric store."

"You'll do no such thing. I'll fix you lunch. No need throwing away our money."

"All right then. It's a compromise. Tomorrow have lunch ready, and together we'll go do a little shopping." She might be seeing things, but it seemed as if the frown lines around her *aenti's* eyes and mouth softened.

Irene nodded and then said, "You should go before you're late."

She wasn't late. In fact she was early and once again caught Eli at his desk eating a caramel cinnamon donut.

"Do you have those every day?"

"I try to." He motioned to the chair across from him and handed her a white paper bag. "Got you one too."

"How can a girl resist?"

"Why would a girl resist?"

They drank their coffees, finished their sweets, and discussed the last clue that they had found on Saturday—a place that Eli called No Man's Land. The strip of land was one hundred and fifty feet wide and separated Summey's land from Davis's. "For many years, no one built there," Eli had explained. "Which is where the name came from."

The three of them had walked up and down the street, trying to figure how this pointed to the sixth clue.

Martha had thought about it many times since Saturday afternoon, but she'd come up with no solutions. She'd continued to puzzle over it as she drove the horse and buggy to work. "What was there before, in No Man's Land? In the beginning?"

Eli wiped crumbs from his face and stared up at the ceiling. "Stores, a hotel, and the old train depot."

"It's like trying to look into the past with our eyes closed." She stood and began picking up their trash. "All of that sugar. I should get twice as much work done this morning."

"Good thing. Duncan is meeting us here at three."

It seemed to her that Eli wanted to say more. Martha remembered his hand on hers the day before and felt a slow blush begin to crawl up her neck. She hurried out of the room before he noticed.

Did she have a crush on her boss?

Confirmed bachelor Eli Wittmer?

What was it he had said the day before? *If we wait, if we are patient, a time might come when a person will change their outlook.*

She'd assumed he had been talking about Irene. Had he been talking about himself?

The morning flew by in a flurry of bills to be paid, correspondence, and shipping invoices. Before she knew it, their office door opened and Duncan stepped inside. As usual, he was dressed in jeans, a T-shirt, and his Cubs baseball cap.

Clutched in his hand were the sheets of paper with the map rubbings, and a giant grin was plastered on his face.

He tugged on his ball cap and said, "I figured it out."

"The final spot?"

"No. Not that. But I did figure out clue number six."

Eli popped out of his office. "Did someone say clue?"

"It's the Davis Mercantile, or what was the mercantile."

"But the fire was—" Eli dropped into the chair across from Martha.

"Twelve years ago. I know. I'm talking about the original complex of stores built by the Davis family in 1891."

"Here we go again," Martha said, her pulse quickening as she leaned forward in her chair.

"So I Googled the original hotel and its owners."

"Googled?" Eli scrunched up his nose as if he'd smelled something offensive. "Speak English, son."

"Oh . . . searched on the Internet. Think of it as a virtual encyclopedia."

"Virtual." The idea reminded Martha of e-readers. She'd never had one, but the idea of a library that had a practically unlimited number of books—that was technology she could embrace.

"And you learned something on this . . . Google?"

"I think so." Duncan placed the sheet of paper on the desk between Martha and Eli. "We thought this clue—Meeting place—meant either a store or church, but what if it meant the hotel?"

Martha had no idea what he was talking about, but Eli had sat back and was running his thumb up and down his suspenders. "That hotel was destroyed in the fire of 2004, and the new Davis Mercantile was built on the site."

"That's all completely true, but the hotel was originally near the train depot."

"They moved the hotel in the 1960s."

"So you think—" Martha struggled to catch up.

"I think our map is referring to the original location of the Davis shops."

Eli popped out of his chair. "Our first stop for the afternoon then is the train depot."

Ten minutes later they were all piled into Eli's buggy.

The depot was easy enough to find. Martha had walked by it a dozen times, and Eli . . . well, he claimed to have played there when he was a young boy and raced his buggy there when he was a teen.

"There has to be something here," Duncan said.

They'd stomped around the entire train depot and found nothing. Martha's thoughts were scattered. She found herself thinking of the sadness in her *aenti*'s eyes, the history of Shipshewana, Duncan's enthusiasm, and the way mysteries—at least in books— often came together in a way quite different from what the readers expected. She felt a prickling along her scalp.

History.

Tears.

Pots of gold.

"The last clue . . ." Martha could barely contain her excitement. "What if, what if it's not a pot of gold at all? What if that's not what we're looking for?"

Duncan had been studying the map, now he brought it closer to his eyes and then held it at arm's length. "What else could it be?"

"What if it's a vessel . . . something to hold a people's tears?"

"We're supposed to find a vessel of tears to the northwest of this spot?"

"*Nein.*" Martha stepped closer and peered down at the faint outline. "But we couldn't think of anything northwest. Correct? And the map began with the statue of Chief Shipshewana."

Eli joined them. "Then it took us through the history of the town."

"And just maybe it ends where it began."

"With the lake."

"Where the tribe originally lived."

Duncan shook his head. "That can't be right though. We can't possibly search around an entire lake."

"If I'm right, we won't have to."

Eli smiled at her.

"You two know something I don't."

"What year were the Potawatomie Indians forced to leave, Eli?"

"If I remember correctly, it was 1837."

"And the Amish moved to the area in 1844. I remember the bishop mentioning that to me when I first arrived."

"What does this have to do with Chief Shipshewana?" Duncan asked.

Eli was already moving back toward the buggy. "The chief and some of his relatives were allowed to return. In fact, legend says he was buried along the banks of the lake."

It was a two-mile drive to the lake, past fields that had been harvested the week before. Fall's work was done. All that was left was to prepare for winter. The lake itself was surrounded by homes and vacation cabins and trees. The day was too cool for swimming, but Martha saw several men out fishing.

"Where do we even start looking?" Duncan was staring out the window, an expression of pure misery on his face.

Martha looked at Eli, who nodded his head once and turned the buggy west. Down the road the mare *clip-clopped* until Eli called out "Whoa" and pulled her into a parking area.

They stepped from the buggy as the sun slipped toward the western horizon.

"Why here?" Duncan asked.

"Makes perfect sense, it's where the monument of the chief sits."

Duncan bounced on the balls of his feet. No doubt he had waited for this moment for many years. He had promised his dad he would solve the mystery of the map. "There's a monument?"

"Indeed," Eli said. "And I think it might have been dedicated around the time our mapmaker began etching his clues into a piece of wood . . ."

"Which was later affixed onto the back of a wardrobe." Martha wanted to run to the monument, which she could now make out in the midst of the trees. She settled for a very fast walk.

Chapter Sixteen

This area is probably where Chief Shipshewana lived out his last years, once he was allowed to return."

"From Kansas." Duncan walked around the monument as if he were looking for a secret compartment.

"Correct. The forced march took sixty-one days and twenty-seven of their people died." Eli studied the inscription. He sensed that they were on the right trail. Maybe it was just Martha's enthusiasm. He had to admit that her eagerness to solve the mystery was contagious.

Duncan wasn't so sure. "Feels like a stretch."

"It could be that we're completely off base," Martha admitted.

The three stood in front of the monument, reading the words inscribed there.

THE CHIEF WAS REMOVED FROM THIS RESERVATION SEPTEMBER 4, 1838 AND WAS ESCORTED TO KANSAS BY A COMPANY OF SOLDIERS. HE RETURNED IN 1839 AND DIED IN 1841.

"I don't see any pots—of gold or tears," Duncan muttered.

Martha took the map from his hands. "But a receptacle like the one drawn on this map—it can hold many things and it can take different forms—a box or a saddlebag or a pot. As to what it might hold, I suppose the owners could use it to store treasure, food, or even tears."

"How do you store tears?" Duncan asked.

"Memories. You could store memories." Eli stepped back, trying to see the monument with the eyes of a visitor in 1931. Finally he shook his head, unable to spot anything out of the ordinary. But what Martha was suggesting pricked his memory. "In Revelation there is a verse . . . something to the effect that John saw twenty-four elders kneeling before the Lamb of God, and each had a harp and a golden bowl."

"I don't remember hearing that in church," Duncan said. "But then I never did understand the book of Revelation."

"The bowls were full of incense," Eli explained. "And the incense were the prayers of the saints."

When Martha looked at him curiously, he shrugged and said, "Bishop Abram enjoys the book of Revelation. He's preached on it several times in the past."

Duncan leaned forward, his fingertips now touching the monument. "So you think the map was made by an Amish person?"

"I think it was made by the father or grandfather of the person who owned the original wardrobe."

For the next fifteen minutes, they each walked in different directions. It wasn't until the sun kissed the western skyline that Martha admitted to herself they might not be able to solve the mystery. But they were so close . . .

An older man was walking past them, leading a small dog on a leash.

After Eli had greeted the man, he explained, "We're on a bit of a quest."

"A good way to spend a fall evening."

"Indeed, it is. At the moment we're stumped. We think that we're looking for something pertaining to Chief Shipshewana, which is why we've come to the monument."

The old man nodded and pulled a pipe from his pocket, though he didn't light it. "Then you know that the Potawatomie Indians once lived along these shores."

Martha and Duncan had joined the two men.

"Yes, we know their history—or at least a part of it. Are there any other plaques or memorials to the chief?" Martha asked. "Something that is very old."

"Probably as old as the monument," Duncan added.

"I can't think of anything like that." The old man slipped the pipe back into his pocket. "I'm sorry. I wish I could help."

Eli thanked him for trying. He turned to Martha, shrugged his shoulders in a time-to-surrender gesture. Suddenly he wanted to take her hand in his, like he had on Sunday. In that moment, as the sun blazed orange and the sky filled with streaks of purple and red, he knew that he didn't want to be alone any longer. His life was fuller, richer with the woman standing in front of him. She was a blessing that had been brought into his life almost against his will, and she was more precious than any treasure they might or might not find.

All those thoughts flashed through his mind quickly, so that at first he didn't realize the old man had turned and walked back toward them.

"There is one thing, but I doubt it holds a treasure."

Duncan was sitting on a park bench, his elbows propped on his knees and his head in his hands. He didn't bother looking up.

"There's a round metal plaque of sorts—impossible to read the words. It's old, that's for certain. For some reason, the grounds crew keeps the grass around it trimmed. My dog Flash is always sniffing around it."

Duncan had stood up, and Martha was now standing right next to him.

Eli said, "That sounds like it might be what we're looking for. Can you tell us where it is?"

"Take this road to the end. You'll see a pasture and then the banks of the lake. There's another small park there—nothing much but a trail and a few benches. The metal plaque is on the west side of the bench farthest from the water."

They thanked him and decided to leave the mare and walk the short distance.

Though the sun had disappeared below the horizon, there was a little light left. A slight breeze rustled the leaves that remained on the trees. As the man had described, there was a round metal disk, approximately the size of a dinner plate, surrounded by a metal rim. The place had sunk slightly over the years, but the area was well maintained nonetheless.

They knelt around the piece of metal.

"Certainly looks old," Martha said.

"And this word, it could be Shipshewana."

Eli pulled his pocketknife out and opened the blade.

As Martha and Duncan leaned even closer, he worked the tip of the knife into the recess between the piece of metal and the rim, which held it in place.

Duncan looked suddenly nervous. "Should we be destroying public property?"

"Not destroying it," Martha said.

Eli paused to wink at them. "We're just looking."

The metal did not yield easily. Years of rains, floods, and sun had effectively sealed it shut. But eventually the blade won. Eli lifted off the round plaque, which they still couldn't read, and set it carefully on the ground. And then they were all three looking into the dark recesses of a metal container, their heads bent together as one. The light was now nearly gone, but there was enough.

Eli reached down and pulled out the ancient wooden box.

Duncan snatched his cell phone from his pocket and took a picture. It showed Eli's hand, the box, Martha's fingers on the edge of the container, the lid lying in the grass.

Unlike the metal, the wooden box opened easily.

Inside was a cheesecloth, and inside of that an object covered with waxed paper like Eli's mother once used to wrap his sandwiches. He placed it on the grass and together they turned the object over again and again until they'd completely unwrapped the thing the owner of the map had hidden.

Epilogue

Two months later

Martha and Eli sat in a booth at JoJo's, enjoying a fresh pretzel and hot chocolate. The day was blustery and quite cold—exactly like December should be. Martha found that she wasn't dreading the shorter days or the wintry weather. In fact, she was looking forward to it. Winter brought its own joys, like time for quilting, preparation for Christmas, and buggy rides through the snow-covered town with the man sitting across from her.

"So it's final?" she asked. "The objects will all be placed in the historical society office?"

"On display for all to see. Hopefully folks will better appreciate the connections between the Potawatomi, Amish, and *Englisch* people."

"Reading those letters—it was better than any mystery or romance novel. It was like actually seeing into the lives and hearts of our ancestors."

Eli nodded. "It's a rare gift."

"The coins—"

"From the *Englisch*."

"Necklace—"

"Made by the Potawatomi."

"And Bible—"

"Which we know belonged to an Amish family."

"Treasure—for sure and certain."

Eli sipped from his hot chocolate, and then he leaned forward in a conspiratorial manner and said, "The mayor, she says that we'll have even more tourists than ever, come to see the time capsule."

"Which means we'll have even more people at the auction." Martha popped a piece of pretzel into her mouth.

"Maybe so."

"Could be I'll need help in the office."

"That's why I got you the kitten."

"The kitten is for everyone, Eli. I'm sure that Socks has already upped our production."

Eli grunted at that, but he smiled at her as he stood and reached for her hand. "I spoke with Jeremiah this morning," Eli said.

"How is Duncan?"

"Turns out the lad has a real skill with woodwork. Jeremiah has decided to hire him on full-time."

"The map—it led Duncan back to Shipshe, to the life he was meant to live."

"I supposed *Gotte* did that, but the map helped."

They walked outside into the blustery day, and Martha marveled at what God had done in her life in so little time. She still loved Melvin. She always would. She and Eli had talked about that.

He'd explained to her his heartbreak as a lad of seventeen, how he'd grown used to being alone, how he'd convinced himself that marrying wasn't a part of God's plan for him. They both had scars, but the wounds themselves had healed, and what remained was a map of its own sort—one chronicling the ups and downs of life.

"How's the dress coming?" he teased.

"Nearly done. *Aenti* Irene is working on it today."

"Is the medicine helping with her blood-sugar problems?"

"It is. The doctor said she might have had diabetes for several years without realizing it, and certainly it explains her erratic moods. Now that she's taking the insulin, she's like a different person."

Eli squeezed her hand, and Martha could feel the warmth spread all the way to her heart. After they'd found the time capsule, Eli had asked her to dinner to celebrate. They'd begun to walk each Saturday on the Pumpkinvine Trail, and he always sought her out on Sundays—whether it was a church day or not. Somehow in only two short months, he'd become an integral part of her life. He made her laugh again, and he said that she made him feel younger and more content than he ever had before.

"She still seems okay?" he asked. "With us marrying?"

"When I told her, it was the first time she hugged me. *Aenti* has kept to herself for so long that she's forgotten how much better it is to share our burdens with one another—our burdens and our joys."

"She's part of the community again."

"I think she's actually looking forward to moving."

"The *dawdi haus* at my place hasn't been lived in for some time. It will be *gut* to have her there."

"And she'll have enough money to last her, now that the sale of the farm to Simon Miller has gone through."

They made an unusual family—a confirmed bachelor,

widowed woman, and crotchety old aunt. But sometimes families were unusually shaped—patched together by God's omnipotent hand.

In many ways, life resembled a mystery.

And this time, Martha was quite satisfied by the way it was solved.

DISCUSSION QUESTIONS

1. At the beginning of this story, Martha doesn't want to move. She doesn't want any change in her life. What scriptures can guide us when we're going through such a time?

2. Have you ever lost something precious? Read Luke 15:8–10. How does this scripture relate to us today? What things should we focus on?

3. *Aenti* Irene is not a pleasant woman, but she does write to Martha and ask her to come and stay with her. In her way, she's asking for help. We learn by the end of the story that Irene has been suffering with a medical condition. So often, we can't really know what another person is going through. In light of that, what are some specific ways we can show grace to one another?

4. This story is a mystery, but it's also a story of romance found again. Are we ever too old to fall in love? And are romantic relationships different as we age? If so, in what ways, and what things can we do to cherish them?

ACKNOWLEDGMENTS

This book is dedicated to Kris Stutzman who owns and operates Lolly's Fabrics in Shipshewana, Indiana. Since the first book I wrote set in Shipshe, Kris has been a joy and a privilege to know. She's quick with a smile, a hug, and an answer to my many questions. I consider it one of life's blessings that I can count her as my friend.

Thanks also to my prereaders Kristy and Janet, without whom I would probably take up professional fishing instead of writing. You ladies always help me meet my deadlines, and your work ethic is awesome. Gratitude also to my agent Steve Laube, my editor Becky Philpott, and all of the awesome folks at HarperCollins Christian Publishing.

I'd also like to thank Janet Schrock, historian for the Shipshewana Area Historical Society. Your publication *Shipshewana, Indiana 1889–1989; A Patchwork Sampler* provided wonderful insight into the history of the area. To the folks in Shipshewana, a special thank-you for welcoming me into your homes and your hearts. Being the grand marshal in your Christmas parade is a memory I will always cherish. You are where my love for the Amish began, and I'm proud to share your little community with my readers.

If you happen to be passing through northern Indiana, I encourage you to take a few hours to visit this small town south of Interstate 90. It is truly a haven of rest in a very busy world.

And finally . . . "always giving thanks to God the Father for everything, in the name of our Lord Jesus Christ" (Eph. 5:20).

Blessings,

Vannetta

ABOUT THE AUTHOR

Photo by Jason Irwin

Vannetta Chapman is author of the bestselling novel *A Simple Amish Christmas*. She has published over one hundred articles in Christian family magazines, receiving over two dozen awards from Romance Writers of America chapter groups. In 2012 she was awarded a Carol Award for *Falling to Pieces*. She discovered her love for the Amish while researching her grandfather's birthplace of Albion, Pennsylvania.

Visit Vannetta's website: www.vannettachapman.com
Twitter: @VannettaChapman
Facebook: VannettaChapmanBooks

Under the Harvest Moon

Pearl's Florentines

Ingredients:

1 ¾ cups sliced, blanched almonds (about 5 ounces)

3 tablespoons all-purpose flour

Finely grated zest of 1 orange (about 2 tablespoons)

¼ teaspoon fine salt

¾ cup sugar

2 tablespoons heavy cream

2 tablespoons light corn syrup

5 tablespoons unsalted butter

½ teaspoon pure vanilla extract

Chocolate Topping, optional:

2 to 4 ounces semisweet chocolate, chopped

Directions:

Position a rack in the center of the oven and preheat to 350 degrees F. Line a baking sheet with a silicone baking mat or parchment paper.

Pulse the almonds in a food processor until finely chopped, but not pasty. Stir together the nuts, flour, zest and salt in a large bowl.

Put the sugar, cream, corn syrup and butter in a small saucepan. Cook over medium heat, stirring occasionally, until mixture comes to a rolling boil and sugar is completely dissolved. Continue to boil for 1 minute. Remove from heat and stir in the vanilla, then pour mixture into almond mixture and stir just to combine. Set aside until cool enough to handle, 30 minutes.

Scoop rounded teaspoons (for 3-inch cookies) or rounded tablespoons (for 6-inch cookies) of batter and roll into balls. Place on prepared baking sheet, leaving about 3 to 4 inches between each cookie since they spread.

Bake one pan at a time, until the cookies are thin and an even golden brown color throughout, rotating pans halfway through baking time, about 10 to 11 minutes. Cool on baking sheet for 5 minutes, then transfer to racks to cool. Repeat with remaining batter. Serve.

Optional chocolate topping:

Put the chocolate in a medium heatproof bowl. Bring a saucepan filled with 1 inch or so of water to a very low simmer; set the bowl over, but not touching, the water. Stir the chocolate occasionally until melted and smooth. (Alternatively, put the chocolate in a medium microwave-safe bowl. Melt at 50 percent power in the microwave until soft, about 1 minute. Stir, and continue to heat until completely melted, about 1 to 2 minutes more.)

For sandwiches: Drop about ½ teaspoon chocolate onto on the flat side of half of the cookies and press together with remaining halves. Return to rack and let chocolate set.

For chocolate decor: Drizzle melted chocolate over Florentines as desired. Set aside at room temperature until chocolate is set.

Busy baker's tips: Store baked cookies carefully, separated by parchment or waxed paper, in an air-tight container for up to 3 days. Florentines are best stored separated from moist cookies and cakes.

Naomi's Roast, Potatoes, and Carrots

1 blade roast about 4 inches thick and weighing approx. 5 lbs.

1 teaspoon salt

⅛ teaspoon pepper

1 cup water

6 medium potatoes, peeled and quartered

6 medium carrots, peeled and cut in 2 inch cubes

3 medium onions, peeled and quartered

Directions:

Sprinkle roast well with salt and pepper, then place in a large roasting pan.

Add water, cover, and cook for 1 ½ hours at 325 degrees.

Uncover and arrange vegetables around roast in pan.

Recover and cook for 2 ½ to 3 hours longer or until meat and vegetables are both fork tender.

Tip: Sometimes Naomi adds 1 can of cream of mushroom soup and reduces water to ½ cup for a creamier gravy. Psst . . . don't tell.

Love and Buggy Rides

Black Raspberry Pie

2 unbaked pie shells
1 cup *Therm Flo
¾ cup water
¾ cup sugar
1 quart fresh raspberries

Directions:

Bring 2 quarts of water to a boil.

Meanwhile, moisten 1 cup *Therm Flo with ¾ cup water.

Whisk together, then whisk into boiling water.

Add ¾ cup sugar.

Remove from heat and add one quart fresh raspberries.

Pour into pie shells (don't overfill, you may have extra).

Top with pie crust; cut holes in dough to allow steam to escape.

Bake at 350 degrees for one hour.

*Therm Flo is a modified food starch derived from waxy maize. It is used in canning and freezing home-prepared foods as a clear thickener.

Barbecue Meat Loaf

1 ½ lb ground beef
1 small onion, chopped
1 cup milk
1 cup oatmeal
1 egg
1 ½ teaspoon seasoned salt
1 ½ teaspoon chili powder
¾ teaspoon pepper

Directions:

In a small bowl, mix together the onion, milk, oatmeal, egg, salt, chili powder, and pepper. Add mixture to a medium-size bowl with the ground beef and combine.

Topping:
1 cup ketchup
½ cup brown sugar
1 ½ teaspoon dry mustard
1 ½ teaspoon vinegar

Mix topping ingredients and spread over meat loaf. Bake for one hour at 350 degrees.

A Quiet Love

⟡

Amish Chicken

6–8 chicken pieces, cleaned
1 cup flour
2 teaspoon garlic powder
1 tablespoon salt
2 teaspoon paprika
1 ½ cups heavy whipping cream
1 ½ cups water

Directions:

Dredge the chicken pieces in the flour and spices and arrange skin side up in a baking dish. Mix the cream and water and pour over the chicken. Bake at 350 degrees for 1 ½ hours or until the skin is golden brown. This chicken makes its own gravy while baking.

*Recipe from Food.com, original recipe found in an Ohio Amish cookbook

Amish Potato Rolls

1 cup mashed potato

1 cup sugar

½ cup butter

3 eggs, beaten

1 ½ teaspoon salt

2 packages yeast

1 cup warm water

5 cups flour

Directions:

Mix together first 5 ingredients. Dissolve yeast in the warm water, then add it to the mixture. Stir in about 3 cups flour. Add the remaining flour while kneading. Knead until no longer sticky but still moist. Let rise until double.

Preheat oven to 325 degrees. Roll out dough to ¾–1" thickness. Cut into bun shapes with round cookie or biscuit cutter. Place on greased cookie sheet about 2" apart. Let rise until puffy but not doubled. Brush with milk. Bake until golden brown, about 12 minutes.

Yield: 3 dozen

*An Amish recipe from Food Network

RECIPES FROM VANNETTA CHAPMAN'S
Mischief in the Autumn Air

⁓⦁⦁⦁⁓

Peanut Butter Chocolate Chip Cookies

1 ½ cups all-purpose flour
1 teaspoon baking soda
1 cup (2 sticks) butter or margarine, softened
½ cup peanut butter
½ cup sugar
½ cup packed brown sugar
1 teaspoon vanilla extract
1 large egg
1 ¾ cups (11.5-oz. pkg.) dark chocolate chips

Directions:

Preheat oven to 375 degrees.

Combine flour and baking soda in small bowl. Beat butter, peanut butter, granulated sugar, brown sugar, and vanilla extract in large mixer bowl until creamy. Beat in egg. Gradually beat in flour mixture. Stir in chocolate chips.

Drop dough by rounded tablespoon onto ungreased baking

sheets. Press down slightly with bottom of glass dipped in granulated sugar.

Bake for 8 to 10 minutes or until edges are set but centers are still soft. Cool on baking sheets for 4 minutes; remove to wire racks to cool completely.

Strawberry Lemon Water

15 fresh strawberries
One sliced lemon
Water

Directions:
Add 15 fresh strawberries, washed and finely sliced to a ½ gallon glass jar. Add one sliced lemon with rind on. Fill with water. Let sit 4 hours (to overnight) in fridge and enjoy.

Homemade Hot Chocolate

1 cup milk
2 tablespoons sugar
½ to 1 tablespoon cocoa powder

Optional Ingredients:
pinch of salt
pinch of cayenne
½ teaspoon vanilla

Directions:

Add the sugar and cocoa powder into a cup with the cayenne and salt.

Mix together with a fork.

Pour the milk into a measuring cup and heat in the microwave for 2 to 2 ½ minutes, or until nice and hot.

Pour milk over dry ingredients and mix with a fork.

9781401685942-B

ENJOY THE FIRST TWO INSTALLMENTS IN THE AMISH HEIRLOOM SERIES!

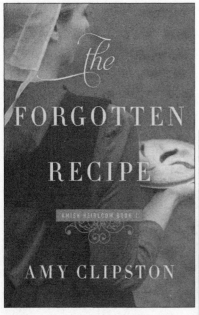

Available in print, audio, and e-book.

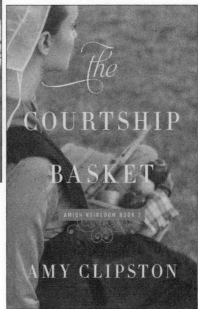

Available in print, audio, and e-book June 2016.

Enjoy
Kathleen Fuller's
Amish of Birch
Creek series!

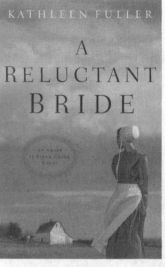

Available in print,
audio, and e-book.

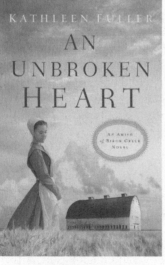

Available in print,
audio, and e-book.

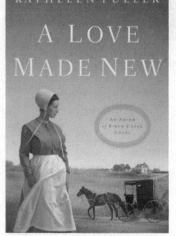

Available in print, audio,
and e-book September 2016.

THOMAS NELSON
Since 1798

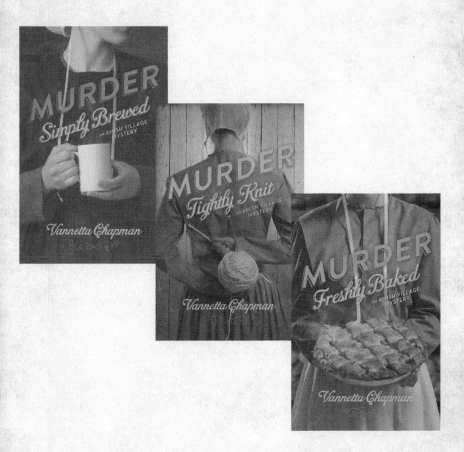